D0808898

George P. Pelecanos is the author of *A Firing Offense*, *Nick's Trip*, and *Down By the River Where the Dead Men Go*, a trilogy featuring PI Nick Stefanos, as well as *King Suckerman*, shortlisted for the 1998 Crime Writers' Association Golden Dagger Award, *The Sweet Forever* and *The Big Blowdown*, all part of his DC quartet and published by Serpent's Tail. Pelecanos has been hailed as "the coolest writer in America" (*GQ*) and "a literary Tarantino with added heart" (*Mail on Sunday*) who "makes Jim Thompson look like Barbara Cartland" (*Mirabella*).

Pelecanos lives in Washington, where he "has carved out a territory – the seedier suburbs of Washington, D.C. – and a language of danger and sadness all his own" (*Chicago Tribune*).

THE
SWEET
FOREVER

A NOVEL

GEORGE P.
PELECANOS

A catalogue record for this book is available from
the British Library on request

The right of George P. Pelecanos to be identified as the
author of this work has been asserted by him in
accordance with the Copyright, Designs and Patents
Act 1988

First published by Little, Brown and Company, New York, 1998

First published in the UK in 1999 by Serpent's Tail,
4 Blackstock Mews, London N4 2BT

First published in this 5-star edition in 2000

Website: www.serpentstail.com

Printed in Great Britain by Mackays of Chatham plc

10 9 8 7 6 5 4 3 2 1

To Rosa

ACKNOWLEDGMENT

The author would like to acknowledge *Dream City*, Harry S. Jaffe and Tom Sherwood's extraordinary account of the rise and fall of Home Rule in Washington, D.C., as a major source of factual material in the writing of this novel.

PART I

FRIDAY

MARCH 14, 1986

ONE

The first time Richard Tutt made it with a suspect's girlfriend, he realized that there was nothing, nothing at all, that a man in his position couldn't do. He'd gotten some just that morning — a high-assed young thing by the name of Rowanda — and the feeling had stuck with him right into this bright, biting afternoon.

Tutt made a left onto U Street, eye-swept the beat that he knew he owned.

The Power. It was a cop thing, but not an across-the-board cop thing. The desk jockeys never had it. The homicide dicks were too tortured to have it. A few of the boys in Prostitution and Perversions had it, but only some of the time. The beat cops, the ones who really knew how to walk it, had it *all* the time.

Tutt dug the free-fall feeling that came with the Power. He even looked forward to the looks he got — the looks of fear and hatred and, yeah, the looks of respect — when he stepped out of his cruiser. He'd been a cop for five years, always in blue, and always out on the street. You could keep your promotions and gold shields. Tutt liked the fit of the uniform. He knew he'd never wear anything else.

Tutt turned to his partner, Kevin Murphy, who was staring through the windshield, one thumb stroking his black mustache. Murphy's head throbbed with a dull ache; he hoped for a quiet day. He'd fallen asleep on the couch with a beer in his hand the night before, trying to make out the blurred images on the screen of his new television set. Murphy's nights had been ending this way for some time.

"Let me ask you something, Murphy."

Murphy exhaled slowly. "Go ahead."

"Got a man-woman kinda question for you."

"All right."

"Had me a little brown sugar action this morning, on the way in to work?"

Tutt, bragging double, not just letting Murphy know he had gotten some pussy, letting him know it had been some good *black* pussy in the bargain.

"Oh, yeah?"

Tutt smiled. "Yeah. Lady took a long ride on that white pony."

Murphy thinking, Yeah, 'cause you promised some poor sucker's girlfriend that you wouldn't bust her old man if she gave a little up.

"Have a good time?" said Murphy.

"Damn straight."

"Good for you, man. So what was that question?"

"Right. So I'm playin' with her privates, see, got my finger right on the trigger."

"Uh-huh."

"I haven't put it in her yet, but even without that, her elevator's gettin' ready to shoot right up to the penthouse suite, you know what I mean? Just about then, the bitch looks up at me and goes, in this real whiny voice, 'Pleeeease?'"

"Yeah?"

"My question is, what was she askin' for? I mean, please what? Please do? Please don't? Please have a bigger dick? I was wonderin' if this was something, you know, the sisters say all the time, something I just don't know about."

"I wouldn't know, Tutt. I only been with one *sister* for the last ten years. Had some *sisters* before I was married, understand, but not every *single* sister. So I can't speak for all of them. And I sure couldn't tell you what this particular sister was lookin' for when she asked you the question."

"I'm bettin' she was begging for it. Had to be 'Please do.'"

"Think so, huh?"

Tutt drove the blue-and-white east on U. Black Washington's once grand street was ragged, near defeated by crime and indifference and Metro's Green Line construction, which had blighted the area for years.

They passed the Republic theater, dark now, where Kevin Murphy had seen classics like *J.D.'s Revenge* and *King Suckerman* and a bad-ass prison picture called *Short Eyes* back in '77. Flyers touting the mayor's upcoming reelection effort were stapled to telephone poles, his increasingly bloated image distorted in a haze of dust kicked up by jackhammers and trucks. Murphy's eyes followed a young dealer stepping out of a drug car parked at the curb.

"Murphy?"

"What?"

"Don't get this wrong, partner . . ."

Don't get this wrong, huh? Here we go.

". . . but all I kept thinking of when I was hammering this black chick is that y'all, what I mean is you brothers, y'all fuck in a furious fuckin' way, you know what I mean?"

"That so. How'd you arrive at that conclusion?"

"Well, okay, here's what got me started. I was watchin' this porno flick the other night. My brother-in-law, the *art* director, brought it over. All-black cast; the star of the flick was hung like a donkey, you know what I'm sayin'? Anyway, this brother in the movie, he was just wailing on this punch, up on one arm, doing some high-ass, violent-ass thrusts."

"Man was goin' at it."

"Like I've never seen. And the way this girl was screaming, now, I shouldn't have been surprised. I mean, I've *been* with some black women, man. So you *know* that I've heard some screams."

"Oh, I *know*."

"But watchin' that porno tape, it made me think of that old expression."

"What expression's that?"

"'I thought I'd fucked a nigger'" — Tutt grinned — "'till I saw a *nigger* fuck a nigger.'" Tutt air-elbowed Murphy, cackled in that high-pitched way of his. "You ever hear that?"

Murphy stared at the Twenty-third Psalm card he had taped to the dash. He made his lips turn up into a smile. "Nah, King, I never did."

Tutt breathed out in relief. Murphy calling him "King" — Tutt's nickname from the Twinbrook neighborhood, where he'd come up — meant everything between them was okay. Course, Tutt *knew* it would be okay. Civilians didn't understand about the shell cops had, the things that could be said between partners. You could use any goddamn words you wanted to use in fun, because those were just words, and there was only one real thing that mattered, one serious task at hand, and that was to watch your partner's back out in the world and know that he would do the same. Sensitivity was for the high-forehead crowd, the ones standing comfortably behind that last line of defense, skinny-armed liberals and ACL-Jews. *Men* knew that words were just words and only action counted — period.

"Hey, Murphy. I was just shittin' around. Hey, you all right?"

"I was thinking on somethin'," said Murphy. "That's all."

I was thinking of my wife . . . my mother, and my brother, and my father. Niggers, all of them. I was thinkin' on how I betray them every day, listening to those filthy words coming out of your fat redneck mouth, doin' nothing, saying nothing to shut you up. . . .

"Hey, Murph. No offense, right?"

"Nah, Tutt," said Kevin Murphy. "None taken."

Murphy noticed the kid wearing the Raiders jacket, maybe ten or eleven, standing outside of Medger's Liquors at 12th and U. He had seen the kid the last year or so, hanging on that corner, often during school hours. No one had the time to bother much with truants anymore, but Murphy wondered what the kid was up to, if he was a runner or a baby foot soldier or just checking out the hustler's map, prepping himself for a lifetime of nothing.

"There's your boy," said Tutt. "Same as always. One of these days we ought to stop, see what his story is."

"I expect we'll be crossing paths someday. When he grows up some."

"Yeah, they all grow up, don't they? Grow up and fuck up."

Across the street, past immobile construction equipment, near the bank on the 11th Street corner of U, flags and balloons announced the grand opening of a new store named Real Right Records. Below the identifying sign, in smaller letters: "African American Owned and Operated," and "Your In-Town Music Connection."

Tutt said, "You believe some fool, opening up a business down here? You got your criminal element and, on top of it, all this construction. How stupid could the man be?"

"Man's name is Marcus Clay."

"You know him?"

"Heard of him. Played ball for Cardoza back in the sixties. I saw him go off in this Interhigh match when I was, like, twelve years old. Got a few years on me, but they still talked about him a little when I was comin' up. They say he could sky like Connie from the key."

"Connie?"

"Hawkins. Clay's got another store over at Dupont Circle, and in Georgetown. Got one in Northern Virginia, too, I think. Tryin' to bring somethin' into the community here, I guess."

"Yeah, I see what he's tryin' to do. Question is, what the fuck for?"

Tutt turned south on 11th. They passed a black Z parked on the left. Tutt slowed down, checked out the driver and passenger, cruised past and went along the strip of two-story residential row houses.

"Rogers and Monroe," said Tutt, and Murphy said nothing.

Down by T Street, Tutt pulled the cruiser over to the curb and cut the engine. Tutt liked to park here and watch the neighborhood. This was his quiet time, an opportunity to engage in what he called his "street surveillance." Tutt still imagined himself to be a good cop. Murphy had no such illusions but was grateful for these rare moments of silence.

Murphy wished he were home, kicking back on his sofa, watching the game. The first two rounds of the tournament were the best, maybe the four best days in all of sports. Maryland would be finishing up with Pepperdine now, and it gnawed at him that he had no idea how Len Bias and the Terps had done. Like most D.C. natives, Murphy was a Georgetown fan, had managed to see the Hoyas edge Texas Tech the night before. Georgetown still had some good players — Williams and Jackson and Broadnax, too — but it hadn't been the same since Patrick had shipped off to New York. Murphy's heart had gone on over to Maryland this year because of Bias alone; there was beauty in the way that young man played.

"Check it out," said Tutt.

Murphy scoped T. His eyes lit on a boy, eleven, maybe twelve, wearing a neon green knit cap and palming something over to another boy, bone skinny, at the head of an alley.

"You recognize them?"

Murphy shook his head. Far as he knew, they weren't part of Tyrell's crew.

7

"Stay here," said Tutt, patting the grip of his service revolver.

"Want me to radio it in?"

"Uh-uh. I got it wired."

Tutt was out of the car and across the street just as fast, one hand on his night stick, keeping it steady at his side as he made it behind a tree and then another, getting closer to the alley. Murphy studied Tutt: careful, but fearless as a mothafucker, too, the kind of partner most cops wanted. That is, if you could get past everything else.

Murphy heard a dull explosion somewhere behind him. He gazed idly in the rearview, saw nothing.

Tutt came up on the two boys, shouted out his warning, took off after the one in the green cap as the other hightailed it west on T. Tutt hit it: chest out, running hard while carrying twenty-five pounds of pack set and gun and assorted cop hardware, blowing and going, almost on top of the kid. Then he was gone into the narrow alley. Murphy did not consider chasing the skinny kid.

In the rearview, Murphy saw smoke rise over a row house roof, back off of U. Several sirens called out from different directions. Murphy adjusted the radio's frequency and listened for the report. He keyed the microphone and informed the dispatcher that they'd respond.

Tutt emerged from the alley a couple of minutes later, John Wayning it across the street. He got into the driver's side, his face pink, his eyes stoked and wide. Murphy noticed the red seeping into the skinned palm of Tutt's right hand.

"Who was he?" said Murphy.

"Nobody we know. Some kid, *young* kid, way out of his territory. I was almost on him, but Tyrell's boys got these old tires and shit spread out all over the alley. Slowed me down."

"That's what they're there for."

"I know. You should have seen the look on his face when I told him to stop, Murph. . . . Ah, Christ. Stupid. I tripped back there, took some skin off on the concrete." Tutt shook the pain out of his hand. "What's all the noise?"

"Just came over the radio. Some kind of accident in front of that new record store. Got a car in flames right in the middle of U. Told them we'd get on it."

"The Third District," said Tutt happily, ignitioning the squad car. "*Always* somethin' goin' on down here."

"Why you love it, man."

"You got that right, partner."

Tutt spun the wheel, one-eightied the cruiser, and punched the gas coming out of the fishtail. Murphy flipped on the overheads and grabbed the door's armrest. Tutt high-cackled as the cruiser left rubber on the street.

TWO

Donna Morgan didn't get downtown much anymore. Her job was in Wheaton and so were the bars where she hung out with many of her friends. But she liked being downtown. In the District the young people talked about music and ideas and took chances on what they wore and how they cut their hair. Donna could remember wanting to live downtown, be a part of it herself. But she was cruising up on thirty now, and figured that her time had passed.

These days Donna Morgan only came downtown every other month or so to go to a club or see a concert. When her regular dealer ran dry, she also came downtown to cop a little blow.

Eddie Golden, Donna's boyfriend and date for the Echo and the Bunnymen concert that night, hated to come downtown. Donna had seen Eddie lock his door as soon as they hit the District line on Georgia Avenue. Eddie told Donna to do the same, as he feared that car-jacking thing he had heard so much about, and Donna locked her door to make him happy, though she doubted anyone would want to steal Eddie's drab four-cylinder Plymouth Reliant. The car had one of those magnetic signs on the passenger door, "Appliance Installers Unlimited" spelled out in red letters, even gave the phone number and address, as if anyone cared. No, nobody would want to steal this boring rag, not even on a lazy bet.

Eddie turned down Missouri, cut south on 13th Street.

"This looks a little better," said Eddie. "More residential."

"I won't let anything happen to you, Eddie. Besides, we're not exactly riding in the inner-city sports car of choice. Maybe if someone's looking to heist some dishwasher hoses . . ."

"Go ahead and make fun. Just remember, we're playin' an away game here." Eddie pushed in on the dash lighter, pulled a Marlboro red from the sun visor where he kept his pack, stuck the filter between his thin lips. "Who's opening for Echo, man?"

"The Church."

Eddie lit his smoke. "Oh, yeah, you played me one of their records, right? It was kind of trippy."

Trippy. Eddie Golden could deal with that. Eddie used to love to smoke a little green, lay back and listen to *Meddle* or some other old Floyd, huff cigarettes, drink some ice-cold beers, maybe pull one off if he was alone. His dust days were over, though; he'd lost too many amigos to that stuff, K-heads who had dropped their bikes doing eighty or taken on the wrong guys in bars or sometimes everyone in the bar behind that crazy shit. So Eddie had made his way over to cocaine. He liked cocaine better because it made him more alert and also less shy. There was that other good thing, too: When he did high-grade C with Donna the two of them could go half the night.

"Eddie, shit, can't we listen to something a little more, you know, hip?"

Donna reached over, flipped the radio off DC-101, where they were playing the new one by the Outfield.

"Sure, babe, anything you want."

Donna went right past the broadcasting of a basketball game that neither of them cared anything about, got the dial over to HFS, caught the Weasel doing his Frantic Friday thing, Lene Lovich singing about her new toy and then right into the Slickee Boys doing "When I Go to the Beach."

"All right?"

"Sure, Donna, this ain't bad."

The truth was, Eddie hated that new-wave shit they played on WHFS, but Donna dug it, and if it made Donna happy, he could stand it for a little while. Eddie liked the newer groups that rocked, Mike and the Mechanics, Mr. Mister, INXS, like that. Donna seemed to be into any group that had fucked up–looking hair.

"Where we goin'?" said Eddie.

"Take this all the way down to U Street, hang a left. My friend works in a record store down around Eleventh."

"This guy white?"

"Greek guy. Works for his best friend. A black guy, Eddie. He *owns* the place. *Four* places now. Real Right Records."

"Greek, huh? How well you know him?"

"I know him, Eddie. He's a friend, he's doing us a favor, and he's cool."

And we used to have a thing. But you can't handle hearing it, Eddie, so —

"He's gonna hook us up?"

"Got a nice, fat gram put aside for us."

"Sounds good to me. What's this dude's name?"

"Dimitri Karras."

"Careless?" Eddie laughed, dragged on his cigarette.

Careless. Eddie, if you only knew.

They were at the top of a steep hill, looking at the downtown skyline and the monuments below, and then over the crest, and the Reliant went down 13th between Cardoza High on the left and the ruin of the subsidized Clifton Terrace apartment complex on the right. Some black kids walked slowly across the street, made Eddie brake, gave him hard looks through the windshield as they passed. Eddie met their eyes for only a second, then looked away.

Donna looked across the bench at Nervous Eddie as he made the turn and took them east on U. Despite the cold March wind, Eddie had his Sonny Crockett thing going on today: a pastel sleeveless T-shirt under a light rayon sport coat — sleeves pushed back on the forearms — and a two-day growth of beard on his hollow cheeks. The look was cool out in the suburbs, but down here he looked like just another guy who picked his attitude up off TV.

Donna had affection for Eddie. On the downside, he was a follower and without ambition, and the guys he partied with were stupid and cruel, but Eddie himself was kind, and he had yet to screw her over in that thoughtless way she had come to expect from men. He was younger than she was by a few years, too, and still eager to please in bed.

Yeah, she had affection for Eddie. Affection, not love. The difference was significant. She never stared at Eddie and imagined what he'd look like with gray hair. Never pictured him at the head of anyone's dinner table. Course, they did have a couple of things in common. Both of them liked to party, for one. And they shared a cockeyed dream of moving to Florida someday, having a modest house with their own swimming pool in the backyard. But this wasn't much to base a future on, Donna knew.

If you asked her what she was looking for, she'd give you the simple response: Love was what she was looking for, to love and to be loved back. And if she was being honest that day, she might have added something else: A guy with money in the bank and the looks to make her wet.

At Donna's instruction, Eddie pulled over near the corner of 11th. You'd barely notice the record store if you weren't looking for it, what with all the construction equipment, bulldozers and such, parked in the middle of the street. Eddie guessed that was why the owner had strung up plastic flags and that big "Open" sign, on account of the store was so hard to see. Dividing the east- and westbound lanes, a platform truck up on leg cranks held a small load of steel I beams on its flat, open bed.

"You want me to walk you in?" said Eddie.

Donna smiled, patted Eddie's cheek like he was some kind of kid or something. What, didn't she think he could protect her if anything went down?

"I'll be okay," said Donna. "Be out in about ten."

"Okay, babe. I'm watchin' you."

That's what he did. Watched her cross the street with that bouncy walk of hers, her ass doing the alternating piston thing inside her skirt, Eddie thinking, God, she's some kind of woman. Man would be a fool to let that shit get away.

Donna was only inside the record store for a minute or so when Eddie noticed the kid in the Oakland Raiders coat walking by his car. The kid had his hands deep in the pockets of the oversized coat and he was smiling at Eddie, checking out the car, smiling back at Eddie in a way that was neither friendly nor threatening but somehow knowing. Eddie figured, smile back, and he did it with a nod, but now the kid had passed. Eddie checked the kid out in the passenger sideview, watched him go and stand on the corner in front of the liquor store, where a couple of older black guys were laughing over something a third one had said.

Eddie looked ahead to the next corner. A young black guy had gotten out of a late model black 300Z and was leaning against the door, his arms folded, just looking around. He caught Eddie's eye for a moment — maybe Eddie imagined it; he couldn't be sure — and glanced away.

Eddie fumbled in the visor for another smoke.

Black guys. Why'd they always look at Eddie Golden like they wanted to fuck him up?

Eddie had nothing against black people; it was just that, growing up where he did, out Layhill Road near Bel Pre, he never had the opportunity to get to know any. The guys Eddie drank with, at Gentleman Jim's in Twinbrook, the Stained Glass in Glenmont, and Hunter's in Wheaton, *those* guys didn't care much for the brothers. Because they were his friends, he listened to their nigger jokes and, sure, he laughed along, but it wasn't like he had a racist bone in his body himself. The thing was, why rock the boat with his buddies for a bunch of black guys he didn't know and who always seemed like they'd just as soon cut his throat as look at him anyway? What would be the point of that?

Through the windshield, Eddie watched the black guy get in his Z and drive off.

Eddie looked in the rearview mirror at the unlit cigarette dangling from his mouth. He dug the way that looked. He turned his head a little, ran his fingers through his straight, thin hair where it had receded back off the top of his forehead. In the rearview he saw a car approaching from two blocks back, coming on at a high rate of speed.

Eddie checked himself out. He knew he wasn't a bad-looking guy. Miss Donna M. could be doing a whole lot worse. The comments she made, about his car and his dishwasher installer's job and his low-rent friends, they bothered him a little, like someone was always pinching his shoulder from behind. It was true that careerwise, Eddie hadn't lit up the town as of yet, but he was a young man, just a hair off of twenty-seven, and he had time. He could score somehow — no immediate prospects, but you never knew — and then Donna would quit cracking on him so much and look at him in a different way. Not that she wasn't a slave to the bone to begin with. But with a little money and success added to the bargain, she'd come all the way over to his side.

Eddie heard a sound like a plane was coming down. He turned his head suddenly, saw that the car that had been coming so fast before was almost on top of him now, up on two wheels, narrowly missing a frantic woman running across the street with her child. The car was right behind him. It was a boxy GM, a Monte Carlo or the hopped-up version of the Cutlass, Eddie could no longer tell any of them apart. All four wheels were off the ground, and the car was in the air.

"Fuck!" screamed Eddie, dropping to the bench seat, covering his eyes with his hands.

An explosion filled his ears, and he felt his own car move a couple of feet as if it had been windblown, the tires abutting the curb.

Eddie sat up. He took the crushed cigarette from his lips, tossed it aside.

Eddie stood in the street. He had stepped out of the Plymouth without knowing that he had. He was thinking, I'm no hero, as he walked toward the car that had crashed. It got hotter as he approached because the interior of the car was on fire. The car had flown right into the platform truck parked in the middle of the street. An I beam overhanging the back of the flatbed had gone through the car's windshield and out the rear window, and now the car hung suspended, smoke and licks of flame coming from the openings made by the beam.

A green rectangular piece of paper blew out of the open windshield and was lifted in the air. It was a coupon of some kind, or one of those things they throw out of skyscrapers at New York parades — no, it was *money*.

Eddie heard people yelling. Black men's voices, the winos, maybe, from outside the liquor store. He saw a tall black guy, broad of shoulder and chest, come from the front door of the record store, walk slowly toward the center of the street.

Eddie pulled back his hand. He had burned it on the handle of the back door of the burning GM. He must have opened the door, because the door was open, and there was a pillowcase spread out on the floor in back. Money spilled out of its open top. Medium denominations, not hundreds and not ones. A black head, its nose flattened, its mouth a stew of bloody, mashed teeth and gums, lay on the backseat. The I beam rested where the head had been, on the smoking shoulders of the torso behind the wheel.

The pillowcase looked damn near full. Eddie's face stung from the heat. His hair seemed to rise momentarily off his head. He was stumble-walking back toward his car, swallowing the bile that had risen in his throat, letting go of the pillowcase gripped tightly in his hand and allowing it to fall to the Plymouth's bench seat. The kid with the Oakland Raiders coat stood just outside the passenger window of Eddie's car, and he was tapping on the window, and there were many people shouting now, though it seemed not at him, and sirens, he had heard them first moments ago, and now they grew loud.

Eddie fumbled the ignition, cranked it, pulled down on the tree, got away from the curb. Donna. He couldn't wait for her. She'd understand. She'd be happy when she saw what he'd done. She'd be *proud.*

He carefully negotiated his car around a cop cruiser that had just pulled in at the scene. A black cop and a white cop got out of the cruiser. Eddie went by them briskly, turning his head so they could not see his face.

He glanced back over his shoulder, caught a glimpse of Donna and some dude with gray hair, coming out of the record store.

Eddie hooked a left on 9th. He floored the Reliant, felt it hesitate and knock. His heart raced. He felt *good.* He checked himself in the rearview: face sunburn-red, his rooster-cut hair black and curled at the ends, his eyebrows singed. The smell of burning things was strong in the car.

Eddie reached to the right, let his fingers go to the money.

Eddie thought of himself dropping to the bench, covering his eyes before the crash. He had been scared, like always. But he had *done* something, too.

Eddie laughed without knowing why.

THREE

Dimitri Karras flipped the switch and extinguished the bathroom light. He stood motionless, savoring the cool drip of cocaine back in his throat, the touch of ice behind his eyes, the charge of energy flowing toward his brain. It was his first jolt of the day, and his first was always the best. The world was better than it had been moments before. The day would surely be more interesting now. There would be interesting people to meet, interesting things to talk about. What did his dealer call it? *Medicinal optimism*. The promise of a clean and deathless future.

He smiled. It was comforting, standing in the darkness. It felt better here, out of the light.

Karras fingered the amber-colored glass vial in the pocket of his jeans. That was the crazy thing about this stuff — well, *one* of the crazy things: Once you did your first hit, you were thinking about your next right away. What you were holding, when you'd get to it, how much you had left, how far it would go . . . you'd get so wrapped up in the plan, it was easy to forget the high itself.

Through the bathroom door he could hear the announcer calling the Maryland-Pepperdine game from the thirteen-inch Sharp set atop Marcus Clay's desk in the back office of the new store. Karras heard the announcer raise his voice, the surge of the crowd, Clay's voice.

"Lord!" yelled Clay. "Mitri, man, come on out, you're missin' this shit. Pepperdine's making a run!"

Marcus — he loved the epic four-day, sixty-four-team first and second rounds of the NCAA tournament. He waited for it like a child does

Christmas morning, called it "the best four days in all of sports." Damned if Karras could disagree.

"I'll be out in a second," said Karras.

"What're you, waxin' your little old carrot in there?"

"I said I'll be right out."

Fuck it. Might as well do another jolt.

He turned the light back on, caught a glimpse of himself in the bathroom mirror. His hair was short and gray and spiked with gel, the post–new wave look for aging rock and rollers. Thirty-seven years old and all gray. Just ten years earlier he'd had a head of long brown hair and a desperado mustache. The hair had come off when a girl in a bar had told him he looked "so seventies" by way of a quick get-lost. As for the mustache, he had removed it when some cowboy hat–wearing gay boys eye-fucked him on the street near his Dupont Circle pad.

Karras retrieved the vial from his black Levi's and unscrewed the plastic top. A tiny spoon dangled from the inside of the top on an attached chain. He dipped the spoon into the vial, removed a miniature mound of coke, fed one nostril, repeated the action, fed the other. He put everything back in place, ran some water from the spigot, wet his fingers, put the tips of his fingers into his nostrils, and inhaled. Karras splashed water on his face, dried it with a towel, and winked at his reflection. He switched off the light and headed out the door.

"Oh, shit," said Clay, pointing at the set. "Lefty, don't be lettin' Gatlin throw that ball in. 'Cause you know Gatlin threw it to the wrong uniform when they played Georgia Tech in the ACC tournament."

"Pulled a Fred Brown," said Karras, moving alongside Clay.

But Gatlin didn't pull a Fred Brown. He got the ball in to Len Bias. Bias drove and was fouled before the shot.

"What do we got?" said Karras.

"Thirty-nine seconds left," said Clay, and Karras grinned at the sight of spit flying from Marcus's mouth. He was just so *into* this shit.

"And?"

"Pepperdine came back from a twelve-point deficit to bring it to within two."

"Your boy Bias gonna let it get away?"

"Man can't do it all himself. Got twenty-four, and he's been pullin' down mucho rebounds, too. Help if he had a center out there. Know how many Terry Long's hit today? Zeee-ro."

"Relax, Marcus."

"Relax? Man, *fuck* all that."

Bias hit the one-and-one, and then the Waves had no option but to foul. Keith Gatlin went to the line, hit both from the charity line, and ended the game. The Terps had made it past the first round. Karras and Clay gave each other skin.

"Well, Georgetown beat Texas Tech yesterday," said Clay. "And we got Duke and Syracuse, Louisville and Navy, too — Mr. Robinson's in his neighborhood, and I do believe he came to play."

"Had thirty against Tulsa."

"*All* my teams made it through. We got us a tournament now."

"Looking forward to the rest of the games —"

"After you get your ass out there to the stores. Need you to look in on Arlington today."

"Shit, Marcus, you know I can't deal with Northern Virginia on a Friday afternoon. Might as well park my car out there on Sixty-six."

"You're my GM, man, you *got* to deal with it, hear?" Clay turned, looked up at Karras. He narrowed his eyes. "Dimitri, you don't mind my saying so, your jaws are lookin' kind of tight."

"Been grinding my teeth is all." Karras felt his forced smile. "The pressure of working under you."

"You ain't been hittin' that freeze back in the bathroom, have you?"

"*Fuck* no, man. Besides, you know I'm just a weekend warrior."

"We're damn near right up on the weekend now."

"I said I wasn't using," said Karras, moving his eyes away from Clay's.

"All right, man, I'm just checking."

Karras moved toward the entrance to the showroom. He could hear the new Cameo coming from the sales floor.

Clay said, "Hey," and Karras turned.

"What?"

"You read the *Post* today?"

"Haven't got around to it yet."

"Houston let John Lucas go. Man went and failed his second drug test."

"That's too bad."

"Yeah, it *is* too bad. Lucas could play. Was a role model, too. I remember seein' him when he was at Maryland, wearin' those crisp tennis whites. He was one of those Gold Coast brothers. Young black men in this town could look up to him, 'cause he had it all in front of him, see? Now he's just another one who went and threw it all away on some powder."

"It's a damn shame."

"Go on and mock it. But I'm just tellin' you because . . ." Clay stood out of his chair and waved his hand. "Ah, forget it, man."

Karras looked at Clay standing in front of his desk, handsome with his close-cut hair and thick mustache. Even if it *was* out of style now, even if it *had* been a gay look for years now, Clay wouldn't have shaved off that mustache for anyone but himself. He wouldn't have shaved it because Marcus Clay knew who he was. Karras had never felt that kind of peace.

"Don't worry, Marcus. I got it under control."

"You do?"

"Yeah."

"If you say you do," said Clay, nodding, "then I guess you do."

Karras and Clay went out to the sales floor, where Clarence Tate, Clay's controller, was talking to the new store manager, a guy who went by the name of Cootch. Cootch smoked Newports and wore long-sleeved Oxford shirts year round to hide his skinny arms. He claimed the girls liked him better like that, covered up, until they got surprised by the rest of him later on. Cootch had a big smile reflecting his positive disposition and a solid work ethic to go with it; Clay had recently promoted him from his six-month stint as a clerk at the Dupont Circle store.

Tate stood behind the new register and explained the order-entry system, once again, to Cootch. Clay watched Tate's face, the sidelong looks he gave Cootch as he tried to keep a lid on his impatience. All right, Cootch was a little slow on the uptake. But he loved music, had a deep knowledge of it, and was pleasant with the customers. Tate had to understand; not everyone caught on as fast as he did with this computer shit. But everyone did have their strengths, which was why Clay had Karras out in the stores, hiring and firing and dealing with personnel, and why he had Tate, who was a man who could deal better with numbers than with people, behind a desk.

You had to give Clarence Tate credit, though. While working full time for Real Right he had done six years of night school and gotten his accounting degree. All that and he had raised young Denice, too, all by himself. Clay had been lucky to find Tate, and keep him, after that bad shit they had all got wrapped up in back in '76.

"Yo, boss," said Cootch. "Wha'sup?"

"Cootch," said Clay. "How you doin' with that, man?"

"He's gettin' it," said Tate, who picked up a tabloid-sized newspaper off the counter as he moved out from behind the register stand. Tate was as tall as Clay, but his schedule through the years had kept him away from any kind of exercise. Unlike Clay, he had let himself spread out.

"Clarence," said Karras.

"Dimitri."

"Any beeswax?" said Karras. Not that he cared much about the numbers, but the coke pulsing through his blood was pushing him to conversation.

"Huh?" Tate seemed distracted. He kept glancing over to the window fronting the store, where his daughter, Denice, stood looking out across the street, her book bag over her shoulder.

"The business," said Karras. "We doin' any?"

"Never enough," said Tate, his standard answer. He turned to Clay, held up the newspaper. "Course, we might be doin' better if we were in *City Paper* this week —"

"Had a full-page grand opening ad in there last week," said Clay. "Can only afford two of those a month."

"What you gotta do, then," said Tate, "is run a half-page *every* week. Got to be in that joint every single week, Marcus."

Karras looked at the two of them. They had this same argument every Friday, usually right about this time.

"I like those big ads, Clarence. Keeps the competition on their toes. Makes us look like somethin'."

"It's like they always told us in my marketing classes," said Tate, "when they were teachin' us print advertising: Frequency beats size, Marcus, every time."

"That's what *she* said," said Karras, and no one responded. Well, Cootch did give him a charitable, lopsided grin.

Clay rubbed his face. "Cootch, turn that music down a touch, will you, man?" The music always got to Clay first, even more so in the last few years, as he neared the end of his thirties.

"This one's gonna be big, Marcus," said Karras, nodding at the wall-mounted speakers where the eight-piece funk was coming through.

"Bigger than the moonwalk," added Cootch.

"Yeah, I know." Clay hadn't paid much attention to this group since *Cameosis* in '80, but even he still knew a hit when he heard one. "Word Up" was going to be the bomb in D.C.

"Better be big," mumbled Tate. "We brought in enough units, man. And too many on the wax side, if y'all don't mind my sayin'."

"The twelve-inch on this one," said Clay, "is going to go large."

Karras had been hoping the conversation wouldn't go in this direction. The product mix had been the most heated debate subject for the last six months. Lately, they had been bringing in about 80 percent vinyl and cassette, 20 percent CD. No one seemed to know for sure the way the software was going to shake out. On top of that, the rumor mill had the national chains headed toward town. It was a crazy time to be in the music business. And a really crazy time, thought Karras, to be opening new stores.

"Hey, Neecie," shouted Tate across the store. "Come away from that window, now, hear?"

Tate knew who she was looking at: that boy leaning against the Z, looked like some kind of drug boy to him, across the street. His girl was too young to be fraternizing with young men. She was especially too young to be checking out young men like *that* one. Far as he was concerned, she'd always be too young.

Denice Tate rolled her eyes and walked toward the men in the center of the store. She was fourteen, tall like her father, and suddenly running more to woman than to girl. Her hair fell in cornrows around a wide and pretty face.

"Denice," said Cootch, saving her from her old man. "Got somethin' for you here."

He pulled a cassette tape from under the counter, handed it to Denice.

"What's this?" she said, inspecting the unlabeled tape.

"Rare Essence," said Cootch, "live at Anacostia Park, nineteen hundred and eighty."

Her eyes widened. "Dag, you got *this?*"

"First generation, off my personal master. Take care of it, girl, it's precious."

"Thanks, Cootch. They say this be bumpin'!"

"They say this *is* bumpin'," corrected Tate, and once again Denice rolled her eyes.

"*Bumping*," said Karras to Tate. "You dropped your *g* there, Clarence. Just thought I'd point it out."

"Thanks, Professor. Was wonderin' why the boss man keeps your Greek ass around."

Clay was looking through the window and out to the street, where a fine-looking white woman had gotten out of one of those Lee Iacocca cookie-cutter sedans and was crossing, heading toward the store. Ankle-high black boots with a short, tight skirt, black stockings, a jean jacket over a purple sweater — one of Dimitri's friends, no doubt.

"Hey, Mitri," said Clay, pointing his chin toward the street. "What you think about a woman wears shorty boots with a skirt like that?"

"That's her hookup, I guess. You gotta admit, on her it looks good."

"Yes, it does." Clay liked the way she walked, too, not just the hip action, but the determination in her step. "You think she's lost or somethin', comin' in for directions?"

Karras smiled. "No, she's not lost. She's comin' to see *me*."

"I'm just messin' with you, man. I knew who she was comin' to see."

"You could tell, huh?"

"Yeah," said Clay. "She looks like one of yours."

Clay expected a response to that one, but Karras hadn't heard the cut. He was already headed for the front door.

Karras chuckled to himself, noticing Donna's Susanna Hoffs–style haircut as she neared the door. It was the medium-length cut from the cover of the *All Over the Place* album, not the redone Hoffs look off the new LP. It would be just like Donna to be a little bit behind in her look. But it suited her, that black hair fluffed out, shorter on the sides and hitting her shoulders in the back, the black a nice contrast to her pale skin. She had the thick black eyeliner going today, too. He liked that.

He held the door open for her. She came in, and they embraced. Karras pushed himself into her for a moment, a habit of his, letting her know that he was still all there. Donna broke off first.

"That you?" said Karras, giving her his patented smile, wide and holding, though a bit tight from the cocaine. "For a minute there, I thought it was that Bangles girl walking across that street."

Donna turned to the side, made forty-five-degree angles with both wrists, did a brief version of the "Walk Like an Egyptian" dance she had seen on MTV. Miniskirted girls were doing it on the floor of Cagney's and Poseurs and the other new-wave clubs all around town.

"Yeah, it's just me," said Donna. "How you doin' Mr. Karras?"

"Doin' good. Come on, say hello to everyone."

Karras introduced her to Cootch, Tate and Denice, reintroduced her to Clay. Clay could hardly keep track of Karras's women through the years, but this one he recalled vaguely, if only for her face. One of his students back when he was teaching at the University of Maryland.

Clay and Tate returned to their argument about frequency versus size, and Cootch asked Denice if she wouldn't mind helping him file some new stock into the racks.

Donna and Karras were alone. Donna leaned forward, put her mouth close to Karras's ear.

"Got something for me?" she said.

"Yeah," said Karras. "Come on back."

Marcus Clay watched them enter the back room.

FOUR

Dimitri Karras pulled the vial from the pocket of his jeans and unscrewed its top. Donna Morgan had a seat on the edge of the sink. It was cramped in the bathroom; Karras took his liberty, brushed the rough denim of his leg against Donna's stockinged thigh.

Donna pulled her leg back an inch. "Isn't Marcus gonna know something's going on?"

"He's out there arguing with Tate. Believe me, they'll keep arguing for the next ten minutes." Karras lifted a spoonful of coke up to Donna's nose. "Here."

Donna hoovered it like a pro. "Mmm." She did a quick shake of her head.

"Another?" said Karras, and she took it in.

"Wow. This is the same shit I'm getting?" Donna pushed her pelvis out to slip her fingers into the right pocket of her skirt. She pulled free five folded twenties.

Karras nodded. "It's cut out of the same eight ball."

"Cool."

Karras fed himself a couple of mounds. He had felt the start of that familiar, sad crash a couple of minutes earlier, and he thought he might as well get back up. He'd be on it into the night now, he knew.

Karras retrieved his wallet, pulled Donna's snow-sealed gram from the secret place behind the photograph of his mom. He handed Donna the gram. Donna handed him the money.

"I don't deal," said Karras.

"I don't *care*."

"I just want you to know, I picked this up from my guy as a favor to you."

Donna put the gram where the money had been.

"What does that mean, you're some kind of angel now? You used to sell pot. I can remember that."

"No one sells pot anymore," said Karras.

"Well, I appreciate it, Mr. Karras. So does Eddie."

"You still with him?"

"Uh-huh." Donna eye-swept Karras. "He's steady."

Karras smiled tightly. "Right."

They heard an explosion. Donna let herself down off the porcelain. The sound did not seem too close, but she had felt a vibration coming through the sink.

"Jesus," said Donna.

"I know. Sounds like someone had a wreck or something out on U."

"We better —"

"Yeah." Karras had the vial out of his pocket again before Donna could step around him. He hadn't been around her for a while, and now that he had her here he didn't want to see her go. "Want another taste real quick?"

"Sure."

They did another round. Karras was rushing hard. The bathroom *was* too small now. He could see Donna was anxious to move. He could hear sirens from out on the street.

"Let's go," said Karras. "We better see what that is."

"What's going on?" said Karras to Cootch.

"I don't know for sure," said Cootch, "but it looks pretty bad."

Karras and Donna went by Denice, who stood by the plate glass window next to her father, a little behind him and to the side, her hand touching his hip.

Karras pushed through the door. Donna followed him outside. A car was in the air, suspended and burning on the end of a flatbed truck parked in the construction median. People stood on the opposite sidewalk, watching quietly, a couple of them just a step or two out in the street, but not too far because of the heat and smoke. A squad car had pulled over and a couple of uniformed cops, one black and one white, were out and asking the ones who had begun to close in to step back. An ambulance was traveling west down U, with the heavier siren of a fire truck not far behind.

Donna saw Eddie's Plymouth going east, then the red of his taillights, then the Plymouth turning left. Donna thought, Maybe the cops told Eddie to get the hell off the street. He'd circle around the block, pick her up.

"Be right back," said Karras.

Donna said, "I'll be here." She reached into her jean jacket and pulled out a cigarette. She lit it, pulled hard on it, kept the smoke deep in her lungs; nothing better than nicotine over cocaine.

Karras met Clay, who was stepping back away from the car, in the street.

"Marcus."

"Hey, man. Where you been?"

"In the back with my friend."

"In the back, huh?"

"We heard the noise and came out. What happened?"

"Damn if I know."

Karras stepped toward the car. Clay grabbed ahold of his arm, held him back. Karras saw something in Marcus's eyes, stopped walking.

"What is it?"

"You don't want to see that, Dimitri. Been a long time since I seen that kind of shit my own self. Saw it plenty in the war, but . . . shit."

"What?"

"Boy got his head tore off, man. One of those I beams went through the windshield of that Buick, ripped that mothafucker right off his shoulders."

"All right," said Karras. "I'm not going near it. I'll stay right here."

They watched the rescue squad clue the fire department in. They watched the fire department extinguish what was left of the flames.

Clarence Tate noticed that the driver of the black Z had come back and parked the car on the south corner of 11th. He watched the driver — tall and slim, not a bad-looking kid — get out of the car. The door on the passenger side opened. A shorter, more muscular kid stepped out, down-stepped around the car to where the taller kid leaned. Despite the cold, the short kid went without a jacket. He wore a white T-shirt clinging to a cut chest and oversized biceps. He wore two gold chains out over the shirt. He wore the Scowl that young boys felt they had to wear these days. Tate thinking, These two here are definitely in the life.

"Daddy?"

"What, Neecie?"

"The person in the car is dead, right?"

The rescue squad people had looked in the Buick. Now they were just standing around. Their squad leader had said something to one of his men over by the fire truck as it had arrived, and now the firemen were putting out the blaze. The smoke was thick and black, and it was rising off the street.

"That's right, honeygirl," said Tate.

Tate could see the shorter kid talking with his hands, trying to make a point to the taller kid. The taller kid kept looking toward the window of the store. He was looking for Denice.

"You know that boy?" said Tate.

Tate didn't have to say *which* boy. Out the corner of his eye he had seen Denice glancing that way.

"I seen him around."

"You don't need to be talkin' to him. He's too old to be talkin' to *you*, hear?"

"Daddy, I don't even know his name."

She did know his name. It was Alan Rogers. He was tall and he was cute. It was good to know a boy like that. She was scared on these streets now, with all the rough boys talking trash to her as she walked back and forth from school, pushing themselves against her in the stairwell *in* school. Hard-looking boys; she heard tell some of them had guns. It was good to know a cute boy like Alan, who was hard, too, but in a different way, who drove a nice car, who had respect, who could protect her from those other boys.

"You hear me, girl? I don't want you talkin' to his kind."

"Oh, Daddy —"

"Daddy nothin'. You mind me now, hear?"

Tate's voice was harsh. But he hoped she understood that he loved

28

her, just loved her so much. He scolded Denice to make his point known. As he scolded her, he stroked her hair.

Officer Kevin Murphy told the usual Medger's winos to get back up on the sidewalk. A couple of elderly men from the residential side of 11th had come over, too, and Murphy ordered them back, too, gently and with more respect. He watched Tutt get close to the burning Buick, and then he watched Tutt make his way toward the Z, where two of Tyrell's boys, Alan Rogers and Sean "Short Man" Monroe, stood against the car. He could see Tutt shake his head subtly to Rogers, as subtly as a clumsy guy like Tutt could manage. Then Tutt started back, stopped to talk to a couple of other uniformed cops, two young white guys named Platt and Thompson, who had just come upon the scene. Platt was all right, hardworking and by all accounts committed; Thompson was mean and stupid, red to the core, just like Tutt.

Tutt looked over at the Buick, said something to Thompson, and Thompson laughed. The kid in the Raiders jacket, the one who always stood in front of the liquor store, walked by them. He stepped out into the street, his hands in his pockets. He walked toward Murphy.

"All right, young man," said Murphy. "Get back over there with the others."

"Sure thing, officer," said the kid, but he didn't move.

"You heard me, why you're not walkin'? Move along."

"I saw what happened," said the kid.

"The accident?"

"After, too."

"Lotta people saw it. You don't worry yourself over this now, hear? Get back up on that sidewalk."

"Whatever you say."

The kid smiled a little, walking away.

Murphy checked the cockiness in the kid's step, pictured himself at the kid's age, on these same streets, twenty years ago. Tried to picture this new world through the kid's eyes.

Murphy called out, "Say, young brother. What's your name?"

"Anthony Taylor," said the kid, still walking, not turning. "Up around my way they call me T."

"You live around here?"

"My corner," said Anthony. "Right over here."

Murphy watched him go there and take his place.

"Dag, boy," said Sean "Short Man" Monroe. "How'd you like to go out like Junie went today?"

"I don't want to go out no way," said Alan Rogers. "I want to live."

"I ain't goin' out like that. Gonna take some *with* me when I go."

"No doubt you will."

Monroe licked his lips. "You know, Tyrell told Junie not to buy that car. Knew it was too much for him. Knew Junie'd fuck his own self up behind the wheel. Don't you know, little nigga like Junie couldn't even reach the pedals and shit."

"Junie did like to drive fast."

"Tyrell *told* him not to be drivin' so fast when he had 'caine or money in the car. Man had twenty-five grand in a pillowcase, goin' to make a buy, doin' seventy down U."

"Didn't listen."

"Never *did* have no control. Grand National and shit. Way he drived, man shoulda been drivin' a Dodge Omni, some shit like that."

The white cop, Tutt, came close by, shook his head slightly in Rogers's direction. Then he walked away.

"Redneck mothafucker," said Monroe.

"*Talk* about it."

"What, he claimin' the money ain't in the car?"

"That's what he's sayin', yeah."

"Tyrell ain't gonna be happy, man."

"Could be in the trunk, you never know. Coulda burned up, too. Tutt'll find out when the smoke clears. We'll talk to Tutt later."

"*You* talk to him. I say fuck that mothafucker, boy."

"Yeah, I know. Come on."

They got into the Z. Monroe saw Rogers take a last look over at the record store before he gunned it down 11th.

"Look at you," said Monroe, laughing. "You still goin' at that young stuff."

"She look good, man."

Monroe pursed his lips. "Clean, too. After you hit that shit, I'll be right behind you."

"She's nice," said Alan Rogers softly.

Monroe said, "Got a good ass to fuck, too."

Marcus Clay stood watching the street scene unfold. He saw the familiar, aging residents who came from their two-story 11th Street row houses to see the action. He saw the beat cops who worked his district, one of whom he recognized as a brother who had come out of Cardoza a few years after him. He saw the kid who always stood on the corner at the liquor store, the winos out front. He saw the drug boys leaning against their pretty sports car, just two of the many who were driving middle-class residents out of the city, keeping them away from U, keeping them and their children from patronizing his shop. Maybe Elaine had been right: He must have been off to think that a new record store could go down here in Shaw.

Clay noticed the white beat cop, a no-neck musclehead, walk over to the drug boys and half shake his head. Clay saw his partner talking to the boy in the Raiders jacket. Clay thought about what he had seen just after the Buick had burst into flames.

Dimitri Karras returned. He had been checking on his lady friend, who stood back on the sidewalk huffing a cigarette.

"Guess the show's about over," said Karras.

"Yeah," said Clay, cocking his head. "Funny thing, though."

"What's that?"

"Your girlfriend, what's her name, Madonna?"

"Donna Morgan."

"Her. She came with that boy drivin' the K car, right?"

"He split. She was just wondering if he was comin' back."

"I don't think he *is* comin' back. Thing is, I saw him pull somethin' out of that drug car while it was burnin' up. Saw him put it in his car — a pillowcase or somethin' — and take off."

"Why do you say that's a drug car?"

"That there's a brand new Grand National, Dimitri. Top of the line. I got close enough to see the hands wrapped around that wheel. Looked like a kid's hands. How you gonna figure a young black kid, sixteen, seventeen years old, gonna afford one of those?"

"Sounds like you're makin' a big leap, just 'cause he's young and black."

"All I see around here every day, it ain't no leap. And don't be throwin' that 'just 'cause he's black' shit up in my face. Remember who you're talkin' to, man."

"Okay, maybe I'm wrong. Maybe I have no idea."

"I do. Trust *me*."

"What're you sayin', Marcus?"

"Just . . ." Clay looked into Karras's eyes. "Shit."

"What?"

"I don't even know why I'm talkin' to you now. You higher than a mothafucker, man."

"I am not."

"Hard eyes, can't stand in one place. Grindin' your teeth and shit. Now you're gonna look at me and tell me, 'I am not.'"

"Marcus —"

"Look, man, I know your girl came down here to cop some blow. I know you were back in the head feeding each other's noses. *Her* boyfriend took somethin' out of a drug car, could've been drugs, could've been money, could've been that dead boy's dirty laundry for all I know, and he booked. What I'm tellin' you is, I don't wanna know. I don't want to know about that kind of trouble, and I damn sure don't want you bringin' that kind of trouble around, hear?"

"I don't know her boyfriend. I don't know anything about him or that car."

"Look —"

"Okay, I hear you, Marcus."

"I got a business to run."

"I hear you."

"You got the rest of the day off, man. Get her out of here and go."

"I'm sorry, man. I'll see you back at the apartment."

"Good."

Karras rubbed his chin. "Marcus?"

Clay sighed. "Ain't no thing, man. Just go ahead."

They shook hands. Clay watched Karras go back and talk to his coke-head girl. He wished Karras hadn't mentioned the apartment. It was bad

32

enough, what with his business troubles, trying to keep his head up, that Elaine had thrown him out of their own house. That he was separated from her and Marcus Jr., their three-year-old son. Now he and Dimitri, a couple of grown men coming up on forty years old, were sharing an apartment.

He didn't need to be reminded of all that. Especially not today.

FIVE

Marcus Clay hit the gas, ascending the big hill of 13th Street that was the drop-off edge of the Piedmont Plateau. His Peugeot fought the hill, knocking all the way. The engine made a sound Clay hated, like the rattle in an empty spray-paint can. He never did like this car. All the buppies in D.C. were buying Peugeots now, from the old money up on North Portal Drive to the suburbanites to the Huxtable-looking trust-fund kids on the campus of Howard U. Elaine had encouraged him to buy his, telling him he'd look like a real businessman behind the wheel of the import. It was what *she* wanted to be seen in when they pulled up to the houses of her attorney friends. It had hurt him to give up his '72 Riviera with the boat-tail rear. There wasn't anything wrong with it that a tune-up and some new rubber couldn't have cured. Goddamn if that Riviera wasn't one righteous, beautiful car.

Clarence Tate sat in the passenger seat. His daughter sat in the back. Clay was giving them a lift home, as Tate's Cutless Supreme was just coming out of the shop. Denice Tate stared out the window, saying nothing. The burned-up boy in the Buick had been her first close-up look at death.

Clay looked left at the Clifton Terrace apartments. Run-down to the point of irreversible disrepair, roach and rat infested, play areas strewn with garbage and needles and broken glass . . . a nightmare for the women and children who lived inside its walls. The second of the mayor's three wives, Mary Treadwell, had skimmed hundreds of thousands of dollars out of Pride Incorporated, the agency responsible for much of the city's subsidized housing. The money she had taken had included Clifton Terrace rent payments. Treadwell had stolen from the poor while living high in the Watergate apartments and cruising the city in her shiny Jag. Treadwell had been sentenced to three years. She was serving it after losing her last appeal in 1985.

Tate looked through *his* window at Cardoza High on the right. Denice would be entering it next fall. More money was available to D.C. schools than to practically any school district in the country. Despite this, Tate knew of no public school system in worse shape. Leaking roofs, broken windows, lack of running water and working toilets in bathrooms, a severe shortage of supplies, in many cases *no* supplies. Tate knew that most of the money had gone to midlevel administrators. And Tate had read in the *Post* how the mayor had awarded many of the major school contracts to minority firms, how those firms had driven up the cost of supplies, materials, and repairs to outrageous levels. Since the well was only so deep, the artificially high cost meant less of everything for the children. Tate was all for brothers giving brothers preferential treatment in business — hell, it worked for the Koreans and Greeks and Italians who had come before them. But the mayor's administration had made a handful of black men wealthy while tens of thousands of black *children* went without across the city. Tate couldn't abide by that. He loved D.C. But he'd be damned if he'd see his little girl have to put up with that kind of day-to-day substandard bullshit much longer. He'd leave the city if he had to, even if it was the last thing he ever wanted to do.

"Daddy?"

"What, baby?"

"I was gonna go over to Ashley's tonight, watch some video."

"Ashley's momma gonna be there?"

"Yes, Daddy."

It ain't *exactly* a lie, thought Denice. Ashley's mom *is* gonna be there, but me and Ash are not. Chuck Brown and the Soul Searchers are playing at the Masonic Temple tonight. We're gonna be *there*. And it is gonna be the *bomb*.

"All right, honeygirl," said Tate. "You can go if you'd like."

Donna Morgan looked across at Dimitri Karras. Karras wore his cat eye–lens Vuarnets, his gray hair moussed and spiked. He sat low in the driver's seat of the 325, his right hand working the stick.

Karras in a Beamer. Spiked hair and Vuarnets. If the yuppies had a coat of arms, it would be those sunglasses, that haircut, this car. She wasn't surprised that Karras had adopted the uniform. Karras had always worn masks.

She had met him at College Park, when she was a student and he taught American lit. That was the seventies, when he still wore the Shaggy Professor mask — longish hair, droopy Wyatt Earp mustache, corduroy sport jacket over Hawaiian shirt and jeans. Clydes on his feet. He had that casual thing down cold with his students — I'm older than you but, hey, I'm *one* of you — and also a rep with the girls. Men who were sexually aggressive didn't scare Donna. They never had. And besides, Karras was cute. The first day of class, when his eyes flashed on hers from the front to the back of the room, she knew he was going to be inside her. It was just a question of when.

Karras wasn't much of a teacher. He claimed to love books, but seemed wary of overanalyzing them. The syllabus required that the students read six assigned novels over the course of the semester and show up for class twice a week. There would be a final because there had to be a final, but Karras assured them it would be lightly weighted against their overall participation in the weekly discussion, which tended to concern the book at hand only marginally. To no one's surprise — he always looked a little stoned — Karras admitted his love of marijuana one day to everyone in the room. At undergrad Maryland U, this was akin to pulling one's finger out of the dike. After his confession, a majority of his students began to meet out on the mall, where kids played Frisbee and caught sun and walked bandanna-clad dogs, and get smoked up together before his class. The discussions thereafter were sometimes heated, momentarily interesting, frequently incoherent, and instantly forgotten. At the time, the word on campus was that Dimitri Karras's class was "really deep."

Donna Morgan nailed Karras behind his desk after class one afternoon about three weeks into the semester. There was little verbal foreplay before she brazenly cupped a handful of his jeans. She straddled him on his chair and gave him the goods, really pushed it out. He had this smile on his face, this I-Don't-Give-a-Fuck-About-Nothin' smile, that should have hipped her to his character. He never even said, "Maybe we shouldn't," or even the more cowardly "Do you think we should?" There was no ethical question raised because neither of them thought to bring it up. Teaching was just something Karras was doing on the way to something else, and Donna attended classes with naked disinterest and a blind eye to the future. Indeed, Karras ankled his position at the end of the semester. Donna dropped out of school at the same time and never returned.

They had stayed boyfriend and girlfriend for a few months into the new year. He began to move dope in quantity, and she took a salesclerk job out at the Hecht's in Wheaton Plaza. They broke up, for reasons Donna could not now remember, sometime in the spring. Donna heard later from a friend that Dimitri had gotten into some unspecified bad shit in the summer of '76, and that he had given up wholesale for retail — records, that is.

Over the next ten years, she ran into him maybe twice. Once down on 19th Street in 1980, when they were both standing in line to see *Raging Bull* at the Dupont. On that night, Dimitri wore a new mask: an Elvis Costello pompadour and a deep-weave overcoat with heavily oilskin shoes, straight off the cover of *Get Happy*, his retro Teddy Boy look. She saw him a couple of years later at the Wax Museum, Graham Parker's *Real Macaw* tour. Karras wore a black sport jacket, pointed Italian shoes, and a skinny black tie, like the *Special Beat Service* boys coming off the plane. Karras had begun to go gray.

On those occasions when cocaine brought them back together, she called him Mr. Karras. It was an unsubtle jab at their age difference, but also a reminder of their teacher/student history. Karras didn't seem to get it. If he did, he didn't care.

Mask or no, Donna had to admit that Dimitri Karras looked good behind the wheel of his BMW. Rumpled, waved out, or yuppified, the man always had style.

"Nice car," said Donna.

"You think?"

"Oh, yeah."

"I didn't want to be one of *them*. But I saw this on the lot and fell in love. The navy over burgundy combo, it's bad, isn't it?"

Donna ran her hand over the leather seat. "It's really nice."

"I been workin' hard these last few years. I had the money. No kids to support, nothin' like that, so . . ."

"You don't have to apologize. Everybody's making money these days.

You gotta spend it on something, right?" Donna looked out the window. They were coming into Georgetown via M. "Where we going?"

"I've got to stop by the store, check in."

Marcus had told him to go home. But Karras would call Marcus from the Georgetown store, score a few points, let him know he was still on the case.

Karras said, "Where were you and Eddie off to tonight?"

"Echo and the Bunnymen at Lisner. I left the tickets in his visor."

"Funny, him taking off like that."

"I know. I wonder why he booked."

Karras looked over at Donna in her seat, the cut of her black-stockinged thigh. Karras hadn't mentioned his conversation with Marcus to Donna. He was glad Eddie Golden had taken off. He didn't care about Eddie heisting a pillowcase out of some drug car. He didn't want to know. He didn't want *Donna* to know, not tonight. He wanted Donna alone.

"Well," said Donna, "I guess that takes care of the concert."

"Look, we'll call Eddie in a little while, find out what happened. With that crash so close to him, he probably got spooked is all. Maybe you guys can still make the show. Anyway, if you ask me, he did you a favor, taking off with those tickets."

"Aw, come on, the Bunnymen rock."

"The Bunnymen suck."

"Okay. What were *you* going to do tonight?"

"I don't know. Check out some music, I guess."

"You know," said Donna, "if Eddie doesn't turn up, I got nothin' to do."

"Eddie doesn't show," said Karras, "it's you and me."

Donna stifled a smile. The situation couldn't be better. She had a virgin gram in the pocket of her skirt, and she was riding in a new Beamer with a good-looking man behind the wheel.

Karras was a sprinter, and Eddie went long distance. She figured, whatever happened tonight, Eddie would be around in the morning. She hoped Eddie wouldn't post tonight.

"Mr. Karras?"

"Huh?"

"If we goin' out, I'm gonna need some cigarettes."

Karras cut up 34th, hooked a left onto P Street, found a parking space up near Wisconsin. Karras and Donna had a couple of quick spoons, left the car. Donna stopped in Neam's market for two packs of Marlboro Lights — she could go through two decks easy behind a night of cocaine — and then the two of them walked south on Wisconsin Avenue toward the store.

They passed a Mean Feets, the city's premier shoe boutique. A salesman named Randolph stood outside, leaning against the display window, smoking a cigarette.

"Hey, man," said Karras, "what's goin' on?"

"Ain't nothin' to it," said Randolph. "Just tryin' to make a livin' out here. How those Zodiacs treatin' you?"

Karras looked down at the black leather lace-ups on his feet, rubber soled, utilitarian. Randolph had sold them to Karras, and they were his favorite pair of kicks.

"Treatin' me good."

"Got some Zodiac boots, too, nice low heels, got your name on 'em."

"I'll be in soon."

"You, too, girlfriend," said Randolph to Donna. "Time for you to come on in and see the footdiatrist."

Donna laughed. "Okay. Thanks."

"I'm serious, baby. Not that those shorties you got on don't look good on them legs of yours. Mm-mm-mm."

"We'll be back," said Karras.

"I know you will. And when you do, don't forget to ask for Shoedog."

They kept walking. They passed Commander Salamander, where rich kids from Potomac and McLean came downtown to get their hair dyed pink and buy their bondage "punk" look from the middle-aged proprietors. Well, thought Karras, at least the kids are having fun. Everyone these days is having big fun.

Karras could deal with Georgetown: the lack of parking, the panhandlers, the gimmick bars serving shitty draft beer to Northern Virginia kids on weekend nights, the suburbanites and the crowds, the Iranian and Iraqi merchants selling off-brand clothing and shoes, the "jewelers" pushing gold chains to the drug kids driving in from across town. Marcus Clay *couldn't* deal with Georgetown, so this had become Karras's turf by default. You needed a record store in this part of town if you wanted to be in the business in D.C.

The demand for music was big down here. Two years earlier, a monstrous crowd had pushed through the plate glass window of Kemp Mill Records during an in-store appearance of Frankie Goes to Hollywood. That same year, when a rumor surfaced that Prince had been seen window-shopping on M Street, scores of purple-clad kids had descended on Georgetown in hopes of spotting His Royal Badness. Yeah, Marcus hated G-town, but Karras never tired of reminding him that Wisconsin and O was his top-volume store.

Karras went into the store. Donna Morgan stayed out front, lit up a smoke.

The store was narrow and deep, generally unclean and dimly lit. The new Falco, "Rock Me Amadaeus," boomed from the stereo and pumped the house. The manager, Scott, greeted Karras right away with a handshake and a smile.

"Hey, Dimitri. What's the word?"

"Johannesburg."

Scott was on the heavy side, his face acned from junk food. He wore his shoe polish–black hair short except for a thick lock that fell in front of his face. Marcus had complained about the look, and Karras had shrugged it off, saying it was "a Flock of Seagulls thing." Marcus had said, "A flock of douche bags, maybe. Tell him to get his hair the fuck on out of his face."

But Scott was a good manager, steady and into it, and Marcus soon forgot about the hair. Karras knew that protecting the good employees from Marcus's sometimes grumpy moods was part of his job. Marcus was under a shitload of pressure these days, and Karras understood.

Karras had a quick look around. Scott was ringing a two-person line at the register. Other customers roved the store, suburban white kids with money to spend. Karras transferred the new Bananarama and the new Miami Sound Machine to the front display. He said hello to a clerk named Mary, a dark-haired Brit with whom he had tongue-wrestled at last year's Christmas party. No regrets.

The coke was good. Karras was moving fast, he could feel the tick-tick-tick of blood through his veins; he five-slapped Mary's palm as he passed her in the aisle.

When Scott had finished, Karras asked him to get a reading off the register. Scott did it, handed Karras the cutoff tape. The numbers were typical for a Friday. Karras dialed the U Street store, asked Cootch for Marcus.

"Marcus drove Tate home," said Cootch.

"Marcus calls in, tell him I phoned from G-town, hear?"

"Sure thing, boss."

"Any business over there?"

"Nothin'. They're still out there, blockin' the street."

"All right, man. You take care."

"You, too."

Karras cradled the receiver. He clapped Scott a little too hard on the arm.

"Okay, Scott, I'm outta here. And don't bother calling the other stores."

"Calling the other stores?"

"Yeah, you know, like you managers always do, to warn them that I'm making the rounds. 'Cause I am gone for the day."

"Okay, Dimitri. See you, man."

Karras gave Mary a nice smile — you never knew — and left the store. Donna was out front, working on her second smoke.

"Come on," said Karras.

"Where to?"

"My place. I need a quick shower. Then we're gone."

"Gonna have fun tonight," said Donna.

"Gonna Wang Chung tonight," said Karras. "Let's go."

Marcus Clay parked the Peugeot near Karras's apartment, walked over to the Metro entrance north of Dupont Circle, picked up a *Post* on the way in, and caught a Red Line train down to Judiciary Square. Clay took a seat next to a thin guy reading a thick novel, its cover illustration depicting a submarine, an aircraft carrier, an American flag, and a hammer and sickle, all about to collide.

Clay scanned the *Post*'s front page: CIA Director William Casey was pushing hard for the upcoming House vote allotting $100 million in aid to the "freedom fighters" of Nicaragua. Casey had been the key architect in promoting the Reagan Doctrine, covert paramilitary operations in

Afghanistan, Cambodia, and Angola. Clay shook his head. All it took was a hostage situation in Iran for a whole generation to get gung-ho and forget the horror of Vietnam. Techno-war books, written by those who had never witnessed the violent, useless death of young men, were all the rage. Kids stood in line at the Uptown for tickets to *Top Gun*. Action in foreign lands, the threat of communism, it stirred the blood. Military buildup spurred the stock market and strengthened the economy. Strong economies opened the door for reelections.

Clay scanned the right-hand story above the fold: Alphonse Hill, D.C.'s deputy mayor, had resigned amidst allegations of receiving kickbacks from an out-of-town contractor. Three months earlier, Ivanhoe Donaldson, the mayor's longtime right-hand man, pleaded guilty to stealing almost two hundred grand in city funds and to tax evasion. Donaldson drew seven years in a minimum-security Virginia prison.

Clay sighed, folded the newspaper, turned to the man on his right. "How's it goin'?"

The man looked over, hesitantly said, "Pretty good."

Clay had broken the Metro rule: no eye contact, no conversation with strangers. Especially not between the races.

Clay said, "Good book?"

"Great."

"Looks very exciting," said Clay. "It truly does."

Clay left the train, got up on the street. He went down to the Superior Court building at 5th and Indiana, had a seat on the edge of a concrete planter, kept an eye on the main doors. Elaine would be coming through one of those doors any minute. He knew she'd be rushing out, like clockwork, to pick up Marcus Jr. at the play-school or the child-development center or whatever fancy name they were calling it this week.

Teenage boys were being hurried along by their mothers or their aunts, who scolded them or looked stone-faced ahead as they walked, the boys trying to maintain the Scowl. Older dudes, waiting for their hearings or to testify, or here to pick up buddies or relatives, stood around smoking cigarettes. Lawyers, rumpled Criminal Justice Act types, stood outside, smoking as well.

Elaine was one of the CJA attorneys, court-appointed lawyers, the ones they called the Fifth Streeters. She never looked rumpled, though, not like the others. And she didn't have the buttoned-to-the-neck business look that so many women felt they had to adopt these days. Clay saw women all over town, looked like they had doilies hanging off the front of their dresses; Karras called them their clown outfits. None of that bib and bow tie stuff for Elaine. Elaine always looked like a woman. She *always* looked fine.

Yeah, Elaine would be coming out that door any second. It was different now, not like before the separation, when she used to work those crazy hours, expecting him to drop everything to pick up M. J., expecting *him* to leave his business while she managed her caseload. That had been one of the problems between them. One of many, and then Clay had done that Big Thing that had severed it between him and Elaine.

Here she was now.

And damn, she *did* look fine. Elaine wore a two-piece rust-colored suit, the skirt clinging to those long, muscular legs of hers, the jacket over a cream silk blouse. She was some kind of woman, *all* woman, taller than the man she walked with, some slick dude in pinstripes, powder blue shirt with white Peter Pan collar — Clay hated that elegant-running-to-dandy look — soft leather loafers on his feet.

Clay stood up, got in their path. Elaine saw him, frowned, then smiled cordially. He walked up to the two of them.

"Elaine."

"Marcus."

Clay cupped his hand around her arm, kissed her check. She took the kiss, pulled her arm away from his touch.

"This is Marcus," said Elaine. "Marcus, meet Eric Williamson."

"Marcus *Clay*." He shook Williamson's hand, released it quickly. Man had a conk, Clay couldn't believe it, and a weak-ass mustache. He turned to Elaine. "How you doin'?"

"I'm doing well."

"Thought we might, I don't know, get a cup of coffee or somethin'."

"Can't, Marcus. Got to pick up Marcus Jr."

"Maybe I can ride uptown with you. I'm on foot, see —"

"I don't think so, Marcus."

Clay put his hand back on her arm.

"Marcus, don't."

Williamson said to Elaine, "You all right?"

Clay felt the warmth of blood in his face. He balled his fist, then relaxed it as he took a breath.

"I'm fine," said Elaine. "Really, Eric."

Clay stepped between Williamson and Elaine. As he did, he put the heel of his shoe on the toe of Williamson's thin loafer. Clay put all his weight on the heel.

"Ow!" said Williamson.

Clay stepped off and smiled. Clay said, "You all right?"

"Marcus, please," said Elaine. She bit down on her lip. "Look, Eric . . . I'll see you on Monday, okay?"

Williamson gave Clay a short look. He said to Elaine, "Okay. You have a good one." He walked away.

Elaine got close to Clay's face, spoke firmly. "Marcus, what the hell do you think —"

"Just wanted to see you is all. Didn't mean to embarrass you in front of your pretty friend."

"My friends aren't pretty, Marcus. We're all just doing a job down here, tryin' to defend these people got no one else."

"Save it, baby."

"And, oh, because my friend is a professional, because he wears a suit, now he's pretty."

"French cuffs . . . man had a *conk* and shit. That ain't pretty? Man walkin' around lookin' like the whole DeBarge family put together."

"Look, Marcus . . ." Elaine waved a hand in front of her face. "You're not making any sense. *This* makes no sense. Listen, I've got to go." She walked off.

Clay said, "Elaine! When am I going to see M. J.?"

"Call me," she said, and kept right on stepping in that sure way of hers. He watched her disappear into the crowd.

Clay stood there for a few more minutes, just shaking his head, thinking how funny it was: Once you fuck up, seems you can't *stop* fuckin' up to save your life.

Anthony Taylor watched the last few minutes of the Alabama / Xavier game on the old set he had on the dresser up in his room. Above his dresser hung a Day-Glo Globe concert poster advertising a D.C. Scorpio show coming to town; Bobby Bennett had been talkin' about that show on the radio for a long time. Anthony had ripped the poster off a telephone pole at 14th and Fairmont.

With 3:10 left to play, it looked like Alabama had it in the bag. He watched it through the end, though, just to see the highlights of the Maryland game earlier in the day, Lenny Bias taking it to the hole against Pepperdine. There he was, too, Number 34. Pretty as shit the way he elevated, and stayed elevated, all the way to the dunk.

Anthony shut off the TV. He went over to his dresser, picked up the letter that had come in the mail that day from his moms, read it over again for the third time. The letter started the usual way, talkin' about how his mother was looking for a job, how the girls were doing good, how it got warmer earlier in the year in Georgia and how it got greener down there than it ever did in D.C. "Maybe when school lets out you can come on down, spend the summer with me and your sisters." Spend the summer, the letter said, not come down to live for good.

Anthony knew there wasn't no room for the four of them in his great-uncle's house, a three-bedroom place on some farmland out in Fulton County. No room and never enough money. That's how his mother had explained it when she had left town with his two baby sisters a year ago, left him with *her* mother, a woman he had always called Granmom. Anyway, she said, he was settled here in D.C., it would do him more harm than good to take him out of his school, pull him away from his friends and the teachers he knew. That's what she told him, and that's how it played out. He didn't argue with his mother. His mother had been on welfare and she'd got to using the checks to buy drugs. The drugs had made her skinny and sick. The last time Anthony'd seen her, she looked like forty years old, and she wasn't no more than twenty-eight, twenty-nine. He understood that she needed to get away from the District, start fresh, get herself well.

Anthony had got himself in trouble a few times this past year. He got beat up twice by his school "friends" and his teacher had told him she didn't much care for his attitude. He wasn't hard, not hard for real like some of the other boys, but he had to act tough because if you didn't those other boys would take you for bad and punk you out. He began to cut the classes he could and sometimes entire days. He spent much of his time in the Martin Luther King library down on 9th, reading sports biographies and old-timey books about the West and black cowboys and such, and the rest of his time he'd hang on the corner of 12th and U, where he had gotten to know some of the winos and the merchants around the liquor store. You *saw* things down there, too. And after a while, the older guys on the corner and in the houses down the way, it got comfortable to be around them, like they were some kind of kin.

Granmom tried her best to keep him in the house, but he hung there less and less. Not that she was weak — she wasn't no Moms Mabley–looking grandmother, neither. She was strong, a Viceroy smoker with big arms who supervised an office cleaning crew. Granmom wasn't too old, after all, maybe forty-six, something like that. She was a good woman, too; he knew she meant well with all those lectures she was always giving him. She was real sorry that one time when she'd gotten so mad at him, said his mama had left him behind because he wasn't no good. She apologized right after, even cried some, which he had never seen her do, but it stuck with him just the same. Made him think, Maybe I *am* no good.

Granmom had this boyfriend name of Louis, no-account hustler type, wore velvet sport jackets, wide-brimmed hats, dressed like old school. Came over Friday nights, helped Granmom spend her fresh paycheck on beer and expensive liquor. The two of them would listen to that old Philadelphia sound and some Stax/Volt jive from the days when they were both coming up, get to dancing as the night wore on. Then some loving, or a big argument, one of the two. Either way it ended, Anthony didn't like to be around the house on Friday nights.

He sure would like to see his moms again. And his half sisters, Keechie and Michelle, fathered by a man named Rondo who used to come around and then was just gone. Least they had seen their father, could recall his voice and smell. Anthony had never known his, not even a picture. When he asked about his father he got no straight-up answers. When he kept asking, his moms and Granmom told him to hush his mouth.

Anthony looked at the time on his clock radio. *Solid Gold* was coming on soon on channel 20, right after the *Benson* rerun, but any minute now Louis would be walking through the front door. Anthony changed his shirt, put his Raiders jacket on, double-knotted his Nikes, told Granmom he was going out for a while, and left the house. It was dark now out on the streets.

He walked east on Fairmont. He crossed 13th, quickened his step when he saw a few Clifton Terrace boys hanging out around some parked cars, fast-stepping by them, but not too fast. Head up, eyes straight ahead. At 11th he turned right, went down the hill to U.

The pedestrians had gone home, and the residents were in their houses. He saw a couple of drug cars he recognized, one cruising and one idling at the curb. He saw a foot soldier on the corner and another at a pay phone. Tyrell Cleveland's, all of them. Anthony walked on.

There wasn't anyone in front of the liquor store this evening, just patrons buzzing in, leaving hurriedly, carrying forties and pints wrapped in brown paper. The cops and ambulance people had cleaned up and left the scene. Anthony had recognized that black Buick. He knew the driver by sight, a boy named Junie, a runner for Tyrell. He'd seen the skinny white guy take the money or the drugs or whatever it was out of the burning Buick. The woman who had been with him, the good-looking white woman wearing that short skirt with the short boots, she had gotten out of the skinny dude's Plymouth before it all happened. She had walked into that new record store, come out with another white guy, gray-haired but not too old, after the crash. By then, her friend in the Plymouth had taken off.

Anthony noticed these kinds of things, standing for hours like he did out on this street. He wondered who else would want to know, and if he told them, would he get paid.

Anthony Taylor put his hands in his pockets, looked across the street at the new record store. No customers, just one young brother working inside. Anthony wondered where the owner was, the tall man with the wide shoulders. The guys on the corner said that the tall man was one of those soldiers in that war, Vietnam, ended about the year Anthony was born. The tall man didn't look like any old businessman. He looked kind of hard, like he could go with his hands if the situation came up.

The night, young as it was, felt cold. And there wasn't nobody out tonight 'cept for drug dealers and drunks. Maybe Anthony should go over to that record store when the tall man came back to close up, introduce himself, warm up. Way the tall man looked, he might turn out to be a good man to know.

SIX

Tyrell Cleveland ran one long finger down his cheek and sat back in his chair. He uncrossed his long legs, stretched them out before him. He cracked his knuckles, then let one wrist dangle off the chair's arm.

Tyrell's cousin Antony Ray, whip thin and dressed in a black shirt and black slacks, sat silently on a hard chair against the wall.

"Chink," said Tyrell, "turn that shit off."

"Tyrell, man," said Charles "Chink" Bennet.

"Turn it off."

Bennet scampered off the couch, went over to the wide-screen, kicking Atari wires and empty Doritos bags out of the way. He stood in the blue light for a moment, watching the Suzie Wong video, *Oriental Jade*, that was playing on the set.

"Damn, Chink," said Mario "Jumbo" Linney. He smiled, leaned forward from his place on the couch, where he sat twisting up a fat bone. "Can't you bring your tiny self to stop watchin' that shit?"

"Look at her, though, Jumbo. She's a straight-up freak." Bennet lifted his arm dreamily and pointed at the set. "She pantin' like a *dog*, man."

"She be takin' it like a dog, too."

"Turn it off," said Tyrell.

Bennet reached down and turned off the set. Tyrell relaxed his shoulders. That was better. The sound from the TV was no longer competing with Whodini's new one, *Back in Black*, coming from the stereo. Tyrell could deal with loud music or loud television, one or the other, but not with both. There were a couple of girls making noise and laughing back in the kitchen, high schoolers from Northeast who Alan Rogers and Short Man

Monroe had picked up on their way out East Capitol. Tyrell didn't mind their voices; he planned to double them up later on.

Chink Bennet went back to the couch, sat down next to his friend Jumbo Linney. Linney handed Bennet the lit bone. Bennet hit it hard, kept the smoke down in his lungs.

Jumbo Linney was dark and round and went three hundred pounds at six foot four. He ate greasy hamburgers and food from buckets and bags. But he still had his youth, and he was hard. He was certain his size would protect him. He was too dumb to know fear.

Chink Bennet was tiny, wiry, light-skinned with almond-shaped Asian eyes. When violence went down or was about to, he got giggly, silly as a slumber-party girl. So far he had always held up his end. Sitting next to Linney, he looked like an Afro-Chinese Webster.

Tyrell said, "Alan."

"Yeah, Ty." Alan Rogers leaned with his back against the front door, looked into Tyrell's strange bottle green eyes.

"You say you didn't get close to Junie's car."

"Uh-uh."

"So you don't know."

"Nah. But I got the sign from Tutt. Shook his head as he walked by."

"So he was tryin' to say —"

"That there wasn't a got-damn thing in the car."

"Damn."

"By now he done checked out the whole car, though, Tyrell. By now he'll know for sure. You say he's comin' out?"

"Should be out here real soon." Tyrell looked through the bay window to the street. A set of headlights, with another set behind it, was coming down the gravel road. "That would be them now."

Short Man Monroe stood out of his chair. "You want my opinion, Tyrell, we don't *need* no mothafuckin' po-lice around."

"Relax, Short Man. We do need them. They're gonna help us carve out our territory down there, and protect it once we do have it carved out."

"Can't stomach that Tutt."

"Relax."

"Like to bust a cap in his fat head, too."

"Just relax."

Alan Rogers shook his head. "Junie, man. I can't believe that young nigga's dead."

Tyrell looked at his manicured nails. "I told that boy not to drive so fast."

Richard Tutt stepped out of his Bronco. Kevin Murphy closed the door of his Trans Am, met Tutt in the yard. They moved toward the house, walking between the black 300 and Tyrell's black BMW 633. To the side of the house, Tutt saw Jumbo Linney's beat-to-shit, primered '82 Supra, the two-tone model that made Spics catch wood.

Tutt wore street clothes, a Members Only jacket over a denim shirt worn out, his .45 tucked beneath the band of his acid-washed jeans. Murphy noticed that Tutt had on those gray ostrich-skin Dan Post boots with the three-inch heels, the ones Tutt thought were so fly. Tutt's flattop was gelled, shaved back and sides, no burns, the back of his neck rolled and pink as a baby's ass.

"Tyrell's gonna be all over it tonight," said Tutt.

"Heard that," said Murphy.

"You let me do the talkin', partner."

"You got it, King."

They had come out East Capitol, crossed the Whitney M. Young Bridge over the Anacostia River into P. G. County, taken Central Avenue for a couple of miles through Seat Pleasant and on into a spare mix of residential and commercial structures, gas stations, half-rented strip shopping centers, and the occasional fast food outlet. Back behind one of those strip centers, where only a TV repair shop and a dry cleaner remained in business, was a rocky field split by the access road. The road continued another quarter mile, went to gravel, ended at an old bungalow backed up to a shallow woods of maple and oak. With the strip center forming a one-story concrete barrier and the stand of trees semicircling the right side of the house, the bungalow could not be seen from 214.

About a year back, a Capitol Heights friend had told Tyrell about the For Rent sign out on the highway. Tyrell liked the idea of being out of the city, and when he saw the house, he especially liked how it was kind of tucked back against the woods. He had this coke-whore girlfriend, white freak, a real estate broker named Kerry King. For the free blow he was laying on her and all that good dick she was getting, Kerry had been more than happy to put her name on the lease.

Tutt and Murphy stepped up onto the bungalow's porch. Tutt knocked, and Alan Rogers opened the scarred oak door and stepped aside. Tutt and Murphy entered the house.

"You don't mind," said Tyrell, "if I don't get up."

"Gentlemen," said Tutt, stepping into the room with his stiff weight lifter's gait, his beefy arms pumping him forward, the arms way out at his side.

Murphy scoped the house. Two large rooms, once used as living and dining areas. A stereo, a wide-screen, and a couch and table arrangement where the dining area had been. Jumbo Linney and Chink Bennet sat on the leather couch, laughing and getting high. They had barely acknowledged the cops' entrance. Beyond the couch was an open entrance to a kitchen. The living room contained Tyrell's reclining chair, several folding chairs, a round oak table, and a fireplace, which Tyrell liked to keep live. Murphy knew the layout of the rest of the house: a hallway to the right of the dining area, a bathroom splitting two small bedrooms, a stairwell leading up to an unfinished attic. Murphy and his wife, Wanda, lived in a bungalow just like this one, on 4th and Whittier on the D.C. side of Takoma Park.

Alan Rogers closed the door, went over to the table where Monroe sat, found himself a chair. Kevin Murphy positioned himself behind Tutt, leaned against the door frame, folded his arms. Tutt stood before Tyrell. None of them had made a move to shake hands. That they wouldn't was understood.

"So," said Tyrell.

"Yeah," said Tutt. "Lotta action today."

Tutt smiled cordially, kept smiling as he had a quick look around the place. Mutt and Jeff were back on the couch, cooking their heads on some ragweed, listening to some kind of mindless rap. Tutt could see a gun, looked like a nine, sitting on the table in front of them amidst the clutter of someone's old lunch. To his right, Tyrell's enforcer, Short Man Monroe, sat at the round table, a toothpick in his mouth, polishing one of his two Glocks with a lambskin cloth. Tutt could have laughed out loud: It *would* be just like a nigger to polish a plastic gun. The Rogers kid — Tutt made him as soft — had taken a seat at the table next to Monroe. On the table: an LED readout scale, a mirror with a couple of grams of coke heaped on top, a blade lying next to the coke, an automatic money-counting machine, a brown paper bag holding cash or bricks. A Mossberg pistol-grip, pump-action shotgun leaned barrel up against the bricks above the hearth. With all the McDonald's wrappers, empty chip bags, and half-drunk Big Gulps sitting around, Tutt wondered if any of these geniuses would be able to find his hardware if anything went down.

"About today," said Tyrell.

"You mean Junie," said Tutt.

"Uh-huh."

"Junie's car was empty."

"No pillowcase. No twenty-five grand."

"Nothin'."

"I saw him put it in the car myself before he left to make the buy."

"Maybe Junie got greedy, stashed the bundle somewhere before the accident."

"I don't think so."

Short Man raised his head. "Junie wasn't smart enough to plan nothin' like that."

"Or stupid enough," said Tyrell, "to try and take me off."

"I don't know what happened to it," said Tutt.

"No?"

Tutt motioned toward Rogers and Monroe. "They were there. Maybe you ought to ask your boys."

Short Man stopped polishing his gun. He stared at the floor, re-arranged the toothpick to the other side of his mouth.

"I'll ask them what I want to ask them," said Tyrell. "Right now I'm asking you."

"Me and Murphy," said Tutt, "one way or another, we're gonna find out what happened to your money, Tyrell."

Tyrell stared at Murphy. Murphy held the stare. "That's what I'm payin' you two for. Right, Officer Murphy?"

Tutt cleared his throat. "Okay. So we'll start with some of those neighborhood rummies down there, see what we can dig up."

"Yo, Tutt," said Alan Rogers. "You might want to talk with that kid, too."

"What kid?"

"One stands out front of Medger's all the time."

"Yeah," said Tutt. "I know the kid you mean."

Murphy thought back on the conversation he'd had with Anthony Taylor. "I saw what happened," the kid had said. And when Murphy had told him that a lot of people had seen what had gone down, the kid had said, "After, too." Like he'd seen something else.

"*I'll* talk to the kid," said Murphy.

"Well," said Tyrell, smiling. "The man speaks."

"That youngun always be there," said Monroe. "Calls himself Tony the Tiger, some shit like that."

"Calls himself T," said Murphy. He repeated, "I'll talk to the kid."

"Don't care who talks to who," said Tyrell. "Long as I get what's mine."

Linney and Bennet laughed raucously from the other room. They had turned the porno tape back on, and Chink Bennet was in front of the set, air-humping Suzie Wong.

"I thought I told y'all to cut that tape off," said Tyrell.

Bennet pointed at Linney. "Jumbo did it, Tyrell."

"Damn, Chink, why you be lyin' like that?"

"Turn it off and come in here. We talkin' business; I want y'all to know what's up."

Tutt nodded at the silent man in the hard chair. "Who's the new man, Tyrell?"

"Antony Ray. Cousin of mine. Just got out of Lorton, three weeks back. Served four on an eight-year armed robbery bit. Not sure what his role's gonna be with us, but I am sure he'll fit in somewhere. Right, cuz?"

Antony Ray nodded.

"Antony's great-uncle," said Tyrell, "was a big man down on Seventh Street, way back in the forties. Fellow by the name of DeAngelo Ray."

"Yeah," said Tutt. "Good to know we got some royalty bloodlines comin' into the organization." Tutt tilted his chin up at Ray. "Nice meetin' you, An-tony."

Ray said nothing.

Murphy said, "Gonna get me some water out the back."

Murphy walked into the kitchen. A couple of girls were back there, couldn't have been more than sixteen. They were dancing in place to the Whodini record playing in the other room. One of them, wearing a tight barber pole–striped shirt, looked him over as he passed. Murphy nodded. The girls giggled. Murphy saw a vanity mirror lying on the kitchen counter with lines tracked out on it, and a rolled twenty lying next to the lines. Murphy found a clean glass in a cabinet, ran some tap water into the glass. He drank the water with his eyes closed as he leaned over the sink.

"What's goin' on, Stuff?" said one of the girls.

"You *big*, too," said the other, and both of them laughed.

This is wrong. I'm wrong. Father in heaven, this is all wrong.

Murphy placed the glass in the sink, walked out of the kitchen and back to the front of the house.

When he got there, Tyrell was looking up at Tutt, saying, "So you didn't catch them."

"No," said Tutt. "I had the one kid dead to rights in the alley. Would've caught his ass, too, if it wasn't for all the obstacles your people got set up back there."

"You know who these boys are?"

"*I* know," said Monroe. "One of them calls himself Chief."

"The kid I chased, he was wearin' some bright green knit cap. Kid might as well go on and wear a target next time."

"They just younguns, Ty," said Rogers. "They be *playin'* like they in the life."

"They tryin' to beat me on my own strip," said Tyrell. "Ain't no game to me."

"We'll take care of it," said Tutt.

"Not if I take care of that shit first," said Monroe.

Tutt said, "This ain't about makin' noise, Tyrell. This ain't about startin' a war. This is about control."

"Man's right, Short," said Tyrell. "We don't want no high drama. Just want to keep everything nice and quiet down there. Under control. Why we got our men in blue here on our side."

Linney and Bennet laughed, touched hands.

Murphy said, "Let's go, Tutt."

"Hey, King Tutt," said Bennet. "Those are some sporty shitkickers you got on, man. Where you goin' tonight, some kind of hoedown and shit?"

"What, you don't like my boots, Chink? And here I was gettin' ready to say somethin' to you about that suit you're wearin'."

Bennet looked down at his lime green parachute-material jogging suit as if he were seeing it for the first time. "This suit is bad!"

"It's bad, all right. Matter of fact, I'd own two of them if I was you."

"Yeah?"

"Yeah. One to shit on and one to cover it up with."

No one laughed. Murphy saw Monroe point the Glock at Tutt, mouth the word *pow*.

"Let's go, Tutt."

"Yes," said Tyrell, "maybe you two better get on your way."

Tyrell stood from his chair, uncoiling his gangly frame. Tyrell went six foot six. He was light-skinned and freckled, with long equine features, a hint of beard, pointed teeth, pointed ears. Reminded Murphy of one of those stone figures perched atop white people's churches.

"We'll talk tomorrow," said Tutt.

"Find my money," said Tyrell.

Tutt nodded and made an elaborate good-bye wave of his hand to Monroe. He and Murphy walked from the house, heard the door shut behind them.

In the yard, Tutt looked back at the house and grinned. "Shit. An-tony Ray. Couldn't be just 'Anthony,' had to be 'An-tony.' And you hear Ty-rell in there? 'I'll ax them what I want to ax them. Right now I'm axin' you.'"

"He said 'ask.'"

"What?"

"Nothin'."

"All right, partner. I'll check with you tomorrow, hear?"

"Yeah. See you then."

Tutt climbed up into the Bronco with the oversized tires. Murphy settled into his new Trans Am. He hit the ignition and drove back out to 214.

From the bay window, Tyrell Cleveland watched the truck follow the car out to Central Avenue while Linney and Bennet returned to the couch.

Tyrell went to the hearth and picked up the poker that lay on the bricks. He squatted down before the fire. He moved the logs around and found new flame.

Short Man Monroe lifted his leather jacket off the back of his chair. He put it on, picked his Glock up off the table, fitted it in the waistband of his Lees. He dipped his finger into the cocaine heaped on the mirror, rubbed a generous amount on his gums. He nodded at Alan Rogers.

"We gone, Ty," said Rogers.

"Where you off to?"

"Gonna check out the Chuck Brown show at the Masonic Temple."

"Make the pickups while you're down there."

"Right."

Monroe walked out, leaving the door open. Rogers opened his mouth to speak. He had practiced what he was going to say, said the words aloud to the bathroom mirror just a half hour before: Yo, Ty, for tonight, why can't I be like any young man, forget about the business, just have fun? He looked at Tyrell, squatting there, his face lit by the flames. Damn if Tyrell didn't look like the devil himself.

Rogers kept his mouth shut. He followed Monroe out the door.

SEVEN

Eddie Golden paused on the steps of his Aspen Hill apartment house, put fire to a Marlboro red, and had a quick look around the parking lot. As far as he could tell, no one had followed him home. No brothers in drug cars, and no cops. No phone calls, either, which meant everything had to be cool. So far, at least, Eddie had made out all right.

He went down to the Reliant, parked by the brown Dumpster in the corner of the lot. He had stopped the car when he had made it over the Maryland line, pulled over on a side street to transfer the pillowcase to the trunk. Leaning into the trunk, he couldn't resist, he had to have a look at the money again. And take a couple of hundred out for his pocket. Walking-around money, that's all it was, until he could figure out what to do next.

Right now, Eddie felt kind of loaded down. There was the money in his wallet, twenties and tens, and it felt fat in the back pocket of his jeans. Also the cocaine inhaler in his front pocket, loaded with blow he had just bought from a neighbor, a scientific-looking guy named Leonard who dealt out of his cat piss–smelling one-room on the third floor. His car keys and Donna's apartment keys in the other pocket. A half pack of 'Boros and a full hardpack, one in each pocket of his jacket. All of this made him feel heavy and slow, a funny feeling for a skinny guy like him. And naturally he felt jumpy, too.

After Eddie had copped the blow from Leonard he had gone back downstairs to his own place, got out of his concert clothes, and changed into Wheaton bar dress, a pair of jeans and a flannel shirt. He cut out a couple lines for himself, snorted them using one of the fresh rolled twenties, had a few drags off a cigarette, then went and had a seat on the can. Leonard's coke was cut heavily with mannitol, and the baby laxative had loosened him up right away. He came out of the head and called Donna, left a message on her machine. He did some more coke, sat on the couch alternately smoking and wringing his hands, then packed himself up and booked, as the closeness of the apartment was driving him nuts.

He drove over to Hunter's, a bar at the corner of Georgia Avenue and University Boulevard, and went inside. The place was loaded with the usual Friday night crowd, young white people, blue- and gray-collar, most of them already half in the bag. Eddie got a beer from the bartender, a guy who wrestled All-County for Northwood High, and found his friends at a four-top near the small stage, where a Southern boogie band in the Marshall Tucker/Rossington-Collins mold was tuning up. The table was crowded with Buds and Miller Lites, a couple of dirty ashtrays, and three shot glasses holding the smell of Jack Black.

"Play some Krokus, man!" yelled one of Eddie's friends to the guitar player, and the rest of Eddie's friends laughed.

Eddie's friends were freelance installers, just like Eddie, who worked on commission for several local appliance dealers. They made half of each installation fee, which sounded good on paper, but there were frequently call-backs and cancellations, which Eddie and his friends always blamed on the salespeople who never bothered to ask the right measurement questions when the customers were in the stores. Many of the salespeople were Jewish, making them the further target of Eddie's friends' anger and jokes. Eddie's friends had a name for Jews: tapirs, after the long-nosed mammals one of them had seen once in a picture book.

Eddie himself was Jewish, but he had never gotten around to telling his friends. A name like Golden, you'd have thought they would have known, but they had assumed that Eddie had adopted one of those Vegas strip, crapshooter-cum-good-time-boy names like Bobby Montana or Nicky Diamond, and Eddie never told them different. He had grown up out in Layhill, in a mostly upper-class Jewish neighborhood, and his family had belonged to that Jewish country club out there, Indian Springs, which Eddie's friends of course called "Israel Springs."

Eddie had been the only one out of all his young relatives to end his education at the high school level, and after a couple of years of watching

Eddie lie around the house blitzed on green, his parents had cut him off and told him he was on his own. This was okay by Eddie, who was embarrassed by his mother's loud manner and his father's loud clothing. He'd had it up to there with his successful cousins and the annual Passover dinner, which he could give two shits about, and the Atlantic City ashtrays and the other tchotchkes spread out all over the house. Eddie was a Jewish boy who had been raised right and with plenty of opportunity. But Eddie didn't want to be Jewish. His secret ambition was to be a redneck, just like his friends.

"Thought you had a date," said Mike Frane, a heavyset guy with big arms.

"Nah," said Eddie. "I didn't want to go to that show anyway."

"Bunch of tail gunners," said Frane, "down in D.C."

"What about your girlfriend, though?" said Dave Marshall, the meanest of the bunch, sharp featured and thin lipped. "She go to that bunny-hop show alone?"

"I guess. I don't know. So what?"

"Bet she's got guys sniffing around her right now like a bunch of *big* dogs."

"She'll be all right."

"Sure she will, man."

"Come on," said Eddie, suddenly noticing his empty bottle and looking around for a waitress. "Let's drink."

Eddie bought a round of beers and shots. They drained the shots and lit up smokes. It was early, but Marshall, Frane, and the third man at the table, a stupid, quiet guy named Christianson, all looked cooked. "Fuck or fight" was their motto, but none of these guys had a chance of getting laid, so Eddie knew the way the night would turn out. He got up and went to the pay phone, dialed Donna's number. He left another message on her machine.

Eddie went back to the men's room off the main bar, got in the stall, did a couple of jolts from the inhaler. Out in the main room he said hey to a nice guy named Tony, lit a cigarette, stepped up to the bar, and ordered another round. He carried the beers back to the table, went back for the shots. He had a ton of energy. He didn't really want to sit down. He didn't know what else to do.

Dave Marshall said something to a weak-looking guy who was on his way out the door. Marshall was a coward and had made sure the guy was alone before he called him a "fucking girl."

The table was completely covered now with bottles and shot glasses.

"Thanks for the beers, man," said Marshall.

"Yeah, Eddie," said Frane. "What'd you do, hit the fuckin' number or somethin'?"

Eddie winked and thought of his parents' address. "Eighty bucks. Played seven-three-seven on the box."

"Well, all right," said Christianson.

"Was wonderin' what it was," said Marshall. "You're spendin' money like a nigger in a Seven-Eleven."

Everyone laughed. Eddie Golden closed his eyes, drank down his Jack. He wiped his chin with his sleeve.

Eddie looked around the bar. He missed Donna. He wondered where she was.

Donna Morgan stood at the left corner of the stage at the 9:30, drinking down the last of her beer. Dimitri Karras was pushing through the crowd, a couple of Buds in his upraised hands, trying to get to Donna.

The bass man, second guitar, and drummer were out and prepping their instruments while "How Soon Is Now" played through the sound system. This would be the single Karras would think of when he thought 1986, the way "Brass in Pocket" would always mean 1980 and "Dancing with Myself" would always trigger 1981 in his head.

He got to Donna, handed her a beer. She leaned against the black wall and drank. Her forehead was bulleted with sweat. The place was ass-to-elbow, humid year round, and always smelled like something between piss and perspiration. It was the best live music venue in town.

Karras had wanted her to see the headliner, Tommy Keene, telling her that this was what the "real shit" was all about. He had talked about it all the way downtown, as they traded hits from Karras's amber vial, and down the long hall entrance to the club, where Cure-cut Robert Smith look-alikes in long overcoats and other kids in mostly black lounged around, talking and smoking cigarettes. Karras was so excited that Donna didn't have the heart to remind him that she had been in the audience the night Keene opened for Graham Parker at the Wax, the same night she had run into Karras when he had affected his new-wave mask. Karras had always been slow on the uptake when it came to memories; he liked to say that he "lived in the moment," which Donna knew was his way of sugarcoating but not excusing his thoughtless nature.

Keene came out in a vintage sport jacket and jeans, and launched into a set of propulsive, guitar-driven pop from his new album, *Songs from the Film*. L.A. and Geffen had him for the time being, but he would always be the mid-Atlantic Alex Chilton, and he would always be D.C.'s After the bridge of "Baby Face," when the break built and crested into the chorus, Keene closed-eyed and singing right up to the mike, the band driving and tight, the whole club had gone forward to the stage, and in the crush, Karras's arm had gotten around Donna's shoulders, and he was thinking, as the cocaine and alcohol married beautifully in his brain, This is One of Those Nights, and maybe I *won't* die, just maybe I will live forever.

Karras leaned into Donna at the end of the first set, told her it was time to go. There was another band he wanted to see tonight across town. Donna shrugged, said all right. Karras tipped Mike, the front-of-the-house tender, on the way out the door. Out in the night, they felt the electric shock of cold air against their sweat. Karras put his arm around Donna to warm her as they walked west on F. Then he stopped, turned her toward him, kissed her at the head of the alley a few doors down from the club. Her tongue, rough as a cat's, slid across his. He could *feel* the warmth of her groin as he pushed himself against her. She moved back a step, brushed damp hair away from her face, and smiled.

All right, he thought. I'm in.

Marcus Clay walked down Indiana Avenue from the courthouse and took the steps up to the second floor of the Dutch Treat, a nondescript neighborhood watering hole near the National Archives. He had a seat at the bar, ordered a beer, nursed it while he watched the end of the Alabama/Xavier game on the house set. This place was okay. He could keep to himself, have a slow glass of cold beer, watch a little ball, let the tension ease on out of his shoulders and back. Forget about how he had acted the fool, once again, with Elaine.

When the game ended, Clay took the Red Line back up to Dupont, picked up his ride, and drove over to U Street. A teenage boy was hanging out front of the store, standing next to the pay phone mounted on the brick wall. This time of night there was always some young drug boy leaning against his car at the curb, waiting for that phone to ring or looking to make a call.

"You got a reason to be out here?" said Clay, his hand on Real Right's front door.

"Just goin' on about my business," said the young man, punctuating his response with a tough roll of his shoulders.

"This here is *my* business you're leaning up against. Don't need you out here scarin' away my customers."

The young man smiled. "I ain't seen no kind of customers, scared or otherwise, in nary a day."

"Go on, boy." Clay took a step toward the young man, who was half his size. "Go."

The young man took his time, but he went.

Clay entered the store. Cootch was behind the register, turning down the volume on the new Africa Bambaata.

"Hey, boss."

"Cootch."

"Anything?"

"Not one customer all night."

"Damn."

"Yeah, I know. Don't worry, though, Marcus. This whole street's gonna turn around, soon as this Metro construction folds up. U Street's gonna come back."

"They been talkin' about that shit for years. Question is, will I be able to hold on until it does."

"I heard *that*."

Marcus rubbed his face. "You got plans tonight?"

"Was gonna take my girl out to a show. *Game of Death*'s playin' down at L'Enfant Plaza."

"Your girl into Bruce Lee?"

"She'd be into Chuck Norris if it meant spendin' the evening with me."

"Go on, then, man, take the night off. I'll count out the drawer."

"Thanks," said Cootch.

Clay said, "Ain't no thing."

After Cootch had locked the door behind him and gone, Clay put the *Impressions: Sixteen Greatest Hits* album on the platter and turned up the amp. He loved his Curtis Mayfield, loved *all* the positive music with the message of uplift and pride that had come up off the streets in the late sixties and early seventies. He knew that he should have kept up with the newer jams, owning four record stores like he did, but the truth was, he just couldn't relate.

A kid knocked on the front door. Clay moved forward, recognizing the Raiders jacket. As he got closer he saw it was the half-pint who hung on the corner down the street. Clay made a cutting motion across his throat. The kid knocked again.

Clay used his key to open the door. "What's up, Youngblood?"

"Can I come in?"

"We're closed. I'm just countin' out."

"I ain't lookin' to buy nothin'. It's just . . . I'm cold, man."

"Name's not 'man.' Name's Mr. Clay."

"I'm cold, Mr. Clay."

Clay had a look around the dark block. The night air had numbed his hand, still wrapped around the door. "You down here alone?"

"Yessir."

"Where your kin at, boy?"

"I live up on Fairmont with my Granmom. She's havin' company tonight."

"You shouldn't be runnin' around out here alone."

"Yessir."

Clay opened the door. "Come on in and warm up. Mind, I'm just about done. You're gonna have to take off then."

The kid came in. Clay noticed he had on those new Michael Jordan Nikes all the kids were into. Clay went back behind the counter and turned down the music while the kid flipped through the records in the racks.

"Dag," said the kid, "you got the new Run-D.M.C.?"

"Got it all," said Clay.

"You wanted to, you could take home *any* of the records in this joint."

"I'd be takin' food out of my own mouth."

"What you mean?"

"I own this place."

The kid cocked his head. "How'd you get it?"

"Hard work."

Clay continued to count the bills from the drawer. He let his eyes drift for a moment, saw the kid dribbling an imaginary basketball in one of the aisles, pull up and shoot.

Clay said, "You play ball?"

"A little," said the kid. "Prob'ly ain't gonna be too tall, though. . . ."

"Yeah, well, hardly anyone gets to the NBA. Nothin' wrong with playin' just for fun, long as you do your schoolwork, too. Ball's healthy, and it keeps you off the streets like these other knuckleheads out here."

"Yeah, I know."

"You know, huh. You watch that Maryland game today?"

"Saw the highlights."

"Lenny Bias had —"

"Twenty-six."

Clay made some markings in his ledger. He closed the book, looked at the kid. "What's your name, Youngblood?"

"T."

"Your given name, not your street name."

"Anthony Taylor."

"How old are you, Anthony?"

"Thirteen."

"Don't be tellin' stories. You look around eleven to me. Am I right?"

"How you know so much, mister?"

"You live long enough, you naturally learn."

"My granmom says the same thing."

Clay eyed Anthony Taylor. "You want to do somethin' for me while I count out?"

"What?"

"There's a broom in the back room, leaning up against my desk. And a dustpan right next to it. You feel like sweeping up out here, I'd be obliged."

"Will I get paid?"

"We'll take a look at the job you do first. Decide then."

Clay watched the kid's miniswagger as he headed toward the back room. This Anthony Taylor was just eight years older than Marcus Jr. Clay wondered, would his little boy be out on these streets someday, just hanging like this kid? He thought of Anthony Taylor on the corner, standing out there in the cold.

"I swear to God," said Clay in a very soft voice, "I'll never let you be that kind of alone."

Richard Tutt parked his Bronco with the oversized tires in a lot filled with trucks with oversized tires and walked into the Gold's Gym on Georgia Avenue. He changed into his shorts and tank top, went out into the gym, did some warm-ups in front of a wall-to-wall mirror, and then began to pump hard iron.

Tutt only did free weights. The Nautilus and the Universal were for beach-boy types, slope-backed lawyers, kids, and girls, and anyway, you couldn't get that vein action going with those machines like you could with the free weights. Or that sound. He liked the clang of the plates.

Tutt did some benches with a spotter he knew, then went to the curl bar to work on his guns. He was proud of his arms; he liked to pyramid the sets, really max it out so the veins popped on his biceps like fat pink wire.

He pushed it hard. It helped when he thought of people he'd like to kill. Like Tyrell's enforcer, Short Man Monroe. Short Nigger was more like it. Like Tutt would ever let some sawed-off little spade give him any kind of shit. And now this toy fuck was going to try and show Tutt up, chase off those kids that were playing dealer down around U, or find the money that was missing from Junie's car. Tutt wouldn't let that happen. He was still a cop, and Tyrell and the rest of them were nothing more than the shit on his shoe. Sure, he'd taken their money, and he'd keep taking it as long as the ride lasted. But they didn't own him. It was Tutt who was in charge. They'd find that out eventually. Then he'd move on to the next bunch of geniuses, because there was always someone out there looking to get shook down.

Tutt finished a full circuit, glanced in the mirror, twisted his torso to check himself out. Was he getting a little small? Hell, he'd never be as big as he was that summer down at Ocean City, when he was working as a bouncer at the Hurricane Club, lifting with those Salisbury State boys with the close-set eyes, shooting monkey hormones, walking down the beach, and looking big as Joe Jacoby. That was the summer they had taken this little waitress out on a boat, gotten her drunk on Busch beer, asked her if she was a good girl or a bad girl. She had smiled coyly and said, "I guess I'm half good and half bad," and Tutt's friend Dewey said, "Is this the bad half?" and put his hand, big as a bear's paw, right on her snatch. Man, did she jump back. And did what they told her to do after that. That was one crazy summer. He'd never be that maxed out again, but he'd sworn off the 'roids ever since, because right after that he had come back and taken the test to be a cop. No drugs of any kind since then. You came up positive on a test, it could get you bounced right off the force.

Tutt wiped his face dry with a towel as he walked toward the locker room. He passed a guy he recognized, good-sized arms but talked kind of funny, like maybe he worked in a library or some shit like that. He stopped to tell the guy a joke.

"Hey, buddy," said Tutt. "Know what 'gay' stands for?"

"No."

"'Got AIDS yet?'"

If the guy smiled then Tutt missed it. "Oh, you mean like an acronym."

"Huh?"

"You know, each letter of the word stands for another word."

"Whatever."

Tutt entered the locker room shaking his head, wondering when they started letting pencil-necks join this place.

Tutt showered. He got dressed next to a Montgomery County cop, last name of Penny. Penny had a second-degree black belt. He claimed the dojo workout made him skinny, so he came here three times a week to pump iron.

"Hey, Tutt. What you carrying these days?"

"Police-issue thirty-eights. But the solid citizens they got us goin' up against got autos holding fourteen to a clip. Mini-Tec nines, all that. So you can believe I'm packin' something else."

"What?"

"Got me a forty-five. A thirty-eight shoots nice and straight and all that, but the Colt's got more stopping power."

"Tell me about it."

"And there's something else." Tutt looked around the locker room, lowered his voice. "When the jungle heats up and boils over, you're gonna see a lot of those candy-ass National Guardsmen dead in the street. *They* carry forty-fives. Gonna be a lot of ammo lying around out there for the real soldiers, the frontline cops, to pick up and slap right into our guns."

Penny low-chuckled. "Shit, Tutt. You better watch what you say with that jungle shit. Anyway, I thought your partner was a brother."

"He is. But he's one of the good ones. You can believe that." Tutt shut his locker. "Take care, Penny."

"You, too."

Tutt went outside to the pay phone. He searched his pocket for a coin, watched a short female lifter walk toward the gym. She had on leg warmers and a sweatshirt worn off one shoulder, her tank-top strap showing. Reminded Tutt of that *Flashdance* chick who everyone claimed was half jig.

"What a feeling, sweetness," said Tutt, giving her a toothy smile. "Ain't nothin' I like better than a woman with nice, strong thighs."

"Pig," said the girl, walking quickly through the front door.

"Yeah, yeah, yeah," said Tutt.

He found a quarter and dropped it in the slot. He made his call.

Kevin Murphy sipped from his beer, watched the point guard take the ball down the court. The guard had a nice way of protecting the ball on the dribble. And his teammate, this Farmer kid from Alabama, he could really play.

Murphy leaned back on the couch, used the remote to kick up the volume on his brand new Mitsubishi set. He didn't want to hear his wife's footsteps. He knew his wife Wanda was in the bedroom doing a little crying this time of night, maybe getting up off the bed, walking around the room, sitting back down on the bed, rubbing her hands together, like that. Hers were ordinary footsteps, nothing unusual in their sound, except that he could picture Wanda's troubled face, all wrinkled up as she made those footsteps in that dark room, not going anywhere, not knowing where to go.

This new set, it sure did have a nice picture. Murphy had read about the special blue picture tube, Diamond Vision, some shit like that, in a magazine before he had even walked into the store. The salesman, sideburned white dude trying to talk black after he had a look at Murphy, called it an 'ass-kickin', booty-whippin'" picture. Went so far as to call it the Cadillac of televisions, winking on the word *Cadillac*, like the mention of that car would trigger a black man's hot button. Murphy stayed cool and disinterested, smiled inside when the salesman thought he had lost the handle and said something good and stupid about how owning this television was like having a "poontang magnet" in your very own home. Despite the fact that he was ignorant, there was something about this salesman's blind determination that Murphy had liked. So he bought the set. But he couldn't let this guy get away with all that fool talk. So after Murphy had paid from a roll of hundreds, he shook the salesman's hand and said, "By the way, haven't heard the word *poontang* in about twenty years. Can't recall if I've ever heard a black man use it." And to the salesman's nervous smirk he added, "Smooth as your rap is, I thought you might like to know."

Yeah, the picture on the set was all right. Truth of it was, though, he didn't enjoy watching the game on the Mitsubishi any more than he had on his old chipped-up-cabinet thirteen-inch Admiral. In that way this new set was kind of like his new black metal-flake Trans Am. He'd always wanted one, sure, and he had it now, and it was top of the line. But he never enjoyed a car like he did his first, a used '70 Camaro, springtime gold with saddle interior. Now *that* was one beautiful car.

Strange about how the money meant very little to him anymore. You couldn't bank too much of it, what with the paper trail and all that. So Murphy had to spend it on things.

Course, in the beginning, the money was going toward the adoption. A baby for him and Wanda. And the baby would need "things," too. When they had first looked into it, after all the fertility quacks with their shots and cycles and drugs had bled his bank account dry, Murphy couldn't believe how much an adoption cost. But he knew he'd have to find a way for Wanda, unhappy as she was.

He'd confided in Tutt about the hole he was in. And Tutt began to talk to Murphy, right about then, about taking a little bit here and there. Tutt said they could control the situation on their beat like that, keep the drug dealers and their foot soldiers and enforcers calmed down, not let them get crazy behind their violent territorial shit. Tutt made it seem sensible, or maybe that's the way Murphy wanted to hear it. He almost had himself convinced it was the right thing to do.

Kevin Murphy didn't think on it all that long. He began to take.

It was about that time, funny how it worked out, that Wanda started to withdraw. She had spent years fretting over their inability to have a child, and now that Murphy was making it possible for her, she was suddenly unsure. And acting weirder than a mothafucker, too, saying how the Lord had "told" her it wasn't in the cards for them to have a child of their own. Even went on to say, during one of their many arguments, "Why would I want a baby, Kev, that someone else gave away?" This was a woman who, just a few months earlier, could no longer bear to be around their friends who had kids. Who had quit her government job because she couldn't hide the shame of childlessness. Maybe Murphy should have seen that she had been fragile all along. Murphy's brother, Ted, the reverend, had claimed when he first met her that Wanda had a "sick heart." Ted always did have a knack for seeing inside people straight away, knowing how to help them before their problems got too bad. In the end, when Ted was down to ninety pounds, the only one he couldn't help was himself.

Kevin and Wanda stopped seeing their friends. After a while, in fear that Wanda would break into uncontrollable laughter or hysterical tears, they couldn't even have neighborhood couples over for barbecues. Out of the office environment and with only family dropping by occasionally, Wanda rapidly lost most of her social skills. Along with any kind of hope.

And though there was no longer a pressing need for the extra cash, Kevin Murphy continued to take. Because once you started, you couldn't stop. There just wasn't any such thing as a "reformed" cop. Sure, there was the option of quitting the force, just walking away. But he would never exercise it. As far back as he could remember, Murphy, just like his damned partner, had only wanted to be one thing. And it was everything now; in the face of what he had lost, being a cop was all he had.

The phone rang on the table beside him; Murphy picked it up.

"Yes," said Murphy. He listened and said, "All right. See you there."

He replaced the receiver. This game was ending, and there would be late games coming up. It would be good, for a little while anyway, to get out of the house.

Murphy walked across the knotty pine finished basement, the room he had redone just a few months back. Had a nice wood bar in it, with a Formica top, like his father had always wanted to own. Redskins memorabilia on the walls, plenty of signed glossies going all the way back to Bobby Mitchell, Sonny and Charley Taylor. And a full-size pool table under a big rectangular lamp.

He went through a door into the unfinished half of the basement, past a locked upright case with a glass front where he kept his shotguns, two Remington autoloads, racked. He brushed against the heavy bag he had hung from the beams of the ceiling. He reached above his workbench to an oak shelf. There were several handguns there: a double-action .380 Walther PPK, two S&W .357 Combat Magnums, and a 92F Beretta nine. He brought down the Walther case, opened it, picked up the PPK, checked the magazine, slapped it home. He safetied the gun, holstered it in his waistband, pulled his shirttails out over the bulge.

Kevin Murphy excelled on the range. He shot regularly and had won several marksmanship awards. He had never killed, though, or wounded a man. Of this he was proud.

Murphy went up the stairs to the bedroom, knocked on the door, and pushed it open. Wanda was lying on the bed, wearing that Kmart housedress of hers, her hands folded across her chest as if in death.

"I'm going out for a little bit, sweetheart."

"Okay."

"Want anything?"

"Uh-uh."

"How about some of those chocolates you like?"

"I don't care."

"All right, sweetheart. I'll be back soon."

Murphy closed the door softly, snatched his car keys off a nail he had driven into the wall. Wanda hadn't asked where he was going. Her eyes hadn't moved toward him when he'd entered the room. She had only stared at the brush strokes on the ceiling of their room. She hadn't even blinked.

Murphy left the house. He walked down the steps to his shiny new car.

EIGHT

Denice Tate first noticed Alan Rogers and that short, mean-looking boy he hung with about halfway into Chuck Brown's show. Brown was doing a call and response to that big hit of his, "We Need Some Money," and the packed house at the Masonic Temple seemed to move in unison as the jam went on and on, building to a sweat-soaked, natural high. Chuck Brown, the Godfather of Go-Go, was set to play with that other Godfather, James Brown, at the Convention Center later in the month, but Denice could not imagine a more bumpin' show than this one right here. She hated lying to her father, but now, 'specially since she had seen Rogers, she sure was glad she had come.

"He's looking at you, girl," said her friend Ashley, doing a kind of deep dip, one step up, one step back thing.

"No he ain't, Ash!"

"Trust *me*," said Ashley.

Alan Rogers had been keeping on the lookout for that cute girl, the one they called Neecie around the way. Nice young girl like that, unspoiled, you could make a girlfriend out of her if you wanted. Now he had her in his sights, standing over there with another girl who didn't look half as fine. Neecie looked *good*, too.

Short Man Monroe turned to Alan Rogers. "You ready, black?"

"Nah, Short. Gonna fuck with the show."

"Gotta get out of here, man. Tyrell 'spects us to collect."

"You go on. I wanna check this shit out."

"I know what you be checkin' out."

"She got a friend, man."

"I ain't interested. Stay if you want. I'll come on around back, pick you up."

Rogers moved through the crowd, careful not to bump anyone hard, make anyone feel like they had to step *to* him. The whole city seemed to be here tonight. He saw some of Rayful Edmond's boys from the Strip, and some Northeast boys out of Montana Terrace, and a couple of leftovers from the old Hanover Place crew on the west side of North Capitol. Rogers was chin-nod familiar with a few of them, but he didn't look any of them in the eye.

You never knew out here anymore. He had seen this one boy shot over nothing but a misunderstood glance at Chapter III one night down in Southeast, convulsing in the parking lot with a bullet in his back, froth and shit coming out of his mouth like overflowed laundry suds as the life leaked right out of his eyes. Rogers had dreamed about it a few times since. Sometimes he'd keep himself awake at night in fear that he'd dream of it again. He had the walk and the look down, because you had to, but Alan Rogers didn't want none of that, the death part of being in the life.

But you had to do somethin', right? Couldn't just be like some raggedy-ass welfare case, or one of those pee-smellin', wine-breath old mothafuckers sleeping on the subway grates in the middle of the winter. You needed things, needed to look sharp to get respect from your boys and the looks from the girls. But how *would* you get those things when you couldn't do much better than write your name? His teachers had moved him up, grade by grade, but they hadn't really taught him shit. Not to read and write all the way, or to add things up in his head, not really. Not even how to go out and get a job.

One time, when he'd applied for this busboy thing at this bar over on 2nd Street, this white boy who ran the place, after he told him he couldn't hire him, decided to give him a little advice. "Next time," the white boy said, "when you're applying for a job, act like you want it. Wear a clean shirt and sit up in your chair; smile, maybe; look the person you're dealing with in the eye. Ask for the job. And don't keep looking at your prospective employer like you want to kick his ass." Right about then Rogers had wanted to kick Pretty Boy's ass, but later, when he was thinking about it, he realized that the white boy had been right. Alan Rogers never had examples. Never had anyone to explain even the simple shit, like what to wear, what to do when you apply for a job, how to act. How to get *along*.

At a house party in Shaw, a friend who was now in jail had introduced him to Tyrell Cleveland. Next day, Tyrell called him up. Asked him if he wanted to make a little bit of change. Rogers knew what time it was as soon as he had met Tyrell, but he couldn't get a clear picture of a future anywhere else. Rogers saw other people looking good, getting new things, wearing designer clothes, driving nice rides, on the streets and every time he turned on the TV. He needed some of those things, too. Decided, yeah, it was time to get paid like everybody else.

"Hey, girl," said Rogers, smiling broadly.

"Hey."

"Been lookin' for you all night."

"You have, huh."

"Lookin' for somethin' jazzy and fine. Didn't know it was you till I *saw* you. You *know* you got to be the finest one here tonight."

"Go ahead, Alan."

"You know my name?"

"Sure. You know mine?"

"Call you Neecie, right?"

"That's right."

"See?" said Alan Rogers.

Denice Tate had her hands clasped behind her back. "See what?"

"You and me, we got that ESP thing goin' on. We was *meant* to hook up, girl."

Denice laughed. Ashley rolled her eyes and giggled.

Rogers said, "Let's go for a walk, okay? This is a bad show, but I can't hear nothin' but the band this close to the stage. I want to talk to you."

Denice looked at her friend for a moment and said, "All right."

They went to the back of the hall, where it was less crowded, and found a place in the corner. Alan Rogers did most of the talking. Denice liked his voice, his style, the way he moved his strong hands in the air to make a point. And his beautiful brown eyes. He made a joke, and both of them laughed. Then he leaned in to kiss her. She closed her eyes and let him. He was a nice boy. The kiss felt good.

* * * *

Clarence Tate looked at the March calendar that the Ibex Club sent out to all the folks on their mailing list. He figured Denice would be out for a few hours at Ashley's house. He thought he'd treat himself for a change, go out, have himself a drink.

He put on a sport jacket over an open-collar shirt, got into his newly tuned Cutlass Supreme, and headed out, listening to an old Stylistics tape on the stereo all the way uptown. He parked off Georgia and Missouri, a block south of the club. He knew one of the club's owners, a dude he had gone to Roosevelt with, now on the D.C. boxing commission. He mentioned this dude's name to the doorman, who nodded to a second doorman, which meant he had beat the cover. The first doorman ran one of those U-shaped metal detectors over his clothes before letting him in. Something new here, but he could dig it, what with all the guns out there now. Still and all, the Ibex was a pretty nice place.

Tate went up red carpeted stairs. He passed the landing on the second floor, where he could see younger people congregated and hear the thump of bass from a hip-hop group playing in the adjoining hall. He continued on up to the third floor and went into the big room. It was people closer to his age here, dressed nicely, drinking from glasses, listening to the man up on the stage.

Tate ordered a Remy with a side of ice water, leaned against the bar. He closed his eyes for a moment, listened to Gil Scott-Heron's rich voice singing the beautiful words to "95 South," one of Tate's favorite songs. Gil was solo tonight, just him and his piano, right for this setting. He looked thinner than the last time Tate had seen him, and his hair had gone gray.

Tate remembered how he used to play the *Winter in America* LP for Denice, sing her to sleep when "Your Daddy Loves You" came around. What was that, ten years gone already? Damn, she was growing up too fast.

At the set break, Tate struck up a conversation with a woman at the bar. She was a handsome woman with a nice way about her, heavy in the hips and with plenty of leg on her, but that was all right. Tate was no show prize either, what with the weight he'd put on.

They talked with one another and had a few laughs. The two of them had a real nice evening. The woman had an easy smile. He got her phone number before he left. She seemed a little surprised that he didn't at least try to make a play for her that night. But he hadn't even considered it. He had to be getting back home to Denice, and anyway, it wouldn't be proper to bring a woman back to the house with him. Not while he was trying to set an example for his sweet little girl.

Dimitri Karras and Donna Morgan stood well to the back of the St. Augustine School auditorium off 15th and V. They could hear fine there, could feel the music pulse right through them as the mostly male crowd got off on the sounds of Scream, one of D.C.'s hottest bands. Karras had gray hair, and Donna was nearly thirty years old. They didn't belong in the fray.

But Karras had wanted to check out this show. Scream, a band on the local Dischord label, was one of those punk-metal outfits that turned it out with melody and drive. He liked the crowd, too — not all the way headbanger or absolute punk. It was a rock-and-roll crowd he could relate to, some sober and some half fucked up and some nearly out of control. Karras didn't exactly get this Straight Edge movement, the postpunk kids who were anti-alcohol and anti-drug. Some of these kids, they'd even put Xes on their *own* hands before they entered the clubs these days, proud to show that they were booze free. Shit, drugs went hand in hand with rock, didn't they? At least in Karras's mind they did. Minor Threat and those other Straight Edge bands, he dug the energy in their music, but the other part he couldn't comprehend. He figured it was just a new generation of kids carving out their own identity, trying to separate themselves from the beards and the potheads who came before them. And though he didn't care to admit it, he knew his confusion had a lot to do with his age. There were plenty of things lately he didn't understand.

The Stahl brothers were up front on stage, Peter at the mike and Franz ripping his ax, with Skeeter Thompson anchoring on bass and Kent Stax's sticks pounding the skins. They were finishing "Feel Like That" when Karras felt a hand on his shoulder. He turned around.

Karras recognized the guy standing before him. Late twenties, black jeans, fifties-style sport jacket over a tails-out oxford shirt. Greek kid; he knew him, but he had aged, changed. . . .

"Nick Stefanos," the guy said, holding out his hand. "Dimitri Karras, right?"

"Right." Karras shook his hand.

"You remember me?"

"Sure," said Karras with a smile.

He did remember him, now. Stefanos was the grandson of this old guy, also named Nick Stefanos, owned a diner down on 14th and S, a place where Karras's father had worked back in the late forties, at the time of his death. The last time Karras had seen the Stefanos kid was Bicentennial weekend, right after that bad shit had gone down with Wilton Cooper and the others. Stefanos had been heading out of town with this friend of his on some road trip, and Karras had gone to see him off. He could no longer remember why.

"How you doin'?" said Karras.

"Doin' good, man."

Karras had a look at the kid. He knew a member of the club when he saw one. He leaned forward, put his mouth near Stefanos's ear.

"Wanna do a bump?"

"Yeah," said Stefanos. "Sure."

Karras pointed Donna to a spot over by the left wall. He winked at her, told her he'd be right back. Her eyes were eager and bright. She was wired, but he knew she'd be okay by herself. No one had even looked at the two of them since they'd entered the hall.

Karras and Stefanos went to the bathroom, found an empty stall. Karras latched the door, leaned against it, pulled his amber vial from his jeans. Stefanos made a fist and turned it up; Karras dumped a mound on the crook of his hand. Stefanos hit it, took in another mound through the other nostril. Karras used the cap-spoon for himself.

"Nice shake," said Stefanos.

"Always," said Karras. "What're you up to, man?"

Stefanos held up his left hand Indian style, flipped it so Karras could see the ring.

"You got married."

"Yeah, last year."

"Congratulations. Greek girl?"

"Nope. White girl named Karen. Met her down at the Local. Teresa Gunn was playing that night. Karen looked just like Chrissie Hynde. That is, she did back then. We partied and, you know, kind of fell in love."

Karras didn't think Stefanos looked to happy about it. He said, "She here?"

"Uh-uh, not her scene. Not anymore, anyway. She's at home. I'm outta here, too, right after the Scream set."

"Not staying for Black Flag?"

"Rollins? Nah."

Karras had the vial out again. He set Stefanos up the same way.

"Thanks."

"*Tipota.*"

"So what are you doing?"

"Good flake."

Stefanos laughed. "Besides that."

"Working with my buddy Marcus Clay. You remember that record store —"

"Real Right."

"Yeah, there."

They were talking awfully fast. Karras did a couple more jolts. Stefanos lit a Camel he had pulled from the inside pocket of his jacket.

"You mind?"

"Uh-uh."

Stefanos hit his cigarette hard. He held the smoke in deep, let it out while he took another drag.

Karras said, "What're you doing now?"

"Still working for Nutty Nathan's."

"On Connecticut Avenue?"

"Yep."

"My dealer's over that way."

"Stop in, man, say hey."

"You were a stock boy —"

"I'm a salesman. Been one for years. Karen wants me to go for management."

"Go for it."

"Yeah, right."

"What do *you* want?"

"Fuck, man, *I* don't know. I been doing this other shit, too, with this guy I work with, Johnny McGinnes? Process serving. We find people. Follow them and find 'em. I don't know, I can't seem to get too serious about anything, you know? Shit, man, I'm twenty-seven years old; I'm still having fun."

"Me, too."

"You're twenty-seven?"

"Get outta here, *re*." Karras wiped at something dripping from his nose. "Am I bleeding?"

"No, you're all right."

"So, what about your grandfather. He still alive?"

Stefanos blew smoke at the ceiling. "Yeah, he's . . . Papou's okay. He sold the grill. He's nearly blind now, walks with a cane. I go over there to Irving Street, have dinner with him once a week."

"Good man."

"Me?"

"Your *papou*."

"The best."

"Want another taste for the road?"

"Okay."

Stefanos pitched his butt in the toilet before they left the stall, had another lit by the time they hit the auditorium. They shook hands and clapped shoulders. Stefanos headed for the stage, where Scream was really blowing the roof off. Karras moved quickly toward Donna.

It was good to see the Stefanos kid. Good, and kind of sad at the same time. He didn't quite know why. Karras made it to Donna, told her it was time to go. He needed air. He needed to be outside.

"Glad you could make it," said Richard Tutt.

Kevin Murphy said, "I needed to get out of the house."

They were driving south on 13th in Tutt's Bronco. They had met at their usual spot, outside a bar called O'Grady's on Longfellow and Colorado, where Murphy had left his Trans Am.

"How's Wanda?"

"She's doin' okay."

Tutt figured Wanda Murphy for some sort of head case. Last time he'd seen her, she'd come to the door in some piece-of-shit housedress, looking like someone's maid. Had some wicked body odor coming off her, too, like she'd blown off showers for a week. Tutt knew from experience that black women liked to smell nice, sometimes even went overboard with that sweet perfume of theirs. But Murphy's wife had long since given up on hygiene or caring for the way she looked. She'd become a wall-hugger, always had to think real hard on what she was going to say. Vacancy signs hung in her eyes. You asked Tutt, she was way past gone.

Tutt made a point of keeping the Wanda conversations to a minimum. Murphy, he was acting kind of touchy lately, too.

"You see the mayor on TV today?" said Tutt.

"Nah, Tutt."

"His deputy resigned under a . . . what do you call it?"

"A cloud of suspicion."

"Yeah, a cloud. Citywide corruption, baby, and now another one of those geniuses went and fell out of the tree. Reporters were askin' questions; the mayor kept on saying, 'You people got no cause to question my veracity.' Pattin' his head with that handkerchief of his. I do believe our mayor got a case of the cocaine sweats."

"Yeah," said Murphy tiredly, hoping to put the conversation to an end. "They got their problems down there at the District Building."

"Problems? Oh, yeah. But you know what the mayor's gonna do tonight, take his mind off his problems? Go on down to This Is It?, do a few lines on his favorite glass table, watch some ho suck his dick underneath. Maybe have a nice *con*-yack to go with his *co*-caine."

Tutt high-cackled and air-elbowed Murphy. Murphy turned his head, looked out the window to his right. That old story about This Is It?, the titty bar down on 14th, he knew Tutt would bring it up sooner or later. The cop who had reported it got busted down to night duty for his troubles, but the story had managed to leak out to the general public anyway.

Kevin Murphy *knew* that the mayor was out of control, an alcoholic, drug-addicted, pussy-addicted monster. But Murphy was old enough to remember the District before Home Rule. He *wanted* to believe that the mayor would wake up and do his job. And he didn't care to hear about the mayor from a racist mothafucker like Richard Tutt.

"Course," said Tutt, "seein' as how the mayor's most likely gonna be tied up tonight, that frees up his wife to go out and hook up with one of her girlfriends, you know what I'm sayin'?"

"Hey, Tutt."

"What, partner?"

"You ever get tired of hearin' your own voice?"

Short Man Monroe spun the wheel, one-eightied the Z in the middle of 11th, headed south. He was through collecting for the night. An orange Nike shoebox filled with cash money sat on the bucket to his right.

Monroe sat real low in the driver's seat, his forearm resting on the lip of the open window, his wrist dangling. Had to have the arm outside the window for the full lean. Monroe reached over to the radio, got it off of KYS and that Billy Ocean bullshit. He punched in his favorite station, WPGC.

It felt good to have the evening's business taken care of, but he wasn't done yet. Had to find those kids, the one called himself Chief and the others, before Tutt did. Ain't no way he was gonna let Tutt, or that other Mr. Charley cop, Murphy, show him up. He had to prove to Tyrell that they didn't need their kind around anymore. Monroe was out there more than Tyrell these days, and maybe Tyrell didn't realize how fast the city was changing. Having a couple of cops on the payroll, it didn't buy you nothin' anymore. Not really. Look at that open-market thing they had goin' on over at the Strip, practically untouched by the law.

Monroe glanced at his watch, the one with the braided gold strap. Almost time to swing back around, pick up his boy Alan Rogers at the Temple.

Rogers. Shit, he'd gone all the way over for that young freak. Monroe, now, he wouldn't let no pussy get his own head turned around. Besides, why waste all that time leading up to it when you could get any ho out here to suck your dick right quick for a little 'caine? Least that's how it was with the girls he knew.

Monroe ran his finger down the trigger guard on the nine wedged tightly between his thighs. The gun felt *good*.

Jumbo Linney and Chink Bennet, now *there* were a couple of niggas who could use some pussy. They had their movies and all that, the ones on tape and the big-screen ones they jacked off to down at the Casino Royal and the Stanton Art. But never any real girls. Course, neither one of them was much to look at. Jumbo was a Fat Albert–lookin' mug, and Chink, well, little and yellow as he was, he looked like that wax doll–lookin' sucker hanging off the lamppost on the cover of that Grandmaster Flash record, the one had "The Message" on side two. Monroe used to wonder if Jumbo and Chink were punks or something, the way they always hung together. But he saw now that they were just used to each other, growing up in the same housing unit like they did. Couldn't separate those boys for nothin'.

Monroe liked movies, but not that porno shit. He liked movies about men who had made it big, who lived large, who got their propers all the time and then checked out right. Like those *Godfather* movies, and especially that *Scarface* nigga, baddest mothafucker ever walked down the street. He liked that *Terminator* one, too. 'Specially that scene where the Terminator walked back into that police station, fucked all those uniformed mothafuckers *up*. He remembered the night he saw the movie out at the Allen theater on New Hampshire Avenue, some of the harder young niggas were standing up during that scene, yelling, "Kill 'em!" and "Kill 'em again!"

Monroe saw two boys down the street near the alley off T. One of them wore a bright green cap.

"Hey, now," said Monroe.

He downshifted coming out of a hard right. The boys looked up at the sound of rubber left on the street.

NINE

Wesley Meadows decided on his street name, Chief, after watching this mean old rottweiler dog in the alley behind his row house on O. This rottweiler, named Chief by his teenage owner, had everyone in the neighborhood all the way shook. Got so after a while nobody, kids or adults, would walk down that alley along the backyard fence where the teenager kept that dog. Didn't matter that Chief, the dog, was tied up to his choke collar by a heavy chain. Way that dog got up on his hindquarters, bared his teeth right up to the gums when you neared the yard, it just plain made you weak with fear. And Wesley, he had the fear more than most. Wesley thought, wasn't nothin' alive badder or more fearless than that dog, so he took Chief's name for his own.

Wesley Meadows and his friend James Willets walked down the alley toward T. They had to step around a bunch of junk — bald tires and old washing machines and shit — put there by Tyrell Cleveland's boys to slow down the cruisers and the foot cops. It wasn't that hard anymore to get around back here at night; by now Wesley and his boy James had memorized where all the obstacles were.

Wesley's friend James went by the name of P-Square. James said he chose the name 'cause it sounded mysterious and all that. He was embarrassed to tell Wesley where he had gotten it, though Wesley knew. P-Square stood for Peter Parker, that boy who was really Spiderman, James's favorite character from the comic books he loved.

James Willets had a Spiderman action figure in the pocket of his jeans, along with several dimes and quarters of stepped-on cocaine wrapped in individual packets of foil, twisted at the ends. Wesley had a few dimes and quarters of the same stuff in one pocket of his sweatpants and an old .22 with a worn-down firing pin in the other. He had traded a half to some no-ass, nose-running junkie over on 10th for the gun.

Wesley Meadows and James Willets were eleven years old.

Wesley didn't want to hurt nobody, but you had to have the gun if you were going to play, so there it was. Course, he and James, they weren't makin' any kind of money at this yet, but it was something to do at night to get away from his little brothers and sisters, his mom and her loud boyfriend who was always just hangin' around the house trying to tell him what not to do. Wesley's older brother, Antoine, now *he* was in the life for real. Wesley took a little bit of Antoine's 'caine every so often, just enough so Antoine didn't notice, and then Wesley would mix in a good amount of that stuff in the blue plastic bottle, the stuff made babies do dookie real quick. Antoine had shown Wesley how it was done.

"We gonna make some change tonight, P-Square?"

"*Large* change," said James, smiling that goofy-ass smile of his.

Truth was, they hardly ever sold any of the stuff they carried. Most of the time, they brought the same stuff out with them two, three nights in a row.

Wesley looked over at James. James was short and skinny, with a mouthful of buck teeth. The other kids at school were always crackin' on him over those teeth, calling him Hee-Haw Willets and shit. James was too small and scared to be useful in a bind, but Wesley had named him his lieutenant anyway. Gave James confidence. One thing you could count on with James, he hung with it, not like their friend Mooty Wallace, who would run home the first time one of Tyrell Cleveland's boys gave them any kind of hard look. Truth was, Mooty was faster on his feet than the two of them combined.

Shoot, they were just out here having fun, basically, gettin' a little bit but not too much, not cutting into Tyrell's turf at all. Tyrell's boys, they could see that Chief and P-Square weren't much more than a couple of kids. Came down to it, they wouldn't waste their time.

Wesley and James came to the head of the alley and heard a screech of tires on the street. They looked up to see a black Z heading straight toward them.

"Buck!" said Wesley Meadows.

They turned and ran.

Short Man Monroe curbed the Z. He pulled his keys from the ignition, came out of the car with the Glock in his hand and pointed up in the air. He ran into the alley.

He could see that green hat even in the dark. The head of some other young boy, too, waggin' back and forth as he ran next to the one who called himself Chief.

"Yo, man, hold up!" screamed Monroe. He jumped over a tire, landed clean, kept going without breaking his stride.

Wesley said, "P-Square!"

"Chief!"

Their voices sounded funny to them, mixed with their hard breath, running all out like they were.

"Go right, man," said Wesley. "I'll meet you on our street!"

"Okay!"

James Willets turned abruptly, ran straight for someone's backyard fence. He had the action figure out of his pocket, clutched tightly in his fist. He knew he'd have to leap that fence clean. . . .

"Peter Parker," said James. "Fly!"

And he was over the fence with barely a touch, heading into the darkness of the side yard and out the front, adrenaline pushing him on, his feet hardly lighting on the dead grass and then the asphalt of the street.

"You!" shouted Monroe. He had let the skinny one go, was concentrating on the one called Chief. He was gaining on him now.

Wesley Meadows cut hard coming out of the alley and booked west on S. A woman was walking down the sidewalk; Meadows danced around her, kept right on.

Monroe came around the corner, almost ran right into some fool woman carrying grocery bags. She looked into Monroe's eyes, looked at the automatic in his hand. Her own eyes widened. She hurried past with her head down, staring at the sidewalk and her feet.

Monroe ran a few more steps, slowed down and stopped. He bent forward to catch his breath.

"Damn," he said.

He stood up straight. That woman would remember him. Stupid to finish this tonight. Kid was plain lucky she came on them like she did. He slipped the Glock in the waistband of his jeans.

Monroe looked down S. Around 12th, under a streetlamp, he saw the kid in the green cap stop and look back, jump up and down cheerleader style, wave his arms. What, did this little mothafucker think Monroe was playin'? And what was that he was holding up in his hand? Looked like . . . goddamn, it *was*, some kind of gun.

"You done sealed your doom, Chief," said Monroe, narrowing his eyes, watching the kid, watching the smoke of his own breath. "Now you're gonna die for sure."

Dimitri Karras leaned forward from his seat on the couch. He used his single-edge blade to lengthen the long line on the mirror. He moved the snow back and forth, making it longer with each stroke. He loved to play with the stuff; sometimes he thought the ritual was the best part of doing coke.

Donna Morgan stood in the center of the room, moving to *No Free Lunch*, the Green on Red EP that Karras had thrown on the turntable. While Donna danced, she stared at the *Miami Vice* episode playing silently on the television. Karras thought it funny — *ironic*, he would have said in his teaching days — that a nation of coke-using young people watched this show every Friday night, religiously following the exploits of these stylish undercover cops. Karras would have said something to Donna about it, but she wouldn't have heard him. The music was up too loud.

They had come back to Karras's apartment at 1841 R Street, nick-named the Trauma Arms by its earlier residents, after Karras had stopped for a twelve-pack of Heinekens. Karras wasn't a power drinker normally, but when he did coke he had a bottomless thirst. Lately he'd been drinking quite a bit. There were five dead soldiers on the table in front of him.

"Here, baby," said Karras when he'd caught Donna's eye.

He watched her walk to the couch. She had taken off her sweater and now had just a white T-shirt tucked into her skirt. Like everyone else these days, partiers and health nuts alike, she had a tight body. Karras could re-member the freckles on her chest, the dark nipples hung like plums on her smallish, hard white breasts. He tried not to think of them or the rest of her. He wanted to party some more, not rush the night.

Donna used a twenty, tightly rolled and taped, to hoover the line. There was a cigarette burning in the ashtray and one still smoking where she had butted it out.

"All right," Donna said, dipping her fingers in the glass of water on the table, putting the wet fingers in her nose. She took a bottle of beer off the table.

Karras sang along to the record: "'Time ain't nothin' when you're young at heart, and your soul still burns. . . .'"

"Yeah!" said Donna.

Karras did half his line into one nostril, half into the other. He dumped some more coke from Donna's snow-seal onto the mirror.

As the music ended, Donna said, "You got any U2?"

"Uh-uh."

"What?"

"I saw them at the Ontario on the *Boy* tour, and then at Ritchie in College Park to make sure I wasn't missing something. The audience was in black leather, all of them pumping their fists in the air at once. It looked like Berlin in thirty-eight."

"You'd know, 'cause you were, like, hanging out in Nazi Germany in thirty-eight."

"Look, I just don't get it."

"Whaddya wanna hear, then?"

"Keep on goin' with that Paisley Underground thing. Put on some Dream Syndicate."

"Which one?"

"*Medicine Show*," said Karras. "A Sandy Pearlman production."

"Huh?"

"Guy who produced that record produced early BOC. Also did that Clash record, *Give Em Enough Rope*."

It was all speed now, Karras knew. His mouth was overloading his asshole. He was spouting useless shit just to hear his own voice.

"What are you talkin' about?"

"Go ahead and put on that Dream Syndicate, Donna."

A couple of beers and several lines later, Karras was in the center of the room air-guitaring the "Merrittville" solo. He caught his reflection in the window, a gray-haired guy running his fingers down an imaginary fret.

"What's so funny?" said Donna.

"Funny? I feel good, that's all."

"I feel good, too."

She'd reached her peak, a kind of desperate and deluded happiness in her eyes. Her smile was glued open. She looked blown out.

Karras wanted more. The time between jolts was getting shorter, and *more* was all he could think of now.

He laid out lines. They talked and talked. Donna jumped up to call Eddie Golden for the third time that night.

"His machine again," said Donna.

"Oh," said Karras. He hadn't told her that Eddie had taken something from that burning car. I'll tell her tomorrow, he thought, or maybe not at all. Why does she need to know? Why fuck things up for tonight?

Karras pulled her to the couch and kissed her. He broke off, gave her the thousand-dollar smile. His charm was full on. They made out until their mouths were dry. Karras put his hand up Donna's T-shirt, massaged her breasts through her bra. Her nipples were pebble hard.

"Mr. Karras," whispered Donna.

"That's me."

They drank some more, talked much more, laughed. They did the rest of Donna's coke. They listened to *Psychocandy*, *The Replacements Stink*, and cranked up *Zen Arcade* in a beer-and-blow rush. Karras finished off the night doing an improvised thrashing jig to a Pogues tune off *Rum, Sodomy and the Lash*, leaving his feet and knocking an old end table over as the last Heineken finally kicked in.

On his ass, feeling the bass of his big Polk speakers, he looked across the room. Donna was standing near the coffee table, her hair in her face, licking the snow-seal clean. When she had gotten every last taste, she dropped the paper from her hands. He watched her eyes sadden as she tracked the leafy float of the empty snow-seal to the floor.

Marcus Clay said, "How's that dog taste, Youngblood?"

"Dog taste *good*, Mr. Clay. Thanks for gettin' it for me."

"Ain't no thing."

They sat at the counter of Ben's Chili Bowl, near the old Lincoln Theater on U. Clay had taken Anthony Taylor there after he had closed up the store. He had given Anthony a five-spot for sweeping the place out, told the boy he'd drop him off at home. But the Taylor kid had hunger in his eyes, so they made a stop down the street. Clay had nothing going on for the evening anyhow, and there wasn't anything much better than a late-night stop at Ben's.

Clay sopped up the chili on his plate using the heel of his bun. "You want another?"

"Okay," said Taylor.

Clay signaled the counterman. "Two more. And another grape soda for the young man."

They were served, and Taylor dug in straight away. He turned his head to look out the window at a Metrobus that was passing on U.

"That's a nice bus," said Taylor.

"You like buses?"

Taylor nodded as he swallowed a gulp of Nehi. "Like to drive one my own self someday."

"Shoot, boy, you could *own* a bus yourself, you work for it hard enough."

"For real?"

"Why not? You can do anything, you set your mind to it. I grew up near here, up around Thirteenth and Euclid. When I was a kid, I wanted to own my own record shop. Now I got four of them myself."

"Dag."

"Just remember, though, it took a whole lot of focus. Wasn't no quick way to get it. These young drug dealers today, living large like they do, it might look real good to you now, but you got to realize, that good life's only temporary. Either death or jail waits for those boys on the for-real side."

"I know. Like that boy got burned up today. Name of Junie, worked for Tyrell Cleveland."

"Cleveland, huh." Clay knew the name.

"Yeah, he's runnin' the action in the neighborhood down around your store. Junie, that boy got burned up today in that fast Buick? He worked for Tyrell."

"You see too much, boy, for your young age."

"I see everything! Saw this white dude get out of a Plymouth, take a pillowcase out of Junie's Buick this afternoon."

"Yeah?" Clay didn't look at the boy.

"Sure. A whole lot of cash money in that pillowcase, too. Saw some of it fly up out of the Buick when it was on fire."

Money. So that's what it was for sure. Clay wondered if Karras knew that his cokehead girl was running with a man fool enough to steal from a dealer.

"Good-lookin' white girl got out of that Plymouth first, went into your shop, came out after the accident with this white dude had gray hair. I seen him over at your shop plenty of times. And somethin' else."

"What?"

"There was this sign on the side of the Plymouth door. I memorized the phone number and the address they had there on the sign. See, I *told* you I seen it all."

"Uh-huh."

"I was gonna tell this po-liceman, too," said Taylor. "Man I seen around, rides with this mean-lookin' white cop in our district. But he didn't ask."

"What you gonna do if he does ask?"

"What *should* I do?"

Clay took a bite of his dog to buy some time. He didn't want his friend Dimitri involved in any of this. And he sure didn't think it was healthy for the kid to get involved, either. But here Clay was, acting the role model to the kid, giving him advice. What was he supposed to do, be selective as to what he told Anthony Taylor when it came to right or wrong?

"This black cop asks you," said Clay, "you tell him to come talk to me."

"Yeah, I figured you'd say that. Way my friends at school tell it, you shouldn't talk to the po-lice about nothin'."

"Your friends are wrong. But in this case . . . it's just better this time, he talks to me. Hear?"

"Okay."

"You want another chili dog?"

"Nah, I'm kinda full."

"Gettin' full myself. But it sure tastes good, doesn't it?"

"*Damn* sure does."

"Watch your mouth, boy."

"All right."

Short Man Monroe hated that Jeffrey Osborne tune, "You Should Be Mine," 'specially when the deejay called it "The Woo Woo Song," which made it sound like something a punk would be into for sure. Monroe couldn't square with that love music. Now he was listening to it, driving down U with Alan Rogers and his new skeezer, the one his boy Alan kept calling Neecie. They were both squeezed into the passenger seat of the Z, Neecie on Alan's lap. Alan was givin' the girl a little tongue.

"Where we goin', man?"

Alan Rogers moved his mouth off the girl's. "Gonna drop Neecie off up around the way. Gotta be gettin' her home, man, 'fore her pops be buggin'."

"Your pops," said Monroe, "he work in that record store, right?"

"He works for *all* of them," said Denice. "He's the controller. Handles the money."

"Didn't know he was so important," said Monroe, chuckling low. He moved his toothpick to the other side of his mouth.

Denice Tate pulled Alan Rogers back to her, gave him a long kiss. It felt so good to kiss him, strong and looking good like he was, and sweet as he had been to her all night. And he hadn't tried anything more than those good kisses he had been giving out for free. A gentleman, that's what he was, someone her father would probably like if he'd only give Alan half a chance.

"Good show," said Rogers, "right, girl?"

"Chuck Brown was the bomb," said Neecie. "Gonna remember that show for a *long* time."

Rogers smiled. "Yeah, me too."

Monroe got low in his seat. Good thing wasn't none of his other boys around to see him drivin' around Rogers and this girl, Rogers actin' like he was livin' in some soap opera, little birds flyin' round his head goin' tweet tweet and shit, everything all pretty and nice. Monroe thought, Why doesn't he just do what he wants to do, get a deep nut with this bitch, hit it and split it and kick her the fuck on out of their ride? They had business to attend to, didn't concern no girls.

Up ahead, a truck parked in front of a late-night market flashed its lights at the Z. Monroe eased his foot off the gas, pulled over to the curb.

"Yo, Short, what you stoppin' for?"

"Man wants to talk to us, I guess."

"What man?" said Rogers.

"Looks like our pocket cop," said Monroe. "King Tutt."

TEN

Marcus Clay first noticed the group standing around the baby blue truck with the big wheels as he cleared the intersection at 12th and U. Rolling nearer to the group, he recognized those drug boys who had been across the street from the store, the short one with the pumped-up arms and the taller one with the gentle face. They were talking with a weight-lifter type, white man with a buzz cut. Clay couldn't be sure — the white man wore street clothes — but it looked to be that beat cop from the neighborhood. The taller boy had his arm around a girl, seemed like he was doing it to keep her warm the way he softly rubbed her shoulder and arm. Clay passed by, looked them all over. It sure was that cop, probably shaking those boys down. And the girl, god*damn*, it looked like — no, it *was* — Denice Tate.

"What the hell," said Clay.

"What's that?" said Anthony Taylor.

"Nothin'."

He punched the gas. No sense in getting this kid Taylor involved in anything. And no reason to stop. While Clay was pretty certain that Clarence Tate didn't know his little girl was out here tonight, Clay didn't believe she was in any kind of immediate danger. What could happen to her? After all, they were with a cop. The cop would make sure she came to no harm. The *cop* would see that she got on home. Denice was a smart girl; she knew how to steer away from trouble. Probably out having a good time is all it was. Maybe she didn't even know this kid was in the life.

The next thing he had to think of was should he tell Clarence, straight up, about Denice?

Clay drove the boy up to Fairmont, kept the Peugeot running outside Taylor's house.

"This it?"

"Yes."

"All right, then, get on inside."

Taylor looked over at Clay. "Can I come by tomorrow?"

"Sure," said Clay. "You come on by."

"Thanks, Mr. Clay."

"Pleasure, Anthony."

Clay watched the boy walk toward his row house. He waited there until the boy had gone inside.

Richard Tutt saw the Z coming down U at about the same time that Kevin Murphy entered the market to pick up some chocolate for his wife. He flashed his lights, and the Z pulled over to the curb. Tutt got out of his Bronco just as Monroe and Rogers and some young girl got out of the Z.

Rogers and the girl hung back as Monroe walked toward Tutt in that slow, deep-dip way of his, a toothpick dangling from between his lips. Tutt thought, What I wouldn't give to slap that toothpick out of that little nigger's mouth.

"Wha'sup, Tutt?" said Monroe. "Where go your darker half?"

"My partner's in the store. He'll be right out."

"What brings y'all out tonight?"

"Just checking out our neighborhood."

"Your neighborhood. You own it now, huh?"

"The good citizens own it. I'm just the caretaker."

"Whatever you say, big man."

Tutt grinned. He reached behind him like he was hitching up his jeans.

"Here's a joke for you, Short."

"I'm listenin'."

"What did Marvin Gaye's father say to him right before he smoked him?"

"What?"

Tutt pulled his gun, racked the receiver, pointed it in Monroe's face, in one fluid motion.

Tutt said, "This is the last forty-five you'll ever hear."

Monroe didn't even twitch. If this white boy wanted to high-noon it out here, he was ready for it any time. And he didn't give a *fuck* if he was a cop.

Tutt laughed. "Don't you get it, *Short*? Marvin Gaye. Forty-five, as in forty-five caliber. As in forty-five RPMs."

"I get it. It just ain't all that funny, Tutt."

Alan Rogers put his arm around Denice Tate. He stroked her arm, could feel her shiver beneath his touch.

Tutt replaced his Colt in the waistband of his jeans. A car approached. None of them looked directly at the car as it slowed and then accelerated and passed. In his side vision, Tutt only noticed that the car was one of those French jobs that were all the rage these days with the city's spades.

Murphy came out of the market holding a package of Turtles, Wanda's favorite chocolate.

"What's goin' on?" said Murphy, trying to break the strange silence he had walked into. He stood behind Tutt, always behind him, because Tutt would cowboy it without thought if anything went down. Tutt would *protect* him, take that first hit. Murphy thought he saw contempt in Monroe's eyes, and maybe disappointment in Rogers's. Both of them knew what Murphy knew himself: that he didn't have the same kind of balls-out courage as the white cop.

"Your partner, he just tellin' jokes, Officer Murphy," said Monroe.

"What you got there, Rogers?" said Tutt, nodding at the girl, looking her over slowly, letting Rogers know, law-of-the-jungle style, that he could make the girl his own if that's what he wanted to do. "Got you some new stuff, man?"

Rogers held Denice close.

"She looks *fine*, too," said Tutt with an ugly smile and a wink at Murphy. "Don't she, Murph?"

Shut your mouth. Just shut it, man, for once. And don't look at her like that. Shit, can't you see that she ain't nothin' but a kid? Even you ought to have enough decency to see that.

"Let's go," said Murphy.

"Yeah," said Tutt. "We got work to do. You geniuses have yourselves a good night."

Tutt and Murphy walked back to the truck. Monroe's voice stopped them.

"Yo, King Tutt. I ran into Chief tonight, that young boy been tryin' to move into our strip."

Tutt turned around. "Yeah?"

"Gonna take care of that my own self, Tutt. Gonna do your job for you, man."

"You ain't qualified to have no job, Short."

Monroe smiled, transferred the toothpick to the other side of his mouth. "We'll see."

Monroe, Rogers, and Denice Tate watched the two cops get back in the Bronco. They watched them drive away.

"I'm cold," said Denice.

"I know it, baby," said Rogers. "So am I."

"I want to go home, Alan."

Rogers said, "Let's go, black."

Monroe said, "We gone."

Clarence Tate pulled the Cutlass up to the curb, cut the engine. He took the concrete steps leading to his row house, entered, hung his coat on a tree by the door. He went up the staircase, knocked on Denice's bedroom door.

"Denice? Honeygirl, you in there?"

He pushed on the door, stepped inside. The room was dark, but light spilled in from the hall. Tate could see his daughter's form beneath the covers of her bed, the cornrows roped on the back of her head.

"Denice?"

She didn't stir. He backed out of the room smiling, went downstairs. He grabbed a beer from the refrigerator, turned on the set in the den. Maybe he could catch one of those late-night tournament games they had playing tonight.

In her room, under the covers with her street clothes still on, Denice felt her heart race. She had just barely beaten her father home. She thought of Alan, and that awful boy he ran with, and that ugly white cop with the small eyes and the pink face.

Denice was scared, excited, and a little bit ashamed. All of those things at the same time. She couldn't stop thinking of Alan. Even with all the bad in his world, she couldn't wait to see him again.

Tutt pulled over alongside Murphy's Trans Am on Colorado Avenue. He looked at his partner.

"Tomorrow we talk to some of those people in the neighborhood, Murph. See what we come up with on Junie's money."

"All right."

"Maybe try and hook up with that little —"

"Little what?"

Little nigger. Say it.

"That little *fuck*, Chief."

"Right."

Murphy stared through the windshield at some clean young brother and his girl, dressed nice, headed over to Twin's Lounge to hear a little jazz. Wasn't that long ago that he and Wanda used to go there, have a nice late evening together, one or two drinks.

"Murphy, you okay?"

"I'm fine."

Tutt said, "You see that little piece of ass hangin' on Alan Rogers's arm? Wouldn't mind cuttin' a slice of that myself."

Cuttin' a slice. Tutt was always quoting that Grease Monkey, or whatever his name was, the deejay on DC-101 that all the white boys loved.

"She ain't but thirteen, fourteen years old, Tutt."

"Yeah, she's young, but you know what the Greaseman says, don't ya?"

Greaseman, that's what the fool's name is.

"No, Tutt, what's your boy say?"

"'Old enough to sit at the table, old enough to eat.'"

Tutt was high-cackling as Murphy got out of the Bronco. Murphy didn't look back or say good-bye. He wanted to forget he knew Richard Tutt. He wanted to scrub down until the skin came off his hands.

Kevin Murphy drove up to his neighborhood, parked in front of his house, slipped his gun beneath the bucket seat. He walked over to Takoma Station at 4th and Butternut, had a beer and then another while listening to the quartet headed by a tenor sax, with piano, sticks, and upright bass backing the reed man up. He drank his third beer quietly, facing the bar. No one initiated a conversation or bothered him in any way. He knew a couple of the folks in the bar. A couple of others he didn't know had made him as a cop.

Murphy bought a six at the corner market. He popped the ring on one as he walked back home. He went to Wanda's bedroom and put the chocolate Turtles on her nightstand. He turned off her lamp. He stood in the dark for a minute or two and listened to her sleep.

Murphy went down to the basement, had a seat on the couch, put the rest of the six-pack on the floor beside him. He turned on the late game, Kentucky versus Davidson, and watched the last ten minutes as he drank.

The game was a rout. Murphy was bored and drunk. He looked around the room. Knotty pine walls, signed Redskins photos, a full-length bar, a beautiful pool table . . . everything he had wanted when he was first coming up.

Everything he'd wanted — every *thing* — and now he had them, and none of these things made him happy. He wondered, What's left to acquire? What could possibly make me happy now?

He thought of a dark and quiet place he called the Peace.

Murphy pulled on the chain of his gold crucifix, let it hang out over his shirt. He fingered the cross and rested his head against the back of the couch. He closed his eyes.

Eddie Golden lay in his bed, his fists clenched tight. He unballed them and tried to relax. He could feel his heart thumping in his chest, his back arching slightly, coming up off the bed. He knew he'd never get to sleep. Goddamnit, he'd be up all night.

Round about now, like he always did, Eddie wondered why he had done so much blow. What the fuck was so good about this shit, anyway?

So now he had money. He had brought the pillowcase inside. He had dropped it in the hall closet. You couldn't spend it, though, could you?

97

He was just an appliance installer, after all, and walking around with a bunch of show money, that would cause suspicion. And you couldn't just put it in the bank. Someone would get hip to that, too.

Eddie Golden didn't want to look at the clock radio on his nightstand. He had been lying in bed for hours now, and looking at the time, it would only get him upset.

Eddie noticed that, once again, his fists were balled tight. He turned over on his side and closed his eyes.

Eddie wanted to see Donna, tell her what he had done, how he had reached into that burning car and taken the money.

What to do with the money, that was Eddie's question now. He'd hook up with Donna in the morning. Donna would know what to do.

Dimitri Karras used a hard kitchen match to scrape the last residue of cocaine from his amber vial. The end of your coke: It was flagged by the hasty exit of friends, the pitifully thin line, the empty inhaler, the final canine lick of the snow-seal. But it was never truly the end. If you went through all your containers, you could always find a little more blow.

Karras managed to create a minimound on the glass paperweight he kept under his bed. He used his blade to chop it further. He spread what he'd made into a short line.

The *tap tap tap* of the blade on the glass. His dealer called that sound the mating call of the eighties.

At the moment, Donna Morgan couldn't hear the call. She was in the bathroom, moving about, getting herself ready for bed. She had run water from the spigot to cover the sound of her urination. Now he could hear her brushing her teeth. Then the click of the light switch by the door.

Donna came out of the bathroom wearing only her black panties and bra. Karras felt his stomach jump; it was always like this when a woman first came to him undressed. It gave him those good butterflies, like when he was eight years old, leafing through *Playboys* against the side of his house, feeling hard in his blue jeans, dizzy and guilty and nearly desperate because he didn't know what to do next. But now he knew. Sitting there in his briefs, stretching them straight out.

Donna stumbled, caught herself as she opened her fist and dumped six aspirin on the bed. Her black hair fell sloppily about her face.

"I'm going to get us a glass of water."

"I'll be here," Karras said.

He listened to *The Good Earth* coming through the Bose 301s wired into his bedroom. He had put it on the platter before they had shut off the living-room lights.

Donna returned, squinted as she picked up three of the aspirin and washed them down with water. She handed the glass to Karras and he did the same. He placed the water on the nightstand, the ice cubes like muted chimes banging against the sides of the glass.

He stood before her and kissed her. He unclasped her bra, peeled it off her shoulders. He kissed her breasts and licked them, going slowly to his knees, kissing her warm belly and the inside of her hard thighs as he tugged at her panties and she stepped out of them. The heat and smell of her hit him as he buried his face in her sex. He split her folds with his tongue.

"Dimitri."

"Been waitin' for you to say my name."

Donna came, gripping his shoulders.

They sat facing each other on the bed. Donna's thighs rested atop his. Karras dipped one finger in the cocaine, rubbed some on Donna's clit and along the silk pink of her lips. Donna followed, touching cocaine to the head of his cock, running the remainder down the underside of his shaft and massaging his balls. Karras's sex felt frozen and hot at once.

He cupped a hand under her ass, lifted her and brought her forward, slipped himself inside her. Engulfed in her warmth, he let out a long, relieved breath.

"Bury it," she said.

There was nothing better than this.

They moved slowly. They moved for a long time. The rhythm and squall of the Feelies was just right. Donna threw her head back, pushed her pelvis out. Sweat flew off her hair. Karras squeezed her breast. She put her hand over his and made him squeeze it harder.

"Go," she said.

"You go," said Karras.

The sounds she made got him closer. It started in his thighs. He bit down on his lip.

He heard that chiming sound and opened his eyes. He saw Donna's hand coming back with a fistful of ice as she reached beneath him.

"What the —"

"No," said Donna. "Now *you* go."

She jammed the ice cubes through his asshole and into his rectum. Karras thrashed, the veins defined on his neck. He came convulsively as Donna laughed from far away.

"Damn," said Karras minutes later. "What the hell was that?"

"Something I picked up somewhere."

"I thought *I* was the teacher," said Karras.

"You were," said Donna. "But not anymore."

Marcus Clay stood out on R Street, his hands buried in his pockets, watching Dimitri Karras through the living-room window that faced out from the third floor of the Trauma Arms. Karras was doing some weird kind of dance. Clay could hear Irish-sounding music all the way down on the street.

Fuckin' Dimitri, man. Thirty-seven years old and up there raising all kinds of hell with that black-haired girl. Probably coked up out of his head, too.

Clay wanted to go to bed. But he figured there was no way he could sleep in there, not while Karras was on that kind of roll. He got back into his car.

Clay thought of going to a bar that had a television, watching the late Kentucky-Davidson game, but he had already had a beer tonight, and one was pretty much his limit. He drove uptown.

He knew where he was going. He went up through Rock Creek Park. He got off near Arkansas Avenue, and then he was on the edge of Mount Pleasant, on Brown, the street where he owned his house. He parked the car a few houses down.

He walked over to a Chevy owned by a good guy named Pepe, a hard-working Puerto Rican he'd been knowing for the last fifteen years. He leaned against the car, looked up at his own house, to the second-story window on the right, the room where Marcus Jr. had slept since he'd been born.

Clay could see Elaine's silhouette in there, Elaine sitting in the rocker, patiently looking at a book — *reading* a book aloud, Clay knew — as Marcus Jr. jumped up and down on the bed.

He could see Marcus Jr.'s nappy head rising in the frame of the window and falling out of the frame as he jumped. Marcus had a big head and nicely formed features for a boy. You could already see the muscles defined in his shoulders and arms. Dark skin — he got that coloring from Elaine. And deep brown eyes. He was going to be a big man, Marcus reckoned, and a handsome one, too.

Elaine, reading that Donald Crews book aloud, one about the kids going back to the country, playing around the train tracks and all that. Reading it while Marcus Jr. jumped around, listening while he jumped because he loved that book, but having too much energy to lie still. By now Clay would have lost his patience, told his little boy to sit his butt down.

Elaine was better with the boy, there wasn't any doubt about that. But a boy needed a father around to make him whole.

It was a lot of little things that had driven Clay and Elaine apart: the fact that they led two separate lives, that they barely made time to talk, that their conversations centered around money when they did talk, that they had become more like housemates than lovers and friends. Stepping around each other, not meeting eyes, always on the way to something else. Details and obstacles, clouding the memory of how it had been when they'd first met. All those little things that weaken a marriage over time. But it was one big thing that had torn them apart.

That girl Clay had met at the Foxtrappe that night, she'd shown him more attention in the hour she knew him than Elaine had shown him in six months. That's how he explained it to Elaine, anyway, after one of those he-said/she-said friends of hers had called Elaine and told her she'd seen Clay and this girl leaving the club and going out to his car. The truth was, this young girl, she looked good, and Clay just had to find out, *could* he still if he wanted to? He'd had four beers, way more than he ever drank, and he supposed his judgment was off, too. Never should have gone out to the Peugeot — that damn car, it always had brought him bad luck — and never should have put fire to that fat joint of Lumbo she rolled while she was smiling and showing him all those perfect teeth. Shouldn't have kissed her when she leaned into him, either, or slipped his hand in her dress and

101

brushed it across that big red titty of hers, but there it was. He'd denied it to Elaine, of course, which had only made the whole thing worse. He never *had* been able to look her straight in the eye and tell a lie.

The hardest part was what he'd learned. Maybe it was self-righteous of him — okay, it *was* self-righteous — but Clay had always thought that he was better than all that. Turned out, you put something fine as that girl in front of him, he wasn't any different than most men he knew. The thing that hurt was he had never imagined himself to be that weak.

Okay, he'd made a lot of mistakes. He'd make an effort to be a better husband if only she'd let him try. As for strange women, never again. One thing that had come out of this: He knew now how deeply he loved Elaine. And God, he loved his son.

The light went out in the window. Elaine would try to quiet Marcus Jr. down now, get him up in that rocking chair, hold him in her arms. It was tough on her, big as Marcus Jr. was, but this always got him down to sleep.

If Clay were in there now he'd offer to help. He'd tell his wife, It's all right, go on downstairs, baby, I'll do this part tonight. He'd sit there in that rocker, hug his boy tight, make him feel loved. Smell his hair.

But he wasn't in there. He was out here, standing on the street.

Dimitri had always warned him, when he'd seen a certain look in Marcus's eye, You don't even want to be thinkin' about messing with any strange. You don't want to end up standing outside your own house, like some kind of heartbroke spy, looking with puppy-dog eyes at our own wife and kid, separated by brick and glass you paid for yourself.

And now that's exactly where he was. Funny how it was that Dimitri, king of the players, ended up being the one to give him that kind of advice.

Not like Dimitri would ever change in that way himself; just look how he was carrying on with that girl up in the Arms. As for Clay, he had no business living in that apartment down on R Street. He had love for his friend, but Clay was all the way past that bachelor thing. He didn't want any part of that world anymore.

Clay turned and walked back to his car. He hit the ignition, rubbed his hands together against the chill as he looked back up through his boy's window.

Clay belonged with his wife and son, behind the walls of that warm house.

SATURDAY
MARCH 15, 1986

ELEVEN

Dimitri Karras had a seat on the edge of his bed. The furnace heat of the sun came through his bedroom window, causing him to lower his head. Hundreds of other cokers across the city were sleeping off their Friday night grams and wouldn't get out of bed until noon or one o'clock. But Karras worked retail, and Saturday happened to be the biggest day of the week. He thought of his mother, always giving him advice, urging him to be a professional. He could see her raised eyebrow, the flip of her hand punctuating her words. "Go to law school, *Dimi mou*, you'll work gentleman's hours. No weekends, nothin' like that." And then he thought, I haven't been out to see my mother for some time.

Karras rubbed his temples. He was suddenly dizzy, and his stomach felt fragile as glass. He burped up some liquid, swallowed it, and fell back on the bed. He passed gas. He wiped flop sweat off his forehead. He forced himself to sit up.

"Ah, Jesus."

Donna Morgan lay behind him, naked under a single sheet. Her lips were chapped from breathing through her mouth. Her breath carried a deep wheeze. Her skin looked grayish in the light.

Karras touched Donna's shoulder, gave it a gentle shake. "Donna. Donna, honey, wake up."

"I just got to sleep," she mumbled. Donna stirred but did not open her eyes.

Karras felt as if he had just gotten to sleep himself. He remembered staring out the window, the feeling of self-disgust at the sight of the false dawn. He had slept two, maybe three hours tops.

"Come on," he said, "you gotta get up."

Karras went to the bathroom, ate three more aspirin, swallowed cold water from the spigot until his head ached. He blew blood from his nose into a tissue. He voided his bowels. He took a long shower, came out, and dressed for work. His clothes smelled of cigarettes.

Karras pulled Donna to a sitting position on the bed, sat with her for a while until she stood up. He watched her grasp the door frame for support before entering the bathroom. He waited to hear the shower run.

Karras walked down the hall to the kitchen. Marcus Clay sat on a stool at the counter, reading the sports page.

Clay looked up from the newspaper. "There's got to be a morning after."

"Maureen McGovern," said Karras.

"Good thing you work in a record store. Otherwise all that useful knowledge you got might go to waste."

Karras poured coffee into a mug. "Thanks for making the extra java."

"Thank *you* for leaving the lights on last night."

"Sorry, man, I forgot."

"I drove by, saw you through the window lookin' like the Lucky Leprechaun, dancing some kind of fool dance, decided not to crash your little party just yet. When I came back, I could hear you all makin' a hell of a racket back there in the bedroom before I even got through the door."

"Just havin' a little fun."

"Sounded fun. What's she doin' now, rinsin' the plaster chips off her forehead?"

"Funny."

Karras took a sip of coffee and screwed up his face.

Clay said, "Taste like dog shit, huh?"

"Yeah, Marcus, it tastes pretty bad."

"I kind of figured you'd be lookin' all rough this morning. Can always tell by the albums you were listenin' to from the night before. Saw that Whoopdie Doo cover lyin' over there —"

"Hüsker Dü."

"Whatever."

"Hey, Marcus, what are ya gonna do, bust my balls forever?"

"I guess I'm done for now." Clay got off the stool, rinsed his cup out in the sink. "You *are* coming to work today, right?"

"Sure."

Clay head-motioned toward the hall. "Your Donna friend gonna be all right?"

"Why wouldn't she be?"

"I'm not even gonna remind you of your age, 'cause we already been down that road. But that woman back there, she's a little bit past the prime of her life, you agree?"

"What's your point?"

"One of these mornings, you keep feedin' their noses like you do, you're gonna wake up next to a blue face. You think you feel bad now, how you think you're gonna feel when you overdose some girl?"

"Shit, man —"

"Shit, nothin'. I'm serious. And while we're on it, I got word on what Donna's boyfriend pulled out of that drug car yesterday."

"What?"

"Cash money. Whole pillowcase full."

Karras stared into his coffee cup. "Well, she's not a part of it. She doesn't even know he took it."

"She will, though. And I'm gonna tell you again: I don't want to have a goddamn thing to do with it."

"I hear you, Marcus."

"Okay. I'll be on U Street if you need me."

"I'll hit Arlington this morning, call you later on."

Clay nodded and went to the front door. He touched the doorknob, turned, and looked back at his friend. "Got some ball today, Dimitri. Hoyas play Michigan State at noon in Dayton. Terps goin' at UNLV tomorrow night around seven."

Karras glanced over at Clay. "What about the late games from last night?"

"Syracuse over Brown, that wasn't no surprise. Arkansas-Little Rock advanced. Auburn took Arizona."

"Kentucky?"

"Put a hurtin' on Davidson."

"The Wildcats are always in there, man."

"You got that right." Clay opened the door. "You take it light, lover. Hear?"

"Yeah, Marcus. You, too."

Dimitri Karras and Donna Morgan drove over the Theodore Roosevelt Bridge into Virginia. Donna stared out the window at the Potomac, the sunlight winking off the swells. She kept a hand up to shade her burning eyes, and also to mask her face. Though she could barely breathe through her nose, she could smell the nicotine and beer on her wrinkled clothes. She looked every day her age and a couple of hundred more. She felt like a twenty-dollar whore.

She appreciated that Karras hadn't tried to engage her in conversation. At least he'd been decent enough for that.

The night before, neither of them had been able to shut their mouths. They couldn't talk fast enough, couldn't wait for the other one to finish a sentence before starting in on one of their own. Every statement, every opinion, had seemed so profound. Donna's jaw ached now from all that talk. She couldn't remember a word they'd said.

She remembered the sex, though. Even from her current perspective, a sick, pale rider with an awful case of cokeover depression, she could still remember the sex. After the ice cubes they had done it straight and sweaty, and it had been good. Her legs kicked out and her toes got pointed, and when it was done, the two of them had managed to move the bed halfway across the room. Yeah, Karras was still a cock star in the bedroom, but there wasn't much more to him than that. When Donna thought of Karras, she pictured a beautifully wrapped present with nothing inside the box.

"Donna?"

"Huh?"

"I was talking to Marcus this morning while you were taking a shower."

"Yeah? What about?"

"Your friend Eddie."

"What about him?"

Karras breathed out slowly. "Marcus saw Eddie take something out of that burning car yesterday. The car was a drug car, Donna. I got to figure that's why Eddie booked, left you down on U."

"A drug car."

Karras nodded, looked straight ahead. "Kid who got burned up was either a dealer or a runner, one of the two."

"You saying that Eddie took drugs out of the car?"

"Marcus thought it might have been money."

Donna felt her heart race. She went into her purse, pushed a crumpled pack of smokes out of the way, found a nearly empty pack, and pulled free a bent cigarette.

Karras pushed the lighter into the dash. "Thought you might want to know."

Donna thought of Eddie, nervous as he was. How it must have been for him, to do the act and then to live with it last night. Eddie doing something bold like that, it must have been something to see.

And Donna thought of Marcus Clay. If Marcus had seen something like that, what would he have done? Donna was certain he would have told his best friend right away.

"So," said Donna, "Marcus just got around to mentioning it to you today, huh?"

"That's right."

"Why?"

"He wasn't *sure* until today, I guess. Or maybe he forgot in all that confusion. Hell, Donna, I don't know."

You know. He told you yesterday, Mr. Karras. You knew I wouldn't have hung with you last night if I had any idea that Eddie was in trouble. You wanted to fuck me first before you cut me loose.

"I want to go home, Dimitri."

"I'll drop you right after I check in on Arlington."

"I need cigarettes."

"There's a Seven-Eleven next to the store."

The lighter popped out. Donna touched the hot end to her cigarette and coughed out her first drag of the day. She looked at Karras full on, no longer embarrassed at her appearance.

Karras cracked the window and relaxed. He'd been silent until they hit Virginia, debating on whether or not to give her the news. He was glad now that he'd gotten it over with. He thought he came off pretty well.

A guy who called himself Dutch ran the Arlington store on Wilson Boulevard. Dutch was one of those names that conjured up barrel-chested beer-drinker types, but Arlington's Dutch was a skinny dude with a strange beanie-top haircut and two hoop earrings in his left lobe. He favored frilly New Romantic shirts à la Adam Ant, worn out over black jeans. There had been a couple of customer complaints about his aloof manner, and those complaints plus his usual appearance put him in the negative column with Marcus Clay. But he showed up six days a week, didn't steal, and managed to hit his numbers every month. Karras thought Dutch was pretty good.

Dutch loved electropop and liked to play it in the store. Clay wanted the managers to play the albums in the current top ten, which naturally were inventoried heavily, but the managers rarely complied, except on those occasions when they had been warned by the other managers that Karras and Clay were making the rounds.

Dutch hadn't been warned, and by the time he saw Karras pushing on the front door it was too late. Dutch had his favorite Talk Talk album, *It's My Life*, on the platter, and he had the volume turned way up.

"Dutchman," said Karras.

"Busted," said Dutch, who shrugged and threw Karras a sheepish smile.

"That's okay." Karras *liked* this album, though he'd never tell Dutch. "Just turn it down some, huh? My head can't deal with it today."

Dutch had a look at Karras before turning down the volume on the house receiver. Karras's shoulders were sagging, and he looked like he'd lost a little weight. Dutch, who listened to druggy music but didn't do drugs himself, figured that Karras had a problem with blow. Blow and women, if you could call the latter a problem. That was the rumor around the company, anyway.

Dutch said, "Got some coffee in the back."

Karras said, "Thanks."

Karras walked into the back room. The place had been a hardware store up until six months ago, and the office area still smelled of fertilizer and cedar. Dutch's assistant manager, a girl named Lori, was sitting at Dutch's desk smoking a cigarette.

"Hey, Dimitri."

"Lori. Don't get up."

Karras tried to smile but couldn't raise the effort. He'd done Lori one night in this very room after an in-store appearance by the Wygals. Looking at Janet Wygal all evening had made him horny, and one thing had led to the last thing, which was Lori bent over a stack of cartons by the back door.

Lori was looking at him now with something close to pity.

"What, I've got something in my teeth?"

"You don't mind my saying so, Dimitri, you're lookin' a little rough today, even for you."

"Late night," he mumbled, or something equally meaningless, as he poured bathtub-warm coffee into a Styrofoam cup. He drank half of it quickly, rushing the liquid past his taste buds and down his throat, then dialed the number for the Georgetown store.

"Scott," said Karras.

"It is me," said Scott, the store manager. Through the phone Karras could hear the new Pet Shop Boys, "West End Girls," playing in the store.

"Any action over there?"

"The suburban children seem to be descending on G-town right on schedule."

"Good. I'll swing by later, okay?"

"We'll be waiting."

Karras hung up, finished the coffee, dropped the cup in the trash. Lori smashed out her cigarette and followed him out to the floor.

"Get the new Simple Minds and the new Hooters to the front racks, Lori."

"Yes, boss."

"And put some of those Windham Hills —"

"Oh, shit, those euthanasia records?"

"I know. Don't ask me why, but the yups are buying them. What's the name of that popular one?"

"A *Winter Snoozefest.*"

"Put a bunch of those up front."

"You got it."

Karras went behind the counter, where Dutch was adjusting the volume on a new record. Karras speed-dialed Marcus at U, got him on the third ring.

"Marcus."

"Mitri."

"I'm in Northern Virginia."

"Any action?"

"Not yet."

"What's that I hear playin'? The Doublemint Twins?"

"No, it's not the Thompson Twins. I believe it's the Blue Nile. *A Walk Across the Rooftops.*"

"I don't care what it is. But maybe you could tell Dutch, if he ain't circlin' around in the sky right now waitin' for permission to land and shit, that what I want played in the store is what we got numbers on, hear?"

"Sure, I'll tell him."

"Good. I'm gonna see you later?"

"Yeah. I've gotta drop Donna off, then I'll be down."

"Got the Hoyas comin' on in a few."

"I'll be there, Marcus. Later." Karras hung up the phone.

"What did Marcus have to say?" asked Dutch.

"Nothin' much," said Karras. "Told you two to have a good day. Be fruitful and multiply, all that."

Karras waved to Lori and Dutch, went out the front door to the lot, got into his Beamer. Dutch had seen a woman in what looked like last night's clothes walk from the 7-Eleven to Karras's car.

"You see the girl he was with?" said Lori.

"I saw her."

"Party girl," said Lori, thinking immediately of that Costello song she liked so much. "Anyway, that's his business. If that's what he likes . . ."

Dutch, who had not yet decided if he was into women or men, or basically disinterested, said, "I guess."

Lori watched Karras pull out of his space. She'd had fun with him that night in the back, but she'd never expected anything more. Not from Karras, anyway.

Lori had met this guy a month ago at the 9353 show down at D.C.

Space. A gentle guy, computer programmer, into music, treated her with respect. Thoughtful and really nice. That was the kind of guy Lori was into now.

Karras took the off-ramp from 495 onto Georgia Avenue north.

"What're you gonna do about Eddie?" he said.

"What do you mean?" said Donna.

"I mean the money. Somebody besides Marcus must have seen him take that money. It's going to get back to the ones that kid ran with. Or it's going to get to the cops. It's bad either way."

"We'll figure it out."

"I don't think you realize —"

"We'll take care of it," said Donna. "Thanks for the advice. And thanks for letting me know about it so quickly, too."

There was enough sarcasm in her voice to convince Karras to end the conversation. Anyway, they were coming up on her place.

Karras pulled into the lot of Donna's garden apartment, a small complex butting up against the Chevrolet dealership at the south end of the Wheaton business district. Eddie Golden sat on the steps leading up to Donna's unit.

Karras pulled up alongside a group of cars parked in front of the steps. Eddie stood but did not move toward Karras's car. Eddie smiled seeing Donna's face. He didn't even bother to look at Karras or shoot him a hard glance. Karras felt an unfamiliar stab of guilt then, thinking, This Eddie character, he seems like a pretty good guy.

Donna shook Karras's hand. "I had a good time, Dimitri. I had fun."

"Wait a second."

"Huh-uh." She reached over and patted him on the arm. "I gotta go."

She was out of the car quickly, closing the door behind her and moving toward Eddie. She had a bounce in her step, a sudden rejuvenation triggered by the thought of the money or the sight of her man, Karras couldn't tell which. He watched them embrace before pulling the BMW out of the lot.

Heading down Georgia toward D.C., Karras pulled into a Shell station to gas up and use the head. In the men's room he blew his nose into some toilet paper and dropped the bloody mess into the bowl.

He washed his face, stared at his wasted reflection in the smudged mirror. He had a long workday ahead of him and some weekend left over after that. He knew what he needed to bring himself back. Not too much, nothing in quantity like last night. Just a little bit would do him right. A little bit of something to clear his head.

Eddie dipped his head, kissed Donna's cool lips. He stroked her belly, took in the pleasure of her naked body beside him.

"I gotta go to work," said Donna.

"I know," said Eddie.

They had made love as soon as they had gotten in the door. Donna was sore from the night before, but she couldn't mention it to Eddie. Her bedside jar of Vaseline helped. Also, Eddie was on the small side, and he never did last too long, a blessing for once.

"Eddie?"

"Huh?"

"I'm proud of you, Eddie."

Eddie Golden smiled. "Thanks, Donna. I don't know what made me do it. I don't know if it was right. I still don't know."

"That's drug money, Eddie." She pointed lazily to the bills spilled out on the carpet beside her bed. Eddie had brought the pillowcase up from the trunk of his car. "It doesn't belong to anybody, not really."

"Who told you that?"

"Karras."

"Your new boyfriend?"

"*You're* my boyfriend, Eddie. Like I told you, nothing happened last night."

She had said they'd gone out to a show and it had gotten too late for Karras to drive her home. She had said that she'd slept out on his living-room couch.

Eddie knew she'd fucked Karras. He knew and he didn't care. He didn't want to lose her. With the money it would be different between them. The money and what he'd done to get it. She respected him now.

Eddie kissed her again on the lips.

"Stop it," she said playfully. "I gotta go to work."

"You don't have to, not really. Not anymore."

"What are we gonna do, run away together?"

"We could."

"How about Florida?" said Donna.

And Eddie said, "Why not?"

Donna showered for the second time that day and changed into fresh clothes. Eddie had cut out a couple of lines from the coke he had left over from the night before. Donna did both lines, figuring it would help her get through her shift behind the novelty jewelry counter at Hecht's. The blow made her feel much better, and she did two more bumps before leaving the apartment with Eddie.

Out in the parking lot, Eddie said, "I've got a dishwasher installation this afternoon. Gotta go over to Beltsville to pick up my tools and my truck. Afterwards I'm gonna swing back by my place, get some clothes. I'm thinkin', till we find out if anybody's looking for me, I'll stay here for a day or two. That okay by you?"

"Fine." Donna touched Eddie's brow, then his hairline where it had been singed. "You okay?"

"It'll grow back, I hope."

"I love you, Eddie."

"We gotta talk, Donna, tonight. We gotta make some kind of plan."

"I get off at six. And I promise, I'm coming straight home."

He kissed her and went to his Plymouth. On the ride out to Beltsville, he pushed in a John Cougar Mellencamp tape and played it loud.

"Little pink houses for you and me," sang Eddie.

He looked in the rearview, checked out his smile. Donna sayin' she loved him, that was really something. He'd been waiting on that for a long time.

Karras studied the checkbook register in his hand. Looking down the withdrawals column, he saw mostly 50s, with the odd 100 inked in here and there. He might as well have written the words *half, gram, half* right next to the numbers. One look at his checkbook reminded him of how much coke he had been doing these last few months. Well, he'd give it up someday soon. He'd get bored with it, most likely, the way he'd gotten bored with grass.

Karras put the checkbook back in his glove box, exited his car, and went up Connecticut on foot. Clouds passed across the sun and shaded the street. He pulled up his jeans, which were hanging loose at his waist. At the ATM by the Safeway he withdrew another fifty, crossed the avenue and headed toward the old apartment house on the corner of Albemarle. His dealer lived on the building's eighth floor. The dealer, a guy named Billy Smith, owned an antique store on 18th Street in Adams Morgan. Sometimes it seemed to Karras that half the antique dealers in D.C. dealt coke.

Near the corner, Karras looked across the street at the Nutty Nathan's on the west side of Connecticut, the electronics store where that Nick Stefanos guy worked. Karras had been there to see him, must have been ten years back, when Stefanos was just a teenager.

A black kid with a bandanna wrapped around his head was standing on the sidewalk outside the store, watching the Hoyas game on the televisions lined up in the display window.

Karras went into the apartment house, sampled a taste of Billy Smith's new batch of freeze, and copped a half.

Driving across town fifteen minutes later, he turned on HFS, heard the intro to "Back on the Chain Gang," and cranked the volume way up. The sun had broken out from the clouds. His head was clear, and he was no longer tired, and the deejay was playing his favorite Pretenders jam.

Karras smiled. He'd felt like roadkill just a while ago. Now, suddenly, there was promise in the day.

TWELVE

Kevin Murphy saw the Taylor kid standing outside the liquor store at 12th and U, his hands buried deep in the pockets of his Raiders jacket. He told Tutt to take the cruiser down the block a ways, and then told him to pull it over to the curb.

"What's up, Murph?"

"I'm gonna talk to that boy back on the corner there. Maybe he saw something with Junie and the money."

"You want me to go with you?"

"Uh-uh. Might be better if I do this one-on-one."

"Maybe I'll find out how Rogers and Monroe are coming along."

"If I don't see you out here, I'll catch you down 11th, near T."

"Where I'll be, partner," said Tutt.

"Right."

Murphy got out of the blue-and-white and walked down the block, one hand steadying his nightstick. A middle-aged MD 20/20 lover tipped his hat, said, "Hello, officer," and Murphy raised his chin. He went by a group of old men sitting on folding chairs set out on the sidewalk. He passed a boy in denim, break dancing to the music coming from his boom box. He came up on the Taylor kid, who was looking in the direction of the record store across the street and jogging in place to keep warm. The clouds had amassed, and now a chill, pushed in on a hard March wind, cut the air.

"Hello, young man," said Murphy.

"Hey, officer."

"Murphy."

"Hey, Officer Murphy."

"Anthony Taylor, right?"

"That's right."

Taylor turned at the sound of a Metrobus headed down U. Murphy saw a small smile form on the kid's face as the tracked the bus's progress.

"That's a nice bus," said Anthony, admiration in his voice. "Clean, too."

"Like it, huh?"

"Gonna drive me my own bus someday."

"Okay."

"I ain't just dreamin' it, neither. For real."

"Don't sound all that fantastic to me."

"Mr. Clay says I can do anything if I set my mind to it."

"Mr. Marcus Clay, works in that record store?"

"He don't just work there. He *owns* the place."

"Well, Mr. Clay is right." Murphy stroked his black mustache. "Look here, Youngblood, you gonna stand on this corner all day?"

"What else I'm gonna do?"

"Now, I don't know about you, but I'm kind of hungry. Was thinking I'd head over to Ben's, get a little lunch. You think you might want to join me for a chili dog?"

"I don't know."

"Lunch is on me, if you want to come along."

Anthony shrugged. "Sure."

They crossed the street together, Anthony Taylor wondering, Why all the sudden is everyone tryin' to fill me up with food?

The guys at Ben's had the Georgetown game playing on the house set. Nearly halfway in, the Hoyas were handling Michigan State. Murphy knew the second half would tell the tale.

"You like Georgetown, Anthony?"

Anthony Taylor swallowed a mouthful of chili beans, bun, and dog. "Not so much since Patrick been gone. I been into Maryland now. Lenny Bias."

"Yeah, I like him, too," Murphy said. "Let me ask you something, Anthony."

"Okay."

118

"Yesterday, after that accident, you told me you saw what happened, and after, too."

"That's right."

"What'd you mean by that?"

Anthony looked straight ahead. "Just, you know, the crash."

"What else exactly?"

"I'm not . . . I'm not *sure*, exactly. Kind of confusing, lookin' back on it, with all those fire engines and shit."

"Anthony."

"I mean, fire engines and *stuff*. Way that car was smokin' and all that."

"But you said —"

"Maybe you better talk to Mr. Clay. *He* saw some stuff. He'll tell you what he saw. I'll go over there with you if you want. I'm practically like, what do you call it, an employee of his now."

Murphy signaled the counterman for the check. The kid was changing his story now, but that was all right. Murphy didn't really feel comfortable getting him involved.

He watched Anthony scarf down the rest of his food. "Hungry?"

"Taste good."

"You eat today?"

"Had some cereal this morning."

"Your mother fix it for you?"

"My moms is down in Georgia, in the country, outside Atlanta. My sisters are down there, too. I live with my granmom, up on Fairmont. Someday I'm gonna go down there and visit my family. Maybe this summer. Maybe stay down there if they got the room, go to school. Gonna take me a Greyhound bus when I go. One of those double-decker models they got, with the windows tinted green."

"What about your father, Anthony?"

Anthony shrugged. "Don't know my father."

Murphy looked at the boy, small in his oversized coat. "Where you live, exactly?"

"Why, you gonna take me home and turn me in?"

Murphy winked. "Just need the information for the official record, Anthony. Case I need to do a follow-up on the investigation."

Anthony gave him his address, and Murphy made a show of writing it down.

Anthony said, "You're nice."

Murphy chuckled. "Thanks. You surprised?"

"I don't know. You ride with that white cop and all."

"Officer Tutt?"

"Whatever his name is."

"Look here, you don't think all white people are bad, do you?"

"I ain't known all that many, tell you the truth. But I do know that one's no good for sure."

"Why you say that?"

"The way he looks. And I just, you know, heard some stuff he said. Like when that boy was burning up in that car yesterday, I heard him talkin' to this other white cop. Heard him say somethin' about 'Those niggers sure do like their barbecues.' Somethin' like that, and then the two of them laughed."

Murphy looked away from the boy.

Anthony said, "So I was just wonderin' why a man like you would ride with a man like that."

"It's like a lot of things in life," said Murphy. "It's complicated."

"Somethin' like that, seems like it would be simple to me."

Murphy didn't respond. He knew the boy was right.

"Come on," said Murphy, "let's go see your Mr. Clay."

Murphy left money on the counter, then got off his stool. He put his hand on the boy's shoulder as he walked toward the door. His hand felt like it belonged there. His hand *fit*. Murphy felt a small shudder enter him then, like when the flu bug first comes, seeping in on the knowledge that he'd never have a boy of his own. Knowing, too, that he had no business being any kind of role model to a good boy like this one.

Marcus Clay felt pretty good about Georgetown's first half. They had held their own so far against Michigan State, with Scott Skiles, the Spartans' star guard, only going one for seven from the field. If the Hoyas could contain Skiles, Clay figured they had a chance.

"Got a whole 'nother half to play, though," said Clarence Tate, who was doing some book work at the desk in the back office where Clay was watching the game.

"Yeah, I know," said Clay. "Want me to turn this up?"

"I can hear it."

"I'm gonna go out and hang on the floor for a little bit while they got this halftime bullshit goin' on."

"Cootch is out there. Ain't all that much to handle."

"Don't remind me. Maybe I'll go out on U, rope some people in."

"Like we used to do, talkin' to the girls walking up the avenue: 'Come on in and get 'em today, ladies, everything is everything at Real Right, we got the sounds gonna help you get down.'"

Marcus chuckled. "Yeah, shit was more simple back in the seventies, wasn't it? And much more fun."

"Don't be layin' that nostalgia trip on me, Marcus. A business either grows or it dies. Remember when you were a kid, how your legs used to ache at night when you were lyin' in bed?"

"Oh, so now you're gonna give me that growing pains lesson again."

"I used that one before, huh?"

"Two or three times since we opened this store."

"Damn. By the way, where's the professor?"

"Karras? He'll be in."

Clay went out to the floor. Cootch was behind the counter, ringing up an Atlantic Starr cassette for a customer. Denice Tate stood by the front door, staring through the window out to U.

"Thank you, brother," Clay said to the customer, trying not to wince at the boy's vines. Jheri-curled fool was wearing a red-and-black leather jacket straight out of a Michael Jackson video, one where Michael danced with all those dead mugs coming out of the grave.

"Thank *you*," said the young man, slipping one fingerless glove on his hand as he headed out the door.

"There's one for you, Neecie," said Cootch. "Was asking after you when he bought his tape. Called you Billie Jean. That your name?"

Denice said, "Be for *real*."

Cootch put a recent George Clinton, *Some of My Best Jokes Are Friends*, on the turntable. Clay felt the urge to dance a little as he walked over to Denice. He never would have imagined a flute solo on a P-Funk jam. But it worked. Long as he had been around, Clinton was still bad.

Clay said, "Hey, girl," trying to open things up in an upbeat way.

"Marcus."

"Good time last night?"

"It was okay. I just went over to my friend Ashley's, watched some videos."

Clay glanced behind him to make sure that Clarence had not come out to the floor. Clay stared into Denice's eyes and said, "Look here. I *saw* you with a couple of boys last night, out on the street."

Denice looked down at the black and white tiles, breathed out slow. Clay let her take her time. He had decided to talk to the girl alone first, see what she had to say.

Denice said, "You gonna tell my father?"

"I haven't yet," said Clay. "Doesn't mean I'm gonna lie to him, either. What I want to talk about here is you."

Denice nodded. "All right."

"That boy you're runnin' with, what's his name?"

"Alan Rogers."

"This Alan Rogers, he's into dealing drugs. You know that, don't you?"

"You don't even know this boy. Alan's good."

"That might be true. I'm old enough to see the world in all kinds of shades. But, good or bad, what he is for sure is trouble. Your father's put in a lot of good years with me, honey, and I love you like my own. Been knowin' you since you weren't nothin' much more than a baby girl. Just don't want to see no harm come to you, that's all."

"I know. And I appreciate it, Marcus. But see, I wasn't in any kind of danger last night. Alan wouldn't let that happen. I saw him at the Chuck Brown show, and he was just ridin' me home."

"With that boy he runs with, tough-lookin' boy. You can't stand there now and tell me *he's* good."

"No, but —"

"What, that white cop who was talkin' to you all, he stop you on some kind of suspicion?"

"You saw that?"

122

"Drove right by y'all."

Denice looked down. "The white cop, they call him Tutt. That man is mean."

"How so?"

"Got mean eyes, Marcus. He and Short Man —"

"Rogers's partner?"

"Uh-huh. Tutt and Short Man were arguing over some kid named Chief. Alan didn't even act like he knew what they were talkin' about. Didn't act like he cared. You know what I'm sayin', Marcus? It was something between *those* two."

"Okay." Denice was clouding the issue, confusing him, avoiding what she had to know was good advice. "Look, Neecie, all I want you to do is think about what you're getting into. Just think."

"I will, Marcus. I promise. And thanks for keeping this between us. Thanks, okay?"

"You hearin' me?"

Denice gave him a quick series of nods. "I'm gonna think real hard on it, Marcus."

"Go on, girl. Don't *play* me, hear?"

"Marcus, I'm not."

Denice looked out the door, saw Tutt's partner, the one named Murphy, in uniform and crossing the street with some kid, headed toward the store. Marcus hadn't asked about the cop named Murphy, and Denice hadn't thought to bring him up. This Murphy, he had been pretty nice last night; in his own quiet way he had calmed things down. But she didn't want to be around the store if he was coming by.

"I'm gonna go for a walk, Marcus."

Clay was looking at the cop and the kid now, too. "Sure, Denice. You go on."

Denice pushed through the door, caught the cop's eye as she went west on U. His eyes met hers, but he didn't say a word. Denice thought it strange.

Clay watched the cop approach. This was the cop who was partnered up with that white patrolman Denice had been talking about, the one named Tutt. Now this uniformed brother was approaching with Anthony Taylor practically under his arm. Clay wondered if Anthony had said any-

123

thing about the drug car, about that Donna girl's boyfriend, or about the money.

Clay figured he was going to find out real quick. He opened the door to let them in.

Kevin Murphy took note of Marcus Clay's height and build as he stepped into the record store with the boy. Clay had kept himself in shape, even with the fifteen, twenty pounds of added weight that a man couldn't help but pick up as he went down life's road. Murphy remembered seeing Clay in this one Interhigh game, when Clay was full grown and Murphy was not quite in his teens. Those five years between them had seemed so much wider then.

"Hey, Mr. Clay."

"Anthony."

Murphy extended his hand. "Kevin Murphy."

"Marcus Clay."

"I know your name."

"You do?"

"I went to Cardoza, same as you."

"Not with me, you didn't. You're too young. I graduated in sixty-seven."

"I came out in seventy-two. But I saw you play. Y'all were up against Spingarn, I think. You had a nice touch from the outside."

"Thanks. You still live in the District?"

Murphy nodded. "Takoma."

"How about that partner you ride with?"

"Tutt?" Murphy smiled. "Not for his likin'. Tutt lives in Silver Spring Towers, little ways over the line."

Clay nodded at Anthony. "He in some kind of trouble?"

"No trouble. We were talkin' about that accident out front of your shop yesterday. Anthony here said I should talk to you."

Clay said, "You ready to do some work today, Anthony?"

"Sure."

"Grab yourself a dust rag and some spray and go over those racks. Cootch will show you where everything is." Clay said to Murphy, "Come on, we can talk in my office."

They walked together toward the back room.

"Nice shop," said Murphy.

"We're tryin'," said Clay.

"You been at this since you got out of school?"

"Made a little involuntary detour overseas first."

"Vietnam?"

"Uh-huh." Clay eye-swept Murphy. "You play for Cardoza, too?"

"Didn't make the cut. Couldn't go to my left is what it was." Murphy touched his mustache. "Still like to play a little bit. And you *know* I like to watch."

"Good. 'Cause I got the Hoyas on the box right now."

"Was watchin' it myself over at Ben's. Took the Taylor kid there for lunch."

Clay glanced at Murphy. "Between the two of us, we're gonna fatten that boy up."

"Good kid," said Murphy.

"Yeah. Figure I can keep him off that corner out there, give him a little busywork around the store."

"Can't hurt."

"Boy wants to be a bus driver when he grows up. He tell you that?"

Murphy said, "He did mention something."

In the back room, Clay introduced Murphy to Clarence Tate, who was seated at the desk, working under a lamp and making notations into a long green book.

Tate lifted himself out of his chair as they shook hands. He had the same raw-material kind of size as Clay, but Murphy saw that Tate's bulk had edged toward fat. Tate's brow was set serious, too, with that pinched, strained look common to numbers men.

Murphy noticed a photograph of Len Bias taped over the desk where Tate sat. It was that one of Lenny that the *Post* had run, where Bias was smiling into the camera, wearing his Terps jersey, palming two basketballs with ease.

"That's my desk," said Clay, who had seen Murphy checking out the shot. "I guess you think it's funny, thirty-seven-year-old man having a picture of a college kid over his desk. I just, you know, haven't seen anything quite like that kid in a long time. Boy's got a lot of promise."

"I don't think it's funny at all," said Murphy.

"Most merchants," said Tate, "got their projections taped over their desk."

"Clarence does half my worryin' for me. Course, he's got a girl he's gonna be sendin' off to college in a few years."

"Oh, yeah?" said Murphy.

Clay said, "Clarence here is the father of that girl you saw walkin' out the store when you came in."

Murphy had recognized the girl as the one who had been with Rogers in the street the night before. He knew the girl had recognized *him*.

Murphy avoided Tate's eyes. "Looked like a nice young lady."

"Denice is her name," said Tate proudly. "And, yeah, she's doing very well."

"Come on over here, Murphy," said Clay, standing in front of the TV set, his eyes widening. "God*damn*, man, you gotta see this, you *know* they're gonna show it again!"

Murphy watched the slo-mo replay, Scott Skiles charging down the court, leading a three-on-one fast break. The guard dribbled behind his back, then went across his body with an on-the-money pass to the forward, who laid it right in.

"Skiles," said Clay.

"Looks like they're on a run," said Murphy.

"Got thirteen minutes left to play," offered Tate, looking up from his paperwork.

Georgetown was down by five. One of the Hoyas signaled the ref for a time-out.

A worn-down-looking white man with prematurely gray hair entered the back room. Murphy looked him over. The guy seemed like he was up on something, dark circles contrasting his overly bright eyes.

"Gentlemen," said the man.

"Hey," said Clay. "Dimitri Karras, meet Kevin Murphy."

"How you doin'?" said Murphy.

"Great," said Karras, shaking Murphy's hand a little too vigorously. "Really great."

No question, thought Murphy, this Karras is up on something for sure.

Clay said, "Michigan State's up by five, Dimitri. Looks like Skiles is gettin' ready to light it up."

"Thompson better slow down the pace," said Karras.

"He just had Broadnax call time," said Murphy.

"Any action out there?" said Clay, his eyes on the game, which had resumed.

Karras said, "Not much," lining himself up next to Clay.

Murphy pulled a chair over and had a seat. He felt comfortable here. Out on the street, in the bars and the lunch counters around town, he always got some kind of reaction wearing his blues. None of these men had backed away or made a thing about his uniform. None of them had made him feel defensive about being a cop.

Skiles hit a bucket from just inside the perimeter, followed it on the next possession with a reverse layup driving to the hole.

"What is he, Dimitri," said Clay, "six two?"

"Six one," said Karras.

"*Damn.*"

The Spartans handled the Hoyas for the entire second half. Georgetown was eliminated from the tournament. Clay turned the sound down as Karras went into the bathroom.

"Now," Clay said to Murphy, "you wanted to talk about something?"

"Right," said Murphy, suddenly remembering why he had come into the shop. He pulled out his pad, the one on which he had written Anthony Taylor's address, and a pen. "Wanted to ask you a couple of questions about that accident yesterday."

"What about it? That *was* just an accident, right? I mean, if it was a homicide or somethin' they'd be sendin' a homicide detective around here, right?"

"It was an accident, far as we know. Procedure, though, you understand." Murphy felt himself begin to fumble. "I need to follow up on a few things about it, that's all."

"Go ahead."

"Well, I need to know, was there something suspicious, anything you might have seen that was suspicious around the scene?"

Clay made a decision. Clay said, "No."

"Nothing at all, right?"

"Not a thing."

Murphy nodded and closed the cover of his pad. He didn't want to pursue it. Suddenly, finding Tyrell's money didn't seem all that important.

"All right. Thanks. I'll be around if you think of anything."

"Glad to help."

"And thanks for the hospitality, hear?"

"Ain't no thing," said Clay. "You come back anytime. Matter of fact, we're gonna be watchin' the Terps tomorrow. Why don't you swing by, you don't have plans."

"I'm off tomorrow," said Murphy. "Maybe I will."

Clay shook Murphy's hand.

THIRTEEN

"There go your girl," said Short Man Monroe. "Young as she is, damn if she don't got some back on her, too."

"I see her," said Alan Rogers.

They sat parked in the Z down on 10th. Denice Tate was walking out of a market on U. She had a bottle of strawberry soda in her hand, and she was headed back in the direction of Real Right.

"I'm gonna go talk to her, man."

"Ain't you done talked enough?"

"Go ahead, Short."

"'Bout time you shut your mouth and busted a nut in that bitch."

"I'll get up with you later," said Rogers as he got out of the car.

Monroe shifted the toothpick in his mouth, watched his boy kick up his heels as he jogged across the street. Damn if anybody'd ever see *him* run after some pussy way Rogers was doing right now.

Monroe sat low in the bucket. He leaned to the right, pushed the Nike shoebox filled with cash underneath the passenger seat. When he came back up he saw Rogers sweet-talkin' the girl, and then he saw him kind of tug on her coat, pull her back behind a solid construction fence the subway people had set up along that stretch of U.

A blue-and-white cruised toward him down 10th, pulled alongside the Z. The uniform inside rolled the window down. Monroe rolled down his. He fingered the Glock tucked tightly between his legs just for fun. He moved his eyes lazily to the cop behind the wheel.

"What's goin' on, Short? You takin' a break from your busy schedule?"

"Doin' a day's work, Tutt. Just like you."

* * * *

Alan Rogers got in close to Denice Tate, draped his extra-large jacket around her shoulders, blanketed them both. They stood behind the fence, hidden from the street.

"Missed you, girl."

"I missed you, too."

He kissed her, sliding his tongue into her mouth. She closed her eyes and kissed him back. He pushed his swelling groin into hers and listened to her moan.

"Want you *bad*, Neecie," whispered Rogers.

"We'll know when it's time," she said in a shaky voice.

"I know now."

She wanted *him*. Kissing him, she felt a warm, wet kind of tickle build between her legs. She kissed him hard once more and broke away.

"Alan."

He slowly pulled her back in against him.

"Tonight, baby. Can we hook up?"

"I don't know. I'm scared."

"What, you scared of me?"

"Course not. I'm talkin' about your friends. Your life."

He tilted up her chin. "I ain't gonna let nothin' happen to you. Don't you know that?"

"I know, but —"

"And you don't have to worry about my friends."

"The man my father works for, he says y'all be dealin' drugs."

Rogers cocked his head thoughtfully. "Just tryin' to make my mark, Neecie. Get some like everybody else. Make enough to break off quick, go on about my business, get a real job. Maybe earn my GED. Don't worry, I know what I'm doin'."

"What about the police?"

"Those ones from last night?" Rogers puffed out his chest. "Shoot, girl, they ain't gonna do nothin' to you."

Denice rested her cheek on Rogers's chest. "I like that you're strong."

"You need a man like me out here. Don't you know that?"

"Yes."

Rogers stroked the top of her head. "So what about tonight?"

"I'll try," said Denice. "Listen, I got to be gettin' back. My daddy'll be all worried."

Rogers said, "You go on."

"Where's your boy Rogers at?" said Tutt.

"Love-talkin' his girl," said Monroe.

"One from last night?"

"Yeah."

"Like to cut me a little slice of that."

"Little on the dark side for you, ain't it?"

"I'm an equal opportunity employer when it comes to pussy. Don't want to deprive anyone of my good lovin'."

"Yeah, you a real fine stud."

"You *know* I am, Short."

"What about *your* partner?"

"Murphy?"

"Uh-huh. Where he at?"

"Talkin' to that kid, always hanging outside of Medger's."

"One wear that Raiders jacket?"

"Yeah. Murphy's got the idea the kid saw something go down when Junie was burning up."

"That's the case, you got the wrong brother talkin' to the kid. 'Cause you know your boy Murphy is way too weak to make that kid sing."

"You talk about my partner, Short, you show respect."

Monroe said, "I'll give it when it's due."

Tutt and Monroe locked eyes.

Tutt said, "Forget about that kid. And forget about Chief and his sidekick, too. You just worry about your runners and collect your junk money and keep pushing your poison on all these other worthless fucks in this neighborhood who ain't never gonna amount to shit anyway. You just concentrate on that. I'll do my job, keeping things together down here. This is *my* district. I rule this motherfucker, you understand?"

Monroe smiled. "Why they call you King, I guess."

Tutt raised his hand and waved good-bye. He pulled down on the shifter and gave the cruiser gas. He drove toward 11th and T, where he and

Murphy had agreed to meet. He chewed on his thumb and spit dead skin out the side of his mouth.

Monroe was right. Murphy *was* weak. Murphy had always been weak. And lately he was acting like he didn't give a rat's ass about the sweet arrangement they'd made with Tyrell. Since they'd been in bed with Cleveland, they'd both been taking home four grand a month, free and clear. Fifty G's a year, that wasn't pocket money, and now Tutt had the feeling that Murphy wanted out. Tutt couldn't allow that. Tutt would have to have a sitdown with Murphy, go eye to eye, let him know how it had to be.

And Monroe. Fuck, that little nigger knew how to make his blood hot. Someday he'd wave good-bye to Monroe for real.

Tutt imagined that Monroe was bending Tyrell's ear every chance he got now, building a case against Murphy and Tutt for sure. Tutt decided that to keep what he had, he'd have to do something quick. Remind them all who was still in charge.

Tutt felt the Power surge through his veins.

Why they call you King, I guess.

Tutt said, "Goddamn right."

Murphy walked down 11th, got into the cruiser. The dispatcher's voice coming from the squawk box described a domestic disturbance called in from the Highland View apartments at the top of the 13th Street hill. Tutt keyed the microphone, informed the dispatcher that they'd respond. He hung the mike in its cradle.

Tutt said, "Anything?"

"Nothing," said Murphy.

"Kid didn't know shit, right?"

"Not a thing."

"We got to find out what happened to that money, partner. We come up with it, it's gonna keep us in good graces with Tyrell. Got to keep provin' our worth, you know what I'm saying?"

Murphy looked at the Twenty-third Psalm card taped to the dash. There was that one sentence toward the end that Murphy loved: "Thy rod and thy staff they comfort me." But Tutt had run a line through it, rewritten the sentence in a childlike scrawl: "My gun and my shield they comfort me."

Murphy nodded in the direction of the radio. "Thought we were gonna take that call."

"In a minute. Ain't nothin' but an argument between a couple of —"

"Niggers?"

"Aw, come on, Murph, don't pull that shit on me. You know me better than that. I'm talkin' about somethin' important here."

"So am I."

Tutt put the car in gear. "We need to have a talk."

"We're on duty," said Murphy. "How about we take that call?"

Rogers and Monroe sat in the idling Z. They had been there for fifteen minutes or so, Rogers keeping the radio up so he wouldn't have to listen to Monroe talking shit about Denice. Monroe reached over and turned the volume down.

"Look what we got here," said Monroe. "Officer Murphy claims that boy there knows somethin' about Junie and the money."

Rogers saw that the kid from outside the liquor store was walking down U.

"Let Murphy handle it."

"Bitch couldn't handle shit," said Monroe, opening his door.

"Where you goin', man?"

"What you think?"

"Short, you don't want to be fuckin' with no little kid."

"Ain't gonna fuck with him," said Monroe, closing the door behind him. "Much."

Moving quick toward the corner, Monroe shouted out some kind of greeting, gave the kid a little come-on-over wave of his hand. The kid hesitated for a moment and looked around, deciding what to do. He stepped off the curb and crossed the street toward Monroe.

They stood together on the corner and talked back and forth. The kid looked scared. He backed up a step. Rogers watched Monroe get real close to the kid's face. He watched Monroe grab a handful of the kid's jacket.

Alan Rogers slid Monroe's Glock underneath the driver's seat. He pulled the keys from the ignition and got out of the Z. Then he broke into a run.

"Short!" yelled Rogers. "Hold up!"

Monroe smiled and threw the kid up against the fence.

FOURTEEN

Anthony Taylor heard that drug boy Monroe, called himself Short Man, yell "Hey" from across the street. Taylor knew to keep walking, act like he thought Monroe was talking to someone else. But there wasn't anyone else around, and that would be a mistake. It would also be a mistake to run, since Monroe would only catch up with him sometime later on. Probably at night, which would be way worse. Anthony thought about it, decided he'd see what this Monroe boy wanted. Maybe, if it was just a question he could answer, he could trade what he knew for something good. Anthony thought if he *did* have something he could trade, maybe he'd get paid.

Anthony crossed the street, looked behind him and down the block toward Real Right, wondering if Mr. Clay was out on the floor or anywhere near the front window. Anthony walked slow. But a car came east on U, rolling along kind of fast, and he had to quick-step to get out of its way. Then he was on the corner before he wanted to be, not quite ready in his mind, without a plan. He found himself standing before Monroe.

"Yo, wha'sup, little man?" said Monroe.

"Ain't shit," said Anthony.

Monroe wasn't so tall, but he had show muscles, and eyes like the kind they put in stuffed birds. Anthony shivered in his coat.

"Heard tell you saw that accident yesterday, one where my boy Junie got himself burned up."

Anthony shrugged. "That's right."

"*What*'d you see?"

"Piece of steel went through the car, took off that boy's head."

"After that."

"Ain't see nothin', man."

"That's some boolshit."

Anthony stepped back.

Monroe stepped forward. "Only gonna ask you one more time."

Anthony felt his legs weaken and begin to shake. He couldn't make them stop. He tried not to let it show on his face.

Gotta be hard. Can't let no one punk you out.

Anthony said, "What you gonna give me, man?"

Monroe looked around, kind of smiled, looked back at Anthony and said, "How about I give you your life?"

"W-what you mean, man?"

"W-w-what I mean? M-m-mean I'm gonna cut your m-m-mothafuckin' head off, you don't start tellin' me what I want to hear."

Anthony looked back toward the store. He felt his eyes tear up.

Monroe said, "Who you lookin' for, huh? Go ahead and cry all you want. Ain't nobody in this world gonna give a good fuck about you, little man. You just another nigga out here, and you are mine. This ain't no bad dream you gonna wake up from, your momma strokin' your head, sittin' by your bed and shit. I'm *real*, hear? Your very own killer-clown."

"Okay." Anthony closed his eyes and swallowed hard. "I saw some shit, okay?"

"Talk about it."

"Saw this white dude, parked on the street. Walked right up to Junie's car while it was burnin', took out this pillowcase and shit, put it in his car. Saw him drive away."

"White dude, huh? What he look like?"

"I don't know . . . white. Skinny, kinda, I don't know. Had a girl with him, but not when he left."

"Where'd this girl go?"

"Came out later, with another white dude, works at the record store."

"What about the car? What *kind* of car? You remember the color, boss?"

Anthony didn't answer.

Monroe grabbed the kid's jacket, turned at the sound of someone yelling his name. Anthony saw the Rogers boy running toward them. Anthony saw Monroe look at his friend and smile. Anthony felt Monroe lift him off the ground. Then Anthony was in the air, feeling the give of the fence as he bounced off it and rolled to the ground. He fought to bring in breath.

Anthony's feet slipped in the gravel spread about the concrete. He tried to get up and run, but Monroe lifted him by his jacket and stood him up against the fence. And there was no place to run; Alan Rogers had arrived and blocked his way.

A vein pulsed in Monroe's temple beside his right eye.

"Gonna fuck you up right quick, little man. You *know* that I'm not playin'. Now, look here: I want to know the license plate off that car."

"Was one of those Plymouths they got, look like all the rest. Gray. . . . Aw, shit, come on, you're hurtin' me, man."

"Wanna know what you saw!"

"Short!" said Rogers, cupping a hand around Monroe's bicep. "C'mon, man, lighten up on that shit!"

"Fuck off me, Alan!" Monroe shook off Rogers's hand. He bunched up Anthony's jacket tight to his neck.

Anthony whispered, "Appliance Installers Unlimited."

"Short!" yelled Rogers.

Monroe ignored Rogers. "Say it again."

"Appliance Installers Unlimited," said Anthony. "That's what it was. What the sign said on the white boy's car."

"Anything else?"

"Had an address; don't recall the numbers. Someplace out in Maryland. Beltsville, wherever that is."

Monroe let go of Anthony's jacket, dropped him on the ground.

"Short," said Rogers.

"What!"

"Look over there, man."

Monroe turned his head. A big, wide-shouldered man was running across the street, straight toward them. Behind him ran a white dude with gray hair.

"I know that nigga?" said Monroe.

"Look like he knows you," said Rogers. "Way he's comin', he don't look like he's gonna stop."

Anthony got to his feet. "Mr. Clay," he said.

Monroe said, "Who?"

"Tried to tell you," said Alan Rogers to Monroe. "You were too busy, though, beatin' up on that little kid."

Marcus Clay had just finished moving the "Word Up" twelve-inch bin to the front of the store when he happened to look out the window. He saw Anthony Taylor a block down, crossing the street around 10th. Then he saw that drug boy, Short Man, standing on the corner there by the construction fence, waving Anthony ahead.

Clay went and stood by the window.

"Turn that music down, Cootch," said Clay over his shoulder.

Cootch cut back the volume on the house stereo. "That better?"

"Yeah. Can't *see* nothin' with that music up so loud."

"What are you lookin' at?"

"You send Anthony out for somethin'?"

"Gave him a couple of ducats for a soda from the market. Told him to buy one for himself, keep the change. There a problem with that?"

"Not sure just yet."

Dimitri Karras came out of the back room. He crossed the floor and stood next to Marcus Clay.

"What's goin' on, Marcus?"

"Just lookin' at —" Clay stopped speaking, noticing Karras. Karras's jaw was knotted tight.

"What?"

"You eat today?" said Clay.

"Had a piece of toast this morning. Why?"

"You don't look so good."

"I feel fine."

"I bet you do. But you sure don't look it. Ought to see just how pale you look. And those jeans of yours are about ready to drop right off your ass. Startin' to look like that Mitch Snyder, been fastin' for twenty-seven days."

"I just need to eat. Food and a good night's sleep, that's all I need."

"Uh-huh."

Karras looked through the window. He squinted his eyes. "That our new employee?"

"That's Anthony, yeah."

"Who's he talkin' to?"

"Goes by the name of Short Man. Deals coke for our neighborhood kingpin, someone named Tyrell Cleveland. That boy got burned up yesterday, he worked for Tyrell, too. Tell me, man, what was the name of Donna's boyfriend again?"

Marcus was getting to something now. It made Karras uncomfortable, that too quiet, too polite tone in Clay's voice. It had been a while since he'd heard Marcus speak that way.

"Eddie Golden," said Karras.

"Eddie Golden. Well, this Tyrell, the one I told you about? He's the one Eddie stole all that jack from."

Clay watched Short Man get up in Anthony's face. Clay made a small humming sound through closed lips.

Karras cleared his throat. "But why's Short Man talkin' to the kid like that?"

"'Cause the kid managed to get himself in the middle. Yesterday, when that boy in the Buick got his head tore off and Eddie Golden took that pillowcase? Anthony saw what went down."

"Damn."

"Yeah, I know."

Karras saw Clay unfold his arms and ball his right fist.

"Thought you weren't going to get involved," said Karras.

Clay said, "I'm tryin' my best."

Short Man threw Anthony up against the fence. Anthony went down, tried to scamper off. The Rogers kid came up on the two of them, blocked Anthony's route. Short Man snatched Anthony by his jacket and stood him back up.

"Aw, shit," said Clay very softly. "You done went and did the wrong thing, now."

Clay stepped quickly toward the door. Karras followed.

"Marcus, what you doin', man?"

"Find out when I get there."

"I'm comin' with you."

"All that energy you got, you might as well."

They pushed through the door and hit the street.

Cootch stepped out from behind the counter and walked to the window, watched Clay and Karras in full sprint.

"Damn," said Cootch. He never would have thought a couple of old-school mugs like Clay and Karras could move so fast.

Short Man Monroe watched the big dude approach, the gray-haired white dude just behind. Big dude was coming on fast. One of those Vietnam-time, Richard Roundtree–lookin' mothafuckers, way past his prime. Monroe figured he'd listen to what the man had to say, then talk him down. If Vietnam wanted to throw a punch, he'd cover up at first, let the old mothafucker punch himself out. Then he'd step *to* him, fuck this old, broken-down nigga up.

The man kept coming, though. Didn't look like he was gonna stop to talk.

"What you want, nigga?" said Monroe.

The man was stepping fast. He was close enough now.

"You don't see no nigger here, boy. The name's Marcus Clay."

Monroe gave him a sucker smile and planted his back foot. He threw a right toward the man's face.

Clay stepped to his side, slipped the punch. He whipped out his hand, turned it for a nice, quick snap at the point of contact, drove his palm up into Short Man's nose. The blow lifted Monroe off the ground.

Monroe flew back, his eyes hot as fire. He watched his own blood splash up before his face, felt it run over his lip and into his mouth.

"Respect!" yelled Karras to Alan Rogers, who had moved forward.

Rogers stayed where he was. The white dude looked like some mad professor and shit, lit by a hundred tabs of speed.

Anthony Taylor backed himself away along the fence.

"How you like that, short stuff?" said Clay. "You like it when a bigger man than you roughs you up?"

Monroe stood up, rolled his shoulders, smiled red. Pain tears streamed down his cheeks. He came forward in a crouch. He brought his hands up to protect his face, bobbed, saw blood hit the sidewalk.

"Stay where you are, man," said Clay. "You don't want no more."

Monroe kept coming. He hooked a right toward Clay's middle. Clay brought his elbows in, took the shot. Monroe led with a left jab, threw another right.

The blow was weak and off. Clay swatted it to the side. He slapped

Monroe hard with an open hand. He backhanded him, hammer-slapped him again square on his broken nose. Monroe yelped like a stick-beat dog and went down to the concrete.

"*Dag,*" said Anthony Taylor.

"Get out of here, boy. Go on back to the store now, hear? Go."

The kid looked at the bloody heap curled on the sidewalk and walked away. A couple of old men had gathered down along 10th, and they were shouting words of encouragement to Marcus Clay.

"You," said Clay to Rogers. "Pick your boy up and get him to a doctor. Now on in, you stay out of sight of my shop. Don't even want to see your kind around this neighborhood, you hear?"

"Tell 'em, Clay!" yelled one of the old men.

Rogers helped Monroe up off the ground. He began to walk him back toward the Z.

"C'mon, Marcus." Karras tugged at Clay's shirt.

"Another thing, Rogers. That your name, right, boy?"

Rogers and Monroe kept walking.

Clay raised his voice. "You keep away from that girl, Rogers. Keep away from Denice Tate!"

"All right, Marcus," said Karras. "You made your point, buddy. Let's go back to work."

They headed across U.

Monroe stopped, pulled his arm away from Rogers. He turned toward Clay. "Gonna fuck you up, nigga!" You hear?" He stared at the old men on the sidewalk, gestured wildly. "Gonna fuck *all* a y'all up!"

The old men turned and walked back toward their homes.

"Gotta get you to D.C. General," said Rogers.

"Gonna doom that mothafucker, Alan," said Monroe.

"All right, black," said Rogers. "Need to fix you up, though, first."

Alan Rogers looked back at Clay and the white dude, crossing the street slow. Clay, he'd *handled* Monroe, crippled his ass and then slapped him down like he was breaking a child. Rogers thought, How'd I ever get with the people I'm with?

Rogers wanted to see his girl. He wanted to run away.

* * * *

Karras and Clay reached Real Right's front door.

"Damn, Marcus, haven't seen you move that fast since —"

"Ten years back? Don't say it, man."

"Where'd you learn that hand strike?"

"Been training a little bit with my cop friend, George Dozier. Just brushin' up, really, on what they taught me in the service."

"We're gonna see those guys again; you know that, don't you?"

"I reckon."

Karras touched the handle of the door. "How'd it feel, Marcus?"

"What?"

"You know."

"Felt good, doin' it. Gonna feel foolish about it later on tonight. Way it always is, Mitri."

"What was that shit about Denice? She hangin' out with that Rogers kid?"

"Yeah."

"Clarence know?"

"Haven't told him yet."

"You just told the whole neighborhood, though."

"I know it. Guess it's time I let Clarence in on it, too."

Karras pulled on the door and held it open. Clay stepped inside.

FIFTEEN

"Mr. Clay," said Anthony Taylor, "I'm sorry."

"Sorry about what?"

"I did wrong."

"No," said Clay, "you did no wrong."

"You did fine," said Karras. "You okay?"

"Back's a little sore," said Anthony.

"You're gonna feel it tomorrow, Anthony," said Clay. "Young as you are, though, you'll rebound quick."

Clarence Tate came into the back office. "What's goin' on, Marcus? Just got back from droppin' Denice at home. Cootch said you had some trouble."

"He didn't have much," said Karras.

Anthony said, "Mr. Clay kicked that boy's ass."

"Anthony."

"Sorry."

"What happened?" said Tate.

"Kid got roughed up by our local drug boys. Had to put one of them down."

"Mr. Clay said *bap*," said Anthony, slapping a fist into his palm. "Broke that boy's nose."

"There's other ways to settle things," said Clay, thinking how good it had felt when Short Man's nose had given way. "You know, talk things out."

"That's what you were doin'?" said Karras.

"Shut up, Dimitri."

"What'd they rough the kid up for?" said Tate.

"Information," said Clay. "Anthony here saw someone pulling something out of that burning drug car yesterday."

"Mr. Clay said not to tell the po-lice."

"You knew about it, Marcus?" said Tate.

"Yeah, I knew. Lots of things I been seein' I should have told you about, Clarence. We get things squared away here, you and me are gonna have a talk."

"I tried not to tell that boy everything I saw," said Anthony. He looked at the baggy-eyed white man with the gray hair. "Had to tell him there was a girl got out of the Plymouth. Told him she came back out the store with you. And I told him what I noticed of the car. I'm sorry, Mr. Karras, I didn't mean to say nothin' about you, only —"

"Don't worry about it," said Karras. "Like I said, you did good."

Cootch put his head inside the door. "Hey, Boss. Cops are here."

"Murphy?"

"Yeah. And that white cop he rides with, too."

They all went out to the floor. Murphy came forward and met the group. Tutt stayed back by the door, glancing around the place like he was looking for something, rocking on his heels.

"Heard you had some trouble, Marcus," said Murphy.

Karras said, "He didn't have much."

"Couple of our neighborhood dealers," said Clay, "they were out there roughin' up Anthony. I kind of stepped in."

"Why were they messin' with you, Anthony?"

"Tried to ask me some questions about that Buick burnin' up yesterday."

"But you didn't know anything, right?"

"Right. And if I did know, I wouldn't have told."

"Anthony's a stand-up kid," said Karras, and Anthony gave him a smile.

"You officers are a little late," said Tate, "aren't you?"

"One of the residents on Tenth phoned it in while we were on another call," said Murphy. "Everybody all right?"

"Yeah, we're all fine."

"Mr. Clay kicked that boy's — he kicked that boy's butt!"

"What boy?" said Tutt from across the room.

"Boy named Short Man," said Anthony. "Mr. Clay broke his nose."

Clay watched Tutt's eyes kind of cloud over.

Murphy said, "That right?"

"I don't know for sure," said Clay. "Put a hurtin' on him, though, I'll admit to that. You need to charge me with somethin'?"

"Not unless this Short Man character files a complaint. And even then I kinda doubt it, considering the circumstances. That sound right to you, Officer Tutt?"

"That's right. Only, Mr. —"

"Marcus Clay."

"Mr. Clay. Here on in, you leave the policin' to me and Officer Murphy. That sound good to you?"

Clay nodded at Tutt. Tutt smiled a little and nodded back.

"Had enough excitement today, young man?" said Murphy to Anthony.

"Yessir."

"How'd you like me to ride you home in my squad car?"

"Yeah! That okay, Mr. Clay?"

"Sure, Anthony, I think it would be all right. You put in a full day."

Anthony went to shake Clay's hand, and Clay gathered him into a hug. Clay patted his back and let him go.

"Thank you," said Anthony.

Clay said, "Go on, boy."

Anthony and Murphy walked toward the front door.

Tutt said, "Nice shop you got."

"Thanks," said Clay.

"Hope you make it down here."

"We will."

Clay, Karras, Tate, and Cootch watched them get into the squad car out front.

Karras said, "That Murphy seems okay."

"Yeah," said Tate, "Murphy's down."

"Can't say nothin' for his Boss Hogg–lookin' partner, though," said Cootch.

"Clarence," said Clay, "let's go in the back and have that talk."

*   *   *   *

144

Anthony Taylor uncurled his fingers from around the criss-cross metal grate. They had put him behind the cage in the backseat. Officer Murphy had turned up the volume on the radio mounted underneath the dash so Anthony could hear. Anthony could see some kind of shotgun propped barrel up next to Tutt, the white cop with the mean eyes. Murphy was driving, sitting up straight. Anthony thought that Officer Murphy looked bad behind the wheel. Murphy stopped the car halfway down Fairmont.

"All right, young man," said Murphy. "This is it right here, right?"

"Yeah."

"Come on, I'll walk you to the door."

Anthony had to wait for Murphy to come around, since there wasn't any handle on the door to let himself out. Anthony figured that this was on purpose, like; it was usually criminals sat back where he was at now.

Murphy opened the door, and Anthony stepped out onto the government strip of grass. A couple of kids from the neighborhood had come close to the car, along with two boys Anthony recognized from Clifton Terrace.

"Don't say nothin', Officer Murphy," Anthony said softly. "Okay?"

Murphy put his hand on the boy's arm, walked him up the sidewalk to his row house. Murphy almost chuckled, watching Anthony affect a swagger as he looked behind him and winked one time at his friends.

Murphy rang the buzzer on the front door.

A middle-aged woman, broad shouldered with large, artillery-shell breasts, opened the door. She registered Murphy's uniform and quickly frowned down on Anthony.

"What'd you go and do now, son?" she asked.

"Ain't do nothin', Granmom."

"He's in no trouble." Murphy extended his hand. "Officer Murphy."

"Lula Taylor."

She wasn't a bad-looking woman. Strong and tall, about ten years past pretty. A large mole lodged against the fold of her right nostril would give some men pause. It looked like a beetle had crawled up and died right on her face.

"Why'd you bring him home, then?"

"Earlier on, some boys tried to rough him up. Thought I'd escort him back."

"Thank you. Appreciate you lookin' out for my boy."

"Pleasure."

Murphy looked past her, into the smoky living room where the *Wattstax* album was playing on the stereo. The figure of a man quickly crossed the room and ducked out of sight.

"Everything all right?" said Lula.

"Yes, ma'am. Was just going to say, might be better if Anthony stays in tonight."

"Aw, man," said Anthony.

"I don't let him out alone at night," said Lula, "if that's what you think."

"Ain't gonna stay around here all weekend," said Anthony, "listenin' to you and your friend argue and —"

"Anthony!"

"But Granmom —"

"Don't you take a tone with me. Now go on up to your room, son. Go on."

Anthony shook his head. "See you, Officer Murphy."

"All right, Anthony. You take care."

Anthony went inside and up the stairs.

Lula looked behind her, then back at Murphy. "That all?"

"Just keep an eye on your grandson, Miss Taylor."

Lula narrowed her eyes. "You sayin' that I don't?"

"No, ma'am, I'm not sayin' that."

"'Cause I do the best I can. Work a full-time job and pay for his food and shelter and clothing, including that NFL jacket and those fifty-dollar sneakers he likes to wear. Give him plenty of love, too. All of this while that daughter of mine cleans herself up down south. I do the best I can."

"Just wanted to mention that it's gettin' awful rough out here. Boy his age shouldn't be runnin' free."

"Good day, officer."

Murphy tipped his head and said, "Good day."

She closed the door. Murphy walked away.

Going down the sidewalk, one of the older boys leaning on an old Datsun asked what the Taylor kid had done. Murphy didn't answer or look the boy's way. He opened the driver's-side door and got behind the wheel of the squad car.

"Still think the kid's tellin' the truth?" said Tutt.

"Yeah," said Murphy.

"I'm not so sure. Let's get to our pay phone. I'll beep Rogers, see if we can't find out what went down. Maybe Taylor did talk. You never know."

Tutt always called from the same pay phone. He made sure none of the runners used the same one.

Murphy ignitioned the cruiser.

Tutt said, "That old man, one who called in the fight? He said Clay had some words with Short Man about stayin' out of the neighborhood. Tyrell's not gonna like that."

"I expect he won't."

"Well, I always said it was just a matter of time before someone shut Short's mouth. Only wish it could have been me."

"You'll get your chance, Tutt."

"Gonna be my pleasure, too. Anyway, he had it comin'."

We all have it coming. It's a vengeful God gonna make us pay.

"Come on," said Tutt, "we gonna sit here idling all day? Or maybe you want to see if one of those geniuses over there wants a ride somewhere, too. Maybe you wanna start one of those, what do you call that, day-care services for all these disadvantaged kids."

Tutt high-cackled as Murphy pulled away from the curb.

"Oh, shit." Tutt wiped his eyes.

"You're cracking yourself up, Tutt." Murphy hung a left. "Where to?"

"Head on down to T, partner. Let's see if we can't do somethin' right before we gotta go talk to Tyrell. Maybe run across that kid in the green hat. You know, the one who calls himself Chief."

Clarence Tate said, "You should've told me, Marcus."

"I know it, Clarence. I apologize."

"I understand what you're sayin', how you thought everything was all right, seeing her out on that street with that cop there and all that. But you should have stopped and checked it out to make sure. Or you should have pulled over and called me up."

"I made a judgment call, Clarence. Last night I thought that Tutt, bein' a cop and all, he wouldn't let anything happen to her. And I didn't think it was right to involve the Taylor kid. But after talking to Denice, and just those few minutes I saw of him today . . . well, if I had known what he was about, I would have done it different. There's somethin' wrong with that cop."

"There is."

"But I wouldn't be too rough on Denice, Clarence. She's got a good head on her shoulders, man. Try to remember how you felt with your first love. How nothin' was gonna stop you from seeing her."

"You don't have to tell me. But it doesn't make it any easier when it's your own daughter and you see her goin' down the wrong road."

"Just go easy on her, friend."

"Yeah, I know."

Crowd noise surged from the television set up on the desk.

"Kansas?" said Tate.

Clay nodded. "They're takin' Temple to school."

Karras came out of the bathroom. He had been in there for the past ten minutes. Clay and Tate shared a look.

"I'm outta here, Marcus," said Karras, speaking rapidly, clapping his hands and rubbing them together with vigor.

"You call your girl Donna, let her know what went down?"

"Left a message on her machine. I'm gonna head over to Georgetown for the late rush, then close things out at Dupont with Cheek. I'll see you there."

"Right."

"Take care, Clarence."

"Professor."

Tate waited for Karras to exit the back room.

"Your boy's in trouble," said Tate.

"Say it again?"

"He's deep into that freeze. Everybody in the company knows it. You know it, too, Marcus."

Clay nodded. "Been recreational up to now. I'm not sure if it's a full-blown problem yet."

"Anyone doin' that shit has a problem, you ask me. You can't tell me any different."

"I hear you. Me and Dimitri are due for a talk."

"Up to you. Thought I'd point it out."

"Clarence?" said Clay.

They shook hands, and then Tate put his arms around Clay and hugged him.

"No problem, brother. We're okay."

"Take the rest of the day off, will you?"

"Planned on it. Gonna go talk to Neecie right now."

Clay walked Tate through the sales floor. He watched him get into his Cutlass and drive west.

Tate's emotions had built on the ride to their row house; as soon as he stepped into the foyer he began to shout. Denice had been caught off guard and unbalanced, and became defensive immediately. Their brief, volcanic conversation ended with the slamming of a door and Denice crying in her room. Tate went down to the kitchen, leaned against the counter, and drank a beer. The beer took him down a few notches to where he needed to be.

He went back upstairs. He pushed open Denice's door. She was sitting on the edge of her bed.

"Neecie?"

"Yes, Daddy."

"Thought maybe you'd like to catch an early movie."

She looked up at him. There were dirt tracks running down her face. "I guess that would be all right."

"Come here." They met halfway in the room. He brought her close and held her tight for a long time, stroking her hair. "I love you, honeygirl," he said.

Denice began to cry again. Tate cried, too.

SIXTEEN

Short Man Monroe walked across the parking lot outside D.C. General. His nose was set, packed, and taped. His eyes were swollen and gorged with blood. Alan Rogers had to move quickly to keep up.

"Slow down, black."

"Fuck slowin' down," said Monroe. "Where go our Z?"

"Round here somewhere."

Monroe took two of the codeines the ER doctor had given him, popped them in his mouth, threw his head back and dry-swallowed the pills. He heard a beeper sound.

"That you?"

"Yeah."

Rogers pulled his beeper off his Lees and checked the number.

"Tutt and Murphy," said Rogers.

"Wonder what they want," said Monroe.

"I'll find out."

"Don't call 'em back. They supposed to be freein' us up to do our business down there. Where the fuck were they when Vietnam came runnin' down the street?"

"Doin' their regular cop work, I expect."

"Yeah, well, Tyrell's gonna hear about this shit, you can believe that."

They found the Z. Monroe tossed dollars at the Ethiopian parking attendant, caught rubber leaving the lot.

"Foreign mothafuckers everywhere you look," said Monroe.

"Man was African."

"Come over here, takin' our jobs."

"You ain't lookin' for no job, Short."

"*Shut* up, man."

Monroe pulled over at the first beer market he saw. He went inside and drew a forty of Olde English from the cooler, raised his voice to the Korean woman behind the counter, told her to get him a Maryland phone book. Her husband and Monroe stared at each other while the woman went to the back room. She returned with the phone book. Monroe opened it and found what he wanted while the woman rang the sale.

"Got the street number of that joint," said Monroe, back in the car.

"What joint?" said Rogers.

"Appliance Installers Unlimited. That's what that boy said, right?"

"I guess. What we gonna do now?"

"Get the ball rollin'," said Monroe. He twisted the top of the malt liquor bottle and took a long swig.

"Maybe we *ought* to call Tutt and Murphy."

"Uh-uh," said Monroe. "We gonna do this mothafucker right."

Chink Bennet said, "Shit, Jumbo, why you gotta be makin' so much noise? Show my girl a little respect."

Jumbo Linney was reaching into his party-sized bag of Doritos, bringing out some ranch-flavored chips. The sound of crushed cellophane competed with the grunts, moans, and short breathing of the men jacking off around them.

"Your girl? She yours now, huh? You think Vanessa know you, Chink? You ain't had no girl since as far back as I can remember. Last time you had a piece of ass was when your finger broke through the toilet paper while you was givin' yourself a wipe, ha ha ha."

"Ain't heard that stupid shit since grade school, man."

"Grade school be the *only* place a tiny mug like you would get some play. Remember that group picture they used to take every year when we was in grade school? How they always put the itty-bitty mothafuckers in the front row? They made a *new* front row for your Tattoo-lookin' ass."

"Quiet down," said someone behind them.

"Take a walk," said someone else from the back of the theater.

"Who gonna walk me?" shouted Linney. "You?"

"Talk about it, Jumbo," said Bennet.

"Nigga tryin' to take me for bad."

Bennett and Linney sat with two seats between them so no one would think they were punks. The Gayety Theatre was half filled for its Saturday matinee. "Ladies Free with Escort," the ads always said, but Chink and Jumbo had never seen a woman in the place, except for the hand-job hookers the patrons brought in and the women up on the screen. Vanessa Del Rio was up there now, sitting on some dude's face.

"*Her Name Is Lisa*," said Bennett with reverence, the way a priest might say "*The Song of Bernadette*" when asked to name his favorite film. "Why don't they call it *Her Name Is Vanessa*, though, Jumbo?"

"'Cause she's playin' a character got the name Lisa."

"There you go," said Bennet, pointing at the screen. "She workin' that mothafucker now, boy."

The actress was saying something like, "Oh, your cock is so big," but Chink Bennet wasn't listening to her words. He studied her mouth, mostly, his favorite Vanessa body part, though he liked her big titties and the muscle action way up on her thighs. Girl had a nice onion on her, too.

A guy two rows up gave a horse-shake of his head and pitched forward as he shot off into a dirty sock. Bennet and Linney laughed. The guy got up and left the theater a few minutes later.

"Hey, Mr. Ed, where you goin'?" said Linney.

"Movie ain't over yet!" shouted Bennet.

"Forgot your Ban-lons and shit!"

Bennet and Linney touched hands.

"Vanessa," said Bennet a little later on. "That there is my girl."

"You ask me, I'd like to have me a girl like Karen Johnson."

"What, you sayin' she near as good as Vanessa Del Rio?"

"Naw, Chink. I'm not talkin' about the way she looks. I'm talkin' about what she did for the mayor. Gave up that pussy and supplied him with cocaine any time he wanted, man. Then went to jail for his ass instead of testifyin'."

"They say the mayor's friends paid her off, Jumbo. The ones he gives those contracts to and shit. Gave her some of that hush money you hear about."

"Why she did it, I don't know. But any man could get with a woman who'd do that for him."

Chink Bennet stroked his chin. "I had a choice, I'd stay with my girl V, right up there."

Out on 9th Street, Bennet and Linney walked toward the Supra.

"Better get over to Tyrell's," said Bennet. "He'll be lookin' for us, man."

"Make a stop first at the Seven-Eleven, okay? Got my heart set on some nachos, man."

"Damn, Jumbo, can't we ever get in the car and drive without stoppin' for food?"

"I guess I just love food the way you love pussy, Chink." Jumbo side-glanced his friend. "Difference is, I can eat any time I want to."

Richard Tutt had an apartment in Silver Spring Towers, just a half mile over the District line on Thayer Avenue. He had stopped at the Safeway across the street on Fenton, bought a few Hungry Man dinners and a box of ice-cream sandwiches, and parked his Bronco in the side lot. He took the elevator up to his place.

Tutt lived in downtown Silver Spring for its proximity to his work. This was as close as you could get to D.C. without actually having a District address. Tutt would never live in a place where he was in the minority, though sometimes it seemed as if Silver Spring was headed that way, too. Looking down to the street, he could see the spics and the spades, the punjabs and the A-rabs, walking up toward the Metro or waiting for Ride On buses, or hauling those two-wheeled carts of theirs up to the grocery store. Tutt was thinking of moving to the country, maybe toward Frederick or out 29, where you could still get a lot of house for the money and some open land. The commute was hell, but at least out there you could wake up in the morning and say hello to your own kind.

Tutt's two-bedroom apartment was sparsely furnished, a floor mattress in one bedroom, a This End Up living-room set and a dining-room table from his parents' old house in the living area. A bench, some free weights, and a floor-to-ceiling mirror sat in the spare bedroom.

Tutt's parents were dead. He didn't have many friends to speak of. He guessed Murphy was his best friend, although Murphy always had some kind of excuse when Tutt suggested they get together outside work. Tutt occasionally saw his sister, who had rowed with one oar in the water since she was a little kid, but only on special holidays and on her birthday. He generally avoided her because her husband, Tutt's light-in-his-loafers brother-in-law, came with the package.

Other than his sister, Tutt never brought girls to his apartment. He didn't like waking up next to a woman he didn't know, and he especially didn't like the awkward way it felt after you pulled out and there was nothing more to say.

Tutt hadn't had a girlfriend since the tenth grade. Tonight, like most weekend nights, he had no plans.

Tutt got back in the baby blue Bronco and drove over to the Erol's on East-West Highway. He picked out a *Death Wish* movie he thought he might have rented before, though he couldn't tell from the box. One of those was interchangeable with the next, and Tutt thought all of them were pretty good. Charlie Bronson wreaking righteous havoc on a bunch of rugheads and Third World cretins. Nothing better than that.

He went back to his apartment, did four sets of fifty push-ups, undressed, and picked up a fuck magazine that lay on the floor by his bed. He leafed through the mag and played with himself a little, but he couldn't make his dick stand up, so he went into the bathroom and took a long, hot shower. Tutt dried off and got into a clean pair of acid-washed jeans, microwaved a Salisbury steak platter, and took the dinner and can of Bud Light out to the living room, and set up in front of the tube to watch the flick.

After dinner he felt kind of tired. He stretched out on the couch and took a nap.

When he woke up, the movie was over, and the VCR had switched back over to TV. *Facts of Life*, a show he couldn't stand, was just coming on. Tutt watched the first few minutes to see if the girls had grown any more tit since the last time he watched, and then he got up, cracked another beer, and went to the window. He looked down to the darkened street and saw that it had begun to rain.

Saturday night. Tutt could put a nice, fat bankroll in his pocket and go out and blow it if that's what he wanted. He could go lean against the bar next to a bunch of pretty guys in some club, but someone might ask him to dance, and he couldn't dance for shit.

Meeting civilians, it wasn't his thing.

He could ask a girl to a restaurant — he could afford any restaurant he wanted, now — but for what, to sit there and listen to some broad run her cocksucker all night? Very, very exciting. He'd rather stick a couple of pennies in his eyes, roll over, and go to sleep.

Tutt had real money for the first time in his life. But when he thought about it, he realized that the only true pleasure he had was his work.

He sat down next to a small table set by the window and turned on the police scanner he had mounted on a shelf nearby. He adjusted the frequency, sat back, and sipped his beer.

Scott ripped the register tape and handed it to Karras. Karras checked it out. The Georgetown store had rung out with pretty sweet Saturday numbers. Marcus would be happy about that.

Karras said good-bye to Scott and to Mary, the cute British clerk, and walked down Wisconsin. He passed the Georgetown theater, where *Caligula* had been playing for years. He bumped into a man and kept walking, through the late afternoon shopping crowds that were bleeding into the early evening party crowds of suburban and city kids beginning their night. Karras went into Pied Au Cochon and had a seat at the bar.

He liked this old place, an English professor's idea of a Parisian café. It had become a ritual to have a drink here on Saturday before his last stop at the Dupont store. Tonight Karras needed the drink. He felt as if his soul was drowning and maybe one drink would lift it back up. He hadn't had a bump for the past hour, having made the decision to cut himself off before he reached the point where he couldn't stop. His body couldn't take one more late night, and he didn't want to see another empty snow-seal lying crumpled in the Sunday morning trash.

"Hey, Bobby."

"Dimitri," said the bartender.

"A Grand Marnier."

"You got it."

Karras watched the tender take a pot off a hot plate and pour steaming water into a snifter. He rolled the water around in the glass and dumped the water out into the sink. Then he free-poured Grand Marnier into the heated glass, eyeballing the level carefully.

Karras watched with interest. He loved the rituals involved in getting high.

"Here you go." Bobby, who looked like a wind-carved laborer in a red vest, set the glass in front of Karras.

Karras tipped the snifter carefully off its base and laid it on its side. The liqueur kissed the very top of the glass but did not spill out by even a drop.

"Perfect, Bobby."

"I know."

Karras sipped the warm liqueur. If he were a smoker he would have lit one now, but Karras had never found pleasure in the taste. Back when he and Clay were serious about ball, Karras wouldn't have even considered smoking, as it would have affected his game. Marcus still played one night a week over at Alice Deal's gym, with a group of longtime D.C. boys — Ted Tavlarides, Adam Young, Sam Pinczuk, and Bill Valis among them. Karras hadn't played pickup for years.

"Hey, how you doin'?" said Karras, smiling rakishly at a leggy brunette who was cruising by the bar.

She surveyed him quickly and looked away. Her date, an impeccably groomed young man, said something funny when she arrived at their table, and both of them laughed.

In the bar mirror Karras looked at his wasted form.

"Goddamn you, man," he said out loud.

"What say?" said Bobby.

"Nothin'."

Karras thought of Donna, rushing off to Eddie Golden, that dishwasher installer, outside her apartment house earlier in the day. He was jealous, and the jealousy confused him. Okay, he'd been with her, and they'd had fun — why would she be different than any other girl he knew? Of course, he didn't love Donna, not in any way he recognized. But he didn't want to lose her so quickly. Or maybe it was just that he didn't want to lose.

Karras threw back his shot. He left seven on four and got off his stool.

"Later, Bobby."

Bobby said, "Later than you think."

You can keep your barroom wisdom, pal, thought Karras, but the tender's words were swimming in his head as he walked out to the street.

* * * *

Kevin Murphy placed a bowl of hot vegetable soup on a TV tray and carried it across the room. He put the tray by the bed. Wanda Murphy sat up, gathered her robe around her nightgown, and pushed her feet into an old pair of slippers.

"Hey, baby."

"Hey, Kev."

She gave him a smile. Her red lipstick was thick and trailed off in places from her mouth, as if it had been applied by a child. Her hair went off in a couple of odd directions, and sheet lines creased her face.

Even with all that mess, thought Murphy, she's still a good-lookin' woman when she smiles. I wonder if she knows.

He said, "You look beautiful, Wanda."

"Go on."

"I'm serious." He lifted the tray so it fit over her legs. "Here's your dinner."

"All that?"

Murphy laughed. "You said you weren't hungry, girl!"

"I know. I'm just playin', Kevin."

He sat next to her on the bed while she ate the soup and watched TV. He rested his hand on her thigh, warm through two layers of cloth. His old thirteen-inch Admiral was set up on her dresser, and Wanda would laugh every so often at the jokes on the show, laugh at things that couldn't even bring Kevin Murphy to smile. She watched the same comedy shows every Saturday night — *Gimme a Break*, *Facts of Life*, *Golden Girls*, and *227*, all in a row. Called it her "lineup." Some real stupid shit, but if it made her happy for a couple of hours, it was all right by him.

"Wanda?"

"What, Kev?"

"Been hanging out with this boy I met, down in Shaw?"

"That right."

"Uh-huh. Eleven years old. Boy name of Anthony Taylor. Goes by T, but I tell him not to use it. Sounds like one of those street names all the kids got now."

"That's nice."

"He's a good boy, Wanda. Not much of a home life, though. Lives with his grandmother down there. She's tryin' and all that, but a boy needs a mother and a father to make him right."

"Why are you telling me this, Kevin?" Wanda smiled at something said on the show. She hadn't once moved her eyes away from the set.

"Just makin' conversation, baby. Just a story is all it is, tellin' you about my day."

"Sounds like you're sayin' we ought to take this boy into our home. That what's on your mind? We're supposed to bring in a stranger you just now met?"

"No, Wanda, I'm not sayin' that. This boy's life is incomplete, but he's got his own kin." Murphy looked down at the carpet. "Look, all I'm sayin' is, there's plenty of boys like Anthony out there in this world, got nobody to guide them, tell 'em what they gotta do to be a man. Babies and toddlers, too, lookin' at a future with no real love. Now, you and me, we can make a home for a child like that. We've got this house, you *know* it's too big for the two of us, and I've got the money put away. Between you and me, we can provide a whole lot of love for some —"

"Kevin!" Wanda laughed raucously. She rocked back and forth and pointed to the TV screen. "You see what that girl did? Oh, Lord, I can't believe it!"

Murphy took the empty soup bowl and water glass to the kitchen. He changed into sweatpants and a T-shirt and went down to the basement. He did some stretches, put on a pair of twenty-ounce gloves, and began to hit the Everlast heavy bag suspended from the ceiling beams near his workbench. The bag had duct tape wrapped around its middle where a split had begun; Murphy had copped the bag from an acquaintance, a karate instructor whose students had given it a punishing hands-and-feet workout over many years.

Murphy started slowly, light brushes and then hard combinations, pounding the canvas with jabs and hooks and straight rights. He broke a good sweat and stopped to catch his breath. He listened to the sound of rain pebbling the glass of the window wells that ran around the house. He relaced his gloves and worked the bag until his shirt was soaked and his head felt light.

Just about then his father phoned about Sunday dinner. Murphy told him he'd try to make it and said good-bye.

Murphy showered, opened a can of beer, and went back down to the basement. He watched a little ball. He got up, grabbed another beer, and carried it to his workbench. There was a cardboard box filled with old lottery tickets from his father's church on it. He put the box on the floor. He opened up a box of Remington ammo and spilled rounds out onto the workbench top. One by one, he clamped the bullets in a vise and cut X's in their heads using a hammer and fine-edged chisel. He brought his S&W Combat Magnums down from the shelf, dismantled them, and used his Hoppe's kit to clean and oil the parts. He reassembled the guns, replaced them in their cases, and put the bullets that he had dumdummed back in the box.

Murphy glanced at his watch. He had been three hours at his bench.

The phone rang in the basement, and Murphy picked it up.

Murphy listened and said, "Lord." Then he said, "I'll meet you at O'Grady's in fifteen."

SEVENTEEN

Eddie Golden turned right off Route 1 and drove his Ford Courier down Sunnyside Avenue toward a concrete horizon of two-story warehouses and fenced-in lots. On weekdays this part of Beltsville's industrial district was traffic heavy, but on Saturdays the landscape was barren and bleak. There'd be tumbleweeds blowing across the street, thought Eddie, if tumbleweeds tumbled in Prince George's County.

Eddie was glad his friends from Hunter's weren't around to see him driving the Jap-made truck. The way the Courier looked, short based and low to the ground, like a kid's toy, they might as well have removed the Ford logo on the tailgate and painted on a rising sun.

Eddie pulled into the lot of Appliance Installers Unlimited, a squat little building not much more than a hollow rectangle of cinder blocks housing two bays. He backed the Courier close to the building, got out, and climbed into the bed, then he pushed an old GSD-400 dishwasher, which he had taken out of a rental unit earlier in the day, to the edge of the tailgate. He pushed the dishwasher off the truck. It landed next to several others where his fellow installers had made a pile.

Eddie locked up the truck. He got his tool belt from the bed and walked toward his car. The Reliant was the sole car in the lot. He had parked it next to a Dumpster set along the building's side wall. A black sports car sat on the street, parked along Sunnyside's curb.

Eddie sang an April Wine tune he liked as he looked up in the sky. Clouds had gathered, and he could smell rain in the air. But he wouldn't let a little weather kill his evening. He was in a really good mood. He hated working weekends, but with the money and all, he wouldn't have to much longer. He couldn't wait to spend the evening with Donna, sit her down, make some plans.

Florida. Goddamn, boy, that would be nice.

He put his key into the lock of the Reliant. He heard footsteps scrape gravel.

Someone grabbed his free hand from behind and twisted it upward. Eddie went forward, his cheek smashed up against the car window, his eyes clearing the roof.

"Whoa," said Eddie, trying to stay on his feet. "Wait a —"

"*Shut* the fuck up," said a voice.

Eddie had a blood rush, hearing the black-man's inflection in the words.

A car pulled from a lot down the street and began to drive away. Eddie panicked and let out a high-pitched yell.

He heard a crack. A fire bolt traveled up his arm, rocketed through his neck, and flared at the base of his skull. He felt his fingers touch the back of his forearm.

Eddie screamed. Eddie went to black.

Eddie stared at the back of a black seat. He was on the floor of a car, and he felt very close to the ground. There was vibration and city music and two men arguing over the music, and when the music stopped there was still the arguing and the sound of wipers on glass.

He was near fetal behind the seats. Something heavy lay across his legs. He moved his arm up an inch and looked down so that he could see what was causing all the pain. His hand was bent too far, and his wrist bone pushed out against the skin where it had snapped. A tear rolled down his cheek.

"Fuck you had to break his arm for, Short?"

"Bitch screamed; I *had* to make him stop."

"What we gonna do with him now?"

"Couldn't just leave him there. Take him back to Ty's, find out what we need to know."

"Tyrell ain't gonna like it, man, you bringin' him to the house."

"He's gonna like how we found the one tried to beat him for his money. You can *believe* that."

"What if someone comes around, looks for him where he parked his truck?"

"Why I had you drive his car and park it a couple miles away, behind that car wash. Anybody comes around, they'll think he got back from work, took off, went and got drunk, some shit like that. That is, if anybody cares."

Eddie Golden closed his eyes. Maybe none of this was real.

Alan Rogers slipped the Z in the space between the Supra and Tyrell's 633. He cut the engine and watched rain cloud the windshield.

"Go ahead, Alan, I'll get our boy inside."

"*I'll* get him, Short. Take his tool belt and go on in. Let Tyrell know we got him 'fore I bring him through the door."

"Right."

Monroe reached behind him and lifted the tool belt off the white boy's legs. He got out of the car and walked through the rain, stepped up onto the porch and into the bungalow.

Rogers looked into the back of the car at the white boy. His eyes were open but set kind of strange.

"What's your name?" said Rogers.

"Ed."

"Ed what?"

"Ed Golden."

"Okay. I'm gonna tell you what's what, 'cause once we get inside I'm just another employee. Can't help you none in there."

Eddie licked some crust off his lips. "I'm listening."

"We know you took the money. All Tyrell gonna want to know now is where it's at. You tell us, you got a good chance to walk away. You don't, well, you think you're hurtin' now, you got a whole world of hurtin' comin' to your ass. Things you can't imagine, hear?"

"Y-y-yes."

"Don't be stutterin' like that, either. My partner, Short, he pick up on that, he gonna run it right into the ground."

"It hurts."

"I bet it do. Short had no call to do you like that. But he did, so there's nothin' we can do about it now." Rogers reached into a cup set between the buckets where Monroe had dropped the last of his codeine pills. "Here you go, eat these. Make you feel better, man."

Rogers put the pills, one at a time, in Eddie Golden's open mouth. Eddie chewed them up and swallowed the bits.

"What's your name?" said Eddie.

"Never mind that."

"Wanted to thank you, that's all."

"Never you mind. Remember what I said. Tell it straight. Be a lot easier on you if you do."

Rogers got out of the car, reached behind the seat, pulled up on Eddie's bicep.

"Uh," said Eddie.

"Yeah," said Rogers, "I know."

He got Eddie out of the car, guided him toward the house. He felt him shake beneath his hand.

Eddie heard bass coming from the house. He saw the silhouettes of two figures behind the curtained front window. For a moment he thought he would break away and run. There were dark woods around the house and tiny lights back beyond the woods. It was quiet, except for the rain. The moment passed. He let the tall kid with the gentle eyes lead him to the front door of the house. They went inside.

A light-skinned black man with very green eyes and sharp, angular features sat in a cushioned chair, looking up at Eddie. The scary one with the fucked-up nose was at a round table, dipping his finger into a mound of cocaine and rubbing the coke on his gums. In another open room, a huge black guy and a tiny yellow black sat on a couch, laughing at something on the television. A thin black leaned against the wall, staring at Eddie with flat, dull eyes.

Eddie saw several guns, shotguns and pistols, scattered around the room.

The light-skinned black uncoiled himself and stood from his chair. He was taller than Eddie by a foot. His ears were long and pointed, like those of a goat.

Eddie's knees weakened. He felt a quiver in his sphincter. He tightened himself and swallowed hard.

"This the one?" said Tyrell incredulously.

"Yeah," said Monroe.

"Don't look like much," said Antony Ray, pushing away from the wall and unfolding his arms. "Hard to believe he took you off, Tyrell."

"Heard that, cuz," said Tyrell.

"Name's Ed Golden," said Rogers.

"Golden," said Tyrell. "What kind of name is that?"

"Jewboy," said Antony Ray. "Ain't that right?"

Eddie lowered his head. Rogers pulled a chair away from the round table and set it by the fireplace. He looked at Eddie and said, "Sit down."

Eddie took a seat. He leaned forward, rested his broken wrist on his lap, and winced. He didn't look anyone in the eye. They were talking, but he couldn't make out much of what they were saying. The music, someone shouting angrily over a bass line and what sounded like a whistle of rockets, was playing too loud.

Eddie saw the one named Tyrell go to the other room and tell the others to come back with him. They turned off the TV and lowered the music and returned. The six of them stood around him then. He kept his head down. The fire shadows played at their feet.

"Eddie," said Tyrell. "You don't mind I call you Eddie, right?"

"No," said Eddie.

"He don't mind," said someone, and a couple of them laughed.

"Look up when we're talkin' to you, boy."

Eddie made himself look at them.

"Good."

"Damn, Short," said Linney, "who fucked up your nose?"

"Shut up, Jumbo."

"For real, man, who fucked up your shit like that?"

"You oughtta go ahead and tell it, Short Man," said Tyrell. "I'd like to know."

"Man by the name of — what's that nigga's name, Alan?"

"Marcus Clay," said Rogers. "Owns this record store called Real Right, down on U."

"You know him, Alan?" said Tyrell.

"My boy Alan," said Monroe, "he knows his name 'cause he's datin' this little girl Neecie Tate. Her father works there."

"That so?" said Tyrell.

"Just this girl I know, Ty —"

"And this one here," said Tyrell, gesturing to Eddie. "Didn't he take me off right in front of that shop?"

"That's right," said Monroe.

"Just tryin' to put all this together. Go ahead, Short."

"I was talkin' to this kid hangs out around the way, boy named Anthony Taylor. Had to get kind of rough with him till he told me what I wanted. All the sudden, this Vietnam mothafucker, Clay, comes runnin' at me, surprises me on the blind side."

"Look like Vietnam did more than surprise you, man," said Linney.

"Nigga did a Billy Jack on your ass," said Bennet.

"*Schooled* you," said Linney.

Linney and Bennet laughed and touched hands. Antony Ray smiled.

Monroe quieted Linney and Bennet with a look. "I got your information for you, Tyrell. Taylor talked before I got blindsided. It's how I got on to this one right here."

"You did good."

"Yeah, I know I did. Far as that Clay goes, I ain't done with him yet. Just gettin' started."

"Maybe you ought to leave things alone. We're runnin' a quiet business. Don't need a lot of drama down there."

"Was Clay who made the noise," said Monroe. "Shoutin' out for everyone to hear 'bout how he didn't want to see our kind in the neighborhood no more. Even had these old niggas livin' down there joinin' in. Next thing you know, you gonna have one of those orange-hat squads walkin' around at night."

Tyrell touched the hairs on his chin. "That's not good."

"Damn right it ain't no good, Ty," said Monroe. "Thought Tutt and Murphy was supposed to keep that kind of shit under control."

"So did I." He looked down at Eddie. "You enjoying this conversation?"

"No," said Eddie. "I'm not listening."

"You haven't heard a thing we've said."

"I can't concentrate. My arm is broken. It hurts. I need a doctor —"

"I can see that. But first we need to talk."

"I'm . . . I'm sorry."

"Oh, I know you're sorry now. Kind of late to be apologizin' and all that. But you did take my money, right?"

"I didn't know it was yours."

"You knew it belonged to somebody, right?"

"I wasn't thinking. I went to help that boy in the car. I saw the money and —"

"You stole it."

"Yes, but —"

"But," said Tyrell.

"Chicken butt," said Linney. "Watch it strut."

Bennet laughed. "Damn, Jumbo, you always be talkin' that grade school shit."

"Y'all are some dumb-ass bitches," said Ray, picking a .38 Bulldog up off the table and locking back the hammer. "Y'all gonna talk shit all night? 'Cause I'll find out where Golden Boy here got the money stashed right quick."

Ray pointed the gun at Eddie. Eddie made a choking sound.

"Wait up," said Alan Rogers, raising his hand. "Tyrell, you ain't even asked him nothin' yet, for real."

Tyrell looked at Rogers and then at Ray. "He's right, cuz. Put it away." Tyrell turned to Eddie. "Where's my money at, boy? Say it and be quick."

Eddie Golden said, "My apartment. In the pillowcase . . . in my bedroom closet."

"Where's that?"

Eddie gave Tyrell the address.

"I got his keys," said Monroe.

"They open your place?" said Tyrell.

Eddie nodded, and Tyrell gave instructions to his men.

Monroe led Eddie Golden back to one of the two bedrooms set off the hall. The room contained a sheeted mattress and box spring on the floor, with a radiator next to the bed. Monroe stood by the door. He left when Rogers arrived with a glass of water, which Eddie drank hungrily. Eddie lay back.

Rogers didn't bother to tie him up. He wasn't strong enough to go anywhere, way he was.

"You be still."

"Thank you."

"You better not be tellin' lies," said Rogers.

"I'm not," said Eddie. "Listen —"

Rogers walked away. He closed the door behind him and left Eddie in darkness.

Eddie listened to their voices from the other room. He breathed out very slowly in relief. It was that same feeling he had once when he'd woken up in the recovery room, after this operation he'd had. The feeling that he'd dodged a bullet. That he'd bought time.

And he hadn't said a word about Donna. Even with the gun pointed at his face, he hadn't thought once of mentioning her.

Despite the rain and clouds, light filtered in through the windows, and as Eddie's eyes adjusted he could make out the angles of the room. His arm throbbed less, but the fear and codeine had made him dizzy and sick.

Eddie stared at the ceiling and tried to forget the pain. He had to think of what he could give them next. He needed to come up with a story, something to tell them when they came back empty-handed. Something that would keep him alive.

Short Man Monroe slid his Glock barrel-down into the waistband of his Lees. He sloppily dumped some cocaine into paper, folded the paper, and put it in his jacket. He put his finger in what remained on the table and rubbed some freeze on his gums.

"Y'all ready?" said Monroe.

"We ready," said Linney.

"Let's go."

"We gone, Ty," said Rogers.

"Call me," said Tyrell, "and let me know."

Out in the yard, Monroe and Rogers got into the Z. Linney and Bennet climbed into the Supra.

"Those two know to follow us?" said Rogers.

"Yeah," said Monroe. "Turn this bitch over, man."

Rogers cooked the ignition while Monroe fingered the cup between the seats.

"Where go my pills, man?"

"You took 'em all," said Rogers.

"Damn, I *must* be lunchin'."

"You swallowed four back there at the hospital."

"Sure you didn't give the rest of my medicine to your girlfriend, so he could feel better?"

"What you talkin' about, man?"

"Saw the way you brought him water and shit, like you was sweet on him or somethin'."

"Go ahead, Short."

Rogers turned the Z around and headed for the road.

"You gettin' soft on me, Alan."

"No I ain't."

"*Yeah* you are," said Monroe. "I got eyes, man. And my eyes can see."

Antony Ray cut a fat line out and spread it the length of the mirror. He picked up a rolled fifty-dollar bill.

"Careful with that," said Tyrell. "It's early yet."

"Got a lot of catchin' up to do."

"That you do."

Ray did half the line. He threw his head back and shook it. He bent down and did the other half. He dropped the bill on the mirror and lit a Newport from his deck.

Tyrell sat in his chair, facing the window. He watched the cars drive away.

"You know, those two shouldn't have brought that thief back with 'em, Tyrell."

"I know it."

"What you gonna do about it?"

"Have to wait and see."

"You think he's tellin' the truth about the money?"

"Gonna find out, I guess."

"I'll find out right now, you want me to."

"For now, let's just do things my way."

"All right. You gotta admit, though, them bringin' him back here, it does complicate the fuck out of things."

"Yes."

"They didn't even think about how we couldn't let that white boy walk away once he done been in this house."

"No, they didn't think."

"You don't mind my sayin' so, those are some simple mothafuckers you got on your payroll."

"What you expect, cuz?" said Tyrell. "They ain't nothin' but kids."

EIGHTEEN

Anthony Taylor was bored just sitting in his room with no one to talk to, so he put his Raiders jacket on and walked quietly down the stairs. Not that Granmom or that hustler friend of hers could hear him, the way they had their music up so loud. Sounded like some church thing they were dancing to, but with more of a rockin' band behind it than the stuff Granmom listened to on that AM gospel station. The singers in the background talkin' about "I'll take you there," over and over again. Whatever it was, Anthony couldn't get into it, but Granmom and her friend, they were back there in the living room kickin' up a storm.

Anthony slipped out the front door.

He turned his collar up against the rain. Cloudy as it was, it seemed awful dark out tonight. Anthony avoided Clifton Terrace, where a whole world of bad things could happen. He walked over to 11th and cut south.

On U Street he saw one of Tyrell's runners using a pay phone, and another standing on the corner near an idling import with limo-tint windows. Anthony went down by Real Right, saw that all the lights 'cept for one or two fluorescents in the back were turned off. Then he remembered that Mr. Clay closed his shop early on Saturday nights.

Anthony crossed the street, stood outside of Medger's for a few minutes, said hello to an old-timer he knew. But the old-timer had to be on his way, with the rain and all. Anthony got tired of getting rained on his own self, so he found a bus shelter and stayed there until a couple of boys who had Trouble stamped on their foreheads came in with him. They started talking to him kind of smart like, askin' him if he had any cash money on him, so he walked out of the shelter, not too fast so they'd take him for bad, and kept going down the street.

He was cold and wet and a little bit afraid, but at least things were going on out here. It was better than being at home.

Marcus Clay and Dimitri Karras met at the Dupont store, as they always did at closing time on Saturday nights, and had a beer with the store's longtime manager, Cheek. Dupont had been Clay's first store, and it would always be his favorite. It only stood to reason that he had his favorite manager in there, too. Cheek had been with Clay for more than ten years, and for every year of service he had put on five pounds.

After the other stores had called in their figures, Cheek closed Dupont and went to make the deposit. Clay and Karras walked the two blocks back to the Trauma Arms, where they both showered and changed clothes.

Karras defrosted a ham bone he had been saving and made a pot of split pea soup. He grilled a couple of tomato-and-cheese sandwiches, put them together with the soup, and he and Clay had dinner.

They watched North Carolina slaughter Alabama-Birmingham as they ate. The food improved Karras's condition considerably, though he was annoyed at the outcome of the game. As a Maryland fan, Karras hated Dean Smith the way most Greeks hated Turks.

"You got to admit, though," said Clay, "whatever they do during the season, Coach Smith does get them through those first two rounds."

"Ah," said Karras, waving his hand at the set. "It's the conference. The ACC just attracts the quality players, Marcus. Look how many go on to play in the NBA. Georgia Tech and Duke both advanced today. The Tar Heels are in, and NC State will crush Arkansas-Little Rock tomorrow. And you know Maryland's gotta go into the Sweet Sixteen."

"UNLV? We'll see. The Terps are gonna need five men to show up, not just Bias."

The phone rang, and Karras picked it up. He talked for a while, wrote something on a message pad, and replaced the receiver in its cradle. He rubbed his face.

"Who was that?"

"Donna. She's worried about her boyfriend, Eddie."

"She should be."

"It's more than that. He hasn't shown up from work yet."

"Maybe he's out havin' a few."

"She doesn't think so. They had definite plans. And she claims he's the puppy-dog type when it comes to her."

"What's she want from you?"

"Guy's a dishwasher installer. I'm gonna run over to where he switches his truck with his car, see if he's knocked off for the night."

"Then you're gonna go see Donna."

"It's not like that, Marcus."

"It's always like that with you."

"Thanks for the vote of confidence."

"The shoe fits, man —"

"I know."

"Mitri?"

"Now you're gonna remind me not to get involved. Like you hung back today?"

"All right. But show some sense."

Karras went back to his bedroom and slipped the snow-seal holding the rest of his half into his jean jacket. He left the Trauma Arms.

Short Man Monroe searched Eddie Golden's apartment and found nothing. He phoned Tyrell. He opened the front door a crack, looked out into the stairwell, and left the place, locking the door behind him before jogging down to the lot. Monroe slid in beside Alan Rogers, who was sitting behind the wheel of the idling Z.

"Boy lied," said Monroe, slipping his gloves off and tossing them on the dash.

"Damn. Tyrell and Ray gonna fuck him up."

"He shouldn't of lied."

"What we gonna do now?"

"Get outta here quick, for one. Makes me nervous bein' out here, all these Maryland farmers walkin' around and shit. Go on down to U, do our job. Want to have me a look around anyway, see if Vietnam is still out."

"Listen, Short . . . I got somethin' I got to do."

"I know what you gotta do."

Rogers said, "You mind?"

"Nah. I better go down in the Supra with Chink and Jumbo, though. 'Cause you know Jumbo can't fit in this here car."

"All right, black. I'll check in with you later, hear?"

"Right."

Monroe reached under the seat, retrieved his other gun, put it up under his shirt before leaving the Z and running to the Supra. The Supra pulled out and headed south toward the District line. Rogers followed them all the way into D.C., turning off of 13th four blocks before the drop-off at Cardoza. He downshifted and slowed the car, pulling over to the curb and cutting the engine a few doors down from Denice's house. He didn't see the old man's car out on the street.

Alan Rogers sat back in the bucket. He pictured Denice in that skirt of hers and, for a little while, anyway, pushed business to the back of his mind. Rogers tried not to think too much about that white boy. He knew what they'd do to him now.

Clarence and Denice Tate discussed the movie on the ride back across town. Denice had enjoyed the romance of it, but for the most part, Tate had been bored to tears. With a title like *Out of Africa*, you'd think they'd have put more into it, but as in most Hollywood pictures he'd seen on the subject, they'd gone and concentrated on how the continent and its people had affected the white folks who had come to live there. Faithful native servants, dewy eyed and head bowed to their Caucasian movie-star masters. All that. The Ward 3 audience had lapped it up. And Denice seemed like she'd had a good time, which was the purpose of the outing, after all. Tate had gotten through it on the music and scenery alone.

Walking up to their house, Tate heard the low rumble of an engine idling down the block. He turned his head, saw exhaust coming from the dual pipes of a black sports car parked along the curb a few houses away. Denice's face brightened, but when Tate glanced over, she tried to bury the look. He hurried Denice up the steps.

With the door locked behind them, Denice said, "I'm gonna go up to bed now, okay? I'm kinda tired and all."

"Okay, honeygirl. I'll be up in a minute to say good night."

"Thanks for the show, Daddy."

"My pleasure."

He watched her go up the stairs.

Tate went down to the basement, found a small key he kept on his ring, put it to the lock of a file cabinet pushed beneath the steps. He retrieved a hot .22 he had bought in the alley behind Real Right just a few months back, and a box of shells. He broke the cylinder open and took some rounds from the box. He clumsily thumbed shells into the chambers and snapped the cylinder shut.

Tate dropped the pistol into his jacket pocket and took the two flights of stairs up to Denice's bedroom. He walked inside. Denice stood by the window in the dark, looking down to the street.

"Come away from the window, girl."

Denice turned, startled. "Daddy."

"Step on back."

Tate moved to the window. The Rogers boy stood on the sidewalk out front of their house. As Tate's figure filled the frame, the Rogers boy took a step back. He buried his hands in his pockets and began to swagger away.

"Daddy, where you goin'?"

Tate pointed at Denice on his way out of the room. "Stay away from that window."

Tate took the stairs, opened the front door, and bolted down the walkway to the street. The Rogers boy was still swaggering, trying real hard not to run, but he had picked up his pace considerably and was closing in on his car.

Tate pulled the .22 from his jacket. He broke into a jog, the cold rain cutting at his face.

"You see this, boy?" he yelled, waving the pistol in the air. "You see this?!"

Rogers looked over his shoulder, ducked into the Z, cranked the engine. Tate heard a window on the second floor of his house open, heard his daughter shout "Daddy" in a pleading kind of way.

"Don't come around here no more, you hear me, Rogers? I'm not playin', you understand?"

Tate's voice, strained and strange to his own ears, was muted by the cry of rubber on asphalt. The black Z shot off the curb and sped away.

Tate stood alone in the street. He looked down at his hand and abruptly dropped the pistol back in his jacket. He glanced around at the houses of his neighbors, turned, and walked back toward his house. He heard the second-story window shut, saw Denice back away and retreat into the shadows of her room.

In his whole life, Tate had never fired a gun in anger. When he was a young man coming up in the District, it was how you went with your hands that made or didn't make your reputation. He knew the playing field was no longer level, which was why he'd bought the .22. But to pull a gun on a kid . . . *damn*, what was he thinking to go and do something like that?

You'd think it would make you feel powerful, in control, to hold a piece of death in your hands, but it only made Tate feel like some kind of coward. Funny how holding a gun could make you so ashamed.

Dimitri Karras knocked on Donna Morgan's apartment door. Though she tried to hide it, he caught the flash of disappointment in her eyes when she first saw his face.

"Yeah, it's just me. Can I come in?"

"Sure. I'm sorry, I thought —"

"I know."

"Come on, take that wet jacket off."

Karras had a seat next to Donna on her living-room couch. Small pillows were spread about on the furniture, and lace curtains hung in the windows. A print on the wall depicted turn-of-the-century women wearing long dresses and carrying umbrellas at the beach. The room smelled of hairspray and butted cigarettes.

"Well?"

"I went by where Eddie works. You say he hung dice from the truck's rearview?"

"Yes."

"His truck's there in the lot."

Donna blinked her eyes. "What about his car?"

"His car's gone."

I went to the Dumpster where you said he always parks it. A crescent wrench and a flat-head screwdriver were lying on the asphalt near the empty space.

"What's it mean, Dimitri?"

Karras shrugged. "He finished work, went back and picked up his car, and took off. That's what you've got to assume. It sure doesn't suggest that anything's happened to him."

But it looks like something did happen to him. Or someone was after him, and he knew it. Like he was in a hurry, or got in a scuffle, dropped his tools, and left them there.

"He would've called me if he wasn't coming tonight."

"You've said that already. Okay, so he wasn't a good Boy Scout and didn't check in. That doesn't mean there's something wrong."

"I was thinking maybe we ought to call the cops."

"And tell them what, that Eddie ripped off a drug dealer? You ready to get him thrown in jail on top of everything else? For all you know, Eddie's out celebrating right now, or shopping for something special, you know, to bring home."

"I'm worried, Dimitri."

"I know you are. And I don't mean to make light of it."

Yes, I do. I can make you laugh, and maybe forget. Whip out this C, get you high. I'm not good for much, but I can do that.

Karras looked down at Donna's wrist. "Hey, kiddo, you aware you got two watches on?"

Donna nodded. "I was trying one on for a customer, and I walked out with it on when my shift was done."

"Got two, in case you're crossing time zones and all that."

"I'm such a world traveler." Donna looked at her wrist. "Jesus, you wouldn't believe it; people are going crazy over these things."

"That's what you do at Hecht's? Sell plastic watches? You makin' a career out of that?"

Donna laughed. "Yeah, I'm the Swatch queen."

"C'mere."

Karras put his arms around her and gave her a hug, kissing the top of her head. He felt himself grow hard as her breasts crushed against his chest. It annoyed him, that his body would betray him when for once he was only trying to be a good guy. He broke away and sat back. He ran his hand through his hair.

Donna grinned. "I felt that, you know."

"Ah, Christ."

"You tried, Dimitri. But you're just not the big brother type." She kissed him on the cheek. "You'll stay here, though, right? Until Eddie calls?"

I don't think he's gonna call, thought Karras.

"Sure, Donna," said Karras. "I'll stay."

Short Man Monroe, Jumbo Linney, and Chink Bennet stood under the narrow awning out front of Real Right Records on U, the Supra idling at the curb. Monroe rubbed the rest of his cocaine on his gums and dropped the empty paper to the sidewalk.

"He closed, Short," said Linney.

"I can see that, man. But maybe he forgot somethin'. Maybe he needs to do some of that paperwork, and he's on his way back."

"Maybe not," said Bennet.

"Need to fuck somebody up tonight," said Monroe, punching a fist into his palm. "Feel like bustin' somebody *good.*"

"We oughtta get on back to Tyrell's," said Bennet.

Short said, "We got time." He looked across the street and narrowed his eyes. "Hey, now. See what happens when you wait?"

"Who's that?"

Monroe smiled. "Calls himself T. And his protector, Vietnam, ain't around right now."

The kid in the Raiders jacket had come around the corner. He froze for a moment, seeing Monroe in front of Real Right. He turned and ran.

"Let's go," said Monroe.

Monroe got behind the wheel of the Supra. He waited for Bennet to scamper over the backseat and for Linney to fold his big self into the passenger side. Monroe slammed the shifter into first, took off. He got around the construction equipment in the middle of U and kicked it south on 12th.

"There he is," said Monroe, pointing at Anthony Taylor, blowing down the sidewalk on foot.

"Haw, shit," said Bennet, nervous and stoked. He began to giggle.

Monroe jumped the curb and got the Supra up on the sidewalk. Anthony was full in the headlights now, the rain falling around him like a net. Anthony looked over his shoulder, his eyes and mouth open wide.

"He movin'," said Bennet.

Monroe downshifted, punched the gas.

"Easy, Short," said Linney. "You don't want to kill his ass."

"I don't?"

Anthony dove right, rolled between two cars parked at the curb, came up on his feet and reached the west sidewalk, beat it toward T.

"Dag, boy," said Bennet. "Nigga can go."

Monroe got the Supra back on the street. He pinned the pedal, skidded into a right at T Street, and came to a stop. The Taylor kid was nowhere in sight.

"Where is he?" said Linney.

"Forget about him," said Monroe. "Look."

Monroe pointed to the head of the alley on T, where three boys stood. Even through the wipers working the windshield, Jumbo Linney could see that one of them had a normal build and one was skinny as a Biafra child. The third wore a bright green cap.

Monroe laughed, working the gas against the clutch.

"Now," said Monroe, "we gonna play for real."

Anthony Taylor heard the Supra scream by. He waited for the sound to subside and crawled out from underneath the car where he had pinned himself to the ground.

He ran.

He ran as hard as he'd ever run, cutting right on 13th, crossing U, going up the hill between Cardoza and Clifton Terrace without breaking stride. He heard boys yelling at him and laughing as he ran. There were ghosts chasing him, the dead, fire, snakes, rats, everything pale and ugly that slept beneath his bed, and every sharp-toothed, rotted thing that had ever waited in the dark corners of the basement of his granmom's house. They were all chasing him now, and he wasn't going to stop, because they had all come out tonight and they were all behind him and close, so close he could feel their stinking, hot breath raising the hairs on the back of his neck.

He heard the crack of a gunshot echo up from the south.

He pounded on the front door of his grandmother's house. She let him in, openmouthed. He brushed by her and ran up the stairs to his room. He took his mother's letter off the dresser and crumpled it in his fist. He fell forward on the bed.

Anthony heard another gunshot.

"God please, God please."

He slammed his hands over his ears and shut his eyes.

NINETEEN

"Got a friend with 'em tonight," said Short Man Monroe, steering the Supra toward the three boys. They were just turning to run, trying to get their footing in the wet street. He was almost on top of them now.

"That's Antoine Meadows's little brother, Short," said Jumbo Linney. "Antoine runs with that crew on O."

"I don't give a *fuck* who it is," said Monroe.

He braked at the head of the alley, kept the Supra running, leaped abruptly from the car. He pulled his Glock from the waistband of his Lees, jacked a round into the chamber, and looked back into the car. Chink Bennet was already slipping between the buckets and settling in behind the wheel.

"Go around the corner," said Monroe. "We'll close 'em up on both sides. Jumbo, use my other gun, man, it's under the driver's seat."

"I don't need no gun, Short," said Linney.

"Yeah, you do. That little mothafucker Chief waved one at me just the other night."

"Short —"

"I'm gone."

Monroe ran into the alley, the gun at his side. Bennet hit the gas, peeled out, hooked left at the next corner. He was giggling as they made the turn.

Chief Meadows, P-Square Willets, and Mooty Wallace bolted into the alley. Mooty was the fastest of the bunch, and his fear had made him jet. Mooty was way out front.

"Buck right, Mooty!" yelled Chief, and Mooty bounded over a low fence.

He was gone into the darkness of a yard and through it quick, out onto the next street west. He stopped behind a parked car, watched the Supra blow by, saw a fat man in the passenger seat and a little boy behind the wheel. He ran in the direction of his house.

"Chief!" said P-Square, running beside his friend. He had pulled his Spiderman action figure from his sweatpants pocket and was gripping it tight. "He comin', man!"

Chief looked behind him. Tyrell Cleveland's enforcer was running straight at them through the rain. Demon had some kind of white mask on his face, covering his nose.

Chief looked ahead. The Supra had pulled in front of the alley and blocked the exit down the street. A big man and what looked like a kid were getting out of the car.

"P-Square," said Chief. "Buck right!"

P-Square turned, slipped, slid onto his side. He scrambled back to his feet. He ran toward the nearest fence. He tightened his fist on his Spiderman and left his feet. It was a good jump; he *knew* he would clear the fence.

"Peter Parker," said P-Square Willets. "Fly!"

Something punched him in the back. He heard a popping sound and felt pain. He saw pink wet things spooling from his chest. He saw the black ground rush up to meet him.

He said, "Gaaaa."

He said nothing after that.

At the sound of the gunshot, Chief Meadows ran into an open yard and slipped in the mud. He slid onto his chest. He stayed there and began to crawl toward the house. A dog was growling somewhere around the outside of the house. The lights in the house had gone off at the sound of the shot. It was dark in the yard, and that was good.

Chief heard someone giggling back in the alley. The giggling got louder, and so did the growl of the dog. Tyrell's enforcer called Chief's name.

God, why, help me, I didn't do nothin' wrong to nobody for real; I didn't mean nothin', God.

Chief couldn't hear nothin' of P-Square. P-Square had gotten away, that's what it was. P-Square was fast like Mooty, and he could sky. P-Square was little, but he was braver than —

The dog, a rottweiler, leaped from the shadows.

Barking insanely, it ran toward Chief, its eyes catching the light from the spotlamp hanging off the next-door house. Chief's blood jumped, and he was up on his feet. He turned without thought and ran out of the yard, seeing the dog behind him, closing in on him, then seeing the dog yanked back by its chain.

Chief stood in the middle of the alley. He leaned over and placed his hands on his knees to catch a breath.

"Lord," he said. "Thank you for that chain."

When he stood up he saw Tyrell's enforcer, smiling at him beneath that mask, standing just ten feet away.

"Dog scare you, man?"

Chief twitch-smiled back. "Yeah. I'm . . . I ain't ashamed to admit it, man, I'm afraid of dogs."

"Got to conquer that fear, Chief." His smile faded. Tyrell's enforcer head-motioned to the yard on the other side of the alley. "Check out your boy, nigga."

Chief looked over, saw P-Square lying facedown, not moving at all, his jacket all torn and shit in the back.

Chief began to cry.

"Aw, look at you. Funny how you ain't mockin' me now."

There was a siren coming from far away. The siren, the rain, and high-pitched laughter. Chief couldn't stop crying.

"Let's go, Short," said a deep voice behind Chief. "We gotta be gettin' outta here, man."

"Step to the side, Jumbo. You too, Chink."

"Short —"

"Do it, man."

Chief heard footsteps moving off behind him. Chief peed his pants. Chief said, "I ain't *mean* nothin', man. I was just playin', see? Look here." He pulled his .22. from his waistband. "This thing here, it can't even fire no bullets, man, for *real*."

"You pullin' that gun on me, Chief?"

"Nah, man, I ain't pullin' nothin'." Chief tossed the gun aside. "See? C-c-come on."

"W-w-where you wanna g-g-g-go? Wanna g-g-g-go see your f-f-friend?"

"Momma!" cried Chief, and the alley flashed white.

TWENTY

Dimitri Karras was chopping out lines when the martial theme music for the eleven o'clock edition of *Eyewitness News* began blaring through the speaker of Donna Morgan's nineteen-inch set. Karras slid the mirror over to Donna.

Donna pushed a beer can aside and fitted a burning cigarette in the U of the ashtray. She used the empty casing of a Bic pen to inhale the coke.

Donna held the plastic tube out to Karras and said, "You ready for a bump?"

"Hold on a second," said Karras, who was squinting at the television screen.

Donna looked at the picture on the set: in the foreground, a solemn reporter holding a microphone and speaking into the camera; in the background, uniformed police, police types in suits under raincoats, wet streets, ambulances, ambulance workers moving slowly, a small lump beneath a sheet.

Karras picked up the phone and punched numbers into the grid.

"What's wrong?" said Donna, but Karras didn't answer.

"Marcus?" said Karras. "Hey, man, it's me. Turn on channel nine." Karras kept studying the broadcast, and after a while he said, "Yeah, that's just a block south of the store. . . . I know it, man. They weren't much more than little kids. No, they haven't released the names. Thought you'd want to know. . . . No problem. Listen, I might not make it back to the apartment tonight. Yeah, you too."

Karras cut the line.

Donna said, "You okay?"

He took a moment and said, "I'm fine."

"Here," said Donna offering him the Bic. "Do this, Dimitri, you'll feel better."

Karras looked down at the snow trailed out on the mirror. "Not right now," he said. "You go ahead."

Tyrell Cleveland put down the phone. He leaned back in his armchair and looked into the fire. He ran a finger down his cheek.

Antony Ray squatted on the hearth, used a poker to lift a log off another. Flames curled upward through the space.

"That was Jumbo," said Tyrell. "We got some serious problems."

"Yeah?"

"Eddie Golden told a lie. Wasn't no pillowcase back at his place."

"Coulda told you that."

"That ain't all. Short Man, he killed a couple kids tonight. Real kids. That boy Chief, been playin' dealer down on our turf? Him and some other little kid. Shot 'em both."

Ray clucked his tongue. "Cold, man. And stupid, too. You'd think Rogers would've stopped him."

"Rogers wasn't with them at the time. They're on their way back in right now."

"You need to get your boys under control, cuz."

"Yes."

"You get any other details?"

"Must be on the TV news by now."

"Gonna watch it?"

"What for? Need to sit here and think on it some."

Ray did a line he had cut out on the mirror. He walked to the hallway, went into the bedroom on the left, and closed the door behind him.

Time passed. Tyrell heard the white boy scream.

The screaming was loud and high pitched, and it bothered Tyrell's ears. He rose from his chair, went into the other room, and turned up the Run-D.M.C. that was already coming from the box. He stood there by the stereo until Ray came back out of the bedroom. Ray's eyes were bright, and he was holding back a smile. Tyrell cut the volume back low to where he could gather his thoughts.

"He talk?"

"Started sayin' somethin' about some white dude, workin' in that record store down on U. Boy passed out cold on me right after that. Guess I put a little too much pressure on that broken wing of his. Way he looked, might be out for the rest of the night."

"He don't look like the hero type to me. Either he's dumb or he's tellin' the truth. He took the money, now, he's said as much. But maybe someone he knew took *him* off after that."

"Maybe that record store dude."

"Have to ask him about it when he wakes up."

"I will."

Tyrell saw that smile again, creeping up. "Don't kill him, Antony."

"Don't worry," said Ray. "Havin' too much fun just keepin' him alive."

Richard Tutt phoned his partner right after he picked up the initial call on his scanner. Kevin Murphy met Tutt at O'Grady's fifteen minutes later. The two of them drove downtown in Murphy's Trans Am. Murphy blew through reds all the way and shut off his wipers as they approached Shaw. The rain had passed.

At the crime scene, Murphy and Tutt showed their badges, clipped them to their belts, and ducked under the yellow tape. Print and broadcast news reporters and their tech crews, meat wagons, neighborhood kids, uniforms and plainclothes dicks from their precinct, forensics technicians, their own Sergeant Miller and his Lieutenant Breen, a media-savvy local reverend, and a prominent city councilman were all on site. The alley was lit now and well protected.

Murphy saw two homicide detectives, George Dozier and Doc Farrelly, talking to residents congregated in one backyard. Several cops were grouped around a boy's body lying facedown beyond a chain-link fence. A dog barked savagely over the squawk of police and rescue-squad radios cutting the night.

Murphy saw Tutt by a second group of cops in the middle of the alley. Tutt was staring down at the body lying there while a uniformed patrolman named Platt talked close to Tutt's ear. Murphy stepped forward and looked through a space between the cluster of cops.

The kid was on his back, his eyes open, his teeth bared in a snarl. His scalp and a portion of his forehead were gone. A bright green cap lay nearby, a piece of red, matted meat lying in its folds.

Murphy turned his head and vomited vegetable soup.

"Come on, partner," said Tutt, grabbing hold of Murphy's arm. "Let's move."

They walked back toward the Trans Am. Murphy stumbled. Tutt kept him on his feet.

"Short Man," said Murphy.

Tutt said, "I know."

"Marcus."

"Elaine."

"What are you doing, coming here this time of night?"

"Wanted to see you. Wanted to see my boy."

"You know our agreement. How you'd always phone first."

"I know, but . . . Elaine, please."

She looked into his eyes. "Marcus, what's wrong with you? You troubled over something?"

"Just need to see M. J. Just need to kiss him good night."

Elaine stepped aside. "Come on, then. And don't wake him, hear? Took me an hour to get him down."

"Thanks."

Elaine watched him walk through the foyer and up the stairs.

Marcus Clay stood in Marcus Jr.'s dark bedroom. Some light streamed in from the streetlamp out on Brown. The light passing the windowpanes threw crucifix lines across the covers of the bed. A bar of pale yellow shone on M. J.'s face. His mouth was open, his breathing deep and wheezy. Clay listened to him breathe, watched the rise and fall of his chest.

Clay got on his knees and kissed his son's warm cheek. He smelled his hair. Elaine must have given him a shampoo or something, because the boy's hair had the scent of coconut. But it also had that goat cheese smell that it had always carried since he was a baby. Clay loved that smell.

He walked from the room, turning once before he left to have another look at the boy.

Elaine hadn't moved. She leaned against the foyer wall, her arms crossed. Clay went and stood before her. He lifted her chin and ran his finger down her strong neck. Elaine's arms dropped to her sides. Clay leaned in and kissed her mouth. She made a low sound in her throat and turned her head away.

"Can I stay?"

Elaine's mouth twitched. "No." She moved her eyes off his.

"Be good for him to see me in the morning for a change."

"I don't think so," she said softly.

"You want me to, Elaine. You *want* me, I know."

"I don't deny that. But it won't fix a thing. It never was the problem between us."

"What was? That girl?"

"That girl was just the last bit of disrespect you showed me. I don't think of her, 'cause I know she meant nothing to you. What I do think about is how you never recognized me for my accomplishments. Who I was."

"I was always proud of you."

"Those stores of yours always came first, but you never thought that what I was doing might be important to me. To our family."

"I know it. But I've learned now, baby, I swear —"

"Don't." She touched his chest. "I'm not ready. Okay?"

Clay lowered his head.

Elaine said, "What's troubling you tonight, Marcus? Why'd you come here, for real?"

"Couple of kids, couldn't have been more than eleven years old or something, got killed down near the U Street store tonight."

"My God. You knew them?"

"I don't think so. But I see kids like them all the time. Got one doin' odd jobs around my store now just to keep him away from the street. These kids got no guidance, Elaine, no one to give 'em examples. I was just, I don't know. . . . It made me want to see my son."

Elaine put her arms around his neck and drew him close. She could feel his strong hands tight on her back.

"Promise me," said Clay, "when you're ready, at least you'll try."

"I promise."

"I love you, baby."

Elaine said, "I love *you*."

*   *   *   *

188

Kevin Murphy walked from the market with a twelve-pack of Miller High Life under his arm. He dropped into the driver's seat of the Trans Am, pulled two beers from the bag, set the bag behind his seat. He opened one of the beers and drank down half of it with one long pull. He wiped his sleeve across his chin.

"Take it easy," said Tutt.

"Too late for that."

He pulled away from the curb. He accelerated through a red and kept the speedometer at sixty going north on 14th. He tossed the empty bottle over his shoulder and cracked the full one wedged between his legs.

"Watch it," said Tutt.

Murphy swerved to avoid a Metrobus coming off a stop. They blew through the Arkansas Avenue intersection and hit the hill. They passed dealers hawking dimes and quarters to the car trade outside a closed liquor store. Murphy nailed the pedal to the floor. Tutt grabbed the armrest.

"Listen," said Tutt as Murphy finally slowed the car for a red light. "Tonight we sleep on it. You go home and get three sheets if that's what the fuck you got to do, but me, I'm gonna go back to my apartment and think."

"'Cause you're one of those deep thinkers, Tutt."

"Yeah, well, at least I'm holdin' onto my shit. And I'm tellin' you, I'm gonna work us out of this."

"Ain't no way out. We're on the payroll of a drug dealer who had two kids killed tonight."

"*We're* not drug dealers. You just keep rememberin' that. We're cops."

"We're nothin'," said Murphy. "And we are *fucked*."

Murphy dropped Tutt at his Bronco without another word. He continued north, killing a third beer by the time he hit Takoma. He parked on 4th, gave a hard look to a young man who had given *him* a hard look as he stepped out of his car.

"You want somethin'?"

"Nah, I ain't want nothin'."

"Then don't be lookin' like you do."

Murphy went into Takoma Station, made his way to the bar, ordered a beer and a shot of Cuervo. He choked the tequila down and ordered another. He said something to the man next to him, and the man picked up his drink and moved away. He saw two couples standing at the service end of the stick, pointing at him and laughing. He drained his shot, finished his beer, and left some green on the wood. He walked toward the front of the club. Groups of people parted and made way for him to pass. Out on the sidewalk, he saw that his badge was still clipped to his pants.

Murphy sat in his Pontiac and had another beer. He drove home and went inside.

Wanda was asleep. Murphy sat on the bed and shook her until her eyes opened."

"Kevin?"

He bent forward, put his mouth on her lips, and kissed her. He was hard immediately. It had been so long. He put his tongue in her mouth and ran it across her gums. He kneaded her breast roughly through her house-dress.

She pushed on his shoulders. He pulled back, saw that he had smudged her lipstick. She looked like an old clown.

"Kevin!" she said. "You reek of alcohol."

"God*damn*, girl," said Murphy, standing straight. "You gonna tell me now how *I* smell? You who ain't even had the pride to take a bath in the last week?"

"Oh, Kevin!"

Wanda's hands fluttered to her face, and she began to cry. Murphy stumbled from the room.

He was in the basement now, and he could hear her still. Crying and pacing across that damn cell of hers she called a bedroom.

"I'm sorry," he said, and then he screamed as loud as he could, "Shut up!"

He had brought the beers down with him. He drank one quick.

He went to the pool table and racked the balls. He got bored and cracked a beer. He watched some TV. He drank another beer. He got up and went to the Skins Wall of Fame, took down his favorite glossy, Number 25, the autographed Joe Washington he had mounted and framed. He stared at it for a while, swaying on his feet. He noticed his shirt was wet all down the front.

Hypocrite.

He was in front of the heavy bag and it was swinging and he was no longer wearing his shirt. He was bare chested and his knuckles were bloodied and he could hear Wanda yelling upstairs in her room.

Stop please stop please stop

Murphy was at the workbench. His gun cases were down on the bench in a sloppy row. He needed to choose one now.

Kid killer you

He picked up one of the Combat Magnums, broke the cylinder, and took a bullet from the pool of them spilled out on the bench. He thumbed a bullet into a chamber. He laughed.

Fuck you laughin' at, man? You seen what a gun-eat does to a man. Brain and skull blown out the back, sprayed up on the wall. Eyes bugged from the gas jolt. Nose scorched black from the flames rushing through. . . . Don't picture it, man. Just think about the Peace.

Tears streamed down Murphy's face. He picked up another bullet. It slipped from his fingers and rolled. His hand crabbed across the bench as he chased the round.

Don't fuck around with too much lead, now. Give you way too much time to think, Kev.

Murphy grabbed the bullet, fitted it in another chamber. He spun the cylinder, slapped it shut. He turned the gun and closed his lips around the cool barrel.

Don't think don't

Murphy put his thumb on the trigger. With his right hand he locked back the hammer. Tears hot on his cheeks. He heard Wanda's laughter. He gagged on the barrel and moaned.

Do it do it do it do it

Murphy squeezed the trigger.

Don't

His eyes crossed, watching the hammer arc forward.

SUNDAY

MARCH 16, 1986

TWENTY-ONE

Sunday morning: cease-fire time in the city. Cars moved slowly and stopped at red lights. Squares rose early, played with their children, read the paper, went to church. Whores and criminals slept late.

Marcus Clay and George Dozier sat at the counter of the Florida Avenue Grill, located at the corner of 11th and Florida on the tip of Shaw. They had seen each other at church, as they did every Sunday, and Clay had followed Dozier to the grill for a late breakfast.

They sat on red stools where the counter jutted in, back toward the swinging kitchen door. Along the wall, front to back, above the grill and sandwich board and coffee urns, hung framed photographs of local and national celebrities who had visited the diner over the years for some of the very best soul food in Washington, D.C. Clay sat before a photo of Sugar Ray Leonard and his boy, Ray Jr.; Dozier's view was of a smiling Johnny "Guitar" Watson. Clay and Dozier had grown up together. They'd been coming here all their lives.

"Thank you, Miss Mary," said Dozier as the waitress set down a half-smoke-and-two-egg breakfast in front of him.

"Sure thing, Detective," said the waitress. "Here you go, Marcus."

Clay thanked her and looked lovingly at the chef's special placed before him: country ham and eggs over easy, redeye gravy, grits, fried apples, and hot biscuits. He dug in.

"So, what do you think?" said Clay.

"We'll get 'em," said Dozier. "We've got to. Too many people interested now. It made the front page this morning, *above* the fold, and you know it's gonna be the lead on the TV news for half the week. The chief already got us together on it late last night. Wait, now, any minute you're even gonna see the mayor chime in with some of his firsthand knowledge of the drug problem plaguing our city." Dozier side-glanced Clay.

"So everything you hear about the mayor's true."

"Overdosed twice in eighty-three. Made it to IAD, too, but the report got buried. They say the mayor's eatin' Valium all day just to notch himself down off the cocaine. Meanwhile, the drug problem keeps festering on. Kids afraid to walk into their own schools."

"It's a damn shame."

"Anyway, we'll get the ones did this."

"What about the gun?"

Dozier shrugged. "Nine-millimeter casings. Gun could be any-where, coulda *come* from anywhere. Anyone can drive over to Virginia, buy a gun, bring it back into D.C., and sell it. Or rent it for the night. Or trade it for a little blow. Gun's got plenty of generations behind it before it gets fired in a homicide."

"So how you gonna solve this?"

"Keep canvassing the neighborhood, talking to people. Clues don't solve murders, informants do. If it's a drug burn, nobody wants to talk, 'cause the citizens and even the snitches got more fear of dealers now than they do the police. And most homicides involve drugs these days."

"You think these kids were into dealin' drugs?"

"They weren't *the* ones dealing drugs down in your neighborhood, no. Fellow by the name of Tyrell Cleveland's growin' a business down there now. Got all sorts of mules around U."

"I know about Tyrell."

"You've seen him?"

"Uh-uh. But I had a good heart-to-heart talkin'-to with one of his sol-diers yesterday afternoon."

"Well, we're gonna get up with Tyrell Cleveland's street army, too, see if they know anything."

"Question is, why would any kid the age of those boys be the target of a drug kill?"

"Kids all ages deep into it now, Marcus. Those boys, both of them, they had cocaine in their pockets, rolled up in foil. Shit wasn't nothin' but baby laxative, mostly, but there it is. And the one got the top of his head blown off, Wesley Meadows, his fingerprints were on this .22 found by his side. Old piece of shit had a bad firing pin on it anyway, couldn't have shot nothin' with it if he tried, but the evidence does suggest that this eleven-year-old kid was carrying a gun."

"Damn."

"Talked to one of Meadows's best boys, kid named Mooty Wallace? Claims he was home last night. Meadows's older brother, Antoine, now there's one we *know* is in the life. We've spoken to him, too, but nothin' there, either. So we just got to keep talkin' to folks. We'll get this one. We will."

Clay and Dozier made a dent in their breakfasts, saying nothing until some activity behind them in the booths turned their heads. The young people sitting there were pointing through the window blinds excitedly at a tough-looking young man who wore the Scowl, standing outside his brand-new import, talking to a girl.

"Who's the celebrity, George?"

"Boy named Tony Lewis," muttered Dozier. "Used to work for Cornell Jones over on Hanover Place, till Jones got busted. Now he's a lieutenant with Rayful Edmond. See how those kids got all bright eyed seeing that boy? Used to be that kind of respect was shown to cops. I remember the first time I saw a brother in a uniform, when my mother took me down to Morton's to shop for some Sunday clothes? I saw that man in those blues, the way people were lookin' at him, I *knew* that's what I wanted to be someday."

"You did it, brother. Got out that uniform and earned your detective's shield quick, too. But what about Edmond? Can't y'all put him away?"

"Workin' on it. But he's got the layers of his empire, and maybe even the people in power, protecting him. Why, at the Strip, over on Orleans and Morton Place, in Trinidad? Cops don't even bother. Edmond's got the alleys trip wired and blockaded so patrol cars can't give chase. Cars lined up there weekend nights with Maryland and Virginia plates, buyin' quarters and halves like burgers at the drive-through. And beyond that, they say he's starting a subdistribution thing with the other dealers around the city."

"Sounds like a real businessman."

"Edmond's become a folk hero, Marcus; I'm not lyin'. Sponsors a basketball team in the Police Athletic league, gives turkeys to the poor at

Thanksgiving, *all* that. Drives a white Jag with gold wheels around town so all the kids can see. A man to emulate, just like Nicky Barnes was up in Harlem.

"I'm tellin' you, Marcus, we're losin' the battle down here. Outnumbered and outgunned. The mayor's been cutting back on the department every year since he's been in office. Every time the new budget comes up, our portion's been less and less. We're low on cars, and we got no new equipment, not even computers linking us to the national crime networks. And what new recruits we do get, why, plenty of them they're lettin' in now are flat unqualified. Heard tell a few are damn near retarded. All of this in the middle of the worst crime epidemic in this country's history —"

"I hear you, George."

"And you think that dried-up old husk of a man down on Pennsylvania Avenue cares? How about those horn-rimmed-glasses economic advisers of his, makin' the rich happy, pushin' the poor back further than they are? You think those Harvard boys care? Or the president's wife? 'Just Say No,' right? Easy to say no when you get born into alternatives and opportunities and a future."

"I hear you."

"It's gonna get worse. You heard about this crack thing, right?"

"Read about it in *Newsweek* magazine."

"It's comin' here, you can believe that. Imagine if they opened a Mac-Donald's in New York and L.A. and Detroit, then it hit 'em they forgot to open one up in D.C. Yeah, rock's gonna be here real soon. And when it is, ain't gonna be no weekend warrior thing, not like it is now for the white people out in the suburbs, using snow in the safety of their own homes. Crack's cheap and highly addictive, a drug tailor-made for the ghetto. Which means nobody's even going to care. Gutters gonna run with blood for real."

"George," said Clay. "Keep your voice down, man."

"I see dead children, I get emotional, Marcus."

"I know it, man. I know."

Clay used his muffin to scoop up some of the rest of his gravy and grits. The big man taking cash at the end of the counter yelled to a waitress, "Miss Mary, by the time you serve this gentleman's food, he's gonna be done eatin'!"

Dozier laughed. "That make sense?"

"To him it did."

"Damn, I love this place."

"Mmm. Me, too. But those half-smokes ain't gonna do your ulcer no good."

"And I guess that gravy's gonna go straight to your heart and give it a nice big kiss."

Clay pushed his empty plate to the side. Dozier sat straight and loosened his belt a notch.

Dozier said, "I don't know, Marcus. Most of the time I can get through all this. But when you see the corpse of a child . . ."

"Got to be rough."

"How's your boy, man?"

"M. J.'s good. Me and Elaine, we're gonna try real hard to work it out."

"My two, I don't have to tell you how much they mean to me. Couldn't sleep for nothin' last night, kept goin' into their rooms, checkin' on them and all that."

"I had to go give my boy a kiss, too."

Dozier turned his knife in the plate. "The Willets boy, got shot in the back? Was clutching this action figure, kind my own kids play with, when they found him in death. Boy had cocaine in his pockets and a toy in his hand. You believe it? Even had a street name; we found out that much from Wallace. Called himself P-Square, whatever that means. His friend Meadows had a street name, too. Called himself Chief."

Clay stopped twisting the napkin in his hand. He'd heard that name Chief before and not so long ago. Probably one of the kids who shopped in his store.

"George," said Clay. "Don't ever feel that what you're doin' out there isn't important. 'Cause it is. I've always admired you for that."

"Thanks, Marcus. But it's hard. I got fifteen years in already. Another ten and I'll have my twenty-five. I'm thinkin', much as I love this city, when I got twenty-five in, I'm gone."

"Lot of people I talk to thinkin' the same way." Clay looked at his watch. "Got to go, buddy. We open at noon."

They signaled the waitress and reached for their wallets.

"Good food, right George?"

George Dozier winked and said, "Make you cry."

Marcus Clay kept seeing Denice, standing next to him on the U Street sales floor. Someone honked behind him, and he moved on the green.

It was the conversation he'd had with Denice about Alan Rogers, that's what it was. Something about driving by them Friday night, seeing them all standing in the street. He could hear Denice's voice now, see her lips moving slow —

Tutt and Short Man were arguing . . .

Clay swerved to the curb.

. . . over some kid named Chief.

Okay, there it was. Didn't prove anything, though. So Short Man knew Chief. Didn't mean he killed that boy.

Short Man dealt drugs for Tyrell Cleveland. The dead kids were dealing on Tyrell's turf.

Tutt and Short Man were arguing over some kid named Chief.

Tutt and Short Man.

"Tutt," said Clay under his breath.

Tutt wasn't just a mean cop. Tutt was dirty, too.

TWENTY-TWO

Cootch had *Young, Gifted and Black*, his Sunday morning LP, going on the house stereo, Aretha's otherworldly voice filling the room, when Marcus Clay entered the store. Dimitri Karras leaned against the front racks, sipping a cup of coffee.

Clay went directly to Karras and clapped him on the shoulder. Karras did the same. Twenty-five years of friendship had made preliminaries unnecessary. Something was happening; seeing each other would make their thoughts complete.

"Good to see you, man," said Clay.

"Been waitin' on *you*."

"Cootch?"

"Yeah, boss."

"We'll be in the back."

Clay poured coffee into a WHUR mug and settled into his swivel chair. Karras had a seat on the edge of Clay's desk.

"You first," said Karras.

"All right," said Clay. "Just had breakfast with George Dozier. Those kids got killed last night? He's workin' the case. Told me one of the kids went by the name of Chief. Denice was with Rogers and Short Man the other night when Tutt, Murphy's partner, came up on 'em. Denice said Short Man and Tutt were arguing over a kid named Chief."

Karras sipped his coffee. "You think Short Man did the kids."

"George said the kids were small-time dealers on Tyrell Cleveland's turf. Short Man enforces for Tyrell."

"What about Tutt?"

"Tutt's dirty."

"Denice tell you that, too?"

"No. Got a strong feeling about it is all."

"Murphy?"

"Just 'cause he rides with the man don't mean he knows." Clay looked into his mug. "Ought to call George Dozier right now, let him and IAD sort it out."

"Why haven't you, then?"

"'Cause I'm not sure."

"Right. And there's something else, Marcus."

"I thought of that," said Clay. "There's the money. And your girl."

"That's right. But there's more you *don't* know. Something's happened to Donna's boyfriend, Eddie."

"The one took off Tyrell?"

"Yeah. I went by where he parks his car. A mechanic takes care of his tools, and his were lying around on the ground. He either left in a big hurry or he got taken real fast. He never phoned her last night, and he's not the type to blow Donna off, not when he's got her close to where he wants her, the way he does now."

"You think Tyrell might have Eddie?"

"It's possible. Sending in the cavalry, it might be a good way to get him killed."

"They might go on and kill him anyway, they don't get what they want. Gonna be on your head if they do."

"I don't think so. They need him alive, long as they don't know where the money is. I just hope he's smart enough to know that."

"You saw the money?"

"In a pillowcase at Donna's apartment."

"If they're after it, it means she's in real trouble, too."

"Yes."

"Bet you took her mind off it real good last night, Dimitri."

"Not the way you think."

"No?"

"You'd be surprised."

Clay set his mug down on the desk. "All of the sudden you goin' all Galahad on me. Why?"

"Just trying to do something right."

"Been a while. Proud of you, man."

Karras said, "Thanks."

"So, what're we gonna do?"

"Maybe we should talk it over with Murphy."

"He's off today. Said he was comin' in to see the Maryland game with us. But I want to be sure about Tutt before I start settin' off the alarms."

"How would you do that?"

"Tutt's off today, too. If Tutt's in bed with Tyrell, and Tyrell had anything to do with those murders, then you know the two of them have got to hook up to talk about damage control. Or maybe Tutt's gonna meet with one of Tyrell's boys."

"Follow Tutt, see where he goes?"

Clay nodded. "Not us, though. He's seen us up too close. You know anybody'd want to follow a cop around for a couple of hours today? I'd make it worth his while."

"You know where Tutt lives? You know his street vehicle?"

"Lives in Silver Spring Towers. Drives a baby blue Bronco. Seen it myself."

Karras thought it over. "There's this one guy I know." He drained his coffee and dropped the Styrofoam cup in the trash. "I'll give him a call."

Nick Stefanos chewed on a breath mint and leaned on the cashier's counter, watching his buddy Johnny McGinnes pitch a nineteen-inch Sharp to a young Indian couple with a baby boy. They had come in for the Sony — a prediction McGinnes had made in his most cartoonish accent as they'd walked into the store — and McGinnes had tried to step them off the Trinitron to the Lynitron, a profit piece carrying a ten-dollar spiff. The couple was slowly edging toward the front door.

Stefanos looked at McGinnes: hair combed diagonally over his forehead in a Hitler hang, polyesters crisp as sheets blowing in a spring breeze, his hands working the air for punctuation. When he worked the floor,

McGinnes was the happiest, most content man Stefanos had ever known. Stefanos envied him for that.

"What's goin' on, Country?" said Andre Malone, the store's stereo salesman. Malone glided gracefully between the glass cases and drew a Newport from his Italian-cut sport coat.

"McGinnes is losing them."

"Can see that. Where's our illustrious manager at?"

"Louie's up at the Van Ness apartments, visiting his girlfriend."

Malone lit his smoke, blew the match out on the exhale. "Brother Lou gonna gyrate, huh?"

"I guess."

Malone eyed Stefanos's jacket. "Where'd you cop those threads, man, Salvation Army?"

Stefanos looked down at the sleeve of his gray-checked Robert Hall, first sold in 1956. "Classic Clothing, out on Benning Road."

"Like I said, Salvation Army."

"We can't all be stylin' like you."

"Tell you somethin' I do know. You never gonna see a brother wearing dead man's clothes, no matter how low he gets." Malone smiled. "Check out our boy now."

McGinnes had the couple backed up near the door. "Remember," he said, grinning stupidly, "the Sharp's only going to be on sale for so long. So, so long."

"So long," said the husband.

"Come here," said McGinnes, bending toward the stroller and pinching the baby's cheek a little too roughly. The boy's eyes bugged out in surprise. "Cutelilcocksucker you got there. You know it?"

"Thank you," said the husband.

"Thank *you*," said McGinnes, still smiling.

McGinnes went to the counter to take his medicine from his friends while the couple left the store.

"Putz," said McGinnes.

"Nice close," said Malone.

"You couldn't close your fly when you first came to work here — that is, till I put you through school."

"Now I close it real good. Woulda closed those punjabi mothafuckers, too, if you hadn't gone and taken my up."

"It might have been your up, if you hadn't been dialing up one of your freaks from the Sound Explosion back there."

Stefanos closed his eyes. He was nursing an alcohol-heavy cokeover, and he didn't feel much like joining in. Their bickering, it was putting a dull ache to his head. That and the electric orange-and-gold signage hung throughout the store.

Stefanos answered the phone ringing on the wall.

"Nutty Nathan's, the Miser Who Works for You. Nick Stefanos speaking." He listened and said, "Dimitri, how you doin', man?"

By the time Stefanos got off the phone, Andre Malone had drifted and McGinnes was putting fire to a one-hit stash pipe he used on the floor. McGinnes took a deep draw, held it in, and blew the smoke into a refrigerator by the cashier's stand.

"Who was that?"

"Guy I know named Dimitri Karras. Called to see if we'd shadow some off-duty cop. Follow him, see where he's going, report back, like that. There's a C-note in it for us. You interested?"

"Yeah, but I gotta make a few deals here first."

"And I want to see the game."

"Maryland?"

"Yeah. You know that kid Freddie, always standing out on the sidewalk, watching ball on the sets in the window?"

"Kid wears that bandanna?"

"Yeah. He's a big Bias fan. I told him he could come inside today, watch it with me."

"This Karras guy say it was okay to get to it later?"

"He said it was cool."

"You got the address of the tail?"

Stefanos patted his breast pocket. "Right here."

"I'm in." A middle-aged black man approached from the Connecticut Avenue sidewalk. "You don't mind if I take this jive turkey, do ya, Jim? One of my B-backs, anyway."

"To hear you tell it, they're all your B-backs, Johnny."

"I'm serious. Was in here a month ago looking for a set. You *know* I never forget a customer's face."

"Yeah, I know. Go ahead."

Stefanos watched McGinnes greet the man, lead him quickly to the Sharps. He'd start the customer on a high-end piece, step him down, tell him he didn't need "that much set," become his friend and confidant. Maybe it would work and maybe not. Stefanos knew one thing: McGinnes would sell *someone* a Sharp television set before the day was done.

"You say this TV's got a good picture?" said the black man.

"Good ain't the word," said McGinnes, smiling broadly. "Ass-kickin', booty-whippin' be more like it."

"Your boy up for it?" said Marcus Clay.

"He and his partner have work to do first. Gonna be a few hours till they can get to it. I told him we'd drop the hundred off at the store later on."

"You know where the store is?"

"Yeah."

It's right across the street from where I cop my blow.

Karras put his arms through the sleeves of his jean jacket. "I'm outta here for a while, Marcus. Check back in with you later."

"Where you off to, man?"

"See my mom."

"Tell her I said hello."

Karras said, "I will."

Dimitri Karras drove slowly down winding lanes cutting through closely cropped acres of lawns and parked his car along the curb toward the rear of the grounds. He got out and walked across the grass, careful not to step on the stone markers or the freshly filled graves. The names on the markers went from Irish to Italian to almost exclusively Greek. It took a little searching, as it always did, but soon he found his parents, separated for so long but now lying next to each other in death. A joint marker memorialized their lives.

Karras took the daisies he had purchased from a roadside stand and placed them in a shallow cup set above Eleni Karras's name. She had always kept fresh flowers in their kitchen, cut from the narrow garden she maintained in their backyard. Karras pictured her standing in the kitchen, her back against the sink, her arms crossed, a crooked smile on her face as she watched him eat. There's no greater pleasure for a Greek mother, thought Karras, than to feed her only son.

Karras spread the daisies and used his hand to brush brown grass shavings off her name. He closed his eyes and pressed his thumb to his two adjacent fingers, touched his forehead, his right shoulder, his left shoulder, and his chest. When he was finished doing his *stavro* he said a silent prayer.

"Oh, yeah, Ma," said Karras, opening his eyes. "Marcus says hey."

He brushed debris away from his father's name. His father, Peter Karras, was killed in 1949, shot to death while killing others in the office of a loan shark named Burke. Dimitri, a baby at the time, remembered nothing of his father, not even his smell. When Eleni realized she was dying from the tumor eating at her brain, she asked Dimitri to exhume her husband's body from the Brentwood Cemetery in Northeast, where Spartan-Americans were buried in numbers, and bring the remains out to Montgomery County's Gate of Heaven, this clean, green place with the pruned, shade-giving trees, where there were no malt liquor bottles and used rubbers strewn about the grounds. Toward the end, holding her bird-claw hand, he had promised that he would.

He had made other promises as well. That he would find a nice *yineka*, marry her, have children, discover the riches of parenthood that she claimed she had found while raising him. That he would go back to school, become a professional, be a good *anthropos*, set down roots.

He hadn't kept those promises, of course. And now he didn't know if he could.

Instead, he'd sold his mother's Northwest home for a healthy profit and received a nice insurance disbursement as the sole beneficiary of her will, gone out and bought the BMW, taken a Hawaiian vacation, and purchased his apartment. Spent money freely in bars, and on clothes and girls and cocaine. He still had plenty, enough to keep a single man with no attachments flush for a very long while.

Karras ran a hand above his lips, wiped at something running from his nose. He looked at the blood smudged on his forefinger and rubbed it off on his jeans.

Karras turned and walked across the grass toward his car, the navy blue Beamer shining in the sun.

Andy Murphy lived in a brick rambler off upper 14th, near the Walter Reed Hospital. In his front yard a group of miniature stone angels faced a small Jesus statue encircled by a wire halo, the word *Son* written in cursive across a wreath. Murphy kept fresh flowers year round in a squat vase behind the shrine.

Murphy stood in the kitchen, basting a chicken while greens cooked in a tall pot atop the gas stove. He was expecting his son Kevin and Kevin's wife, Wanda, for dinner; he'd spent the morning and afternoon reading the Sunday *Post*, attending services at his Baptist church, and preparing the meal. They'd come over, recite the Twenty-third Psalm with him, and all of them would sit down to eat.

Cooking for three, it wasn't so difficult. Not like when Teddy, his older son, used to bring his wife and children by, too. Teddy was a reverend and a fine young man, steady and strong of will. The lymphoma had taken him three years back, and shortly thereafter his wife had gone off with a slick young insurance man, gone and left without a word to some town up in New Jersey. Andy Murphy had received a card and photograph from his grandchildren that first Christmas and nothing since.

He often thanked the Lord that he still had Kevin and Wanda. Cooking for them once a week, it gave him a little something to do. And it seemed to comfort Wanda. He expected it wouldn't be long before God called him home to be with his wife, Paulette, gone ten years. But until then, a man needed distractions to pass the time. Maybe he shouldn't have retired so quickly — he'd been an engineer at the old Brown Building on 19th, between M and N, for the last fifteen years of his career — but you had to step aside eventually, make room for the young. It was their world, after all. He was only renting a small piece of it now.

The bell chimed. Andy Murphy went through the living room and opened the front door.

"You're early," he said.

"Can't make dinner today. Thought you and I could kneel down and say the psalm."

"You don't look well."

"I was troubled," said Kevin Murphy, smiling strangely. "But I'm better now."

TWENTY-THREE

Tyrell Cleveland cradled the phone on the table beside his armchair.

"Who was that?" said Short Man Monroe.

"One of our runners," said Tyrell. "Cops been shakin' most of them down this morning, askin' questions about Chief and his friend. Askin' about me."

"Those runners don't know shit," said Monroe. "And if they did know, they'd know better than to talk."

"I ain't worried about them. You hadn't gone and done those young-uns, they wouldn't have nothin' to talk *about*."

"Little nigga had a gun, Ty."

"Hmm. Hope you threw that gun of *yours* away."

"Damn sure did. Pitched it in the Anacostia."

"No witnesses and no weapon. We shouldn't have no problem, then." Tyrell looked at Alan Rogers. "And where were you when all this shootin' was goin' down?"

"Seein' his girl," said Monroe.

"Tyrell —"

"Got to get your priorities together, Alan. You do have yourself together, right?"

"You *know* I do."

"That's good. Real glad to hear that, Alan."

Antony Ray, Rogers, and Monroe sat at the round table near Tyrell. Chink Bennet and Jumbo Linney were sitting on the couch, quietly playing a game of Atari.

"How's our boy Eddie doin', Antony?"

Ray snapped ash off a cigarette. "Sleepin' again."

"Look like he's hurt bad," said Rogers. "Could be goin' into shock."

"Don't worry," said Ray. "Gonna put him out of his misery soon enough."

"Not yet," said Tyrell. "Alan, you know anything about a white dude, works at that record store?"

"He knows," said Monroe. "White boy with the gray hair stood his ass down."

"Nothin' I could do, Ty —"

"Here's the thing. Antony got a little too rough with our boy Eddie last night. But before he passed out, Eddie said something about that white boy and the money."

Rogers shrugged. "Maybe he took it from Eddie's girl."

Tyrell looked into the fire. "Seems like it all leads to that record store, y'all know what I'm sayin'?"

Monroe smiled. "I do."

"Maybe we ought to pay that Marcus Clay a visit. Meet him and his people all in the same room. Talk about money and some other things, too. 'Bout how we gotta . . . co-exist there in that neighborhood. 'Cause, you know, way things are goin' with him, shootin' his mouth off 'bout how he don't want to see our kind around no more, one of us is not gonna last down there. Think if I talk to him, maybe he'll see the light."

"Sounds like a plan to me," said Monroe.

"How about you, Alan? That okay? Or would that, how they say it in those soap operas, jeopardize your relationship with that girl?"

Ray and Monroe laughed. Rogers's lip twitched as he forced himself to break a smile.

"We go now?" said Monroe.

"Nah," said Tyrell. "Wanna catch that Maryland game first. I'll call Clay after the game, set it up. Tutt and Murphy's supposed to come by later, too. Need to talk to them, make sure we still got our understanding in place. Even bad cops get nervous when you start cappin' mothafuckers on their beat."

"I'll say it again," said Monroe. "We don't need those two, Tyrell."

"Relax, Short. I'll throw a little more money at 'em. That's all they really care about. All anybody cares about, you get down to it." Tyrell stretched his long frame. "Anyway. With all these distractions and shit, I almost went and forgot about the business. Chink! Jumbo!"

Bennet and Linney made their way over to Tyrell. Linney carried Cheetos with him, his hand rustling the bag.

"Y'all busy?" said Tyrell.

"Nah, Ty, we ain't busy," said Bennet.

Tyrell eyed them with amusement. "You don't mind, I need you two to go down and collect what you *didn't* get last night while you were busy fuckin' up those kids."

"We ain't have nothin' to do with that," said Linney.

"Hey, Short," said Bennet, "let us take the Z, man. Think we ought to chill with the Supra down there, for a little while, anyway. Someone might have seen it last night."

"You know your boy Jumbo can't fit in that Z," said Monroe. "Take the mothafuckin' Supra."

"Tyrell," said Bennet, "we gotta go now?"

"Yes," said Tyrell. "Now."

Kevin Murphy said hello to Cootch and walked into the back room of Real Right. Marcus Clay, Dimitri Karras, and Clarence Tate sat in chairs semicircling the store's battered television. Anthony Taylor stood beside Clay, sipping from a can of Nehi grape.

"Officer Murphy!" said Anthony.

"Anthony," said Murphy. "Wha'sup fellas?"

"You missed the first half," said Clay.

"Had some things to do. Listened to it on the radio on the way down. Maryland's down by six, right?"

"Yeah," said Clay. "St. John's lost to Auburn today, you believe that? Chuck Person had twenty-seven, made Walter Berry look like nobody's All-American."

"Big East is out of the tournament," said Karras. "Didn't even place one team in the Sweet Sixteen."

"And that means Bias ain't gonna have that hookup with Berry," said Clay, "everyone's been waitin' for."

"Don't look like Maryland's going to the next level anyway, Marcus," said Tate.

"Gotta think positive, Clarence. Lenny's gonna turn it on second half. You wait."

"UNLV's holding 'em pretty good, though," said Karras. "Seems like they got two men on the ball handler every possession. Tarkanian's coaching a good game. And Anthony Jones is hot."

"Jones is a Washington boy," said Tate for the third time that day. "Out of Dunbar."

"Bias is the key," said Clay. "He's keepin' 'em in the game. Pull a chair up, Kev."

Murphy drew a chair beside Clay. Clay looked him over.

"You lookin' a little rough, man."

"Drank too much last night. Was at the crime scene down the street."

"Need to talk to you about that, just you and me, when we get a chance."

Murphy stared at the action on the set. "Okay."

Len Bias drove the baseline, went up against three defenders, sank the pill.

"Number Thirty-four," whispered Clay.

"Here we go," said Karras.

"Check out Tark," said Tate. "Gonna bite right through that rag, man."

"Go on and bite through it, Kojak!" said Anthony, and Clay tapped him on the head.

The Terps scored the next fourteen without an answer from the Runnin' Rebels, bringing it to 41–33, Maryland's way. Maryland's players were high-fiving at midcourt.

"What's Lefty so mad about?" said Anthony.

"Coach thinks they're celebratin' too early," said Clay.

Armon Gilliam, UNLV's big forward, and Jones began taking it to the hole. The Runnin' Rebels went on a 17–2 run: 50–43, UNLV.

Bias cut it to three. Derrick Lewis, the other half of Maryland's inside game, fouled out.

"Is this a game?" said Karras.

Murphy slapped Karras five.

Clay said, "Got to get it to Lenny now. He can win the game for 'em if they keep dishin' him the rock."

"God*damn* — sorry, Anthony — look at Jones. He's hittin' at will from downtown!"

"D.C. boy."

"Out of Dunbar, Clarence. We *know*."

"It's all Bias now."

"Number Thirty-four."

Len Bias had scored the last thirteen of Maryland's points. The Runnin' Rebels missed the front ends of three one-and-ones. The Terps brought it to within one with forty seconds to go. Jones hit four foul shots. John Johnson, a Terp reserve, stepped up to the free throw line. Tark called a time-out to let the freshman shooter think about it. Johnson bricked the shot.

"Aw, no!" said Karras.

Maryland guard Jeff Baxter drove the lane.

"Dish it to Bias!" said Murphy.

"Look out," said Clay, "man's got position in the paint!"

Baxter was called for the charge. The buzzer sounded. Maryland lost the game.

"Damn shame," said Clay. "Bias had thirty-one points and twelve rebounds. And they *still* lost."

"Got beat by the better team," said Karras. "Outcoached, too."

"Can't wait to hear what Glenn Harris got to say about it tonight on HUR," said Clay.

"*Let's Talk Sports*," said Tate. "The man knows his ball."

The group scattered. Anthony Taylor asked Murphy for a ride up to his place, and Murphy told him to wait out front. Clay and Murphy remained in the back room.

"Kid's afraid to walk home," said Clay. "He heard those gunshots last night. Was chased by some boys in a car, too."

"He say who chased him?"

"He's afraid to say. Even too scared to tell me. But I figure it had to be Short Man Monroe. Take it to the next level, you gotta believe it was Tyrell Cleveland and Short Man were the ones involved in those murders."

"How you make the leap to that?"

"Had breakfast with George Dozier this morning. You know him?"

"Homicide. Good man, got a good rep in the department. Went to Cardoza, about your age. Must have come up with you."

"Right. George told me those kids were playing dealer on Tyrell's turf. One of those kids called himself Chief. Short Man's job is to keep that turf free and clear."

"Keep going."

"I was out the other night, came up on Alan Rogers and Short Man and Clarence's daughter, Denice, out on the street. Your partner, Tutt, he was with 'em."

Murphy shrugged, trying to hide the empty feeling in his gut. "Some kind of shakedown, I guess."

"Plainclothes shakedown? Tutt's a uniformed cop."

"Tutt's a little aggressive."

"Denice," said Clay, "she said Tutt and Short Man were arguing over a kid named Chief."

Murphy's heart jumped in his chest. He stared at the floor.

"Tutt's dirty," said Clay. "You must know it."

"He's my partner. And that's a serious accusation."

"Ain't like you haven't suspected it yourself. I told you just now, there wasn't a whole lot of surprise on your face. Murphy? I'm talkin' to you, man."

Murphy felt himself break a sweat beneath his shirt.

"Okay," said Murphy, "ain't gonna deny that I've suspected it. What're you gonna do?"

"What are *you* gonna do, Kevin?"

Murphy rose from his chair. "You tell George Dozier?"

"No. Was waitin' to talk to you."

Murphy buried his hands in the pockets of his jeans. "Give me the rest of the day, Marcus, that's all I ask. I need to confront Tutt my way. Need to settle things. By tonight I'll have this whole thing worked out. Tomorrow I'll go to George Dozier with what I know. That sound fair to you?"

Clay looked at Murphy. "Okay. A few hours isn't gonna make any kind of difference. I'll give you that."

"Thanks," said Murphy.

"Come on," said Clay. "Sounds like you got a day ahead of you. And Anthony's having Sunday dinner with his grandmother. He needs to be gettin' home."

They walked out to the showroom. Cootch had the new Prince,

214

"Kiss," cooking on the house stereo. Karras and Tate were behind the counter, working on some numbers.

"Anthony," said Clay.

"Yeah, Mr. Clay."

"You dust out those racks?"

"Yes, sir."

"You took the records out first, right? Didn't just dust around them, did you?"

"Cleaned 'em like you said to."

"Here." Clay gave Anthony a ten-dollar bill. "Good job."

"Thanks!"

"Let's go," said Murphy.

"Call me later," said Clay.

Murphy said, "I will."

Clay watched Murphy and Anthony get into the black Trans Am parked out front. He turned toward Cootch and raised his voice over the music.

"Any customers, Cootch?"

Cootch shook his head. "Not a one."

Murphy pulled to a stop in front of Anthony Taylor's row house.

Anthony pointed to a gauge in the dash. "What's that?"

"Tachometer. Call it a tach. Measures the RPMs. You know, like when you rev up the engine? Like that."

"This a nice car, Officer Murphy. *I'm* gonna have me a nice car like this. To go with that fleet of buses I'm gonna have, too."

"A fleet now, huh?" Murphy chuckled. "I believe it, boy. Just remember, though, flashy cars, nice clothes, they don't mean a thing unless you earn the money to buy them. Earn it through hard work."

"Like Mr. Clay did. Like you."

Murphy looked away. "Anthony?"

"Yes?"

"Mr. Clay told me some boys chased you last night. Was the boy who chased you the same boy roughed you up yesterday on the street?"

"I . . . I don't know."

"Yes, you do. And you need to tell me so it doesn't happen again. Was it the one called Short Man?"

Anthony nodded slowly. "Yes. But . . . what happens if he comes after me now? What happens if you can't fix things with him?"

"I'm gonna fix things, Anthony. You don't have to worry about that. And you don't need to be afraid anymore."

"It ain't just him. It's everything down here. I wish it was summertime, so I could be with my moms and my sisters, down in the country."

Murphy smiled at the boy. "You keep wishin' on it, summer might come sooner than you think."

"For real?"

"Just might." Murphy reached across Anthony and opened his door. "Go on, son, you got dinner waitin'."

"Thanks for the ride, Officer Murphy. Take care."

Murphy said, "You, too."

Murphy watched Anthony's grandmother step aside and let him in the row house. Lula Taylor stayed in the doorway, staring at the black Trans Am idling on Fairmont. Murphy drove away.

Karras, Tate, and Clay were in Clay's office when the phone rang. Clay picked it up.

"Real Right."

"Marcus Clay?"

"Speaking."

"Tyrell Cleveland."

Clay adjusted the receiver against his ear. "Go ahead."

"You and me, we need to have a talk."

"What we got to talk about?"

"You got a white boy works there?"

"*Man*'s name is Dimitri Karras."

"He *does* work for you."

"So?"

"This Karras, he's got twenty-five thousand of my money."

"That right."

"Boy by the name of Eddie Golden told me. He ain't talkin' so good right now, but we been able to put enough together to make your boy Karras for the second thief. Karras took off this girlfriend of Eddie's, after Eddie took *me* off —"

"I don't know what you're talkin' about."

"Sure you do. Course, we can go back and twist Eddie's arm a little more, see if he's tellin' the truth. Don't think he'd care for it much. Wrist is startin' to look like a football right about now."

"You holdin' him?"

"Got no choice. And don't get a mind now to call the police on me, Marcus Clay. I'd have to finish Mr. Eddie Golden quick, you know what I'm sayin'?"

"What do you want?" said Clay.

"A meeting. In your store on U. This evening, after you close. Got a few things to discuss. Might as well do it face-to-face."

"Who's gonna be there?"

"Me, Alan Rogers, and Short Man Monroe. He's been anxious to see you again, after you went and schooled him yesterday."

Clay thought it over. "No guns."

"What?"

"No guns."

"What about y'all?"

"I said no guns. Give you my word."

"Okay. Have my money ready, Mr. Marcus Clay. We'll work a trade. My money for Eddie Golden's life."

"Don't kill Golden."

"Don't force me to," said Tyrell.

The line went dead. Clay racked the receiver.

"What was that all about?" said Karras.

"That was Tyrell Cleveland on the line."

Tate dropped his pencil and looked up at Clay.

"What'd he want?"

"Has it in his head that you got his money, Dimitri. Eddie Golden gave him that notion. You were right: They got Eddie. Cleveland told me they'd kill him if I went to the cops."

"Who's Eddie Golden?" said Tate.

"Explain it to you later, Clarence." Clay looked at Karras. "Cleveland wants to come in and talk to us tonight."

"And you said what?"

"I said we would."

"Who's Tyrell coming with?" said Karras.

"Couple of his boys."

"What boys?" said Tate.

"Short Man. Alan Rogers, too."

"I'm in," said Tate.

"Figured that, Clarence," said Marcus Clay.

TWENTY-FOUR

"So I'm in this bar," said Johnny McGinnes, "and I order a Leon Klinghoffer cocktail from the tender. 'What's that?' he says."

"Well," said Nick Stefanos, "what is it?"

"A Leon Klinghoffer cocktail?" McGinnes grinned. "Two shots and a splash."

"Funny, Johnny. Okay, so that's your *Achille Lauro* gag. What's next, a *Challenger* joke?"

"Oh, I got a couple of those, too, you wanna hear 'em." McGinnes popped the top on a sixteen-ounce can of Colt 45. "Thirsty, Greek?"

"Might make my head feel better."

"You could take something for it instead. I think I got a couple of TTs in my pocket here."

"TTs?"

"Tainted Tylenols."

"Just give me the Colt."

McGinnes pulled a tallboy from the bag at his feet. He passed the can over to Stefanos, who cracked it and took a long swig.

McGinnes pointed through the windshield. "That him?"

"Uh-uh."

Stefanos's Dart was parked on Easley Street, across the road from the back lot of Silver Spring Towers. The baby blue Bronco was parked nose out in the lot.

"We're just tailin' this guy, right?"

"Right."

"Don't need to paper him?"

"What, you think we're gonna serve a cop?"

Stefanos produced a Camel filter from the inside pocket of his Robert Hall sport jacket and pushed in the dash lighter. He lit the cigarette, took a deep drag, held the smoke in his lungs.

"This process serving, though," said McGinnes, "you gotta admit, it's like cuttin' butter. See, I got the whole thing figured out. . . . Hey, Nick. Nick?"

"Yeah."

"Okay, you're not that interested right now. But I can tell by lookin' at you, every time we get going after one of these guys, you get juiced real quick."

Stefanos hit his Camel, blew smoke out the open window. "All right, I like the challenge of it. When you find someone it feels like more of an accomplishment than just, you know, closing a deal."

"Maybe you ought to think about doing it full-time. Since you been so unhappy lately, I mean."

"*That* would make my wife real happy. Karen's already all over my ass, pushing me to get a professional job, like all these other guys my age, got Brylcreem in their hair."

"Mousse."

"Whatever. Look, man, I don't know."

"Maybe you're all right, Nick. Maybe it's your wife that's got the problem and not you."

"Yeah, lately I been thinkin' the same thing."

McGinnes scratched between his legs. "Makin' money's easy. The hard part is finding something you like to do every day. Look at me, Nick; I *love* what I do."

"I know it, Johnny." Stefanos noticed a beefy guy coming out of the apartments, watched him cross the lot and head toward the Bronco. "There's our man."

"What is he, the missing link or somethin'?"

"Check out those acid-washed jeans."

"Dress slacks for today's redneck."

Stefanos ignitioned the Dart, pitched his cigarette out the window.

He let the Bronco get up toward Fenton Street before he put the Dodge in gear. The Mopar engine knocked as he gave the car gas.

"Gotta get this thing tuned up," said Stefanos.

"You ask me," said McGinnes with a slow smile, "it's the O-rings need to be replaced."

"What's this we're listenin' to?" said McGinnes.

"Thin White Rope," said Stefanos.

"Sounds like the singer's on the toilet, strainin' one out."

"Tight group. Saw 'em at the 9:30 last week. Guy named Petersen, used to be in the Insect Surfers, opened up for them. Davey Con Carne, he calls himself now. Bad show."

"Yeah, okay. Slow down, Nick, you're gettin' too close. He's gonna make us, man."

"'Make' us? Nice expression, Johnny, real street. What, did you hear that on *Hardcastle and McCormick* or something?"

"I think it was *Scarecrow and Mrs. King.*"

Stefanos pulled over to the curb as the Bronco turned left off of 14th and went down Colorado. The driver stopped behind a black Trans Am that was parked in front of an Irish bar.

"Salt-and-pepper team," said McGinnes as a mustached black man stepped out of the Pontiac, locked it, walked over to the Bronco's passenger side, and opened the door.

"Here we go," said Stefanos.

The Bronco headed south. Stefanos and McGinnes did the same.

"Man's takin' the scenic route," said McGinnes as they drove down Pennsylvania Avenue near the White House. Across the street, in Lafayette Park, a city of tent dwellers covered the green.

"Reaganville," said Stefanos.

"What am I supposed to do, take the day off and shed tears?"

"Oh, so they're not really hungry, long as the rest of us are doing okay, right?"

"You're losing them, Nick."

"No, I'm not."

Ten minutes later both cars were on East Capitol Street, driving toward the Anacostia River.

"Looks like we're leaving D.C.," said McGinnes.

Stefanos said, "I know."

In Maryland, along Central Avenue, Stefanos eased up on the gas and pulled into a half-vacant strip mall off the highway. He had hung back, watching the Bronco roll down the service road behind the mall. He parked in the last space in front of the mall and cut the Dart's engine. They could still see the Bronco as it came to a stop beside a few black imports in front of a bungalow backed by a small forest of trees.

The two men got out of the Bronco. McGinnes watched the black man with interest as he and the white man walked toward the house, stepped up onto the porch, and went through the front door.

"Nick?"

"What?"

"Nothin', I guess."

Stefanos and McGinnes sat there for the next ten minutes and killed the rest of the six.

"You get the address?" said McGinnes, crushing an empty in his hand and tossing it over his shoulder to the backseat.

"Got it."

"Then that's it. We did what we said we'd do."

"I guess."

"What's wrong?"

"I don't know. Just don't feel like we're finished yet, Johnny, you know what I mean?"

"Yeah, I do. It's funny, I feel the same way." McGinnes put on a pair of shades. "I gotta take a piss."

"I gotta take one, too," said Stefanos.

They got out of the Dart, walked to the side of the strip mall, stood side by side, and urinated on the bricks.

McGinnes pissed his initials on the wall, then zipped up his fly. "Now that we're out here —"

"What?"

"You're curious, aren't you? Don't tell me you're not."

"Okay, I'm curious. And that malt liquor's fucked with my head just enough to make me do something stupid."

"I just wanna see what's what. Maybe there's some extra geld in it for us."

"Maybe."

"I'll do the talking."

"Wasn't any doubt in my mind that you would."

They turned and walked toward the bungalow at the end of the road.

"Where is he?" said Richard Tutt.

"Who?" said Tyrell, sitting in his chair.

"Don't be cute. On the phone earlier you told me you had the thief."

"You mean that little white bird dropped out of the sky?" said Antony Ray. "One with the busted wing? Cheep, cheep, cheep."

Ray laughed, reached across the table, and touched Short Man Monroe's hand.

Alan Rogers sat in a chair pushed against the wall. He looked at Kevin Murphy, standing back by the door.

"Kidnapping's a capital crime," said Tutt, "case you geniuses didn't know."

"Thanks for the tip," said Tyrell.

"You better hope he lives. Add murder to the charges and you're lookin' at an automatic death penalty."

"What charges? You gonna charge me with somethin', Officer Tutt?"

"This ain't D.C., Tyrell. Here in Maryland they don't fuck around. Better tell that miniature psycho boy of yours and cousin An-tony the news."

Monroe sat back, moved his toothpick from one side of his mouth to the other. He spun the Glock slowly on the table so the grip came to rest in his hand.

"Yeah, yeah," said Tutt, "I see the gun, *Short* Man. You're one tough case, aren't you? Real tough with little boys. Oh, but look what happened to you when you came up against a full-grown man. That record store owner cut your little ass down to size real good and quick, *didn't* he? Had to go and kill a couple of kids just to make yourself feel tall."

"Come on," said Monroe, rising from his chair. "You wanna go, let's go."

Antony Ray put his hand on Monroe's chest, pushed him down in his seat.

"This ain't the time," said Ray.

Monroe stared at Tutt and smiled. Tutt breathed out slow. Tyrell looked into the fire, ran one long finger up and down his cheek.

"Where's Golden?" said Murphy in a very quiet way.

"Our voice of reason," said Tyrell. "Always glad to know we got an ice-cool mothafucker like you on our side."

"Where is he?" said Murphy.

Tyrell made an elaborate motion with his hand. "Bedroom on the left."

"He gonna make it?"

"Far as I know. Alan been takin' care of him, givin' him water and food. Alan's in love with a girl, case you haven't heard — turned him all sensitive and shit."

Murphy nodded at Rogers. "Alan did good. Because you have to keep him alive. My partner here spoke the truth. It's important for all of us that he lives."

"I couldn't agree more, Officer Murphy," said Tyrell. "Golden's worth nothin' to me dead. 'Specially since Clay and that white dude he works with still got our money."

"Who told you that?"

"Eddie told us. And me and Alan and Short are going to see Mr. Marcus Clay after dark and talk about a trade. See if we can't get together on some other points, too. Might take a little persuadin', understand, but he'll come around." Tyrell looked curiously at Murphy. "You got a problem with that?"

Murphy said nothing.

Antony Ray's fingers spread the blinds on the bay window. "Aw, shit," he said. "What the fuck we got here?"

They all looked through the window. Two white men, one nearing middle age and one on the young side, walked the gravel road toward the house.

"Cops," said Monroe.

"Are they?" said Tyrell.

Tutt squinted. "None I ever seen."

"This some kind of bust, man? 'Cause if it is —"

"I'm tellin' you, Tyrell, I don't make those two as cops."

"You and Murphy get your asses to the back till we figure out what the fuck they want."

Alan Rogers stood up and pressed his back to the wall. Antony Ray stayed in his seat. Monroe picked a towel up off the floor and draped it over the automatic he held in his hand.

"Come on, Murph," said Tutt, making a head motion to the kitchen.

"Right behind you, man," said Murphy.

Tutt walked around the couch, stepping over Atari wires, and went into the kitchen. Murphy started off behind him but broke away and entered the hall. He passed the bathroom, opened the bedroom door, and stepped inside. He closed the door and looked at the figure lying on the bed.

There was a knock on the bungalow's front door.

"Short," said Tyrell Cleveland. "Get back there behind me. I step out the way and signal, you shoot these mothafuckers straight away. Two quick shots to the head. Don't waste no time."

Monroe nodded, adjusted the towel so that it covered the barrel.

Tyrell uncoiled himself from his chair. He stretched to his full height. He opened the front door.

Murphy knelt by the mattress. Eddie Golden was on his side, his knees drawn up to his chest. The wrist area of one hand was like a twisted gourd, orange and purple and black. Eddie looked up at Murphy, his eyes jittery and unfocused.

"Who are you?"

"Name's Murphy." He pulled his badge from his jacket and put it close to Golden's face. "I'm a police officer. Tyrell thinks I'm with him. But I'm *not* with him. I'm here to help *you*, Eddie. You understand?"

Eddie's head came off the mattress. "G-g-get me outta here."

"Can't now," whispered Murphy. "Gonna come back for you later on."

"Not later . . . now."

"Eddie, I need to know where the money is. Gonna bring it back with me and trade it for your life."

"Money's with Karras. That record store guy —"

"Bullshit. You ain't talkin' to them now, you're talkin' to me. I know Karras. And I damn sure know Marcus Clay. Those two didn't take no one off, Eddie. Now, where's that money at, Eddie? Where's it *at?*"

They heard loud laughter from the other room. Eddie winced and fluttered his eyes.

"The money, Eddie. The money, man, it's gonna save your life."

Eddie licked his lips, stared straight ahead. "Donna," he said. "You can't let anything happen to her."

"I won't. I promise you, man, she won't come to no harm. Tell me where this Donna lives."

Eddie gave Murphy her address.

"When she gonna be there?"

Eddie told him the knock-off time of Donna's shift at Hecht's.

"What's she drivin'?"

"A red RX-7. An old one —"

"Now listen," said Murphy. "I'm comin' back later. Meantime, you let Alan Rogers keep takin' care of you. And do what Rogers says, hear?"

Eddie nodded.

Murphy went to the sash window, looked through it, judged the distance to the ground. He unlatched the lock, ran the window up and down in its tracks. It made a harsh scraping sound. He walked to the door and opened it. Murphy glanced back at Eddie once more and stepped from the room.

Out in the hall, he saw Short Man Monroe raising a towel-draped hand. He could see the grip of a gun beneath the towel. The two who'd been walking toward the house were on the porch. Monroe was pointing the gun at *them.*

Nick Stefanos stood on the porch beside Johnny McGinnes, jingling the change in his pocket as McGinnes knocked on the scarred oak door. Stefanos could hear the low thump of bass coming from behind the bungalow's walls, and as the door swung open he recognized the shout of Kurtis Blow: *"It's tough, like Muhammad Ali./It's rough, like the Oakland Raiders. . . ."*

Once he saw the man standing in the door frame, and those grouped around him, he barely noticed the music at all.

The man before them must have stood six and a half feet tall. His ears and chin were pointed, and his eyes were bottle green. Gargoyle, thought Stefanos, looking at the man.

A young black man, short and muscular, stood behind Gargoyle, his nose packed with gauze and criss-crossed with tape. He held his towel-wrapped hands in front of him. Whatever had happened to him, Stefanos guessed his hands had been injured, too.

A dark-skinned black man, also long of feature, sat at a round table, staring at them with hard black eyes. A very young man stood against the wall, looking down at his shoes. Atop the table was a scale, the kind Stefanos had seen in many apartments where he scored cocaine.

A drug house, thought Stefanos, and they're not even trying to hide it. He knew then that it was time to go.

"How's it going?" said McGinnes, extending his hand to Gargoyle, who ignored the gesture.

"What you want, man? This here's a private residence."

McGinnes smiled. "Exactly why we're paying you a visit today. My partner and I, we're real estate brokers. With Cushion and Pushin'."

"Who?"

"Cushion and Pushin'. The name's Richard Long. I didn't catch yours."

"I didn't pitch it."

Nose-Mask smiled.

Gargoyle said, "Say your name again?"

"Richard Long," said McGinnes. "Like the actor. One played in *The Big Valley*? Most people go ahead and call me Dick."

"Who don't know *that*," said Gargoyle, and everyone laughed.

McGinnes cleared his throat. "Anyway, we're canvassing the area, seeing if any home owners are looking to put their houses on this seller's market we're having now. Way it is these days, you can get more than your asking price. Lot of folks are taking advantage of the situation —"

"Really?" Gargoyle raised his voice. "Seems to me you'd be workin' off a list, makin' sure you're not wastin' your time callin' on people like us. And by people like us, I don't mean niggers. I'm talkin' about renters, *Dick*."

"Nice day out," said McGinnes, "that's all. Thought we'd make some cold calls."

Gargoyle's eyes deadened. "I don't think so."

Stefanos watched Nose-Mask raise one of his hands. He saw the muzzle of a gun peeking out from beneath the towel.

"Let's go, Dick," said Stefanos, wanting to run but not able to leave his friend.

"You ain't goin' nowhere," said Gargoyle, stepping away from the door frame and turning his head back toward Nose-Mask. "Ain't that right, Short?"

Short Man Monroe could see that the young white dude with the fucked-up jacket knew what time it was. It was all in his eyes, the way they went quick from his partner, one who called himself Dick, back to Tyrell. Trying to get old Dick's attention, wantin' to say, *Fuck* it, man, let's just buck and run.

Monroe figured he'd shoot the younger one first, blow a hole through his temple as he turned his head. Then the silly-ass one with the shades and the Evel Knievel sideburns and the hair combed slanted-like across his forehead. Do them quick, *bap-bap-bap*, before they could scream.

Monroe raised the gun to hip level, sighted it best he could. He'd practiced hip shots out in the woods, blowin' bottles and cans off stumps, and he'd gotten pretty good. Still, it was a tricky shot from here. But if he missed he could chase those two down easy, head-shoot 'em out in the yard.

He curled his finger inside the trigger guard, pressing his palm tight on the Glock's grip.

The young dude said something, and Tyrell said something back. Then Tyrell stepped off, turned his head back, smiled and said, "Ain't that right, Short?"

Tyrell's smile faded as he looked past Monroe.

Monroe felt sudden pressure on his shoulder, fingers digging deep at the base of his neck.

"You won't be needin' that," said the voice of Kevin Murphy.

Monroe lowered the gun.

Murphy walked by him to the front door. He looked at the white men standing on the porch, a guy in his twenties and some joker wearing shades.

"Whatever it is," said Murphy, "we ain't interested, fellas," and he closed the door and latched it.

Tyrell gave Murphy a hard stare.

Monroe said, "Fuck you do that for, man?"

"Stupid," said Murphy. "Y'all ain't thinkin'."

"They *had* to be cops," said Tyrell. "You gonna let 'em just walk away? Said they were salesmen, some bullshit story about real estate."

"They *were* salesmen," said Murphy. "You see those clothes they had on? Ain't no cop smart enough to think up a perfect disguise like that."

"Those *were* some seriously fucked up vines, cuz," said Antony Ray.

"That white boy wearin' that old jacket?" said Monroe. "He'll never know how lucky he was today."

Nick Stefanos watched his hand shake as he pushed in the dash lighter. He pulled down on the tree and swung a U toward the highway. The Dodge spit gravel coming out of the lot, its rear end swerving as Stefanos gunned it west on 214.

"Slow down, man."

"*Fuck* slowin' down." Stefanos lit his smoke and shot McGinnes a look. "*You* had to have a look in that house."

"You were as curious as I was. Anyway, relax, will ya? We're here, aren't we?"

"Barely. If it wasn't for that guy with the mustache, we'd still be there on that porch, not knowin' whether to shit or go blind. If he hadn't shut the door in our faces —"

"Yeah, he threw water all over the fire, didn't he? But why? Funny thing about that guy."

"What?"

"I don't know. Haven't figured it out yet." McGinnes rubbed his chin. "But I do have a hunch."

Stefanos slowed down for a red.

"Nick," said McGinnes, "we're not goin' back to work, are we?"

"I told Louie we weren't coming back in."

"Why don't you pull over, then. I want to call Andre about that hunch of mine. And I could really use a beer."

"Yeah, I could use one, too." Stefanos laughed. "Dick Long. Shit, man, how'd you come up with *that?*"

"It's *Richard* Long to you, Greek."

Nick Stefanos saw a market with a pay phone out front. He cut across traffic and pulled into the lot.

Tutt walked from the kitchen and stopped in front of Kevin Murphy.

"Where were you?" said Tutt.

"In the head," said Murphy.

"Who were those guys at the front door?"

"Couple of salesmen. Come on."

They went and stood before Tyrell, who had dropped back into his chair.

"We're outta here," said Tutt. "Remember what I said about Golden. Can't be holdin' him back there much longer. You understand?"

"Don't worry, officer," said Tyrell. "We gonna wrap everything up by tonight. Right, Antony?"

Antony Ray said, "Right."

"I'll call you later," said Tutt. "See how it went with Clay."

Tutt eye-swept Monroe before he walked from the house. Murphy chin-nodded Rogers; Rogers looked away.

Out in the Bronco, Tutt fitted the key into the ignition and looked over at Murphy, settled in the passenger seat and staring straight ahead.

"You're pretty cool about all this all of a sudden," said Tutt. "Big change from last night."

"Had to catch my breath is all."

"Good you're keeping your head. Because we've got some hard decisions to make, and I mean soon."

"Yeah?"

"Tyrell and the rest of them, they're out of control. What happens when you crawl into bed with a bunch of —"

"Bunch of what?"

"*Geniuses* like them."

"So what're you fixin' to do, Tutt?"

"I don't know yet. Got a general idea, but I gotta think it through. Be ready to move when I get it all together. You gotta tell me that you're with me, partner. I mean, whatever it is I say, you gotta be there. Are we clear?"

Murphy gave Tutt an odd smile. "Yes."

"I'll drop you off at your car, then call you later on with the details."

"Give me some time," said Murphy. "There's a few things I need to do."

Tyrell Cleveland punched a number into the phone, waited for the signal. He punched in a new set of numbers and cradled the receiver.

"Who you callin'?" said Monroe.

"Tryin' to beep Chink and Jumbo."

"Probably at one of their movies," said Alan Rogers.

Tyrell sat low in his chair. He touched a finger to his cheek.

"You know, Short?" said Tyrell. "Beginning to think you were right about our policemen friends. They're trouble. Not sure we need 'em anymore."

"Tutt," said Monroe.

"It's Murphy I'm thinkin' of. You see his eyes today? Like one of those church-kneelin' niggas, gives himself all the way over to God. Man got no fear anymore, he's capable of anything."

The phone rang. Tyrell picked it up. He listened for a moment, said, "Nah," then slammed the phone down.

"That our boys?" said Monroe.

"Wrong number," said Tyrell, agitation wrinkling his long face. "Chink and Jumbo. *Damn*, boy, where those simple mothafuckers at?"

TWENTY-FIVE

"That you?" said Chink Bennet, hearing the sound of Jumbo Linney's beeper.

"Yeah," said Linney, taking the beeper off his waist and squinting to read the numbers in the dark theater. "Tyrell and shit."

"Let's don't answer it just yet."

"I hear you, man. Just want to forget about that bullshit for a while."

"Jumbo?" said Bennet, staring with disinterest at the close-up of a woman sucking a ten-foot dick.

"What?"

"Can't stop thinkin' about last night. Way that boy looked with a piece of his head blowed off."

"I hear you, Chink. Couldn't sleep my *own* self last night."

"You think . . . you think that boy even heard the sound of that gun goin' off?"

"Can't tell you."

"Think he saw anything at all? Or was it just, you know, one minute he was cryin' for his momma and then nothin'? You think it's like that? Just nothin'?"

"*I* don't know. My aunt used to sing this one gospel song in church, back when she was in the choir? They'd be singin' about goin' to the sweet forever, over and over again. All of them gospel ladies looked so *happy* and shit, singin' that song." Linney rubbed his face. "Sounds nice, don't it?"

"Anything'd be better than this world we got here."

They watched ten more minutes of the feature, *Delicious*, without speaking. The Sunday crowd at the Casino Royal theater was listless and few in number.

Bennet said, "You like Desireau Cousteau?"

"She all right."

"She ain't Vanessa, man."

"Heard *that*."

"Come on, Jumbo, let's go."

They found the Supra parked on 14th. Bennet got into the driver's seat, and Jumbo fitted himself in the passenger bucket. He hit his head on the evergreen deodorizer getting in, and the little tree cutout swung back and forth from the rearview where it was hung.

"Guess we better get back to the house," said Bennet, "get this money in to Ty." He touched the orange Nike box filled with cash, which he had slipped beneath the seat, making sure it was still there.

"Yeah," said Linney, "guess we should."

Bennet cranked the Supra and pulled away from the curb. A gold Monte Carlo did the same a hundred feet back.

Bennet felt better driving, going around the Capitol and taking Maryland Avenue through Northeast, across town to Benning Road. Linney had found an Experience Unlimited tape in the glove box, and they were playing it loud with the windows down. It wasn't too cold a day; just looking at the sunshine made them feel warm.

"EU is doin' it," said Linney.

"Bad jam," said Bennet, touching his friend's hand.

Bennet saw a girl in a tight pair of blue jeans walking down the street. He eased off the gas.

"Hey, check it out, Jumbo, it's one of them Jordache girls."

"Why you slowin' down, man, you gonna ask her for a date? Better get you a phone book to sit on first, so she can see your little head over the window ledge."

Bennet ignored Linney and sang out the open window: "You got the look I want to know bet -tah. . . ."

The girl rolled her eyes and stopped walking until the Supra had passed.

"'Too early in the day to be talkin' to the girls," said Bennet. "'Cause you *know* the freaks come out at night."

"Yeah, we'll come back later when it's dark, Chink, so I can watch you work your magic."

They drove on into the Kingman Park area. Jumbo rubbed his stomach and pointed to a corner market.

"Hey, pull over, nigga, I need to get me somethin' to eat."

"Shit, Jumbo, ain't you had enough today? Saw you put down five chili dogs at Ben's after we collected all that money."

"Pull the fuck on over, Chink. *Damn.*"

Bennet parked in front of a market with a riot gate pulled halfway down over its front window.

"They look like they closed," said Bennet.

"They ain't closed yet. Come on, man."

"I don't want nothin'."

"Come on."

Bennet and Linney went into the store.

A couple of minutes later the gold Monte Carlo came to a stop behind the Supra. The man behind the wheel cut the engine. He and the man who sat beside him got out of the Chevy and walked toward the market. They pulled black stockings over their faces and drew pistols as they entered the store.

"Hey, mama san," said Linney, "where go your sodas?"

"Soda in back," said the round-faced Korean woman behind the counter. Her four-year-old son ran a toy car around her feet on the grease-stained tile floor. She and her father watched the fat black man move to the back of the store, also keeping an eye on the little light-skinned man who had walked in with him.

Through the slats of the riot gate, Bennet saw a gold Monte Carlo ease along the curb and stop behind the Supra. He had a look around the market, noticed the outline of a three-letter logo, long since removed, that had hung at one time on the wall.

"Hey, Jumbo," said Bennet. "This here used to be one of those DGA stores they had all over town. Had one near Barry Farms, remember?"

Linney ambled down the aisle with a bottle of Yoo Hoo in his hand, his hips barely clearing the racks on either side. He snatched a large cellophane bag of pork skins off a shelf without breaking stride.

"Look at you," said Bennet, "grazin' and shit."

"Ain't you gettin' nothin'?"

"Wanna stay lean for the girls."

"Aw, go ahead with that, nigga."

Linney and Bennet stepped up to the counter.

Two men with stockings over their faces and guns in their hands came charging through the front door.

"Back the fuck on up!" yelled the lead man, pointing his gun, a revolver with black electrician's tape wrapped around its grip, at the woman behind the counter.

Linney and Bennet moved back a step, Linney cradling the pork skins and bottle to his chest. Bennet began to giggle. He did his best to suppress it, but the sound built and echoed in the room.

The woman picked her boy up and turned her back on the men. The old man raised his hands above his head.

"Take money!" said the old man. "No shoot!"

"We ain't want your got-damn money, Chang. Get y'alls' asses into that back room. Come on, now, move!"

The Koreans hurried back to the stockroom. The second gunman went behind the counter and followed them into the back.

"Fuck you laughin' at, little man?" said the leader, moving the gun from Linney to Bennet and back again.

"Can't help it," said Bennet, trying to stop laughing, unable to stop. "Ain't mean nothin' by it!"

Linney looked in the leader's eyes. "Just calm down, brother," he said.

"Brother?" said the man. "Nigga, I ain't *got* no brother. *Had* one by the name of Wesley Meadows. *You* know — Chief. But he got murdered last night, by the two of you."

Antoine Meadows yanked his stocking mask up, showed his face.

"Aw, shit," said Bennet.

"We ain't have nothin' to do with that!" said Linney.

"You a lyin' mothafucker, too," said Meadows.

The Yoo Hoo bottle slipped from Linney's hands and shattered on the tile floor.

"Chink," said Linney, moving to the side, his huge torso shielding Bennet.

Meadows shot Linney through the bag of pork skins; the round blew a hole through his heart.

Blood Rorschached out into the gun smoke as Linney stumbled back. He took his last sharp breath in pain and surprise, his arms pinwheeling at his sides.

Chink Bennet backpedaled, tripped, and fell to the ground. Linney came down on top of him, pinning Bennet to the floor.

Antoine Meadows stepped forward, his gun hand shaking wildly. He looked around the market. He looked out to the street. His eyes were feral and afraid.

"Look at you. Like some itty-bitty cowboy. Your own horse fell on you and shit! Ought to see how you look now, little man!"

Chink Bennet couldn't move his legs. He couldn't stop laughing. He was laughing, and there were tears streaming down his cheeks.

Meadows locked back the pistol's hammer.

"Why you still laughin', man? Don't you know you're about to die?"

Bennet watched the hammer drop.

Bennet wondered, would he hear a sound?

TWENTY-SIX

"Hear anything?" said Dimitri Karras.

"Not a thing," said Marcus Clay, looking around his empty store.

"I called the place where Stefanos works. Talked to a guy named Andre. Said they called in, asked a couple of questions. Said they're not coming back today."

"Is Stefanos gonna call me?"

"He'll call. But I was thinkin' I'd drop his money off for him at his grandfather's place. Wanted to see the old man anyway. I was thinking of him earlier, when I went to see my mom. My father used to work for him, back in the forties. Lunch counter called Nick's Grill, down on 14th and S."

Clay smiled. "I remember that place. Me and George Dozier used to go down there when we were kids, play that pinball machine they had. Always wondered about that cast of characters behind the counter, a couple of Greeks off the boat cooking soul food for the brothers. Matter of fact, the man you're talkin' about, he caught me tryin' to drop a slug in that pinball machine one day. Made me sweep the place out and then he gave me a roll of nickels to play. Combination of tough and kind. Best thing that man could have done for me then."

"Feel like taking a ride?"

"Sure," said Clay. "Drivin' me crazy, sittin' around here with nothin' to do."

Karras parked the BMW at the intersection of 17th and Irving in Mount Pleasant, and he and Clay walked up 17th, where they cut into an alley. Karras had visited Big Nick Stefanos once since Stefanos had asked him to counsel his grandson ten years back. Karras knew that the residents of the row houses on Irving used the alley as their primary entrance. Four houses deep into the alley, he saw Big Nick's house.

Karras knocked on the front door. Through the windows he and Clay saw an old man coming slowly toward them, leaning on a cane. Two locks were undone, and the door swung open.

"Mr. Stefanos?"

"Yeah?"

The old man squinted, his milky, glaucomic eyes staring past Karras's shoulder. He had lost all of his hair except for a few strays combed across the spotted dome of his scalp. He had lost a few inches of height as well, though none of the immensity of his hands. His thick horn-rimmed glasses hung crookedly on his large nose.

"Dimitri Karras."

The old man showed his wide-open smile. "*O yos tou* Panayoti Karras?"

"Yeah, it's me. Pete Karras's son. Got a friend with me, Mr. Stefanos."

"Marcus Clay." Clay reached out and took the old man's hand. Stefanos shook it.

"*Ella*," he said, making a come-on gesture with his free hand. "Come on in. I was jus' makin' a little *cafe*."

They entered a room that had been a sleeping porch, now finished off with paneled walls. An old couch covered with afghan blankets sat next to a green leather recliner patched with duct tape. The television played on a stand set against the wall. Steve McQueen was engaged in a card game with Eddie Robinson onscreen.

"Have a seat," said Stefanos. "You two want coffee?"

"That would be good," said Karras as he and Clay took a seat on the couch.

"Watch a little TV if you want. *Playhouse Five*, they used to run Randolph Scott Westerns on Sunday afternoons. No more. But McQueen, he's all right. Makes a pretty good cowboy, too."

"We're okay," said Karras. "Take your time."

Stefanos returned ten minutes later with a tray of three tiny cups and saucers, the cane hooked over his forearm. They didn't rise to assist him.

He placed the tray on a small end table by the couch. They helped themselves as Stefanos took his cup and saucer and settled in the recliner.

Clay looked in his painted ceramic cup, small as a doll's set. The cup was half filled with something thick and black as tar. He took a sip of bitter caffeine.

"What brings you here today?" said Stefanos, looking toward the sunlight coming through the porch windows.

"Wanted to drop this by," said Karras, leaning forward and pressing a folded bill in Stefanos's big hand. "I owe your grandson some money. Good excuse to come by and see how you were doin'. I was visiting my mother today, and I thought of you."

"Where's Eleni, Gate of Heaven?"

"She and my father both."

"Uh. Me, I'm gonna be in Brentwood, with all my friends." Stefanos slipped the bill into the breast pocket of his flannel shirt. "What is this, so I can tell Niko, in case he calls."

"Hundred dollars."

"C-note, huh?" Stefanos grinned. "What'd he do to earn it?"

"Followed someone for me and Marcus."

"Him and that *bufo* friend of his, McGinnes, right?"

"Yeah."

"Goddamn joker." Stefanos turned his head. "You see Niko, or just talk to him on the phone?"

"I saw him the other night."

And I fed his nose with some high-octane flake.

"How'd he look to you?"

Wired. All twisted up inside.

Karras said, "He looked good."

"He ain't happy," said Stefanos. "He married this *Amerikanitha*, she's always pushin' him to work harder, climb the ladder, get more serious, like that. I raised him, you know; he's like my son. He *is* my son. I'm worried about him."

"Gotta find his own way," said Karras.

"Young people today, they're so set on makin' *chrimata*, like the money is the whole point. It ain't the money. It's the journey, *katalavenis?*"

"Sure, I understand."

"It's enjoying what you do, every goddamn day." Stefanos drank some of his Turkish coffee. "Aaah. Anyway, what you up to, *re?*"

"I work for Marcus here."

"*O Mavros?*"

"*Ne.*"

"What kinda work you do, Clay?"

"Own a few record stores, Mr. Stefanos."

"Call me Nick."

"Okay. Nick."

"*Bravo.* Good to own your own business, eh?"

"Yes, it is. Little nerve rackin' when payroll comes due every week. But, yeah, it's good."

"Had my own place on Fourteenth and S."

"I know the place. Nick's Grill."

"Right!"

"You and me had a good talk one day, when I was a kid."

"Hope I treated you okay."

"You did."

Stefanos smiled crookedly. "Yeah, nothin' like havin' your own place. 'Specially from where I came from, just a stone hut in the mountains, to having a store of my own. Just to put my key in the door, to my place, every day . . . it was somethin'."

"You make it sound easy," said Clay.

"Not always." Stefanos frowned. "There was this one time, these men came and tried to shake me down in my own grill. Your father was there, Thimitri; this must have been, I don't know, nineteen forty-nine. God*damn*, almost forty years ago. *O patera sou,* and Costa, and a man named Lou Di-Geordàno. And this big *mavros* named Six, bouncer I had at the time. I remember the way I felt, that these men were going to take away a piece of my business, something that I had built up with my own hands and sweat."

Clay looked at the old man. "How'd you handle it, Nick?"

We slaughtered them like animals in the back of the store. We killed them with machetes and pistolas *and cut them into pieces.*

Stefanos placed his cup and saucer on the end table. "We convinced them to leave us alone." He looked in the direction of Clay. "It was important to send them a message. *You* know what I'm talkin' about, Clay. You got a business yourself."

"Yes," said Clay.

Karras drained his coffee. "We better get goin', Nick."

"Hokay, boy. Appreciate you lookin' out for Niko."

"Sure thing."

"Nice seeing you," said Clay, taking the old man's hand. "We'll find our way out."

"Good meetin' you, Clay. Thimitri."

They left him there on the porch, staring at the blurred images on the television screen. He listened for the door and their footsteps going down the iron stairs to the alley.

Nick Stefanos closed his eyes. He smiled slowly at the pictures running through his head: blond women in flowered dresses, men in pinstriped suits and felt hats, a crisp white apron, a cold bottle of Ballantine ale, a shiny Buick Roadmaster, red and black chips and face cards spread on green felt, bacon sizzling on a hot grill, a ceiling of stars over Meridian Hill Park, warm breezes drifting off the water at Hains Point . . . wide, clean streets, running through a city of promise forever gone.

"I'm trippin', man," said Clay. "'Bout ready to bite down on my tongue."

"That Turkish coffee," said Karras, taking the hill down 16th alongside the park, once called Meridian Hill, now named Malcolm X.

"Guess that's why they only serve you half of a half a cup."

"Uh-huh."

"Drink enough of that, you wouldn't need that powder of yours to get up."

"I'd probably still need it," said Karras, speaking softly. "It likes me too much, if you know what I mean."

"I do," said Clay. "Never did take to that drug myself. I tried it a couple of times, but I figured something made you feel that good just had to be wrong. And I was right. I mean, look at the things it makes people do. Now, smokin' herb was all about gettin' together, sharing. With cocaine, you go to a party these days, everybody's always disappearin, duckin' off, so preoccupied with their next jolt they can't even relax around their own friends. That is if they still *have* friends."

Karras felt Clay's stare. "You talkin' about you and me, Marcus?"

"No. You and me are always gonna be friends, I expect. But I been watchin' you go down this road for a long time. Wastin' money your mother saved her whole life. It's hard for me to see it. . . . Anyway, you're a grown man. You know you're gonna have to give it up someday. The thing I wonder is, do you ever think about how you usin' that shit affects the world around you? How every time you cop a gram you feed the dragon that's makin' kids kill other kids all over this city?"

"I have thought about it. And I'm not proud of myself."

Clay leaned toward Karras. "You know the worst thing, Dimitri? You been lyin' to me, man. It's what that drug makes you do. And you never did lie to me before."

Karras nodded. "I know what I've got to do. Only thing I can promise you is I'm gonna try."

They drove down a quiet and nearly empty U Street. Karras parked the 325 in front of the store. Clay stayed in his seat, staring through the windshield.

"You comin'?" said Karras.

"Yeah. Can't get that old man out of my mind is all." Clay cocked his head. "What he said about those men shakin' him down in his own store, it hit me deep. Made me think about back when I was first gettin' started. How much I wanted this business I got. How I been layin' down lately, lettin' it get away from me. Made me think real hard about tonight, too. How Tyrell Cleveland and them think they're gonna come into my place and tell me what to do."

"What are you sayin'?"

"Not gonna let that happen. And you, me, and Clarence could use a little help."

"Help from *who?*"

"Al Adamson," said Clay. "Remember him?"

Al Adamson had his head under the hood of a '63 Lincoln when the phone rang in his garage. He moved the drop light, wiped his hands on a rag, and picked up the phone.

"Yeah. . . . Marcus, how you doin', man?"

Adamson listened until Clay had finished speaking. He said, "I'll be there. You want me to bring anything? . . . You sure? . . . Okay, I'll see you then."

Adamson took a shower, changed into dark clothing, and went back down to his garage. He'd only seen Marcus Clay a couple of times since Vietnam. Once on the street in 1982, and with that trouble they'd had during the Bicentennial weekend, back in '76. Al Adamson's brother, Rasheed, had worked in Marcus's first record store over at Dupont Circle. When Rasheed saw tragedy at the hands of some hard mothafuckers up from the South, Marcus had stood by Al to see that Rasheed had been avenged. Al didn't have to see Marcus that often for their bond to hold; Marcus knew that whenever he needed him, Al would be there.

Al Adamson found his sheathed Ka-Bar knife in the bottom drawer of his tool cabinet. He put the sheath in a kind of holster he had rigged to hang under his armpit and fitted it so the handle of the knife sat fairly flush against his chest. He put on a black sport jacket over his black fishnet T-shirt and shifted his shoulders. Later, in his bedroom's full-length mirror, he admired the jacket's drape. He pulled on the laces of his oilskin shoes and tied them tight.

Marcus had said no guns. He hadn't said nothin' about knives.

Marcus Clay stared out the window at the gathering darkness on U. Cootch had finished his paperwork and gone home. Clay and Karras were locked inside the store. Karras stood on a ladder taping a big Janet Jackson poster, given to him by an A&M rep, to the wall.

The phone by the cashier's stand rang.

"I got it," said Clay, going to the counter and lifting the receiver. He put his hand over the mouthpiece and said to Karras, "It's that McGinnes guy."

Karras climbed down from the ladder and walked across the room.

Clay said, "You can talk to me. Speak up, man, I can't hear you."

"That's 'cause I'm in a bar," said McGinnes, who stood at the pay phone of La Fortresse, holding a full tumbler of scotch. Nick Stefanos, half in the bag, leaned against the wall, a glass of bourbon in his hand, a burning Camel lodged between his fingers.

"Give me what you got," said Clay.

"We followed your boy. Here's the address."

Clay wrote it down. "Who'd he go to see?"

McGinnes described the men they had seen, the cars, the scale on the table, the gun beneath the towel.

"Good work," said Clay.

"You hire the best," said McGinnes, "you get the best. Wanna talk to Nick?"

Clay said to Karras, "You got anything you want to say to Stefanos?"

"Tell him to go visit his grandfather," said Karras.

"He says for Stefanos to go see his grandfather. He's gonna have to anyway, 'cause that's where we dropped the hundred. And he *should*."

"Thought maybe you'd sweeten the hundred," said McGinnes, "all the extra info we got."

"You want more," said Clay, "you gotta give me some more."

"Okay," said McGinnes. "How about this. Your muscle cop, he met someone first before he met with those dealers. Black guy, handsome, with a mustache. They drove together to the house. I thought I recognized him, so I called the store, had a salesman go back through my tickets. Turned out I sold this guy a TV set, nice Mitsubishi, a couple of months ago. Guy by the name of Kevin Murphy. Yeah, Murphy. No, I'm not mistaken. Like I'm always tellin' Nick, I never forget a customer — hey, you there? Hello?"

"What happened?" said Stefanos.

"He hung up on me. How's that for gratitude?"

"Prob'ly just got cut off. Anyway, we got the money, right?"

"Yeah, it's over at your papa's."

"*Papou*'s."

"Whatever. Have a drink with me before you go. Got to get down when you're at La Furpiece."

"I'm already drunk."

"Just one more, Greek."

"Okay," said Nick Stefanos. "One more."

"What's wrong with you, Marcus?"

"Hold on," said Clay. "Need to make one more call."

Clay misdialed, cursed, and dialed again.

"Clarence Tate."

"Clarence, it's Marcus."

"Marcus, I'm on my way down."

"Fine. But I called for Denice. She in?"

"Right here."

"Put her on."

Clay tapped a pencil on the counter. "Denice? I'm fine. Listen, I got a question for you."

"Go ahead."

"The other night, when that cop Tutt was in the street talkin' to you and Rogers and Monroe, did you happen to see Tutt's partner, Kevin Murphy?"

"Yes," said Denice. "He was in the market for most of it, but he came out after. Kind of calmed everyone down. He was real nice —"

"Why you didn't tell me this before, Neecie?"

"You didn't ask. Why you gettin' so upset, Marcus?"

"Never mind that. Thanks. That's all, I guess . . . all I need to know." Clay cradled the receiver. He looked at Karras.

"Call Donna," said Clay.

"She's probably not back from work."

"Then leave a message on her machine. Tell her not to let anyone into that apartment of hers, no matter who it is."

"Anyone?" said Karras, who saw something shadow Clay's face.

"That's right. Not even cops."

"So this is about Tutt," said Karras.

"Not just Tutt." Clay looked down at the floor and shook his head. "Murphy."

TWENTY-SEVEN

Kevin Murphy stood on the open-air third-floor stairwell of Donna Morgan's apartment building, looking at the north-south traffic on Georgia Avenue, stroking his mustache. He checked his watch: She'd be here any minute now if she was coming straight from work. When he raised his head, he saw an early model rust-pocked red RX-7 roll across the parking lot and swing into a space in front of Donna's unit.

Murphy leaned back against the bricks. He watched Donna lock her car and move up onto the sidewalk, stepping light, nice pins coming out of a short black skirt, black stockings matching the black of her rock-star hair. Not a bad-looking woman. Sure, the odometer had turned on her long ago — no one except a blind man would ever call her a girl again — but she was fine in a scarred-leather, tough-running-to-hard kind of way. He was going to have to come up on her real sudden now, and maybe, if he was lucky, this tough girl might not freak.

Murphy started down the stairs of the unit like he belonged there, chin up, giving her a friendly smile, neither flirty nor threatening, getting close enough to smell her now as she stepped up onto her landing. She had her keys in her fist, holding one of them point out, returning his smile cordially as she made her way around him to her apartment door, number 21.

Murphy glanced out to the lot and caught hold of Donna's arm as she passed. He pressed a finger into the pressure spot behind her elbow joint, not enough to give her great pain but enough to let her know he could. He placed his other hand across her mouth.

She bucked beneath him as he pushed her toward her door.

"Don't panic, Donna," he said softly, his lips close to her ear. "Let's just get inside."

She nodded. He pulled his finger away from the nerves bundled at her elbow and saw the muscles of her face relax. He kept his palm sealed over her mouth, watching her key hand, making sure she didn't try to take out one of his eyes.

She fumbled with the keys.

"Quick," said Murphy. "I'm not playin'."

A moment later they were in the apartment, and Murphy closed the door behind him. Donna flattened herself against the foyer wall.

Murphy reached into his jacket.

"No," said Donna.

Murphy produced his badge and held it in front of her face. "I'm a police officer. Here to *help* you, Donna. You and Eddie."

Donna blinked rapidly. "Where's Eddie?"

"Never mind that. Where's the money?"

"I don't —"

"Don't let's waste too much time on this, Donna. I need to see the money, right now."

Donna was frozen to the wall. She wanted to move. She didn't want to show fear. But she couldn't move.

"Donna!" yelled Murphy, her name echoing in the apartment.

His voice moved her off the wall. Murphy followed her through the living room. Donna saw the red light blinking on her answering machine as she passed. She stopped at her open bedroom door, felt a quiver in her knees.

Don't go in there with him. Don't. Anybody can buy a phony badge —

Murphy put the flat of his hand to her shoulders, gently moved her through the doorway. In the bedroom, Donna turned to face him.

"The money," he said.

Donna found the pillowcase in her closet and handed it to Murphy. He placed it on Donna's bed and reached inside. He pulled out a stack of bills held together by a rubber band, counted it, pulled another stack, counted that one. He studied Donna, tears breaking from her eyes and rolling down her face.

"What, you think I'm stealin' your dreams?"

Donna shook her head. "It's not that. I'm thinking of Eddie."

"Good. Who you *should* be thinkin' of. Now, he's alive. But the ones who took him, they really put it to him. And you know what? He never *did* give up your name. Led those boys right off your trail." Murphy thought of Wanda, lying flat on their bed. "You find someone who loves you that much, keeps lovin' you in the face of all that pain, you oughtta hold onto him, understand?"

"Eddie did that?" said Donna.

"Yeah," said Murphy, dropping the two stacks of banded bills to the bed.

"I . . . I want him back."

"Gonna *bring* him back, Donna." Murphy pointed his chin toward the money. "There's five thousand there. You and Eddie need to take it and leave town. Everything's about to blow up, hear? And the ones he took off, they won't forget."

"You taking the rest of it?" said Donna, ashamed she had asked the question as soon as the words had tumbled sloppily from her mouth. Ashamed at first, and then afraid.

Murphy stood straight, strengthening his grip on the pillowcase, his mouth set tight. He stepped forward, stopping a foot shy of Donna.

Donna's shoulders began to shake. Her eyes were swollen with fear and drunk with confusion. Murphy raised his hand to wipe the tears from her face. Donna recoiled, stumbling back to the bedroom wall.

"Please don't hurt me," she said.

"I'm not gonna hurt you," said Murphy, tilting his head in a funny way. "I'm a cop."

Clay, Karras, and Tate stood at the window, watched a canary yellow Lincoln with suicide doors come to a stop across U Street. Al Adamson, shaved bald, with a closely trimmed beard and wire-rimmed glasses, got out of the car and crossed the street. Karras noticed the cut of Adamson's biceps beneath his black sport jacket.

"Al's lookin' serious," said Karras.

"Yes," said Clay.

"See he still works on those Continentals."

"His specialty."

"That," said Karras, "and fuckin' people up."

"Feels like we got an edge, now, doesn't it?" said Clay. "Just knowin' he's on our side."

Tate let Adamson in the front door. Adamson shook Tate's hand, then gave Clay a handshake that the two of them had invented back in their unit.

"Good seein' you, man."

"Good to see you."

Adamson nodded at Karras, a light in his eyes. "Long time, Karras. Where your Hawaiian shirt at?"

"*Has* been a long time," said Karras.

"Ya'll heard the radio?" said Adamson.

"What?" said Tate.

"Another shooting today, this one over in Kingman Park. Two young brothers got smoked in a market. Triggerman left the proprietors alone. Sounds like a gang hit. Add them to those kids last night and half a dozen others around town, and it looks like we're about to set some kind of record here in D.C. Man on the radio said they're callin' this the 'Red Weekend' and shit."

The men were silent as Adamson removed his glasses and steamed the lenses with his breath. He rubbed them clean on the lapel of his jacket. He fitted the glasses back on the bridge of his nose.

"Marcus," said Adamson, turning to Clay. "Let's talk about your problem."

"They'll be down here soon, I reckon," said Clay. "We best get it together, figure out what we're gonna do."

Night had come quickly; its chill and darkness had emptied the Sunday evening streets. There was little activity on Fairmont, just a couple of hard cases hanging out up around 14th. Kevin Murphy killed the Trans Am's engine, lifted a gym bag off the passenger seat, and set it in his lap. He pulled one stack of bills from the bag and slipped it under his seat. He got out of the car with the gym bag in his hand.

Murphy took the walkway up to the Taylor row house and rang the bell.

Lula Taylor opened the door and stood in its frame. A burning cigarette hung from the side of her mouth, her eyes squinting against the smoke curling upward, curtaining her face. Her fingers cradled a half-gone pack of Viceroys. Up one step, she cleared Murphy's head by a quarter foot.

"Yes?"

"Kevin Murphy. The police officer who brought Anthony home yesterday."

"And again today. I remember. Took me a minute, you bein' out of uniform."

"Yes, ma'am." Murphy glanced behind him at the quiet street.

"Can't ask you in," said Lula, removing her cigarette from her mouth and tapping ash out onto the stoop. "And I don't want to disturb Anthony. He's up in his bedroom doin' his mathematics. You must know how hard it is to get that boy started on his homework. Don't need to be interruptin' him now."

"Didn't come here to see Anthony, Mrs. Taylor."

She looked him over. "What kind of business could you have with me?"

Murphy held the gym bag out. "Came here to give you this."

She nodded at the bag. "What's in it?"

"Damn near close to fifteen thousand dollars."

Her lips twitched involuntarily, causing the beetle mole lodged beside her nose to notch up a quarter inch. She looked past him, trying hard to appear disinterested, and dragged on her cigarette.

"Lot of money," she said, smoke spigoting from her flared nostrils.

"Yes, ma'am."

"It's unclean, I expect."

"That's right. Drug money, you want it plain. Much bad as it does, I thought it might be time to put it to some good."

She looked past Murphy. "What would you have me do with it, Officer Murphy?"

"Use it to get Anthony out of here, for starters. Right away. Send him down to the country, where it's safe. To be with his mother and sisters, where he belongs."

Lula snapped ash off her Viceroy and studied the night. "What, just pull him out of school in the middle of the year?"

"The Social Services people down there, they'd work it out. He can

250

start fresh in school in the fall. Ain't gonna hurt nothin', right? Let him breathe fresh air for a while, play in the woods, make new friends. Take walks at night without fear."

Lula closed her eyes, imagining it. "You make it sound nice."

"*Has* to be better than this." Murphy shifted his feet. "Mrs. Taylor?"

"What?"

"You did the best you could. You brought him to the point where he is, and he's a fine young man."

"Thank you. I do love that boy."

"But the streets are *stronger* than you. And it's only gonna get a whole lot worse in this town. You understand that? For the good of Anthony, you've got to let him go."

Lula breathed deeply, her ample chest rising and falling. "Fifteen thousand dollars."

"Wouldn't object if you took a small piece of it, to make things easier for yourself."

"My baby girl could use *all* of it. And I believe she'd use it for her children now."

She hit her cigarette and dropped it on the concrete, where she killed the butt with the sole of her shoe. She looked at Murphy and nodded one time. He handed her the bag.

"Tomorrow morning," said Murphy, "you put him on one of those Greyhound buses. The double-decker kind with the green-tinted windows. A window seat, too. Make sure he gets that."

Lula Taylor wiped a tear that had threatened to fall. "All this money, I could fly him down there, first class, still have plenty left over."

"Put him on a bus," said Murphy, squeezing her hand.

He turned and headed toward his car.

"Officer Murphy!" shouted Lula Taylor.

But Murphy kept walking. He got into his Pontiac and drove away, not glancing back at the light in Anthony Taylor's room.

Richard Tutt thumbed hollow-point rounds into a magazine, palmed the magazine into the butt of his Government Model .45. He turned the gun in the light, admiring the Colt insignia set in the walnut stock. Beautiful weapon. Some preferred the Lightweight Commander, which came in at twenty-seven ounces against the Government's thirty-eight. But Tutt liked the heft of this gun.

He slipped the automatic in his holster, clipped to the belt line of his acid-washed jeans.

Tutt lifted his throw-down piece off the table, an F.I.E. six-shot .25 he had taken off some spade on 14th and T. Rughead had said, "You take care of my Astra Cub, now," his face smashed up against the squad car window as Tutt patted him down. Had the pistol tucked in his drawers, right up alongside his snake. Fuckin' niggers and their guns.

The .25, it fit nicely into the side pocket of Tutt's Members Only jacket. He dropped it there and checked himself in the mirror. He looked fine.

The .45 held seven. That and the six-shot made thirteen. Murphy would post with his .357s, adding twelve. You could bury a few bootheads real easy with twenty-five rounds. Surprising them would be the key. But, Christ, you could fight a fuckin' war with twenty-five.

Tutt picked up the phone and dialed Murphy's house. He was surprised to see his hand shake. He'd never killed anyone, but in a strange way he felt he'd been waiting to all his life. Anyway, it would be a relief when it was done. No other way out of this one — a clean break and then move on. He could use a beer or something, but not yet. He'd celebrate later with Murph.

"Hello," said Wanda Murphy on the other end of the line.

"Hi, Wanda, it's Richard."

"Richard, how *are* you?"

Tutt tapped the toe of his Dan Post boot on the floor. He wasn't up for small talk with Wack-Job Wanda tonight.

"Kevin in?"

"He just walked through the door," she said in that too-happy, sing-song way of hers. "Let me get him for you."

Tutt heard conversation and footsteps. Murphy came on the line.

"Tutt."

"Murph. Been out?"

"Got the money, Tutt. Got Tyrell's twenty-five."

"Goddamn, boy! How the fuck —"

"Eddie Golden hipped me to it, back at the house."

"Why didn't you tell me?"

"Wanted to make sure. But I've got it. Got it right here. Was thinkin' we'd take it to Tyrell tonight. Make a trade for Golden."

Tutt said, "But we're not really gonna make a trade, *are* we Kev?"

"No," said Murphy.

Tutt relaxed. Murphy was with him all the way.

"The money will keep them busy," said Tutt. "But you *know* what we've got to do."

"I know."

"Then you and me are square on this."

"Yes."

Tutt smiled. "Like you were, buddy. Been waitin' a long time for you to come back around."

Murphy relaxed his tightened jaw. "We're gonna need help. Was thinkin' about Rogers. He can bring Golden out, get everybody together in one room. He's the weakest of the bunch. Won't be hard to convince him we're gonna cut him in."

"We *can't* cut him in, though, Kevin. He's one of *them*."

"That's right."

"I'll beep Rogers," said Tutt, "clue him in."

"Let me talk to him, Tutt. You're not exactly the right guy to be talkin' Rogers into anything. He can relate to me."

"You handle it, then." Tutt looked at his watch. "Meet me at O'Grady's in an hour."

"Make it two. I got some things to wrap up."

"All right, partner. See you there."

Tutt racked the phone and looked down. His hand wasn't shaking anymore.

Murphy placed the phone back in its cradle. He glanced across the room. Wanda sat on the edge of the bed, her old Kmart housedress hanging loosely over a faded cotton sleeping shirt, pink slippers on her feet. The TV set threw colors on her face.

The laugh track swelled, Wanda's laughter riding above it. "Oh, Kevin! That Punky Brewster girl is so cute tonight!"

"Want something to eat, sweetheart?"

"Had a grilled cheese before you came home. I'm feelin' kind of sleepy. Gonna watch *Silver Spoons*, and then I'm gonna take a little nap."

"Don't sleep too long. You'll be tossin' all night."

"I won't."

"Wanda?"

"What?"

"I'm goin' out tonight. Got some police business I got to take care of with Tutt."

Wanda's eyes stayed on the television screen. "Okay."

"Picked up something for you at the market today. I'll bring it to you before I go."

"Thanks, Kev."

"Love you, girl."

"I love —" Wanda's hand jerked to her mouth. "Kevin, this little girl is fuh-*nee!*"

Murphy changed into a pair of jeans, running shoes, and a short-sleeved polo shirt. He walked from the room.

Murphy wrote a one-page letter in longhand, standing at his workbench, and signed his name. He sealed the letter in an envelope and addressed it to George Dozier in care of Marcus Clay. Murphy had little respect for his superiors and none for the suits in IAD; Clay's endorsement of Dozier, and Dozier's rep, had sealed things in his mind.

Murphy lifted the pillowcase from where it sat heaped at his feet. He set it next to the box containing his father's church lottery tickets and dumped the lottery tickets into the pillowcase. He dropped the last stack of banded money in as well.

Murphy brought his S&W Combat Magnums down from the shelf, took them out of their cases, and laid them on the bench. He picked up one of the .357s and turned it in his hand: six-inch barrel, squared butt, checked stock. The stainless steel satin finish winked in the overhead light. He thumbed back the grooved hammer, sighted down the barrel, and dry-fired at the wall. He opened the box of Remington rounds and located the bullets with the Xs etched in their heads. He broke the chambers of the guns and loaded six hollow-point dumdum bullets into each. He wrist-snapped the chambers shut.

Murphy found his gun belt. He buckled the belt to his waist and slipped the guns into the holsters, one on each side, steel scraping leather on entry.

He turned to the wall, where he had taped a Jesus card he had picked up at the Jarvis Funeral Home on the night of his brother's wake. Murphy raised his hands, his palms facing the paper icon, and closed his eyes. Standing there, his guns heavy on his hips, he prayed.

The Lord is my shepherd; I shall not want. . . .

Murphy unbuckled his holster belt and dropped it in the pillowcase. He got a good grip on the load and headed up the stairs.

The TV was still on in the bedroom. Wanda was asleep on her back, her arms folded across her chest. Murphy turned off the set and walked across the room. He placed a red-and-white package of chocolates on the nightstand, next to her lamp. He knelt beside the bed.

"Brought you some Turtles, baby. Your favorite."

Murphy ran a hand through Wanda's coarse, dirty hair. He brushed dandruff off her housedress. He kissed her on the side of her mouth, her breath warm and sour on his face.

Murphy got to his feet and looked down at the husk on the bed. He switched off the light.

Short Man Monroe studied Tyrell, slumped in that big chair of his, running one of his long fingers down his cheek. Big man like Tyrell, it was strange seeing him look so weak. The call from Chink Bennet's aunt, it seemed to take time off Tyrell right in front of Monroe's eyes.

Alan Rogers stood against the wall, looking down at his shoes, smears on his face where he'd tried to wipe tears away. Rogers was nothin' *but* weak; Monroe could see that now. You had to be hard, realize that death was just another day-to-day reality of the street.

Now Antony Ray? *That* was one hard nigga, boy. He'd snorted, laughed shortly, said something about "those simple-ass mothafuckers" when Tyrell had gotten the call. Now he was over by the table, doin' a line through the tube of a ballpoint pen. Havin' no feelings at all, it was something to reach for. No feelings meant no fear. Bein' that cold, it could keep you alive.

"Alan?" said Tyrell.

"Yeah, Ty."

"Tomorrow morning you send some flowers over to the funeral home, hear? I'll put a couple hundred in an envelope, you run it over to Jumbo's moms and Chink's aunt."

"Can't believe it," said Rogers.

"One of those accidents," said Tyrell. "They just got in the way of some niggas doin' some mayhem in one of them shops."

Ray dropped the pen casing on the mirror, rubbed his nose. "Figures fat boy got smoked in some food store."

"Wouldn't of happened," said Monroe, holding up his Glock, "he'd been carryin' his gun."

Monroe looked at Ray for approval. Ray's eyes, heavy lidded with pinhead pupils, smiled.

"Seems like all our shit's just flyin' apart," said Tyrell.

"Can't let it slip away altogether, cuz," said Ray.

"Heard *that*," said Tyrell, rising from his chair. "We best get on our way."

Monroe released the magazine of his nine, checked the load, slapped it back inside the butt. He slipped the Glock barrel-down behind his Lees.

"Thought you said no guns," said Rogers.

"Did I, Alan?" Tyrell eased himself into his leather jacket. "Yeah, well. *Fuck* all that."

Ray laughed. "Wisht I was comin' with you."

"Need you to stay here and take care of our boy, Antony."

"Oh, I will."

"Give him water," said Rogers, "he asks for it. Last thing we need's another death on our hands."

"Yeah," said Monroe, "take care of Alan's other girl."

"Come on," said Tyrell. "Let's go."

Rogers said, "Gonna take my Z, Tyrell, that's all right. Need to do somethin' after."

"Fine."

From the window, Antony Ray watched the two cars drive away.

Ray did a couple more lines of coke and had a seat in Tyrell's chair.

Felt *good* sittin' there, too. Tyrell ever got tired of it, or went down, maybe Ray'd make this seat his own.

Ray shook a Newport from his deck, lit it, and dragged deep.

Tyrell, he'd always had brains. Could've been a real businessman, wearing a fine suit and shit, he'd had the opportunity. But he'd never been incarcerated, and it showed.

Ray, he'd been on the soft side himself when he'd first gone in on that armed robbery beef. Course, he'd had his priors, done plenty of violent shit before he took the long one. Wasn't till he was *in* Lorton, though, that he killed his first man. Had to prove yourself real quick in there, sleepin' in that dorm-style room in the Occoquan facility with all those other hard brothers, most of them scared inside but even more afraid to let it show. So you had to make a point. Ray made it when some skinny, light-skinned nigga cut across him in the prison barber shop, took the chair he'd been next in line to get. Friends of this light-skinned boy, they laughed right in Ray's face, all of them tryin' to take him for bad. Ray figured that before he knew it they'd be punkin' him out in other ways, too. So he waited for that light-skinned boy when he was comin' out the showers, and Ray cut him with a razor blade he'd melted into the stem of a toothbrush, slashed down with pressure and ripped him open from his chest down to his cock. Mothafucker bled right out, his legs kickin', screamin' for his God to save him, tryin' to hold his hands over the long slice while the blood pumped out from between his fingers, and his life left his eyes. None of his niggas talked, either. And nobody laughed at Ray after that.

Ray closed his eyes. It wasn't *all* bad inside. There was this one bitch he had, his very own house mouse, with these thick, fine-ass lips. . . . Ray could almost see him there in front of him, wearin' eyeliner, how pretty he looked.

Antony Ray stroked his cock through his jeans. He butted his cigarette and got up from the chair. He walked to the window and stared at the night.

"Fuck it," he said.

Ray went back to the hall, opened the bedroom door, walked inside. He switched on the light.

"Golden boy," said Ray, moving toward the bed. "That wing of yours is lookin' like some August fruit."

Eddie's feet sought purchase on the mattress.

"Where you goin'? I ain't gonna *hurt* you, boy."

Eddie lay still. "I'm thirsty."

"Figured you would be." Ray chuckled. "Why I came in here, matter of fact. Gonna help you out there, Golden boy."

"Please."

Ray moved closer and smiled. "You ever suck a dick, Eddie?"

"No," said Eddie, making a small choking sound.

"Get ready, then," said Ray, unzipping his fly. "'Cause you gonna suck a good one now."

TWENTY-EIGHT

"Go ahead, Clarence," said Marcus Clay. "Unlock the door."

Tate turned the key on Real Right's front door as Clay, Karras, and Adamson stood at the window, watching the men get out of two cars parked on the south side of U.

"Tall, ain't he?" said Adamson.

"And ugly, too," said Clay. "Tyrell Cleveland."

"Tall man like that, you take out his kneecap quick, he'd fall like one of those California redwoods."

"Thought we were gonna talk to 'em," said Karras.

"Just makin' an observation," said Adamson.

"Al," said Clay, "you watch Rogers, the young man on the left."

"*I'll* watch him," said Tate.

"Let Al watch Rogers, Clarence. You and Dimitri keep an eye on Tyrell. I'll watch Short Man."

"That's what the one with the nose mask calls himself?" said Adamson.

"Yeah."

"Now, how'd I know *that*?"

A small bell jingled as the three men pushed through the door. Tyrell ducked his head coming in. Rogers and Monroe followed, Rogers standing to Tyrell's right, and Monroe standing to his left.

"Gentlemen," said Tyrell.

Karras and Tate stepped forward, close to Tyrell. Al Adamson walked to the side of Rogers, and Clay moved up and stood two long steps away from Monroe.

Get right up on them, thought Karras, like Marcus had said. Put them on the defensive right away.

"Heard of hospitality," said Tyrell genially, "but what ya'll fixin' to do, give us a kiss? Ain't you got a back room or somethin', someplace we can sit quietly, get off our feet?"

"You ain't stayin' long, Cleveland," said Clay.

"You must be Mr. Marcus Clay," said Tyrell, appraising him. "Can see how you handled Short Man here."

"Wasn't nothin'," said Clay.

Monroe shifted his toothpick from the left to the right side of his mouth.

"Prefer you don't call me Cleveland, either, Mr. Clay. I go by Tyrell. Cleveland's one of those Caucasian names." Tyrell's eyes slid over to Karras and back to Clay. "They was gonna name me after a city, should have been New York, or Hollywood. They was gonna name me after a president, should have gone ahead and named me after a famous one, don't you think?"

Clay didn't answer.

Tyrell looked around the room. "Okay, you're Karras. That one's easy. And you're —"

"Tate," said Monroe, smiling. "Father of Alan's girl."

Tate glanced over at Rogers, who looked away. The boy wasn't so cocky now; matter of fact, he looked about half ready to turn and run.

"And what about you?" said Tyrell, his eyes on Adamson. "*Damn*, you're about the blackest mothafucker I seen all day."

Adamson's jaw muscles bunched.

"Let's get on with it," said Clay.

Tyrell took a deep breath. The buzz of fluorescence and the tick of the wall clock were the only sounds in the room.

"Okay," said Tyrell. "Let's do that. We'll talk about the money in a minute. First thing, though, wanna talk about a problem you have with my operation down here. Heard you were shoutin' out in the street yesterday how you didn't want our kind around."

"That's right," said Clay. "After tonight, I don't expect to see you or your boys again. And don't want those sold-out cops you got in your pocket anywhere *near* my shop. I earned *all* this. Proud of it, too. Don't need you contaminatin' what I built myself."

"That a fact."

"Yes."

Tyrell's lip twitched. "We ain't nothin' but two sides of the same coin, Mr. Clay. Couple of businessmen tryin' to get along —"

"Uh-uh. You and me got nothin' in common. You poison your own people, Cleveland. You're a killer of children, *Cleveland.*"

Monroe said, "I'll fuck him up, Ty —"

"Shut up, boy!" said Clay. "Don't make me open-hand you again."

"Easy, Short," said Tyrell. "Let's just keep talkin'."

Karras was afraid, but a rush of pride had swelled in him, too, standing next to his friend. He studied Tyrell, his long frame, his knees, thinking that Al had been right. If it came to it, hit Tyrell low.

"Sorry you feel that way," said Tyrell. His eyes narrowed, and he forced a smile. "Well, let's move on. Let's get off that other thing and get to the money."

"The money?" said Clay. "We ain't got no got-damn money."

"But you said —"

"I said nothin'."

Al Adamson saw Tyrell's eyes dart over to Monroe. He watched Monroe use his right hand to hitch up his jeans, and then he saw Monroe's hand kind of snake around the belt line toward the back.

"What about my money?" said Tyrell.

"*Fuck* your money, Cleveland. Ain't got nothin' to do with me."

"Marcus," said Adamson, trying to move Clay's attention back to Monroe.

"What?" said Tyrell. "I'm just supposed to turn around and walk away?"

"You mean you ain't gone yet?" said Clay.

"Marcus!" said Adamson. "Short Man's goin' for his —"

"I see him," said Clay, calmly stepping in and back-fisting Monroe square in the middle of his face, aiming for two feet behind the mask, connecting deep, the nose giving like the shell of an egg.

Monroe screamed and fell to the floor.

Adamson stepped behind Rogers, twisted his arm up, used his other hand to pull the Ka-Bar knife from where it was sheathed. He put the serrated edge to Rogers's throat, put pressure on the blade, moved it a hair so it drew a drop of blood.

Tyrell looked at Karras and Tate, who had moved in very close. Tyrell raised his hands.

The packing in Monroe's nose turned black with blood. He whimpered, got up on one arm, began to reach behind him once again.

"Don't do it, boy," said Clay.

"*Don't* do it, Short," said Tyrell, slowly lowering his hands. "Mr. Marcus Clay is a quick one. There'll be another time for all that."

"Tyrell," said Rogers, off balance, up on his toes, his eyes wide.

"Looks like they got you, Alan," said Tyrell.

"Your boy goes for that gun again," said Adamson, "I'm gonna cut this one's throat. I'll kill him, Cleveland, I swear to God."

"*Kill* him, then," said Tyrell.

"Tyrell!" said Rogers.

"You heard me." Tyrell looked at Clay. "Think I give a *fuck* about that boy? Got young niggas all over this city give a nut to work for me. Lost two today, and it don't mean a *motha*fuckin' thing to me." Tyrell looked at Adamson. "So go ahead, man, cut him open! Do it —"

"No!" shouted Tate. "Let him go, Al. Can't stand to see another young man die."

Rogers rubbed at his neck as Adamson set him free.

"What I thought," said Tyrell. "Y'all ain't hard. Not really."

"Get out," said Clay.

Tyrell smiled, reached down, and helped Monroe to his feet. Monroe spit blood on the black-and-white tiles, turned and followed Tyrell out the door. Rogers nodded at Tate and left the store.

Out in the street, Tyrell and Monroe stopped at Tyrell's car, waited for Rogers to join them. But Rogers kept walking straight for the Z, put his key to the door.

"Alan!" said Tyrell.

"What?"

"Why you trippin', man? You know I didn't mean nothin' in there. Just makin' a point."

"Get up with you later on," said Rogers. "See you back at the house." He got into the 300 and turned the ignition.

"Alan's turned punk," said Monroe, blood still streaming into his mouth, the wet gauze hanging from beneath the tattered mask.

"Boy's too emotional," said Tyrell, "that's all. Not hard like you. You did good, Short. We get back, give you somethin' to drink, swallow some pills I got, do a couple lines, you'll feel a whole lot better."

"Feel better when I fuck that nigga up," said Monroe, looking with malignance toward Real Right.

"He can't win. We gonna take over down here. Give it a little time, let him get comfortable, then catch him walkin' out his shop one night. Gonna put him on his knees in the alley and let him look at you before you bust him in the head. You'd like that, wouldn't you, Short?"

"Yeah," said Monroe, smiling at the thought, his teeth pink in the light of the streetlamp. "Think Clay was lyin' about the money?"

"I don't know," said Tyrell. "We get back, gonna take my cousin off his leash. Find out the truth once and for all."

"My knees were knockin' together," said Karras. "Guess you could hear 'em, right, Clarence?"

"Thought that sound was comin' from me," said Tate.

Karras, Clay, Tate, and Adamson stood at the window, watching Tyrell and Monroe talking in the street.

"You told a lie, Marcus," said Adamson.

"What lie?"

"You told that boy you were gonna open-hand him. Could be wrong, but it looked to me like you struck him with your fist."

"Did I?"

"Uh-huh. And you hit him right where his nose was already broke, too. Couldn't you see that was gonna hurt real bad?"

"Meant to just tap him a little."

Adamson adjusted his wire-rimmed glasses. "Wonder who did the original damage to that boy's face."

"That was Marcus, too," said Karras.

"See?" Adamson smiled. "Cleveland was wrong. You *are* hard, Marcus."

"Nah," said Clay, trying not to grin. "Not really."

TWENTY-NINE

Looking down from her bedroom window, Denice Tate watched Alan Rogers approach her house. With his head down and his shoulders kind of slouched, he looked different coming up the walk, not his usual confident self. She heard a knocking sound from one floor below.

Denice went down the stairs. She stopped in the foyer and leaned against the door.

"Alan?"

"Neecie, it's me. Open up, girl."

"Can't. My father's gonna be comin' back any minute now, Alan. You got to go away."

"Get on down by the mail slot, Neecie."

Denice sat on the linoleum and lifted the rectangular copper flap. Alan had a seat on the cold concrete in front of the door. He unbuttoned his shirt cuff and put his hand through the slot. Neecie held his fingers. Through the space she saw Alan's spent, bloodshot eyes.

"You okay?"

"Came to say good-bye, Neecie."

"Alan —"

"Quiet, now, let me say it. Shouldn't have been messin' with you to begin with, young as you are." Rogers blinked slowly. "You're good. What you got to do is stay away from boys like me. Ain't nothin' up the road but trouble in that. You hear me, girl?"

"I hear you, Alan." Denice swallowed. "But Alan, you got good in you, too."

"No, I don't."

"Yes, you *do*. You don't belong with those boys you run with. You can change. Find yourself a real job."

"You *know* I can't hardly read."

"Go back to school, then. Get that GED you been talkin' about."

"Too late for me."

"It *isn't*."

"Go ahead, girl." Rogers tightened his fingers in Denice's hand. "You listen to your father, now, Denice; let him guide you. Never was lucky enough my own self to have someone like that." He tried to smile. "Want you to know somethin' else. I cared for you, for real. Wasn't just that you were so fine."

Denice's eyes welled with tears. Rogers pulled his hand back through the slot.

"Alan, wait. Where you goin'?"

"Back out here, where I belong."

"Don't go."

"Got to," he said.

Denice pressed her ear against the door. She listened to the sound of his footsteps receding on the concrete.

Rogers walked to the Z, parked halfway down the block. His beeper sounded as he dropped into the driver's seat. He switched on the interior light and read the numbers off the display.

Rogers frowned and said, "Tutt."

But when Rogers found a pay phone and dialed the number, it was Murphy on the other end of the line.

"Need to talk to you, Alan."

"What about?"

"I'm takin' Tyrell down tonight."

"That right."

"Yes. Wanted to give you the chance to walk away."

Rogers licked his lips. "What I gotta do?"

"I'm alone," said Murphy. "I'll be sittin' in my Pontiac at Fifteenth and U."

Rogers said, "I'll be right down."

*　　*　　*　　*

"That's what I been tryin' to impress on you," said Kevin Murphy after Rogers had told him about Bennet and Linney. "That life you're in, it only ends one way."

"I know it," said Rogers, staring through the windshield at the lights of U.

"Gonna show you the way out, Alan."

"They'll kill me if they find out I'm plottin' against them," said Rogers. "And I don't mind tellin' you, Murphy, I'm afraid to die."

"It's what makes you human, Alan. Not bein' afraid, it means you got nothin' inside, or nothin' left. I was in that place my own self last night."

"What happened?"

"Spun the chamber and got lucky. Lost the nerve to do it again. Woke up and saw that I still had time to make up for the wrong I've done." Murphy looked across the buckets. "Gonna give you that opportunity, too."

"How?"

"You know those woods around Tyrell's bungalow?"

"Yeah."

"What's behind them?"

Rogers shrugged. "'Nother residential street. I walked through 'em once; ain't nothin' but a hundred yards —"

"Okay. Want you to go back to Tyrell's, park your car on that street, face it into the woods toward the back of Tyrell's. Then I want you to go in the house and wait. Tell Tyrell we're comin' out with the money. Tell him you saw it, hear? Maybe it'll stop 'em from hurtin' Golden more than they already have. You with me?"

"What if they ask where my car's at?"

"Tell 'em it broke down on Central Avenue and you walked the rest of the way. Tell 'em anything, man, *you* figure that out."

"What about you?"

"Me and Tutt'll be there straightaway. When we come in, I'm gonna ask you to go bring Eddie Golden out. But I don't want you to bring him out. I want you to get him out that bedroom window back there and take him through the woods to your car. Now, I don't know how bad they've fucked him up. You might have to carry his ass —"

"He ain't that heavy."

"Good."

"What'll you and Tutt be doin' in the meantime?"

"I'll be positioned so I can see through to the kitchen window back there. I'll be waitin' for you to flash me your headlights, let me know you got out."

"Then what?"

"Gonna take Tyrell and the rest of them in."

"Arrest Tyrell?"

"Right."

"But you were with him." Rogers looked into Murphy's eyes. "What, you fixin' to turn your own self in, too?"

"Yeah."

"What about Tutt? Can't believe he's down with that."

"He doesn't know. Thinks we're goin' out there for somethin' else."

"How you gonna deal with *that?*"

"Haven't figured it out yet. You with me, Alan?"

Rogers nodded. "Yes."

"You got good in you, boy."

"What people been tellin' me."

"Whatever happens," said Murphy, "you get Eddie out of there. You hear things start to come apart, you keep goin'. Don't even look back, hear?"

"I understand."

"Get Eddie to an emergency room; just drop him off. Then you call this number" — Murphy handed Rogers a slip of paper —"and tell the woman who answers where you dropped him. She's waitin' for the call. That clear?"

Rogers nodded, his hands fidgeting in his lap. Murphy noticed the cut on Rogers's neck.

"Who cut you, Alan?"

"Ain't nothin'. Got it a little while ago at Real Right."

"Yeah? How'd that meeting turn out?"

"Clay and the rest of them, they schooled us, man."

"Had no doubt that they would."

"Clay knows about you and Tutt. Said something about Tyrell's sold-out cops back there."

"Figured he'd get onto it sooner or later." Murphy reached across Rogers and opened his door. "Time to go."

"Where you headed now?"

"Got one more stop to make. Then I'm headin' uptown to meet Tutt."

"Murphy?"

"Go on, boy. You'll do fine."

Alan Rogers got out of the Trans Am and jogged across U street to his car. Murphy watched him drive away.

Karras and Clay stood behind the cashier's counter, drinking a couple of beers. Tate and Adamson had each downed a bottle and gone home.

"Marcus?"

"What?"

"Look who's comin' our way."

Clay watched Kevin Murphy walk toward the front door.

"Don't think I want to see him right now," said Clay.

"You heard what Donna said about him."

"Yeah."

"Maybe we ought to let him in, see what he has to say."

"All right, Dimitri. Go ahead."

Karras walked to the door, turned the key in the lock. He stepped aside and let Murphy pass. Murphy nodded at Karras and went straight to the counter, where Clay stood up straight.

"Marcus."

"Murphy." Clay looked him over. "What you doin' here?"

"Came by to give you somethin'." Murphy glanced over at Karras.

"You can talk free," said Clay. "He knows all about you, man. Matter of fact, I was just talkin' about you to your boss Tyrell. Tellin' him how I didn't want to see his pocket-cops around here anymore. I meant it, too."

Murphy did not respond.

"Donna called us a little while ago," said Karras. "Said you took the money. You told her you were going to trade it for Eddie's life."

"That's what I said."

"She also said you gave her five grand out of the twenty-five."

"That's right."

"Your boss ain't gonna like that you gave the five away," said Clay.

"Wasn't just the five. I went and gave the rest of it away, too."

"So now you got nothin'," said Clay. "How you gonna make a trade with air?"

"Figure it out when I get there, I guess."

"Just you?"

"Convinced Alan Rogers to come over to my side. And Tutt."

"What, you gonna tell me that Tutt's found religion, too?"

"No. But he's gonna be there with me just the same."

"They've got guns."

"We've got guns, too."

"Ain't you done enough damage, Murphy?"

"I have. Now I'm lookin' to make some kind of peace with what I've done."

"What I ought to do," said Clay, "is call the real police soon as you leave, get them out to that house right quick. Let you ease your conscience some other way than how you're fixin' to."

"You won't do that, though."

"No?"

"You told me earlier that you'd give me the rest of the day to sort things out."

"That was before I knew who you were."

"You gave me your word, Marcus. It means somethin' to you."

Murphy reached behind him, pulled the envelope from his back pocket. He handed it to Clay, who read the writing on the front.

"George Dozier? What's this got to do with George?"

"Just put it in his hands. That's all I'm askin'. You'll do that for me, right?"

Clay and Murphy locked eyes.

"Thanks, Marcus."

"Ain't no thing."

"I best be goin'," said Murphy.

"Kevin," said Clay.

But Murphy turned and left the store. They watched him pass beneath a streetlamp. They heard the Trans Am's engine come to life.

"Kind of hard on him, weren't you?"

"Yes, I was."

Karras opened the last two Heinekens and put one in Clay's hand.

"Cheers, Marcus."

"Cheers?" said Clay. "Right."

Karras did some paperwork in the office while Clay paced around the store, moving records from one bin to another and back again. When Clay could stand that no longer, he went to the back room and dropped the letter on the desk in front of Karras.

"Can't stop thinkin' about Murphy, Dimitri."

"I hear you. I been workin' on the same purchase order and not gettin' anywhere for the last half hour." Karras rested his pen on the desk. "What do you think's gonna happen to him?"

"You heard the man. He went to make his peace."

"With a gun?"

"That's one way."

"Ah, shit." Karras ran a hand through his hair. "Look, you know where he's goin', right?"

"Yeah. Your boy McGinnes gave me Tyrell's address. Got it written down here somewhere."

"Call George, Marcus."

"Mitri, I don't even know what's in that letter."

"Read it, then."

"That letter's *sealed*, man."

Karras picked up the envelope and tore it open. "Here."

Clay unfolded the letter. Karras watched his face as he read it.

"Come on, Marcus, what's it say?"

"It's a confession. Murphy implicates himself and Tutt as willing employees of Tyrell's drug operation. Puts the finger on Short Man for the murder of Wesley Meadows and James Willets."

"What're you gonna do?"

Clay looked up. "Guess I'm gonna have to go ahead and break my word."

Clay picked up the phone and dialed. Karras listened to him tell George Dozier about a couple of rogue cops who were taking it upon themselves to arrest the killers of Chief Meadows and P-Square Willets, holed up in a house in PG County.

"It's goin' down *now*, George," said Clay, and he gave Dozier the address. He cradled the phone.

"Didn't hear you mention the part about Murphy and Tutt bein' on Tyrell's payroll."

"Must have slipped my mind."

"Gettin' forgetful in your old age, Marcus."

"Yeah," said Clay, tearing up the letter and dropping the pieces in the trash. "And clumsy, too."

Clay began to punch another number into the phone's grid.

"Who you callin' now?" said Karras.

"Elaine," said Clay. "Murphy's gonna need a good lawyer, he makes it out alive."

THIRTY

Kevin Murphy curbed the Trans Am at Colorado and Longfellow and killed its engine. He got out of the car and crossed the street. The Bronco was idling out front of O'Grady's. Murphy showed the last stack of bills to Tutt through the driver's-side window. Tutt nodded. Murphy dropped the pillowcase in the back of the Ford, came back, and got in the passenger seat.

"Ready, partner?" said Tutt.

"Yeah. Let's move."

They took 14th Street downtown, turned left on Florida Avenue, went past Gallaudet College and Trinidad, and drove east.

Murphy told Tutt about Bennet and Linney as they hit Benning Road.

Tutt said, "That's a damn shame."

The Bronco rolled onto the Allen and Benning Bridges. Murphy cranked his window a quarter turn, the air crisp on his face. The moon reflected pearl off the Anacostia River below.

"What's so funny?" said Tutt.

"How's that?"

"You're smiling."

"Was I? Didn't mean to be. Just thinkin' back on somethin'."

"Must be a good memory."

"There was this time when I was a boy, I went with this girl to her house. Older girl, used to tease the young boys in the neighborhood. Afterwards, my father found out and made me go to our reverend, tell him what we'd done."

Tutt smiled stupidly. "D'you fuck her?"

"Nah, Tutt, it wasn't nothin' like that. It was one of those 'you show me yours, and I'll show you mine' kind of things. Real innocent, lookin' at it now. But I thought I had committed an awful sin, and it was weighin' on me hard. The point I'm tryin' to make is, after I talked to my reverend, I had this, I don't know, *clean* feeling, see, like I had got it all out, and there wasn't nothin' dirty left inside me. Like everything was in front of me again."

"Way you feel tonight, huh?"

"Yes."

Tutt looked over at Murphy. "You're scarin' me a little bit, man. We ain't goin' to no revival meeting here."

"I *know* where we're goin', Tutt."

"'Cause we gotta be together on this. You gave Rogers the instructions just like we said?"

"Alan knows what to do."

"He brings Golden out, we smoke 'em all at once. Has to be that way, Kev. I'll do Rogers if you want, 'cause I know it's gonna be hard for you. And I'll do Monroe, too. Want to see his face when I wave good-bye to him."

"Take your time in there, Tutt."

"They'll live a few minutes longer, long as they don't fuck with me too much. But I ain't gonna take any of their insults. You just remember, they've *all* got to be put down."

"Like animals."

"What?"

"Forget it."

"Afterwards," said Tutt, "we arrange it so it looks like a hit. Bury our guns somewhere."

"Whatever you say."

"Tell you one thing. Someone did us a big favor today, evened the odds when they blew up Chink and Jumbo's shit. That's just two less to worry about, right?"

"Two more dead ones," said Murphy, looking at Tutt. "It's a start."

"What d'you say?"

"Heard you tell that joke one night in the FOP bar when you thought I wasn't listenin'. 'What do you call a hundred niggers chained to the bottom of the ocean: A *start*.'"

"Jesus, Murph, you gonna get up on that soapbox again? Thought you and me were square —"

"Just wanted you to know."

"Wanted me to know what?"

"That I hate you, Richard. Truth is, I always have."

"Fine." Tutt squirmed in his seat, the green dash lights tinted his reddening face. "Long as we got an understanding about tonight."

"Don't worry," said Murphy, his eyes level and calm. "Everything's clear."

The Bronco crossed the Maryland line.

Tyrell Cleveland squatted on the hearth and placed a fresh log on the fire. The flames heated his rayon shirt and beaded his forehead with sweat.

"Damn, cuz," said Antony Ray. "Don't need no radiators in this joint, way you keep that bonfire goin'."

"Like it, man," said Tyrell. "Makes me feel good."

"How this gin make me feel," said Short Man Monroe, seated next to Ray at the round wooden table, a plastic cup of Gilbey's and pineapple held loosely in his hand. "*Cash* good."

"You don't *look* so good, black," said Ray.

"I'll take care of my shit tomorrow," said Monroe, his face ugly, twisted, streaked with dried blood. "Gimme some of that boat, man."

Ray handed Monroe a lit joint and dipped his index finger into the coke heaped on the mirror. He rubbed some freeze on his gums. He swallowed half his drink and shook a Newport from the deck. Ray put fire to his smoke.

Alan Rogers came out of the bedroom, shutting the door behind him. He had tried talking to Eddie, but he wasn't certain if he had gotten through. Golden's eyes had crossed in on each other all the way, and he was lying funny on the bed, like one of those retards Rogers had seen once. There were bruises and shit all around his mouth. And Golden's arm, it looked fucked for *real*.

Rogers walked slowly to the living area, where Tyrell stood to his full height.

"How's our Golden boy doin'?" said Tyrell.

"Not so good," said Rogers, looking at Ray.

"Did exactly what you said to do," said Ray, elbowing Monroe, who coughed out a hit of pot treated with Raid.

"He shouldn't have lied," said Tyrell. "You ain't got no problem with the way we been hostin' him, do you, Alan?"

"Nah, Ty," said Rogers, trying to smile. "You *know* we all right."

"Good. 'Cause you don't like things around here, you can always *think* about goin' somewhere else."

"Have to get his ride fixed first," said Ray.

"Get that raggedy-ass piece of shit towed off the highway where he left it," said Monroe, dropping the joint in the ashtray and resting his hand on the grip of his Glock.

"Go on, boy," said Ray, motioning toward the dining area. "Make yourself useful and put on some music."

"Yeah," said Monroe, picking up his toothpick off the table and fitting it in the side of his mouth. "And quit actin' like a bitch."

Rogers went back to the stereo, slipped Trouble Funk's live album out of its sleeve. He placed the record on the platter, dropped the tone arm onto the vinyl, and turned up the volume. The multilayered go-go sound came forward: drums, then bass, then call and response.

"This shit is live," said Monroe.

"*All* the way live," said Ray, touching Monroe's hand.

Tyrell went to the bay window, looked at the headlights coming down the gravel drive. The Bronco came to a stop within the arc of the porch light.

"Here come our boys," said Tyrell.

Tyrell eyed Tutt and Murphy as they stepped out of the truck. Murphy went around the Bronco, dropped the tailgate, took off his jacket, and threw it in the back. He retrieved a pillowcase and set it on the ground, pulled a double-holster gun belt from the pillowcase, and buckled the belt around his waist.

"What are they doin'?" said Ray.

"Officer Murphy's strappin' on a couple of revolvers," said Tyrell. "And now he's puttin' on his badge."

"Fuck's he doin' that for?"

"I didn't know better," said Tyrell, "I'd say he was gettin' ready to make an arrest."

"Fuck you doin', Murph?" said Tutt, a catch in his voice. "Tyrell's right there in that window, lookin' right at us."

Murphy did not look up at the house. He buckled the gun belt tightly to his waist and unsnapped the holster straps.

"I'm talkin' to you, man!"

Murphy took his shield from his pocket and pinned it to his polo shirt.

"Murphy! I asked what you were doin'!"

"My job."

Murphy grabbed the pillowcase off the tailgate and walked toward the house. Tutt fell in beside him.

"You goin' in like that?"

"Yeah," said Murphy. "And you better do the same. Don't want to be fumblin' with your shit if this goes wrong."

"But they'll know."

"They'll know anyway when they see your eager eyes."

They took the steps up to the porch.

Tutt drew his Colt. He pulled back on the receiver and jacked a round into the .45.

They stopped at the scarred door, bass thumping through the bungalow's walls.

Tutt's face was ashen in the porch light. "They got that music up loud."

"Guess we better pound real hard on the door, then."

The lights went off inside the house. Murphy's eyes went serene.

Murphy balled his fist, rabbit-punched the door three times.

"I'll go first," said Tutt, inhaling deeply.

"No," said Murphy as the door began to open. "Not this time."

Tyrell stood in the frame of the bay window. He watched Tutt gesture angrily to Murphy, and then he watched Tutt and Murphy move away from the Bronco and walk toward the house.

Tyrell turned and nodded at Ray.

Ray stood up, taking hold of the table for support, dizzy from the gin and the green. He lifted his .38 Bulldog off the table, opened the chamber, spun it, snapped it shut. He fitted the snub-nose in the front of his slacks, the grip and trigger showing just above the waistband, thinking how *bad* it looked like that. Always did have that fantasy, too, of drawin' down on a cop. He hotboxed his cigarette and stabbed it savagely into the ashtray.

Monroe checked the magazine of the Glock, palm-slapped the seventeen-shot load back in the butt. He thumbed off the safety, worked the slide, racked a jacketed round into the chamber, and stepped away from the table.

Tyrell went to the fireplace, where the Mossberg twelve-gauge leaned barrel up against the bricks. The barrel's heat shield was cool to the touch. Tyrell wrapped his hand around the wood stock of the pistol grip, racked the pump, eased a double-aught shell into the breech. He laid the shotgun on the table so that its grip cleared the edge.

"Alan," said Tyrell, "turn them lights out, man."

Rogers extinguished the lights in the room, leaving only the orange strobe of the fire. Monroe fanned out to the right, his finger curled inside the trigger guard of the nine. Ray stood alongside Tyrell.

They heard a pounding on the door.

"Go ahead, Alan," said Tyrell. "Let 'em in."

Murphy came through the doorway first, Tutt behind him. Rogers closed the door and stepped back into the darkened room.

Murphy squinted to adjust his eyes. Monroe was off to the left, hip cocked, an automatic at his side, his face a ruined, rubbery mask. Ray stood beside Tyrell, staring at Murphy and Tutt with murderous, laughing eyes. The trigger of a revolver showed above the belt line at the front of his slacks. Ray looked drunk to Murphy, unsteady on his feet. Or maybe he was cooked on dust; the sweet smell of green hung in the air.

"Welcome, officers," said Tyrell, standing a head above them, two feet away from the round table where a pistol-grip shotgun lay.

The fire threw dancing shadows out beyond the hearth. Tyrell was a black spidery outline, his green eyes wet and luminous in his long pointed face.

"We came for Golden," said Murphy.

"Yeah?" said Tyrell. "Why the guns?"

"Don't want any misunderstandings. Want to walk out of here nice and clean."

"You don't trust us?"

"No." Murphy's eyes went down to the pillowcase in his hand, back to Tyrell. "Let's get on with it. Got the money right here."

"All's I see is some old cloth bag."

"You'll see the money when I see Golden."

"I'll see it now."

Murphy dropped the pillowcase, opened it, reached inside and extracted a stack of bills. He tossed the bills onto the table.

Tyrell looked at the banded green without moving.

"Short," he said. "Bring him out."

"No," said Murphy. "Want Monroe where I can see him. Send Rogers back there."

Tyrell smiled. "Damn, Murphy, you really steppin' up and takin' charge. And all along I thought you were the strong and silent type."

"Send Rogers."

"All right, Alan. Go ahead."

Rogers brushed by Monroe. Monroe gave him a hard look as he passed.

"Hurry up, boy," said Murphy.

Rogers picked up his pace.

Monroe watched Rogers go into the hall, open the bedroom door, shut it behind him.

Tyrell's eyes went to Tutt's ostrich-skin boots. "Lookin' clean tonight, Officer Tutt. Got those shitkickers on your feet, I see."

Don't do that. Don't insult Tutt.

Tutt stepped up and stood beside Murphy. He didn't look ashen anymore. Murphy *felt* Tutt's energy change.

"Say it again, Ty-rell," said Tutt. "Couldn't hear you with that jungle-jump you got playin' so loud."

Monroe shifted his toothpick to the other side of his mouth.

"Curious," said Tyrell, looking at Murphy's guns. "Why you go so formal on us tonight, Officer Murphy, with that utility belt, your badge, and shit? Bet you even got a set of cuffs hangin' on the back."

278

Murphy moved a foot to his right and spread his feet. His vision line between Ray and Tyrell was clear now; he could see the kitchen window, and the black woods beyond, from where he stood.

Tyrell said, "Got yourself customized tonight, too, with that extra revolver."

Let's go, Alan. Step it up.

Ray said, "Man be walkin' in here, six-gunnin' it like the Josey Wales."

Ray and Monroe laughed.

"Cut the bullshit," said Tutt to Tyrell. "Where the fuck's Rogers?"

Relax, Tutt. Breathe deep.

A scraping sound came from the bedroom.

The window. Get him out that window now. Drop him; it ain't that far. Pick him up if you have to and carry him through those woods. Run —

"Check on Rogers, Short," said Tyrell.

Monroe turned.

"No," said Murphy.

Monroe stopped, shifted his shoulders.

Murphy said, "I told you I didn't want Monroe out of my sight."

"You told me?" said Tyrell. "You told me? Boy, you ain't tellin' me a *motha*fuckin' thing." Tyrell blinked hard, chin-nodded toward the pillowcase. "I want to see the rest of that money, Murphy. Give it here."

"Gotta do it, partner," said Tutt, speaking low. "We gotta do it *now.*"

"What'd he say?" said Tyrell.

Run, Alan. Run.

A faint crying sound rode above the music pounding in the room. Tyrell cocked his head. "I asked you what he said."

The Lord is my shepherd; I shall not want. . . .

Tutt high-cackled, took a couple of steps toward Monroe. "I *axed* you what he said."

He maketh me to lie down in green pastures: he leadeth me beside the still waters. . . .

"The *money,* Murphy," said Tyrell.

Murphy kicked the pillowcase to Tyrell's feet. Tyrell bent down and looked inside.

He restoreth my soul: he leadeth me in the paths of righteousness for his name's sake. . . .

279

Tyrell stood up, his jaws tight, spent lottery tickets bunched in his fist. The crying sound grew louder.

"Sounds like sirens, cuz," said Ray, locking back the hammer on the .38.

"Fuck is this?" said Tyrell, ignoring Ray, shaking his fist and then throwing the tickets into the fire.

"Yeah," said Tutt, smiling strangely at Murphy. "What *is* it, partner?"

"What the *fuck* is goin' on!" shouted Tyrell. "Short, check on Rogers, man!"

Yea, though I walk through the shadow of the valley of death . . .

Monroe went back to the hallway, kicked open the bedroom door. Murphy heard him curse, then watched as Monroe came back into the room, emerging from the darkness and stalking back into the jumping orange light.

I will fear no evil. . . .

"Golden's gone, Ty," said Monroe, his eyes shifting nervously between Tutt and Tyrell. He tightened his grip on the Glock. "That bitch Rogers took him out the window and bucked."

Murphy saw headlights flash in the kitchen window.

For thou art with me. . . .

Murphy drew his Combat Magnums.

Thy rod and thy staff they comfort me.

Murphy said, "You're all under arrest for the murder of Wesley Meadows and James Willets —"

"Aw, *fuck* all that, Kev," said Tutt. He raised his Colt with one hand and waved good-bye to Monroe with the other.

Monroe shot from the hip.

The bullet blew four fingers off of Tutt's waving hand, entered his neck, and pierced the carotid artery. Blood sprayed out into the strobing light.

Tutt stumbled forward and squeezed off two point-blank rounds from the .45; the hollow points imploded Monroe's rotten-fruit face. Monroe's heels rattled at the hardwood floor.

Tyrell snatched the Mossberg off the table while Ray fumbled for the .38 lodged in his slacks.

Murphy shot Ray in the chest, the dumdum bullet flattening on impact and punching out fist sized through his back. Ray staggered, yanked at the trigger guard of the gun, yanked the trigger instead. He screamed as the round entered his groin and blew his balls to chowder, the muzzle flame igniting his pubes. Foam spilled from Ray's mouth as he pirouetted to the floor.

A shotgun blast roared in Murphy's ears.

Murphy dove sideways, hot shot peppering his right shoulder.

Tyrell kicked the table up on its edge and fell behind it.

Murphy stood, raised the .357 in his right hand. His shoulder nerves spasmed, jerking his hand straight up. Murphy's gunshot ventilated the bungalow's roof. The Magnum slipped from his hand and clattered to the floor.

"Murph."

He turned his head. Tutt was on his back, his eyes rolled up into his head. He was pushing the stump that had been his hand against the neck wound, now hosing blood.

Murphy heard the *snick snick* of a shotgun pump.

He raised his left hand, squeezed the trigger three times, spacing for the Magnum's recoil. The shots splintered the wood table in a clean, close pattern.

Tyrell came up screaming, blood pumping from his stomach and spiraling from a steaming black gash in his cheek.

Murphy pulled off two more rounds as fire erupted from the shotgun. Murphy felt a part of himself stripped away.

Tyrell fell and rolled onto the hearth, one arm coming to rest in the fire. Flames crawled up his sleeve, melting the rayon shirt to his heaving torso. Tyrell gurgled as the fire claimed him.

Murphy felt unbalanced. He felt nothing on his left side. He looked for the damage to his arm.

"Lord!" he screamed, spinning in a circle through the cordite, the action sending a wash of blood bucketing onto the bay window.

Murphy dropped into Tyrell's chair. He looked down. His left arm was lobster meat, shredded and red and slick, gone below the bicep. Blood flowed freely into his lap.

He managed the phone with his trembling right hand. He punched in 911.

Think of sensations. You feel things and you are alive: revolving blue and red lights striping the room, the smell of gunsmoke and burning flesh, the cat wail of sirens against the bell toll . . .

"Your name, please."

Murphy gave the dispatcher his name.

"Your address."

Murphy gave the dispatcher the address.

"What is the nature of the emergency?"

Murphy gave the dispatcher the numbered code.

"Repeat," said the voice on the other end.

"Officer down," gasped Murphy as uniforms kicked in the scarred oak door.

PART II

TUESDAY

JUNE 17, 1986

THIRTY-ONE

"There goes Brad Daugherty," said Dimitri Karras. "You believe he went first?"

"Cavaliers needed a center, " said Marcus Clay. "Not a bad choice, you think about it. Got that Dean Smith pedigree, too. And you *know* Bias is goin' next."

Karras stood beside Clay, who was seated at his desk in the back of Real Right. They were watching the televised NBA draft selections on the beat-up house set.

"Look at that," said Clay. "One of Red Auerbach's people is whispering something in Bias's ear."

"'Get ready to go,' he's sayin'."

"Most likely. Damn if that isn't a pretty ice green suit Lenny's got on."

"Should be *Celtic* green. The color of money."

"Here we go," said Clay.

Bias's name was announced. Karras clapped Clay on the shoulder and watched his friend smile ear to ear.

"From Northwestern High School to the world-champion Boston Celtics. Can you believe it, Dimitri?"

"With Bird and McHale and Parish down below, he's gonna have to start off as the sixth man."

"Be better for him that way."

"Wonder if Clarence is watchin' this," said Karras.

"He's probably sittin' in traffic right now, tryin' to get into town. Since he moved out to Maryland he's been spendin' most of his time in his Cutlass."

"He did the right thing. With the schools here the way they are, it's better for Denice in the suburbs."

"Seems like everybody's either movin' out of D.C. or thinkin' on it."

"Speaking of that, I got a letter from Donna Morgan a few days ago."

"What, from Florida?"

Karras nodded. "Outside of Orlando. She and Golden are renting a little house. Got a swimming pool in the backyard under one of those bug tents."

"Sounds like a winner."

"She always wanted to go to Florida. She's selling watches in a department store. And Eddie's installing dishwashers. Takes him a little longer than it used to on account of that bum wrist of his. But as far as I could tell, they're doin' all right."

Applause came from the television's tinny speaker.

"There goes Chris Washburn," said Clay.

"Golden State. Bet it's nice out there in California."

"Oh, so you thinkin' of leavin' town, too?"

"You know me better than that."

"'Cause I need you, man."

"I *am* the glue that holds this operation together."

"Wouldn't go so far as all that."

The phone rang on the desk, and Clay picked it up. "Real Right. Hey, Cheek. Any action over there? Good. Uh-huh. . . . How's our boy doin'? That right. Well, you make sure and praise him when he's on it and point out to him when he's not. I want him to stay with it. . . . Yeah, me and Dimitri were just watchin' it. Happy for him, too. Take care, Cheek."

Clay cradled the phone.

"What's up?" said Karras.

"Cheek says they're doin' some business over at Dupont Circle."

"How's it goin' with our new employee?"

"He says he's comin' along. Yeah, I think Alan's gonna be all right."

Karras grinned. "Long as you can keep him away from Denice."

"Knock that shit off, man. Rogers backed away from that his own self. Boy's got self-control, unlike *you*."

They watched Chuck Person get called up by the Pacers; then Kenny Walker went to the Knicks.

"We doin' anything out on the floor?"

Clay shook his head. "Cootch says we haven't rung but one or two sales all day. If it wasn't for Georgetown and Dupont, we'd be hurtin' bad. We're hurtin' as it is."

"You still talkin' to Record City?"

"They're comin' back in next week. Say they're interested in 'testin' the urban waters' with a couple of small locations before they come to town with that superstore concept of theirs. They're talkin' buyout, but we'll see."

"Would you do it?"

"Get out of the way or get run over, that's the way I'm lookin' at it now. Like I say, we'll see."

Karras frowned, looking at the set. "Phoenix took William Bedford over Ray Tarpley?"

"I'm a little surprised at that one myself."

Cootch's head appeared in the doorway. "Boss?"

"Yeah."

"Got a man out here from the mayor's campaign office, wants to put some of those posters in our window."

"Tell him we don't do that," said Clay. "We don't do it for anybody. Explain it to him like that."

"Right," said Cootch, returning to the floor.

"He's gonna get reelected," said Karras. "You know that, don't you?"

"Sure. Runnin' against Mattie Taylor in the primaries and Carole Schwartz — a white Jewish Republican from Ward Three — in the general elections? Damn right he's gonna win. Meanwhile, city services are down to nothin', and the school system is fallin' apart for real. And George Dozier tells me that crack's already come to the District, ahead of schedule. Murder rate's gonna accelerate now like we've never seen."

"And the people are gonna put the mayor back in office."

"Nero fiddled while Rome burned, Dimitri; our mayor took cocaine." Clay looked up at Karras. "But you know somethin'? We're *all* to blame. 'Cause in the end, years from now when it's way too late, we're gonna see that we did nothin' to stop all this. We were so busy makin' money, ignorin' the ones who needed help, lookin' out for ourselves. So busy lookin' the other way."

Karras jingled the change in his pocket. "Yeah, well, what're you gonna do?"

"Just keep talkin' about it, I guess."

"Look, I gotta jet. Gonna make the rounds, check on the stores. There's that Replacements show I want to catch at the 9:30 tonight, so I won't be back in."

"You talkin' about that guy, looks like he can't get a comb through his hair?"

"Westerberg. Steve Earle's openin' things up. Should be a helluva show."

"Whatever."

"Nice day out. You ought to see some sunshine yourself."

"Fixin' to, man. Gonna do some ball." Clay eyed Karras. "You're lookin' a little on the thin side, you know it?"

"Way you're workin' me, man."

"I'm serious. You all right?"

"I'm fine," said Karras, avoiding Clay's eyes. "Listen, you think you could come by one night this week, get the rest of your shit out of the apartment?"

"Why, you expecting company?"

"You never know."

"Okay, man, I'll try. Know how tidy you like to keep things over at the Trauma Arms."

"Thanks, Marcus."

"Ain't no thing."

Clay and Karras locked hands, gave each other their old double-buck shake.

"Take care, man."

"Yeah. You, too."

Clay watched Karras leave the room. He turned to the corkboard over his desk, stared at the *Washington Post* photo of Len Bias smiling into the camera, palming two basketballs.

Clay's eyes moved to the photograph pinned to the right of Len's: a grinning, happy Anthony Taylor, holding up a catfish he had hooked from a Georgia creek, his sisters on either side of him, his mom behind him, her hand resting on his bare, wet shoulder.

Marcus Clay leaned back in his chair, laced his fingers behind his head, and smiled.

Clay parked his car on Takoma Avenue, along the railroad tracks in Takoma Park. He locked the car, stopping to admire it before he crossed the street to Jequie Park.

Kids played on brightly colored equipment while parents sat on nearby benches reading paperbacks. In the open field a dozen shirtless El Salvadorians were engaged in a game of soccer, while at the adjacent roughed-out baseball diamond a father pitched a whiffle ball to his young son. A freight train passed, its *click-clack* muting the children's squeals and laughter and the bird sounds coming from the tall trees at the edge of the park.

Clay went to the half-court square of asphalt set near a sheltered picnic area, where a man dribbled and shot, laying the ball up off the painted wooden backboard and getting ragged net.

"Marcus."

"How you doin', man?"

"*Workin'* on it."

"You up for a game?"

"You ain't gonna play me soft, are you?"

"Wouldn't do that."

Kevin Murphy bounced the pill to Clay. "Go ahead and shoot for ball."

They played to eleven, Clay coming out on top by four. The second game was more even, with Murphy tying it up, ten-ten.

"Gotta win by two, right, Marcus?"

Clay nodded. "Your ball."

Murphy won the game on a shot from the top of the key.

"You gave me that one."

"No, I didn't."

But Clay was lying; he *was* playing Murphy soft, avoiding contact with the man's left side. It bothered Clay, seeing Kevin like that, knowing that this was Murphy now, and it was him forever.

Murphy's game, though, it was improving fast. He'd spent the last month dribbling, getting his balance back, driving to his left, learning how to *move* in a different way.

"Rubber match?" said Murphy.

"Right."

They sweated through their T's, going full out in the best of three. Murphy made a good effort, but he lost his wind halfway into the game, and Clay turned it on. He rejected the ball when Murphy drove left and tried to lay it up. Clay sank the next bucket, a shot that bounced straight up off the rim, came down, and went right through.

"Got some forgiving buckets here," Clay said, shaking Murphy's hand. "You almost had me."

"Never could go to my left. *Told* you that."

Clay and Murphy had a seat on a grassy slope by the street.

"So how's it goin'?" said Clay, lifting his T-shirt and wiping the sweat from his face.

"It's okay. Workin' this summer youth program down in Ward Eight. Got plenty of young brothers I'm tryin' to guide. Funny how quick I got attached to 'em." Murphy looked out across the park. "Almost like havin' sons of my own."

"Thanks for that picture of Anthony," said Clay.

"Thought you'd like it," said Murphy. "Lula Taylor sent me an extra."

Clay spit to the side. "They payin' you down at that program?"

Murphy shook his head. "It's volunteer work. I don't need the money. Got my pension, and the disability payment alone's gonna carry me for a long time. You lose a limb, man, it's more valuable than if you lose your life."

"Sweet how the department took care of you."

"Had to. Oh, they knew somethin' was off about me and Tutt. Couldn't prove it, but they knew. Course, you went and tore up that note. Another thing I need to thank you for, besides sending the troops in like you did. Them gettin' there so quick, it saved my life."

"Good thing you passed out."

"Yeah, IAD never did have a chance to talk to me alone. When I woke up in the recovery room, Elaine was right by my side, holdin' my hand, tellin' me to keep my mouth shut. She and that other lawyer —"

"Williamson?"

"Yeah, him. One who looks like El DeBarge? He did a helluva job for me."

Clay laughed. "Man does look like DeBarge. But he's a damn good lawyer."

"And Elaine, don't forget her. None better than your wife."

"She is somethin'."

Murphy stroked his mustache, salted now with gray. "In the end, I guess the department figured it was easier to give us medals than it was to prosecute. Considering what's goin' on out there now, they thought it was better for the public's morale, too. Made heroes of me and Tutt. You believe that?"

You *are* a hero, thought Clay.

Murphy pulled grass from the ground and shook his head. "One thing's for sure. Tutt would have loved that fancy procession they gave him, all those officers cryin' over him and shit."

"'When the legend becomes fact, print the legend.' Heard that in this Western I saw one time, down at the Keith's."

"What's that mean?"

"Hell, man, I don't know."

Clay and Murphy smiled.

"How's Wanda doin', Kevin?"

"She's got her days. They're tryin' to treat her with pills now, so we'll see. I'm not givin' up, Marcus. No matter what goes down in this life, there's always hope."

"There it is."

"Come on, man. Got to fix Wanda dinner. Need to be gettin' home."

"Yeah, I need to be gettin' home, too. You got wheels?"

"Not anymore. I walked over from Whittier."

"I'll drop you, man. My short's right across the street."

"It's all the same to you, I'll walk home. But I would like to check out that ride."

They crossed the street and stood by the trunk of the car, the boat-tail rear waxed and beautiful in the golden-time light.

"Damn," said Murphy. "That's a pretty-ass Riviera. Seventy-three?"

"Seventy-two. Elaine bought it for me. It ain't exactly like the one I owned. But it's close enough."

"Tell you somethin'. You got a woman like that, you don't ever want to let her go."

"I know it, brother. Believe me, I know."

"See you next week?" said Murphy.

Clay said, "Bet."

Kevin Murphy turned and walked east along the railroad fence, the atrophied stub of meat dangling from the sleeve of his T-shirt.

Clay watched him go, then drove away.

Marcus Clay slipped the sound track to *Claudine* into his tape deck and headed down to Mount Pleasant. Gladys singin' Curtis, nothin' could be better than that. He bought a couple of Boston creams — Elaine's favorite — at Heller's Bakery and then stopped at Sportsman's Liquors, where he picked up a bottle of cabernet on the recommendation of Tasso and Leo, the genial brothers who owned the store. He drove over to Brown and parked his car.

Elaine sat on the stoop out front while Marcus Jr. ran around the rectangle of worn front yard, a small burgundy-and-gold football tucked under his arm. Clay took the concrete steps, waving to Pepe, his neighbor, who was working on a bottle of beer out on his porch.

"Daddy!" said Marcus Jr.

"What's goin' on, M. J.?" said Clay, going up the walk and handing the Heller's box, cross-tied with string, to Elaine, who was moving one foot to "Black Satin," coming from the open door of the house.

"What's that I hear, *On the Corner*?"

"I do love my Miles." Elaine felt the weight of the box. "Thanks for thinking of me, Marcus."

"I'm always thinkin' of you, girl. Proud of you, too."

"Come here."

They kissed and then Clay went out into the yard. Marcus Jr. threw him the football. Clay threw an underhand spiral back.

"I'm the Redskins," said Marcus Jr.

"I know you are, son."

"Who are you?"

"Anybody but the Cowboys."

"Tackle me, Daddy."

"Okay."

Marcus Jr. took off toward his father, and Clay caught hold of his arm. But he *didn't* tackle him; he hugged him tightly and kissed him roughly on the cheek. He smelled his son's hair.

Clay remembered, just then, the words that Kevin Murphy had spoken: *No matter what goes down in this life, there's always hope.*

"Daddy, you sad? Why you cryin'?"

"I'm not cryin'," said Clay. "I'm happy, that's all."

THURSDAY
JUNE 19, 1986

THIRTY-TWO

The sun woke Dimitri Karras early Thursday morning. Raising himself up on one arm, he read the face of the watch strapped to his wrist: ten A.M.

Karras licked his dry lips. He'd been dreaming of cool water in a tall glass, out of reach.

He withdrew a tissue from the box on the nightstand and blew blood from his nose. He dropped the tissue on the floor and sat up on the edge of the bed.

Karras rose and took a long shower, hot water first and then cold. His stomach flipped, and he leaned his weight against the tiles.

"Stupid," he said.

He dressed and walked out to the kitchen. The message light on his answering machine was blinking; it was Marcus, most likely, calling to find out why he was late. He decided not to listen to the message. He'd think of something or other to tell Marcus by the time he got down to U.

Karras tried to drink a cup of coffee but couldn't get it down. He poured the coffee out in the sink and rubbed his face.

God, he felt like shit.

It was going to be a long workday on three hours' sleep. He could use a little bump to get through it. Just a little, to straighten out his head.

Karras took Connecticut Avenue uptown, the air conditioner's blower the only sound in the car. He turned right on Albemarle Street and parked near the entrance to the Soapstone Trail. He got out of the BMW and walked west toward the apartment building where his dealer, Billy Smith, had his place.

While waiting for the light at the corner, Karras looked across Connecticut to the Nutty Nathan's store. Nick Stefanos stood on the sidewalk out front, his hand resting on the shoulder of some bandanna-wearing black kid, both of them watching the bank of televisions in the display window of the shop. Karras hadn't seen Stefanos since March, or thanked him for the work he'd done.

Karras crossed the avenue, approaching Stefanos and the kid from behind. As he neared them, Karras saw the televisions in the window were all tuned to the same image: Len Bias, wearing that jazzy ice green suit of his, standing out of his chair at the calling of his name.

All right, it was news. But why were they running the draft highlights again, two days after the fact?

"Nick?" said Karras.

Stefanos and the boy turned their heads. The black kid was crying freely, tears running down his cheeks.

"Dimitri," said Stefanos, his eyes hollow and red.

Karras felt hot and suddenly nauseous in the sun. He backed away to a government oak, leafy and full, planted by the curb. Karras stepped into its cool shade.

He closed his eyes and drew a deep breath. It was better there, standing in the darkness pooled beneath the tree.

U - A - 1

OEUVRE

OUEVRE